The Bells of Little Woodford

CATHERINE JONES

HEAD
of ZEUS

First published in the UK in 2019 by Head of Zeus Ltd
This paperback edition published in the UK in 2019 by Head of Zeus Ltd

9 7 5 3 1 2 4 6 8

A catalogue record for this book is available from
the British Library.

ISBN (PB): 9781784979836
ISBN (E): 9781784979812

Typeset by Divaddict Publishing Solutions Ltd

Printed and bound in Great Britain by
CPI Group (UK) Ltd, Croydon CR0 4YY

MIX
Paper from
responsible sources
FSC® C020471

Head of Zeus Ltd
First Floor East
5–8 Hardwick Street
London EC1R 4RG

WWW.HEADOFZEUS.COM

*To Ian, who still hasn't told me to go and
get a proper job.*

1

On the first Sunday in September Heather Simmonds, the vicar's wife, headed down the path from her home and towards the church for matins. The sky above the squat Norman church tower was speedwell blue, dotted with a flock of puffy clouds. The leaves on the trees in the churchyard had lost the vibrant shade of green of a couple of months earlier and now some had a distinctly yellow tinge. Not long till autumn sets in, thought Heather. The air was filled with the joyous sound of the ring of six bells calling the townsfolk to prayer. Bing-bong-bing-bong-bing-dong, bing-bong-bing-bong-bing-dong, as the bells rang down the scale from the treble to the tenor again and again. Every few minutes the order of notes changed – the ringers weaving them into intricate patterns like a tweed fabric; only a limited number of colours to work with but producing a beautiful finished product nonetheless. Heather stopped beside an ancient yew to enjoy the sight and sound.

'Glorious, isn't it?' It was her best friend, Olivia Laithwaite, who, as always, was immaculately turned out in a crisply ironed blouse, blazer and smart pleated skirt.

Beside her Heather felt a tad dowdy, dressed as she was in an elderly frock and distinctly threadbare cardy, but it was the best she could do given Brian's income. She ignored her feelings and said, cheerily, 'Makes you glad to be alive.'

Olivia smiled and nodded. 'But we can't stand out here all day.' She glanced at the church clock on the tower. 'Come on, Brian will want to start the service shortly.'

The two women, not wishing to keep Heather's husband waiting, headed for the porch and entered the church. Above them, up in the bell chamber, the six ringers were also keeping an eye on the time. In a couple of minutes five of them would need to cease pulling the bell ropes and leave the treble bell tolling on its own – the minute bell; the warning to any latecomers to get a move on.

The bell-ringers were a good team although the ringer of the number three bell, a young girl called Sarah Hitchins, was the newest recruit. She was the leader of the local Girl Guides and had brought them on a visit to the bell tower a year previously. She'd been so enthralled by the bells she'd signed up there and then to learn the ancient art of change-ringing. She tugged on the bell rope in her turn but as her bell swung there was an almighty crack from somewhere above her head and the rope, with her still gripping it, clattered and rattled uncontrollably upwards through the ceiling. Sarah shrieked in shock and fear as she was lifted clean off her feet.

'Let go!' yelled Pete the bell captain and steeple keeper. The tail of her rope thrashed around, hitting two other of the ringers, and then Sarah plummeted over a dozen feet to the floor and landed in a heap. The bells fell silent except for hers which clanged wildly on, until it ran out of momentum.

As the ringers gathered round the motionless body on the floorboards and Pete rang 999 there came the sound of footsteps up the twisting stone steps from the body of the church. Heather, followed closely by Olivia, appeared in the doorway.

'What's happened?' she asked as she gazed at the white and shocked faces of the ringers. 'Is Sarah OK?' Heather ran across to the casualty and knelt beside her, feeling for a pulse.

'The ambulance is on its way,' Pete told her.

2

'Well, she's alive,' said Heather. 'Out cold but alive.' She gazed up at the bell captain. 'What happened?' she repeated.

'The stay snapped,' said Pete. 'It happens, it's rare but it happens, but I've never seen a ringer injured like this. I think she must have pulled too hard, newbies do that, and she didn't have the experience to let go. Without the stay there's nothing to stop the bell carrying on turning full circle, again and again, wrapping the rope around the wheel. She got lifted clean off her feet.'

Heather transferred her gaze to look up at the ceiling of the bell chamber and at the multicoloured sally of Sarah's rope, now filling the hole that guided it into the belfry. She looked back at Sarah. 'Poor kid. How terrifying.'

In the distance they could hear the wailing ululation of an approaching emergency vehicle. Sarah groaned and her eyelids fluttered.

'Lie still,' said Heather, patting her hand. 'You're going to be OK. Help is coming.' She turned to Olivia. 'It might be an idea to tell Brian – or anyone for that matter – to meet the ambulance and show them how to get up here.'

'Of course.' Olivia rushed off.

Sarah groaned again and opened her eyes properly. Tears slid down her temples and into her hair. 'It hurts,' she whimpered.

'What does?' asked Heather gently.

'Everything. My back, my legs.'

Heather looked at Sarah's legs which were encased in jeans and saw her left ankle was at a hideous angle and blood was seeping into the denim covering her right shin. Heather was pretty certain that Sarah's ankle was broken and she'd put good money on a compound fracture of her right tibia too. But even more worrying was the matter of Sarah's back. And good luck to the ambulance men who would have to find a way of getting her, immobilised, down the tower steps.

When the ambulance crew arrived Heather and Olivia rejoined the congregation which was buzzing with curiosity as to what had happened.

'How bad is it?' asked Brian who was waiting at the bottom of the steps.

Heather shook her head. 'Not great. Definitely one broken leg, possibly both of them are but her back hurts – that's the really worrying thing. Pete said she fell quite a distance.'

Brian ran his fingers through his sparse grey hair and made his fringe stand on end like Tintin's quiff. 'I think, under the circumstances, we might abandon matins. Maybe just all of us join together and say a prayer for poor Sarah and suggest that everyone comes back for evensong...' He looked at his wife. 'What do you think?'

Heather nodded. 'I think that sounds like a very excellent plan.'

The next day, another of the town's residents, Bex Millar, stood in the primary school playground and watched her two young boys, Lewis and Alfie, hare around, like overexcited puppies, as they greeted friends they hadn't seen during the long summer break. What a difference, she thought, from the start of the previous term when they'd just moved to Little Woodford and they'd been new and shy. She wondered how her sixteen-year-old stepdaughter, Megan, was getting on at the comprehensive at the other end of town. Hopefully, now the class bully had been put in her place, Megan would slot back in with the same ease her half-brothers seemed to be displaying – only possibly with less shrieking and running. But Bex was reasonably confident Megan would be OK. When her alarm had gone off that morning and she'd pottered up to Megan's bedroom in the attic she'd found her stepdaughter already awake and showered.

'Gosh,' she'd said. 'You're keen.'

Megan had nodded. 'Don't get me wrong, the holidays were lovely, especially Cyprus, but I'm looking forward to seeing all my friends.'

'Good. And Cyprus was grand, wasn't it.' It had been... for the kids. They'd loved staying with their paternal grandparents but Bex always felt as if Granny Helen and Grandpa Phil were watching her, mistrusting her, waiting for her to mess up and prove them right that their son's second wife *was* a gold-digger who'd only married him for a cushy life. Bex sighed. She was sure they wished that it had been her that had gone under a truck and not their son and that they only tolerated her because she'd produced Lewis and Alfie. She was certain that once all the children were adults, Helen and Phil would cross her off their Christmas card list without a second thought. Bex wasn't entirely sure she'd mind.

The school bell rang and all the kids left off their games and ran to line up. Bex noticed the new ones, starting in reception, standing solemnly in line, most looking apprehensive and some looking tearful. Hovering nearby were their mothers and a few fathers who mirrored their kids' emotions. Been there, done that, thought Bex, sympathetically. But now she was accustomed to having child-free days, she couldn't wait to get home and get to grips with the worst of the mess downstairs – the result of having three children off school for six weeks. And the house needed some serious tidying if Amy, who was due to clean for her that afternoon, was going to be able to see the carpet, let alone vacuum it. And after that, she could return to her job at the pub. She'd missed working there over the summer holidays; the grown-up conversation with Belinda, the landlady; the banter from the regulars. In fact, it hadn't been just the pub she'd missed – she'd missed the whole town. Yes, it had been lovely to see her parents up in the Lakes, and to have a holiday in the Med – even if it had involved her in-laws, but it was even lovelier to be back here again. It had made her realise that, despite having only lived in Little Woodford for six months, she felt more at home here than anywhere she'd lived before.

It would be hard, she thought, not to like Little Woodford with its quirky high street filled with little independent shops selling everything from boho fashion to handmade greetings cards via cut flowers, car spares, pizzas, ice creams and books and everything in between. And it was undeniably pretty – an archetypical, middle-England market town with wiggly roofs, honey-coloured stone buildings, a myriad of hanging baskets, tubs and window boxes all filled to bursting point with flowering plants. And then there was the play park and the nature reserve and the utter Englishness of the cricket pitch down by the church... Such a contrast to their bit of London they had left behind with its pollution, two-tones, congestion and chain stores that made it a clone of every other street in every other suburb. Moving here had definitely been one of her better decisions in life.

She waved goodbye to the boys – both engrossed in chatting to their mates in their lines and both oblivious of her farewell – before she made her way out of the playground and began to head down the hill towards the centre of the town and her house. As she turned onto the main road she glanced across it to her friend Olivia's vast barn conversion. The estate agent's shingle, hammered into the front lawn, announced that it was 'sold subject to contract'. Olivia must be moving out soon. Bex paused and thought for a second about the mess her house was in and how she ought to be dealing with that... sod it, the mess could wait. Checking for traffic, she crossed the road then scrunched up the gravel drive. She hadn't seen Olivia for weeks and she might well want a hand if she was in the middle of packing up. To offer some help was the least Bex could do for her friend – after all, when Bex had been swamped by her own unpacking, and Olivia had been a complete stranger, she'd come to introduce herself to the new arrival in town and ended up spending the evening with Bex, helping to unpack and organise the kitchen. When Bex had first met Olivia she hadn't been sure she was going to like her. It had been obvious from the start that she was somewhat bossy and opinionated and, with her blonde bob and skirt-blouse-and-court-shoe apparel, she looked every inch the town busybody she so obviously was. But she was a doer and grafter and, even more than that, she was kind. And when Olivia had discovered that her public-school son had a drug habit and her husband had gambled away their life savings, her dignity in the face of such a crisis had been admirable. She was even making the best of having to sell up her 'forever' home to stop the family from going bankrupt. Bex was very fond of her.

She rang the doorbell and waited patiently for it to be answered. She was slightly taken aback when it was opened by Olivia's son, Zac.

'Hi, Zac – no school?'

'St Anselm's doesn't go back till next week,' he told her.

'Hello, Bex,' called Olivia from the other side of the monstrous sitting room. She was busy wrapping up an ornament in newspaper. 'Long time no see. How are you?' She pushed a stray lock of hair off her face. 'Zac, be a love and put the kettle on.'

Zac loped off into the kitchen area on the far side of the room, skirting piles of cardboard boxes and a massive roll of bubble wrap.

'St Anselm's always gets a bonkers amount of holidays,' said Olivia. 'It seems to me that the more you pay for a child's education, the less time he spends in the classroom.'

'Quality not quantity,' contradicted Zac over the gush of the tap as he filled the kettle.

Olivia raised an eyebrow. 'I don't think your last year's exam results back up that argument.'

'No... well...' The back of Zac's neck glowed pink. He flicked the kettle on. 'I'll take Oscar out for a walk if you two are going to talk.' He grabbed his dog's lead and whistled. Oscar, a black and white border collie, bounded out of his basket and headed for the front door.

When they'd left, Olivia crossed the room herself and got a couple of mugs out of the cupboard.

'How's it all going?' asked Bex, following her.

7

'What? The move, paying off Nigel's debts or Zac's recovery from drugs?' Olivia sounded weary.

'Oh, sweetie...' Bex gave Olivia a hug. 'I'm sorry.'

Olivia gave her a thin smile. 'Don't be. Honestly, we're getting there. Zac's fine – still clean – and I think I should be grateful he's sowed his wild oats in a safe little place like this and that the guy who supplied him with all the drugs is doing time in the nick and out of the picture. Without him around I think the chances of Zac backsliding are pretty slim although I don't think he will anyway – he's learnt his lesson. I dread to think what would have happened if he'd got addicted at uni where he'd have been just another anonymous junkie student.'

'True,' murmured Bex. That's one way to look at things, she supposed.

'And Nigel's debts will be cleared once we've got the money for this place and move into our new home.'

'And that'll be...?'

'In a fortnight if all goes according to plan.'

'Do you know who's bought this?'

Olivia shook her head. 'Not a clue – to be honest I don't want to know. The estate agent handled all the viewings and Nigel's dealt with the paperwork. I... I...' She stopped. 'I found it all a bit upsetting.'

Bex reached out and squeezed her friend's arm.

'I suppose I'll find out what the new people are like when they move in.' She looked around the huge living space. 'I hope they're happy here. I certainly have been... well, mostly. The last few months weren't a barrel of laughs.'

'No.' And nor would they have been for anyone with Olivia's problems. 'But at least you managed to sort things out.'

Olivia shrugged. 'If you call moving into a horrid little modern box down by the station "sorting things out". Although in some respects it's ideal because there's no chain, and Nigel's creditors will be off our backs once and for all.' The kettle boiled and clicked off. As Olivia began to make the tea she said, 'It would have been nice to have had the time to hold out for somewhere better but...' She sighed. 'The worst of it is trying to get rid of stuff. We're going from five bedrooms to three, from' – she gestured with her free hand – 'all this, to a poky little kitchen-diner and a squitty little sitting room. Half the furniture has got to go, to say nothing of everything else.' She poured milk into both mugs. 'I keep telling myself they're only things...' She stopped and swallowed. 'Just things.' She handed Bex her mug.

Bex took it. 'I came to ask if I can do anything to help. I haven't forgotten how you came to my door the day I moved in and got my kitchen organised. I think I'd still be unpacking boxes now if you hadn't spurred me on.'

'Don't be daft.' Olivia smiled. 'But if you're serious... how long have you got?'

'A couple of hours. I'm due at the pub at midday.'

'You're still going to work there?'

'Of course. I love it. Belinda found a few uni students who wanted holiday jobs but they'll be going back to college soon so I'm back on the lunch shift.'

Olivia looked sceptical. 'I suppose working with Miles helps.'

Miles was Belinda's business partner and pub chef. And a good friend of Bex's.

'Naturally.' Bex sipped her coffee and grinned. 'Perks of the job. Not that he spends so much time in the kitchen these days. The new guy they got in, Jamie, is terrific. It's nice that Miles has more evenings free.'

'I bet it is.'

Bex ignored Olivia's implication, mostly because their relationship was still at the 'just good friends' stage although Bex sometimes felt that it might be quite nice if it moved forward another few inches. But, hey, it was lovely that Miles was a friend and she wasn't going to rock the boat by trying to force the pace. 'Right, what do you want me to do?'

*

9

Across town, at the comprehensive school, Megan pushed back her mass of jet black locks to peer at her class tutor with her smouldering eyes and answer to her name.

'Megan Millar?'

'Present, Mrs Blake.'

Megan, who reminded everyone of her parent's generation of a young Sophia Loren and her own of Kim Kardashian, was about as different from her stepmother as it was possible to get. Bex was blonde, blue-eyed and curvy while her daughter was sultry and leggy. And it had been her stunning looks which had made her integration in the local comp difficult the previous term as she'd aroused the jealousy of Lily, the class beauty who was also the class bully. But after a particularly ugly incident Lily had been removed from the school, the equilibrium of the class had been re-established and Megan had made new friends – foremost amongst these being Sophie, who was as much an English rose as Megan was exotic, and who now sat next to Megan.

It wasn't just good looks that the two girls had in common – they'd both had to cope with more than a fair share of personal tragedy; Megan had lost her father, killed in a ghastly traffic accident, while Sophie's mother had been struck down by multiple sclerosis and was confined to a wheelchair. They shared a sisterhood of adversity.

Mrs Blake handed out the new timetables. Same old, same old, thought Megan as she scanned the subjects. But, yuck, double science last thing on a Friday. Was the school having a laugh? From the look on the faces of the girls sitting near to her, her opinion was pretty much universal. At the front of the room their class tutor droned on about other admin arrangements, including dates for their year group assemblies and the parents' evening.

'Of course, emails will be sent to your parents to remind them...'

Megan leaned across to Sophie and pointed out the scheduled science lesson. 'That's well rotten on a Friday,' she whispered.

'Do you want to share your conversation with the class?' said their tutor, from her desk.

'Er... no.' Megan felt her face flare. Bloody Mrs Blake, she thought. She'd been horrified to discover that this school's policy was for the class tutor to remain with the same group of children from Years Seven to Eleven; better pastoral care, apparently. This was fine if your class tutor didn't hate you which, Megan reckoned, Mrs Blake did.

'Then shall we get on?'

Megan nodded.

'So...' And Mrs Blake read from her list of admin points and the teenagers in front of her fidgeted. Ashley Pullen, the first friend that Megan had made at her new school, sent her a sympathetic look.

The bell went and finally they were released.

'That was a bit harsh of Mrs Blake,' said Ashley, catching up with Megan as she left the classroom.

'She's never liked me,' said Megan.

'True. She always thought the sun shone out of Lily's arse.'

'Yeah,' said Megan gloomily. 'She probably blames me for allowing myself to get bullied by Lily.'

'Well, she's at St Anselm's now.'

'Lucky St Anselm's. Lily's poison.'

Megan peeled off to walk to the next class with a group of boys. 'See you after school?' said Ashley over his shoulder. 'Meet you at the gates?'

'Cool,' said Megan. She stared after him. He was still, she reckoned, the hottest boy in the school; those grey eyes, those dirty blond curls and those eyelashes! But while they were friends he'd never shown an interest in being more than that. She sighed.

At the vicarage, Heather was tidying up the Sunday papers which were still strewn around the sitting room although they were mostly unread. She and Brian had spent most of the previous evening going over the ramifications and implications of the accident in the bell tower as well as making a phone call to the hospital to find out how Sarah was doing. She had, as Heather had suspected, broken both her legs but her back was just severely bruised. Her prognosis was good – which was a blessed relief. However they also had to face the fact that the broken stay might have caused other damage or that the stay broke as a result of other underlying problems with the bells. She bundled the papers together and was about to carry them through to the pantry to drop them into the recycling box when the doorbell went. She tucked them under one arm as she went to open it.

'Hello, Bert,' she said to the churchwarden. 'You've heard how Sarah is, I take it?'

Bert nodded as he wiped his feet and came into the hall. 'Better than we had a right to expect, given the tumble she took. That was a bad do. I can't believe it took so long to get her out of the bell chamber; the best part of two hours, I heard.'

Heather nodded. 'It was like a mountain rescue exercise. They had to strap her to a special stretcher and lower her through the trapdoor.'

'Poor kid. On top of everything else.'

'Still, it'll be something to tell her grandkids.'

Bert snorted. 'Mebbe she'd rather she'd not had the accident *or* the tale to tell.'

'Point taken. Anyway, you're here to see Brian, no doubt. He's in his study. Go on through.'

Bert headed for the study door. 'Only me, Reverend,' he said as he knocked and then opened it.

Heather walked to the kitchen and dumped the papers. The doorbell went again.

'Oh, for heaven's sake,' she grumbled as she retraced her steps. Honestly, she thought, it would be quieter to take up residence at Clapham Junction. She opened the door again. It was her cleaner, Amy Pullen, the town gossip and mother of Megan's friend Ashley. 'Amy? But it's not your day to do for me.'

'No, you're all right, Mrs S. I've just popped over to ask you a big favour.'

'Ask away,' said Heather.

'Well, Olivia's going to be moving out of her gaff soon and she's said she'll recommend me to the new people, write me a reference, but she's got a lot on her plate and… well…'

'You think she might forget.'

Amy nodded. 'And then there's that business with my Billy.'

'Indeed.' Amy's Billy, who had been a part of a local crime wave. Amy's Billy, who had been mates with the local drug dealer. Amy's Billy, who had broken into the vicarage one Sunday morning and nicked a load of Heather's stuff including her mother's antique silver clock. Heather glanced over her shoulder to where it had been reinstated on her sitting room mantelpiece.

'Not that he's my Billy now,' said Amy. 'I'm never having nothing to do with him no more.'

'I should hope not,' said Heather.

'But if the new people get to hear that I went out with a bloke who got sent down for three years… well, it stands to reason, don't it, that they mightn't want me to work for them.'

Heather nodded. Amy might have a point. Guilty by association even though she'd had nothing to do with the break-ins. 'So what do you want me to do about it?'

'Could you write me a reference? Please. What with you being the vicar's wife and everything, it'd give me a better chance.' She gave Heather a winning smile.

'Of course, I will.'

'You're a star. And I'm going to ask Jacqui an' all. I mean, it can't harm to have a doctor's wife onside too, can it?'

'No. So, have you heard from Billy?'

'No, and I don't want to. I saw his mum the other day – she says he's finding the nick tough. And so he bloody well should, if you'll pardon my French. When I think what he did. And there was me hoping he might pop the question. I tell you, I had a lucky escape there.'

'You did. He was a wrong 'un.'

Amy shrugged. 'But I miss the company. Don't get me wrong, I know I'm better off without him but it was nice to have a grown-up to go out with. He used to take me to some well-lush places.'

'I'm sure.' Heather didn't point out that it was probably paid for out of his ill-gotten gains as a thief and a fence.

'I'm thinking about trying one of those dating websites.'

'Really?' Heather was aghast. 'Is that wise?'

'Well,' said Amy folding her arms. 'I can't do any worse than Billy, now can I?'

Heather thought there was every likelihood that she could, but she kept her counsel. 'Good luck, then.'

Amy glanced at her watch. 'I'd better be off. See ya. I'll pick up that reference when I come to do for you next.'

'See you then.' Heather closed the door. She liked Amy and admired her for the way she held down innumerable jobs to keep a roof over her and her son's heads, but she was inclined to be impulsive and Heather was certain she wasn't the best judge of character – not if Billy was anything to go by. Frankly, she thought, Amy's foray into online dating might be doomed but there wasn't much she could do, except be there if – and when – it all went wrong.

2

Brian and Bert were both puffing like steam engines when they got to the belfry. Neither was in their first flush of youth and Bert might have the weather-beaten complexion of an outdoorsman but most of that came from pottering about on his allotment. A sportsman he wasn't, as his slight paunch attested. Brian wasn't much better as regards to fitness but, not being a regular at the Talbot, he didn't have Bert's beer belly.

A pigeon exploded out through a damaged portion of the louvres leaving a solitary feather floating to the floorboards which were dotted with bird droppings. In the centre of the belfry there was a lattice of heavy timbers that formed the wooden bell frame supporting the six bells. Around the edge was a gap of just a couple of feet which enabled Pete, the steeple keeper, to get to the bells to inspect them and their wooden frame which was something he did every few months.

'We ought to get that fixed,' said Brian, looking at the gap in the wooden slats. He moved towards it and stooped slightly so he could see through it, taking in the view across the cricket pitch to the Georgian town hall which rose above the higgledy-piggledy roofs of the town. On a level with him he could see the rookery in the upper branches of the oaks that formed the boundary between the churchyard and the road, and in the distance were the hills that sheltered the town from the worst of the north-westerly winds. It had been a while since he'd been up here and he'd forgotten what a stunning view it was. He turned and patted the nearest bell. 'It always amazes me to think that these were here when James the First was on the throne. The history...' He turned around and looked at the tangle of rope wound around the wheel of the number three bell. Beneath the bell was the broken stay. Brian bent down and picked it up. 'You wouldn't think that a little bit of wood like this could cause such trouble, would you?'

'Yeah, well, that's the thing, Reverend, it's not the only bit of wood that's about to cause trouble. Look at this. Here,' said Bert who was crouched by a bell. He picked up some fine sawdust that was on the floorboards and showed it to the vicar.

'So?'

'So, it means the joints are moving, rubbing against each other. It's got to be fixed because it'll only get worse. And that's not the only place like it.'

'That's not good, I take it.'

Bert shook his head. 'We might be able to put wedges in but it's a temporary fix. We need it properly done, if you ask me. There comes a point when we can't tighten up the bolts no more. I spoke to Pete who says it ought to be done sooner not later cos once a bell frame starts shaking... All that weight swinging out of kilter...'

'So what's the solution?'

'Pete reckons that we need to put some girders in, under the bell frame, that'll stop the movement. He knows of another church with a problem just like ours – that's what they did, he says. You see, Reverend, now the joints have started to move, every time we ring the bells it makes it worse and worse. These bells are blooming heavy buggers and when they swing... well...' Bert shrugged.

Brian stared gloomily at the bells. 'It sounds expensive.'

Bert nodded. 'Anything involving the bells is expensive.'

'I'm going to have to get advice on this,' said Brian. 'Firstly we need an expert to tell us how bad it all is, secondly I need to find out how we can get money to fix it.'

'Yeah, but that's not the worst of it.'

Brian stared at Bert. 'There's worse?'

'Well, not in money terms.'

'In what terms, then?'

'Pete's worried that if we keep ringing the bells, with the bell frame in this state, we'll do damage. Real *permanent* damage. Structural damage.'

Brian looked at the ancient masonry of the tower. It looked solid enough but even he knew that the physics and forces involved with bell-ringing could change that. 'So what's he suggesting?'

'No bells. Not till we get it sorted.'

Brian stared at the bells. No bells? He felt a whoosh of irrational sadness. The bells were an integral part of Sunday; change-ringing was part of what made English church services so *English*. The people of Little Woodford loved the sound of the bells as they drifted across the town; it was as much a part of the fabric of the place as the town hall and the weekly market.

'The ringers,' continued Bert, 'agree with Pete. What if something more than a stay breaks? A ton of bell and only a few floorboards between it and the ringing chamber? It's not worth the risk. They're going to offer their services to some of the other parishes in the area – to keep their hand in – but, I'm afraid, Reverend, no one ain't going to be ringing ours till they're fixed.'

Amy let herself in to Jacqui's house, calling out a cheery 'coo-ee' as she did. Silence. Jacqui must be out, she thought. Good. Time was, a few months back, when Amy was making a start on the cleaning, the doctor's wife would have just been getting up, looking bleary and hung-over and staggering downstairs to make a coffee but, since the summer, she'd quit the booze, cleared out the bedroom of her dead daughter and gone to work part-time at her husband's surgery.

Amy opened a couple of cupboards in the kitchen, took out the spray polish, some multi-surface cleaner and grabbed a couple of cloths. She dumped these on the counter before she filled the kettle and flicked it on. Then she opened the laptop that had been left on the kitchen table and watched it boot up. Once it had stopped whirring she tapped in 'Lisa1998' and hit the return key. The screen flicked to the desktop icons. Good. Amy had been worried that clearing out her dead daughter's bedroom, which had helped Jacqui to finally move on, might also have caused her to change her password which was her daughter's name and the year of her birth – but, thankfully, she hadn't moved on that much. As the kettle boiled, Amy clicked on Google, entered the name of a dating site and logged in. While the little hourglass spun round she made herself a cuppa before she sat at the table. She could do this on her phone, of course she could, but it was so much easier and the pictures were so much clearer on a decent-sized screen. And she was sure Jacqui wouldn't mind... well, not much. Amy sipped her tea and looked at the talent that was on offer. After a few minutes she got up, went to the doctor's study and grabbed a couple of sheets of paper. Returning to the kitchen she began making notes. Eventually she logged off, and switched off the computer. Amy glanced at the clock. Bugger. She was going to have to shift if she was going to get the house cleaned in the time she had left.

Across town, in the offices of a local solicitor, Amy's mother, Mags Pullen, was busy signing the paperwork to allow the sale of her hairdressing salon to a new proprietor. Some months previously she'd made her mind up to retire, sell her business as a going concern and then plough the proceeds into a house on Beeching Rise – the new development behind the station. Quite apart from the security home ownership would give her, it would also make for a tidy legacy to pass on to her daughter when she died. Now her plan was all falling into place and in a couple of weeks, when the money from this sale was in her account, she could buy the house of her dreams.

Fancy that, she thought, as she signed the last of the documents.

She left the solicitor's office and made her way down the stairs and exited into the side-return between the bakery and the card shop. She walked down the alley into the street and immediately turned into the bakers.

'Three chocolate éclairs,' she said to the shop assistant, 'and three almond slices.' She'd treat Amy and her grandson Ashley to a slap-up tea later today by way of a celebration.

Bex finished helping Olivia and walked down the hill to her own home. Her hands were grimy with newsprint from helping wrap up Olivia's best dinner service and dozens of glasses in paper and bubble wrap prior to stacking it all in packing cases.

'Not that I'll ever need sixteen of everything again,' Olivia had said sadly as they worked. 'We'll be pushed to squeeze all six of us around the sort of table that'll fit into my new kitchen-diner – loathsome phrase that that is. And when the children get married and have their own families...' She sighed. 'No way will we be able to have them to stay and have the big family Christmases I'd planned. Still, water under the bridge.'

Bex had nodded and wrapped up another couple of veg dishes in silence.

'At least you haven't said anything like "things might have been worse",' added Olivia.

Bex hadn't admitted that she almost had but she'd stopped herself because she couldn't think how things *could* be much worse for her friend – death and disease excepted. Poor Olivia, she thought as she let herself into her own house. Moving from The Grange to Beeching Rise was going to be such a comedown. Worse was the fact that there were those in the town who would get a kick out of the schadenfreude Olivia's changed circumstances would bring. Tongues had wagged enough when her house went on the market but, if the talk in the pub was anything to go by, most inhabitants had assumed she was going to be moving into something even bigger and swankier. When they realised she was on the new estate in a modest three-bed house the gossips were going to have a field day.

Bex washed her hands and ran a comb through her hair, checked she looked clean and tidy then pottered next door to the pub. She banged on the door to be let in.

'Hello, Belinda.'

'Bex. Right on time as always. It'll be so good to be working with you again. The students were fine—' Belinda stopped, mid-sentence.

'But?'

'—but they weren't you. No attention to detail, no spotting things that needed seeing to *before* it all happened. I was forever chasing my tail with them – reminding them to bottle up, clean the tables, refill the salts and peppers...' Belinda sighed. 'But it's all better now you're back.'

'Well, that's some welcome,' said Bex, grinning. 'It's nice to be appreciated.' She slipped off her cardigan and made her way to the bar. 'After six weeks with the kids I've been feeling increasingly taken for granted.'

'Oh dear, that sounds a bit heartfelt.'

'Not really but when the weather was rubbish or if I hadn't made plans to fill every waking moment of every day then I was deemed to be a bit of a failure. I think mothers should be issued with magic wands.'

'Never mind, they're back at school now.'

Bex nodded happily and began looking at the shelves. 'Bottling up first?'

'Yes, please.'

The kitchen door opened and Miles poked his head round it. 'I thought I heard your voice. Welcome back – we've missed you.' His very blue eyes crinkled up in genuine delight at seeing her.

He had, thought Bex, and not for the first time, such a nice friendly face. No one could help but like him. And considering he worked with food, all day and every day, he was in remarkably good shape for someone of forty.

'You make me sound,' she said, 'as if I've been up the Amazon not in the house next door, nor that you've been popping in and out a couple of times a week.'

'That's different. You haven't been *here*.'

'Stop it, you two. Or my head will get too big to go through this door,' she said as she opened the door to the cellar and switched on the light. She pattered down the steps and reappeared with a tray of tomato juices which she dumped on the bar before she retraced her steps, this time to bring up a load of bitter lemons. With practised skill she ripped off the shrink wrap and, grabbing a couple of bottles in each hand, began stacking them on the shelf under the bar. As she worked Belinda cleaned down the tables and Miles disappeared back into the kitchen from where came the sound of him humming a happy tune.

Five minutes later Belinda opened the door to the pub and five minutes after that in came one of the regulars.

'Hello, Bex. Decided to come back to us, have you?' said Harry.

'I only took the summer off because of the school holidays. The usual?'

Harry nodded and Bex took a glass off the shelf and began to pull him a pint of best bitter.

''Tweren't the same without 'ee. Them students are all too busy on their phones and screens. They weren't interested in talking to us old 'uns.'

'Oh dear.' No, well, she couldn't see that twenty-somethings would take the same interest in the whitefly epidemic on the allotments or the cricket club tea-rota. She filled the glass to the brim and handed over the pint. 'Three sixty.' Harry gave her the correct money and Bex rang it up.

'Do you remember,' said Harry taking a slurp and then wiping his top lip with the back of his hand, 'when you started here?' He chuckled. 'You made a rare old hash of things for a while.'

Thank you, Harry, for reminding me of how bad I was, thought Bex. But she smiled at him benignly.

'You're quite the pro now, ain't you?'

'If you mean I can ring up a sale without making a complete idiot of myself then, yes, I am.'

Bert came in. 'I suppose I'd better buy him a drink and all,' said Harry.

'After the morning I've had,' said Bert, 'I reckon I deserve it. Pint please, m'dear.'

'What's up?' said Harry as Bex pulled the pint.

'Had to go up the belfry with the Reverend.'

'Ain't that part and parcel of being churchwarden?'

''Tis, but I ain't getting any younger. Them steps are a right bugger. Anyway, at the top we found we've got dodgy joints.'

'Shouldn't you be seeing old Doc Connolly about that?' Harry hooted at his own joke.

Bert gave Harry a hard stare. ''T'ain't no laughing matter. Pete the steeple keeper says we can't have no bells and the Reverend agrees with him.'

'No bells. None!'

'Not a one. Not till we've got them fixed at any rate.'

'But what about on Sundays?' said Harry.

'Just got to hope the faithful can find their way to the church without 'em. But it's a bad do,' grumbled Bert. 'A bad do.'

3

Heather stared at her laptop screen as she ate her cheese and tomato sandwich at the kitchen table. She'd Googled the question 'Problems with church bells' and had been rewarded with a plethora of sites, many of which, she was discovering, seemed to be concerned with how members of the public could complain about the noise. She scrolled down the page to find something more appropriate. She clicked on a link and took another bite of her sandwich as it loaded. She quickly read the salient points.

'There's this,' she said, swivelling the computer around so Brian could see the screen too.

He scanned the website that she was showing him. 'Still nothing about grants or handouts for church bells and a lot about fundraising,' he said morosely.

Heather nodded as she chewed and swallowed. 'I think we're going to have to face the fact that we might have to raise the money ourselves.' She sighed. 'It's that or give up with the bells full stop.'

Brian thought about the two options. 'Let's face it, these days there are many causes more worthy of funds than sorting out half a dozen big lumps of metal. Just think about the people at the food bank in Cattebury each day, the homeless, the underprivileged… and that's before we get onto what's happening abroad – disaster victims, refugees, orphans...' He looked at his wife and ran his fingers through his increasingly sparse hair. 'Can we really justify asking people to raise thousands for such a cause when there's so much misery around?'

Heather shrugged. 'Have we any idea what it's going to cost?'

Brian shook his head. 'I spoke to someone at the bishop's office who gave me the number of a specialist. They're going to send out an advisor to come and inspect the bells and tell me quite how bad it is.'

'So we don't know for certain that this is really serious.'

Brian raised his eyebrows. 'Well, if you want to think that you're welcome, but I know what Bert and I saw... and it's not looking good. And let's face it, Pete knows what he's talking about and if he thinks it's bad, it probably is.'

Heather sagged back in her chair. 'We're going to have to raise thousands, aren't we?'

Brian remained silent for a second or two. 'I think,' he said gently, 'it's going to be more like tens of thousands – maybe a hundred.'

Heather gazed at him in horror. 'I don't know I've got the energy for this any more,' she said. 'The very thought is making me feel exhausted.'

'And I need to tell the PCC,' said Brian. 'This isn't the sort of thing for a unilateral decision from me. I'll send an email to everyone and see if we can't get together sooner rather than later.'

'In the meantime,' said Heather, 'I think you'd better pray that the bell-frame problem isn't as bad as you think it is.'

After lunch Heather left her house, walked past the cricket pitch to the main road and then up the hill to Olivia's house. She knew she couldn't possibly ask Olivia to help with any fundraising – not if the worst came to the worst and the bells were going to cost as much as Brian feared – no, that wouldn't be fair, given what her friend was coping with… but she could pick her brains for ideas. She'd had some thoughts herself – no one who had been a vicar's wife for the best part of thirty years was going to be a stranger to fundraising – but mostly the sums she'd been faced with finding had been a few thousand at the most. Tens of thousands, maybe a hundred thou… that was in a different league.

Puffing slightly from her brisk walk up the incline Heather turned onto Olivia's drive and walked over the gravel to the front door. She pressed the bell firmly.

Olivia opened it after a pause of a few seconds.

'Heather, how lovely. What can I do for you?'

'I came to see if I could do anything to help, in exchange for a few of your brain cells.'

Olivia snorted. 'If you can find any live ones you're welcome to them. Honestly, I have never felt more brain-dead in my life. There is *nothing* so mind-numbingly boring as packing.'

'Oh,' said Heather, as she stepped over the threshold, 'you obviously haven't taken the minutes at PCC meetings, have you?'

Olivia laughed. 'Well, if the parochial church council is as dull as the town council…'

'Duller,' said Heather. 'It has to be. At least the town council involves proper politics, not church politics.'

'I'll take your word for it. Tea? I was going to put the kettle on.'

'Love one.' Heather looked at the organised chaos, the piles of boxes, the tape, scissors and packing materials set out tidily on the dining table. Then at the full boxes, the empty shelves… 'You've done an awful lot. When are you actually moving?'

'The weekend after next. Nigel's hired a van and the kids are all coming to help. Mike, Zac and Nigel should be able to manage all the heavy stuff and Tamsin, Jade and I will sort things out at the other end.'

'Sounds like a plan.'

Olivia nodded and filled the kettle. 'It will be if I can ditch all the things we don't need or won't have room for before the big day.' She plugged it in and leaned against the worktop. 'But that's a big *if*. Having all the kids around for a couple of days will be lovely – even if we're going to be in the throes of a house move. Anyway,' she said, trying to sound cheery, 'enough of that. What did you want to pick my brains about?'

'Fundraising.' Heather held up her hand. '*Not* that I expect you to do anything – you've far too much on your plate – but I'm after some ideas.'

'Okey-dokey.' Olivia got out the tea caddy and the teapot and Heather smiled to herself. In amongst all the upheaval Olivia still wasn't reduced to mashing a teabag in a mug. 'So what's the cause?'

Heather outlined the problem as the kettle boiled and Olivia made the tea.

'Bloody hell,' said Olivia as Heather fell silent. 'That's going to be expensive.'

'Very. Well, *if* it's as bad as Brian thinks... And, let's face it, he's not generally given to exaggeration.'

Olivia passed Heather a mug and offered her the milk. 'Let's go and sit down.' As she moved away from the counter she picked up a notebook and pencil and turned to a clean page.

'Right,' she said as she sat down. 'Jumble sales, coffee mornings, a two-hundred club with a weekly draw...' She jotted down her ideas as she spoke. 'Cake sales...' She paused and tapped her teeth with the pencil. 'It's a bugger it's autumn otherwise I'd suggest treasure hunts and barbecues.'

'Put 'em down,' said Heather. 'I can't see this being over and done with this side of next year. I've a horrid feeling it's going to be like the Great War; everyone said it'll all be over by Christmas but no one said which one.'

'Do you think it'd be worth getting some merchandise in? Mugs? T-shirts?'

Heather considered the option. 'The trouble is we'd be spending money in the hope of making money... and we may not. Supposing no one wants a *Save Little Woodford's Bells* mug.'

'Good point – but we can think about that if the campaign gets some momentum. What about sponsorship?'

'What about it?'

'You know – a buy-a-brick scheme or, in this case, buy-a-bell. There must be some filthy rich people round here who'd like to have their name associated with a good cause.' Olivia put the pencil down. 'Earlier this year I'd have suggested tapping up Nigel for a fat donation. Heigh-ho.'

There was silence for a few seconds.

'Right,' said Heather, putting her mug on the table. 'I've picked your brains, now it's time for me to roll up my sleeves and help. What would you like me to do? We can see if we can't brainstorm some more ideas as we work.'

'I've got a whole load of clothes upstairs that I can't see me wearing again. I've shoved them in the spare room but I need to sort them into the ones that I can take to that posh second-hand dress shop which might be able to sell some for me, and the ones that are only fit for Oxfam. I could do with a second opinion and then someone to hold open the bin bags for the Oxfam ones.'

Heather picked up her mug and got to her feet with alacrity. Despite being a good friend of Olivia's, she'd never seen the spare room that, she'd heard from Amy, was monstrous. 'Lead on.'

The spare room was, indeed, vast, made to look bigger with a huge wall of mirrored doors on a built-in wardrobe.

'Bloody hell,' muttered Heather, as she took in the door that led to the en suite and the large picture window with views across the open countryside. She reckoned she could have fitted the whole upstairs of the vicarage into this space. No wonder Olivia was struggling with downsizing.

On the back of the bathroom door Olivia had hung some seriously swanky and expensive-looking dresses. Even with a cursory glance Heather spotted a beaded cocktail dress and a long ballgown. She went over to examine them more closely and rifled through the hangers. There were some beautiful fabrics and – oh look – some labels with names that even she, a vicar's wife, recognised.

'Blimey,' she said. 'Where on earth do you go wearing frocks like these?' She hoped she sounded casually interested not green with envy.

'Golf club ball, the Lord Lieutenant's Christmas party, that sort of thing. But Nigel has resigned from the golf club and I doubt if we'll get another invitation to Ashbury Manor. I can't see the others at Gamblers Anonymous throwing the kind of parties that'll need a posh frock.'

She detected a note of bitterness in Olivia's voice. Not totally surprisingly, thought Heather. 'Maybe not.'

'Shall we make a start?' Olivia pushed back one of the sliding mirrored doors and revealed a rack of smart suits, coats and day-dresses. She picked out the first outfit. 'Sell or Oxfam?'

'Sell,' said Heather. 'Still very smart and looks almost new. I'd pay good money for it.'

'Would you like it... as a gift?'

For a second Heather was seriously tempted but she knew the suit was a favourite of Olivia's and others in the town would recognise it. Her pride stopped her from accepting it, aware that everyone would know it was a cast-off. 'You're very kind but I couldn't. Besides, you're a size smaller than me, at least,' she lied, to make her refusal sound more plausible.

Olivia laid it on the bed. 'OK. And this?' She picked out another suit.

How many suits did one woman need? Heather had two; a winter one and a lighter one for summer – both ancient. Heather considered the one Olivia was holding up. 'Maybe a bit dated?' Which it was, but not as bad as her own ones.

'Oxfam, then.' Olivia took it off the hanger and folded it while Heather shook open a black plastic bag and the pair shoved the skirt and jacket in.

'And this…?'

And so it went on until there was a pile of about another twenty items to go to the second-hand shop, six binbags full of other clothes and the wardrobe stood empty.

'Thank you,' said Olivia, finally, pulling out a dressing table stool and sitting down. Heather drained her now stone-cold tea, leaned against a chest of drawers and wished Olivia's taste in clothes wasn't so distinctive. There were a couple of things that were destined for Oxfam that she would have dearly liked to have snaffled for herself. She knew Olivia would have gladly given them to her. But it was bad enough being poor, she thought, without shamelessly advertising it to all and sundry.

4

As Heather finished helping Olivia sort out her surplus clothes Bex finished her shift at the pub, went home and apologised to Amy for the state of her house, before she made her way back up to the primary school to collect her two boys. She'd barely got into the playground when the bell jangled to signal the end of lessons and a couple of minutes later dozens of children, chattering and shrieking like starlings, tumbled out of the doors and began searching for their mums or dads. The ones outside the reception class looked both relieved and delighted to see their offspring returned. The parents of older children took the lunch boxes, damp paintings and coats that their kids thrust at them with barely a greeting, and then resumed their conversations with other mums and dads while their children ran off for a last game of tag or football before it was time to go home.

She felt someone tugging at her sleeve. 'Oh, hi, Lewis, sweetie.'

'Mum, Mum, can Noah come and play?'

Bex looked down and saw a lad with bright carroty hair standing next to her son. 'I suppose – if it's OK with Noah's mum.' She bent down to talk to her son's playmate. 'You'll be very welcome to come to our house, Noah, but I need to check it's OK with your mum. Can you take me to her so I can meet her?'

Wordlessly Noah took Bex's hand and led her across the playground. As she walked Bex cast about her for Alfie and finally spotted him on the climbing frame, looking as happy as Larry.

'This is my mummy,' lisped Noah, stopping in front of a stoutish redhead with a beaming smile.

Bex liked her at first sight. She stuck out her hand. 'Hi, I'm Bex – Lewis's mum. My son's asked if Noah can come and play for a while. I'm more than happy if you are. I can drop him back to your place in a few hours if you're OK with that?'

'If you're fine with that. I'm Janine, by the way. I don't suppose you'd fancy taking the rest?'

'Sorry?'

'I've got three other kids. They're a right handful.' As Janine spoke several other red-headed kids swarmed up to her. Bex was reminded of the Weasleys.

'No offence but maybe just Noah today.'

'I live in hope. That's fine, though. I live just down the road from here – those houses on the Cattebury road, number seven.'

'I know the ones. If I drop Noah back about six, I can feed him if you'd like – it'll only be something like spag bol.'

'Really? You sure? He'll eat anything, honest.'

Bex nodded.

'Noah'll be your friend for life. He loves anything with mince. Here...' Janine pulled a scrap of paper and a pencil out of her handbag and scribbled down a number. 'Just in case you need to get hold of me.'

Bex took the scrap and got her mobile out. She rang the number. 'Now you've got mine.'

'Ta. See you later.'

Bex collected Alfie from the climbing frame, made sure all the children had their coats, lunch boxes, school bags and reading-book folders before she herded them out of the playground and down the hill, taking a note of where Noah's house was en route.

When they reached The Beeches she closed the gate, told the two oldest to make sure they didn't leave Alfie out of any games they might play, and left them to it. The boys all ran into the garden to make a den and Bex let herself into the house then flopped, exhausted, onto a kitchen chair.

Five minutes rest, she thought, before I make the kids' tea. Just five minutes.

She heard the front door bang open.

'Hello, Bex,' said Megan as she clattered into the kitchen. 'I've brought a friend home. Hope you don't mind.'

Bex saw a blonde with huge blue eyes behind her raven-haired stepdaughter. Disney could have used the pair as models for Snow White and Sleeping Beauty, she thought.

'Bex this is Sophie, Sophie this is Bex.'

'Of course I don't mind. Hello, Sophie.'

'Hello, Mrs Millar.'

'Call me Bex, please.'

Sophie smiled shyly.

'I said she can stay to supper. She can, can't she, Bex?'

Bex made a rapid calculation as to how much mince she had and reckoned she could stretch it to feed five children – but she'd probably have to find something else for her own evening meal. She had bread, she had beans, she had eggs... 'Of course, as long as Sophie's family are OK with that. Anything you can't eat – don't want to poison you or make you ill?'

'No, nothing. I mean, I'm not a huge fan of liver...'

'Don't worry, I'm not going to give you that. And your mum won't mind?'

Megan jumped in before Sophie could reply. 'Yeah, we texted earlier. Soph's mum was cool. Right, come on, Soph – let's go up to my room.' Megan whirled out of the kitchen followed by her new best friend and a minute later the sound of feet thundering up the stairs to the top of the house was replaced by a One Direction hit wafting down them. Bex felt even more drained. Still, it was great her kids had got off to such a flying start this term. At the beginning of the previous summer term, when they'd just arrived, she'd been assailed by doubts about moving to this little town: was it the right thing to do following the death of the children's father; would they make friends; would they settle in? No two ways about it now – definitely the right call.

Bex leaned back in her chair and shut her eyes as tiredness and contentment flooded through her in equal measure. From the garden the boys' happy shouts, yells and squeals drifted in through the open front door. Bex got out of her chair to go and shut it – there was a distinct draught nipping her ankles. And while she was at it she'd check that the boys weren't doing anything silly or dangerous.

She looked into the garden and saw the three lads hiding behind a tree using sticks as guns to battle it out against an unseen enemy.

'Bang, bang,' they yelled, as they 'shot'.

'You got me.'

Bex spun round. There was Miles, by the gate, staggering, clutching his heart, before he did an elaborate pirouette and slumped to the ground.

The boys ran out from their hiding place and jumped on him.

'Hey, careful,' he said grinning and pushing them off. He levered himself up onto an elbow. 'Howdy, Bex.'

'Howdy, partner,' she said. 'What a nice surprise.'

'OK, boys, I want to talk to your mum now. Maybe we'll have another gunfight later.' He walked over to her, dropped a friendly kiss on her cheek as he followed her into the kitchen then sat down opposite her. 'Who's the redhead?'

'A friend of Lewis's. Some kid called Noah. And upstairs with Megan is another stray called Sophie and both have been invited to tea and I am a tiny bit worried about making the mince I bought stretch to feed five.' She led the way back into the house.

'Got any loaves and fishes?'

'It's not funny, Miles.'

'So, if you haven't got loaves and fishes in your fridge, what have you got? Can I?' He headed towards the fridge.

'Be my guest.'

Miles had a rummage.

'I could always pop up to the Co-op – leave Megan in charge.'

'No need.' Miles drew out a punnet of mushrooms. 'This'll bulk up any mince nicely.' He also picked out an onion. 'What were you planning on doing with the mince?'

'Spag bol.'

'I suppose.' Miles had another look in the fridge. 'OK if I use this?' He held out a tub of crème fraîche.

'Of course, but if I were you I'd check it's not gone green and fluffy. I'm not quite sure how long it's been there.'

Miles took the lid off and sniffed. 'It's fine. Perfectly OK.'

'So what are you planning instead of spag bol?'

'I thought a minced beef stroganoff. I've never known it not to be popular.'

'I suppose.'

'You sound doubtful.'

'I think I'll just check with Noah's mum that he doesn't have any allergies – like lactose or mushroom. She said he'd eat anything but... I asked Sophie and she assured me that she is fine with everything but I'd better be safe than sorry with Noah.'

Miles picked up a chopping board and got a knife out of the block while Bex made the call.

'No, he's fine,' she told Miles a minute later, by which time the onion and most of the mushrooms had been reduced to tiny, neatly chopped morsels. 'And you shouldn't be cooking for my kids and their friends.'

'Why on earth not? Besides, at the risk of sounding a bit personal, you look dead beat.'

'Do I?'

Miles nodded.

'I shouldn't be. But you're right, I do feel quite knackered. I think it's the shock to the system of getting back into the old routine.'

Miles stood behind Bex and gave her shoulders a rub.

'Hmmm, that's nice,' she said.

'Yeah, well, this isn't getting supper cooked.' Miles went back to chopping the veg, leaving Bex feeling a little bereft.

'I'll make a salad, shall I?'

'Please.'

The pair worked in silence for a couple of minutes until Miles asked where Bex kept her pans and the cooking oil. A few moments later the onions and mushroom were sizzling on the hob.

'I do love the smell of frying onions,' said Bex.

'One of the main reasons I became a chef.'

'Really?'

'No, I'm joking. But it's a perk of the job.'

Bex thought about the perk of her job; the one she'd admitted to enjoying when she'd chatted to Olivia earlier – that of working with Miles. 'Yup, a job with a perk is always a bonus.'

'So what's the perk of working at the pub?' asked Miles.

Bex was glad she had her back to him because she could feel her cheeks burning. 'Oh,' she said, trying to keep her voice light, 'I don't think there is one. Maybe it's not necessary when the job is only part-time.'

'Maybe. Or maybe I should make sure there are a couple of perks in your contract.'

A couple of totally inappropriate ones flashed through her mind. Should she tell him? Out loud, she said, 'I have a contract?'

Miles laughed. 'Obviously not – unless it's some kind of zero hours one.'

'That's more like it.'

Miles swept the mince into the pan and stirred the mix vigorously while the meat browned before adding the crème fraîche. He tasted it and then switched off the gas. 'That can sit there till you're ready to cook the rice and dish up. You can heat it through in a matter of a couple of minutes.'

Bex stopped slicing tomatoes and turned around. 'Thank you. You didn't have to do that.'

Miles pushed the pan to the back of the hob. 'Hey, cooking is like breathing to me – no effort at all and, besides, I rather like it. I'm never happier than when I'm knocking up a meal.'

'Even so…' Bex smiled at him.

Miles stared at her and the atmosphere got slightly heavier. For a second Bex wondered if he might kiss her.

'Mum, Mum, come and look what we've found.' Lewis, tousled, dishevelled and more than a little grubby, crashed into the kitchen.

'What? What have you found?'

'A snake. And it's this long.' Lewis stretched his arms as far apart as he could.

'A snake? Really?!'

'Really, *really*, Mum. Come and look.' Lewis grabbed his mother's hand and dragged her out of the kitchen, followed by Miles. When they got to the corner of the garden where Alfie and Noah were standing Bex could see that her son wasn't lying – something large and coiled was lying on the grass. As her heart thumped, she approached the creature. A grass snake – or at least, she was pretty sure it was. No zigzags so definitely not an adder and unless it was some non-native pet that had escaped she couldn't think what else it might be. The feeling of relief was quite strong.

'OK, boys. It's a harmless grass snake but he's probably quite scared of you lot so how about you all play at the other end of the garden and let this chap find somewhere quiet to go and hide away.'

'But I want to keep him, Mummy,' said Lewis. 'Please. I found him. I'd look after him properly, honest I would.'

'I don't think that's fair,' said Miles. 'This is a wild creature and he wouldn't like to be in a cage.'

'O-oh.' Lewis frowned and stamped his foot. 'But it's mine.'

'It's no one's,' said Bex firmly.

'And what would you feed it on?' said Miles.

'Grass?' he said hopefully. 'You said it's a grass snake.'

Bex tried not to laugh. 'No, I don't think so. They eat other critters, like frogs. Alive.'

Lewis wrinkled his nose. 'That's yuck.'

'It's the way nature is,' said Bex.

Lewis stared at the snake which began to uncoil and move towards the herbaceous border.

Miles whipped out his phone and took a picture of it. 'I'll send this to your mother and then you can take a copy to school and show your friends. Lewis Millar – snake charmer extraordinaire.'

Lewis cheered up at this. 'Cool,' he said.

The snake disappeared and Bex looked at her watch. 'OK, boys, another half hour of playtime and then I'll do supper. Miles has cooked up something special as a treat.'

'Is Miles your boyfriend?' said Noah, staring at Bex.

'Good heavens no,' said Bex. 'Whatever gave you that idea?' But she couldn't look at Miles and rather wished she hadn't sounded so completely dismissive.

It was an hour or so later, long after Miles had returned to the pub to start the prep for evening service, when Bex called her children and their friends to sit at the table for supper. She dolloped the mince stroganoff and rice onto their plates and put a large bowl of salad in the middle.

The kids, all chattering ten to the dozen, fell on the food. Sophie and Megan helped themselves to the salad – 'I've heard it's dead good for your skin,' said Sophie – while the boys shovelled in forkfuls of meat and rice and ignored the one-of-your-five-a-day option.

Bex caught Megan's attention. 'Can I ask you and Sophie to keep an eye on Alfie while Lewis and I take Noah back home?'

'I suppose,' said Megan. 'When?'

'After supper.'

The girls nodded.

'And if you could be downstairs rather than up in your room, Megan...'

'Oh.'

'If you've got music playing you won't hear if Alfie does something silly.' Which he'd done before, namely climbing on the furniture, falling off and cutting his head open.

'That's fine, honestly, Mrs... Bex,' said Sophie.

'Good.'

'Bex?' continued Sophie.

'Yes, sweetie?'

'Can Meg have a sleepover at mine at the weekend?'

'Please, Bex,' pleaded her stepdaughter.

Bex looked at Sophie. She seemed a nice enough kid and Megan liked her but... but she knew nothing about her family. Sophie's parents might be awful. Yes, it was unlikely but you couldn't be too careful these days. There were some dreadful stories in the papers...

'Tell you what, after I've taken Noah back home, why don't I walk with Sophie to her house and check that it's all OK with her mum?'

Sophie and Megan exchanged a look. 'I suppose,' said Megan.

Half an hour later, after supper had been demolished, the dishwasher stacked and Noah delivered back to his home, she walked Sophie back to hers.

'Is it far?' Bex asked as they headed towards the high street.

Sophie shook her head. 'Nowhere's far here, is it?'

'No, that's true.'

'Megan said you used to live in London.' Bex nodded. 'I've never been. It must be well fun.'

'It's noisy and dirty but there's a lot to do – museums, cinemas, theatre...'

'Not like this place then.'

'Maybe. But this place is a lot safer. I let Megan take the boys to the play park here. I wouldn't have let her do that where we used to live. The roads were a nightmare and there were some seriously odd types who used to hang around.'

'Yeah, but Little Woodford is *sooo* boring.'

Bex laughed. 'When you get to my age you'll find that boring can be rather nice.'

Sophie gave Bex a look which clearly implied that she thought she was off her rocker, then she turned down a side road.

'We live along here.'

Bex looked at the houses – a row of nice 1930s semis with tidy front gardens. Sophie opened the garden gate to one of them, got out a key and let herself in. 'Come in,' she said, holding the door wide. 'Come and meet my mum.' She led the way into the sitting room and there in the corner was a woman in a wheelchair.

'Mum, Mum, this is Bex. Bex, this is my mum.'

Bex looked at Sophie's mum. 'Lovely to meet you.'

'Likewise. I'm Lizzie. Sorry I can't get up.'

'No, that's fine.' She couldn't help staring at the wheelchair.

'It's all right – it's nothing catching. It's MS, which is a bit of a sod for poor old Sophie, especially as I've got bugger all upper-body strength these days so I find it tough to wheel myself about. I don't know what I'd do without Soph.' She smiled at her daughter. 'And talking of Sophie – I hope she behaved herself.'

'She was the perfect house guest.'

'Mum, can I have Megan for a sleepover on Saturday?'

'If you don't mind making up the spare bed,' said Lizzie.

'You know I don't,' said Sophie.

'She's a good girl,' said Lizzie. She turned back to her daughter. 'And you might have to get a few other bits and bobs from the Co-op. I did an online shop but I just did it for the two of us.'

'That's fine, Mum. And it's OK with you, is it, Bex?'

Bex nodded. 'Of course. Right – I'd better get back to my lot. I'll let myself out. Lovely to meet you, Lizzie.'

As Bex closed the front door behind her she felt really sorry for Lizzie – MS and so young. And it sounded as if Sophie was her carer... no dad. Tough on them both, she thought.

5

A couple of days later Olivia looked at the pile of bin bags that, with Zac's help, she'd finally got around to hauling downstairs and which were now heaped in the corner of the living room. God, how she hated this process of clearing out, of getting rid, of downsizing. There was no joy to be found in anything to do with this house move. The fact that Amy had cheerfully informed her that she could look forward to less carpet to hoover hadn't helped matters either; if they weren't moving and if Nigel wasn't broke she wouldn't *have* to face hoovering her own bloody carpets. And as for the fact there were going to be three adults crammed into a poky little house that was about a quarter the size of the space they now occupied... Gah.

Olivia flopped onto the sofa and thought about the future – and didn't much like what was on offer. On the positive side Nigel still had his job and he earned a decent wedge but Zac's fees still had to be paid and if they wanted any sort of security, when Nigel retired, he had to rebuild his pension pot – the pension pot he'd raided, along with almost every other asset they'd possessed, to fund his gambling habit. Their financial advisor had told them what Nigel ought to put away each month to give them any chance of a comfortable old age so, after that and the school fees had been creamed off – and, presumably, Zac's subsequent uni fees – the leftovers meant they'd all have to tighten their belts. No more exotic holidays, no more city breaks, no skiing holidays, no Michelin-starred restaurants, no life's little luxuries – like having a cleaner...

Olivia sighed. She was being self-pitying, she knew. They would still have a roof, they would still have enough food on their plates and, dear God, they'd still be better off than millions of the world's population, but she'd got used to life's little luxuries, she liked not having to worry about money – huh... that ship had sailed. It had not only sailed but it was halfway across the Atlantic. She sighed again. If she wanted to have a chance of a sniff of those things, ever again, she'd have to find a way of getting some more cash in the bank every month, and even she could work out that there was only one way of achieving it: she'd have to get a job.

Olivia flopped back against the cushions and considered the prospect. A job? For a start, was she even employable? She had a decent degree from a good university and she could operate a computer. She was good at organising things, she was literate, numerate... But she was also the wrong side of fifty and hadn't had a paid job for thirty years.

She got up and walked over to Nigel's desk in the corner of the sitting room and sat down in front of the computer. She typed 'Jobs – Little Woodford' into a search engine and then scanned the results. Data entry clerk, no... hairdresser, no... greenkeeper, no... ooh... now that looked hopeful – receptionist wanted at Woodford Priors. Olivia clicked on the link and read the job spec: reliable person wanted for front-of-house duties at a country house hotel. Good interpersonal skills essential, as is English as a first language... Olivia read to the end of the ad. As far as she could see she ticked every box. And, what was more, she could cycle to work. She gazed at the screen and thought about all the implications of taking on this job. For a start it would involve shift work. Would that be a problem? Not for her, but how about Zac and Nigel? An inner voice said that both were perfectly capable of looking after themselves but would

Nigel really want to come home after a hard day at the office and start cooking? Maybe he'd have to. And Zac could lend a hand instead of playing stupid games on his computer.

Olivia made her mind up. She was going to apply for this job.

Half an hour later, dressed in a smart skirt and blouse, her make-up immaculate and her hair tidy, Olivia cycled along the Cattebury road to the turning to Woodford Priors. She knew perfectly well that she could have downloaded an application form on the computer but she didn't want her application to be just one other on the pile. She was well aware that her CV would probably be the thinnest but she was also well aware that first impressions counted for a lot. As did enthusiasm, charm and good grooming – none of which would be apparent on an emailed proforma.

She cycled along the avenue of copper beeches that flanked the drive to the honey-coloured stone mansion, past beds filled with dahlias, chrysanthemums, autumn crocuses and verbena. In the car park to her right she saw a fleet of luxury vehicles – the type of guests at this hotel didn't turn up in family saloons. At the front door, Olivia dismounted carefully, flicked down the stand and pushed open the door.

Despite the fact that it was still mild, a huge fire burned and crackled in the enormous Tudor fireplace. Thick Persian rugs and deep sofas were carefully placed in the vast hall and a discreet sign at the far end of the cavernous space indicated where to find the reception. Olivia walked towards the desk, her footsteps clacking across the ancient stone flags before being muffled by a carpet.

A young girl in a black blazer looked up and smiled. 'Good morning,' she said.

'Good morning,' Olivia responded. 'I was wondering if it might be possible to see the duty manager?'

A frown creased the young girl's forehead. 'May I ask what it concerns?'

'Yes, of course. I want to apply for the vacancy as a receptionist.'

'Let me give you a form.'

'No, thank you.'

'But—'

'But, it will save everyone a great deal of time and effort if I could speak to him.'

'*She* is extremely busy.'

'We all are, and this won't take long.' Olivia smiled. 'Please,' she added in a tone that indicated she wasn't going to be shifted.

The receptionist blew hard down her nose. 'I'll ask Mrs Timms if she can spare a minute.' She disappeared into the office behind the desk.

Olivia could hear a low rumble of voices and then an older woman in an identical blazer to the receptionist appeared.

'Now then,' she said. 'What can I do for you?'

'I want the job of receptionist. Honestly, I am perfect for it. I fulfil all the criteria; I live locally, I am utterly reliable, honest and trustworthy. I speak good French and a smattering of German, I am in robust good health and there is no chance of me going off on maternity leave.' Olivia shot a look at the duty receptionist.

For a second Mrs Timms looked stunned then she regained her equilibrium. 'In which case I can let you have an application form.'

'And how many of the applicants are you planning on interviewing?' asked Olivia. 'Even if it's only a handful it's going to take a morning of your time – and I am sure a busy woman like you, running a hotel like this, has better things to do than that.'

'Well...'

'Precisely. So, as the deadline for submitting applications isn't until the end of next week, I suggest you give me a week's trial. If at the end of the week I haven't carried out the required duties to your entire satisfaction then, by all means, show me the door, interview the other applicants and employ someone else.'

'But...'

'And you needn't pay me. Call it an internship.'

'But…'

'I'm a quick learner and I can supply any number of references.'

Mrs Timms looked shell-shocked.

'What have you got to lose?' Olivia smiled at her.

There was a pause while Mrs Timms thought about it. 'Nothing… I suppose.'

'Indeed. Mrs Timms, I'll be frank with you, I want this job, very much. If you give me a chance, I won't let you down.'

'Mrs…'

'Laithwaite. Olivia Laithwaite.'

'Mrs Laithwaite, I can see that. Your drive and determination are commendable but the decision isn't mine.'

'But you will have a say.'

Mrs Timms nodded.

'Then all I ask of you is that you relay this conversation to the person who has the ultimate responsibility for filling this post.' Olivia pulled a card from her jacket pocket. 'All my contact details are here. If I could ask you to let me know as soon as you have made a decision. Thank you for your time and I look forward to hearing from you.'

Olivia turned and retraced her steps. When she got outside she leaned against the wall by the front door. The show of confidence and bravado had left her feeling completely drained. What was more she was completely unsure whether her approach had been a ghastly mistake or a stroke of genius.

Later that day Olivia got back from a trip to the second-hand dress shop feeling quite up-beat as the dress-shop owner had offered her rather more for the dresses than she'd been expecting.

'It is, of course, dependent on whether they sell or not,' she'd been told, 'but from experience, your outfits are exactly what tend to have a quick turnaround.'

As she dropped her handbag on the coffee table she could hear music playing from Zac's room. She was glad he was home as she had a couple of jobs for him – one of them being to give her a hand with all the bags for the Oxfam shop. She might as well make the most of having another pair of hands before he returned to school in a few days. But first, she needed a coffee before she carried on with the packing and the sorting. As the kettle boiled she noticed the light flashing on the answering machine. She hit the playback button.

'This is a message for Mrs Olivia Laithwaite,' said an unknown voice. 'I am ringing you from Woodford Priors and I have been asked to contact you regarding an interview with Mr Jameson, the manager. Please will you ring back and arrange an appointment with him at your earliest convenience.'

Callooh-callay, thought Olivia as she spooned coffee grounds into the cafetière. Maybe her brass neck had paid off after all.

A few minutes later, she took a sip of her coffee followed by a deep breath, then she phoned the hotel.

'I had a message to call Mr Jameson,' she said to the operator. 'It's Olivia Laithwaite.'

'Please hold while I put you through.'

Awful plinketty-plunk music came down the line. That's got to go, thought Olivia. Who on earth had thought this ghastly racket was appropriate for a hotel like Woodford Priors? No, they should have something like Bach's Double Violin Concerto; something classical and soothing.

There was a click. 'Mrs Laithwaite?'

'Yes, you asked for me to ring you.'

'Indeed. Mrs Timms passed on your message. I have to say that your approach to answering a job application is a first.'

'Yes, well…'

'But your enthusiasm is to be commended.'

'Thank you.'

'As is your offer to work unpaid for a trial period.'

'It seems only sensible.'

'So, unconventional though it all is, we have decided to give you a trial of one week, starting Monday, with the strict understanding that if we find your work unsatisfactory in any way, the arrangement will be terminated with no liability on either side.'

'I completely understand, Mr Jameson. What time do you want me on duty on Monday?'

'Eleven o'clock.'

'Eleven?'

'The staff will be very busy checking out guests before that and will not have the time or the manpower to start training you or look after you.'

'Yes, yes, I fully understand.'

'And please wear either a black skirt or trousers and a white blouse. We will provide you with the appropriate jacket.'

'Yes, yes of course.' For a second Olivia panicked that she'd got rid of her black skirt but then remembered that the Oxfam bags had yet to be delivered to the charity shop. Thank goodness for that.

'Right, we'll see you on Monday.'

'Yes, Mr Jameson. And thank you.'

Olivia put the phone down and grinned. Yes!

6

Heather was busy trying to decipher the handwriting of a parishioner who had sent in an article for the parish magazine – a piece about the wild flowers to be found in the graveyard. She wished everyone who liked to contribute had access to computers and email. While she and Brian were always desperately grateful for anything to fill out the meagre pages of their quarterly newsletter, there were times when she wasn't sure that the contributions were worth the time and effort required to put them in to legible, grammatical and correctly spelt English. She squinted at a word which was, like the rest of the piece, written in thick black pencil. What the heck could it be? She read the sentences either side of it to see if she could work out what it might be from the context. Nope.

The doorbell rang so Heather dropped the piece of lined notepaper on the table and got up to answer it. A stranger stood on the doorstep. Nothing unusual there – one of the 'joys' of living in a vicarage.

'Can I help you?' said Heather.

'I'm from the bell foundry.'

'About the bells?'

The man grinned. 'Well, I'm not here to give advice on drains.'

'Sorry. And, although there is *a lot* wrong with this house, the drains, touch wood,' Heather touched the door jamb, 'are functioning just fine. She smiled. 'My husband didn't tell me you might be calling.'

'No, he wouldn't have. To be honest I didn't know I'd be calling either but I saw a sign to the town on my way back to the foundry from another job and I thought I might as well drop in while I was passing. This will only be an initial inspection and I may not be able to give you a proper heads-up to the extent of the problem but, if it looks serious, I'll know what equipment I'll need to bring with me to give you a proper report and estimate of the cost. And I'm Graham. Graham Kennedy.'

Heather opened the door wide. 'Come in. Come and talk to Brian about the bells.'

She showed him into Brian's study and offered the men coffee.

'Tea, please,' said Graham.

Heather retired to the kitchen to make it and glanced again at the scrawled page of nature notes. She felt any energy she might have had drain out of her. She made the men their drinks and noticed as she did that they were almost out of milk. She carried through the two mugs then picked up her purse and headed out of the front door – go and buy milk or deal with the nature notes? No contest. She knew this was displacement activity and she'd have to face the near illiterate scribble later but the sun was shining, the weather was still warm and buying milk was a legitimate excuse to bunk off for a few minutes.

She walked up the road, past the cricket pitch, past the ancient oaks and the stand of yew trees and stopped to look back at the church. It would be, she thought, such a shame if the bells were silenced. This was such a quintessentially English scene and when the bells rang and there was a cricket match being played she sometimes felt there wasn't a more perfect spot in the world. Yes, without the bells the church with its fat Norman tower and the nearby cricket pitch would still be there but it wouldn't be the same. A proper peal of bells was the epitome of England. Nowhere else in the world did bells like the

English did, she thought. She made her mind up – she would do her very best to raise the money. Whatever it took, it would be worth it.

The energy that had been sapped by the awful article she was supposed to type up was replaced by firm determination to succeed in her mission. She strode on towards the Co-op, up to the end of the road, onto the high street and then she made her way along the pavement to the little supermarket. Her way was impeded by a pile of black bin bags outside the Oxfam shop. She was about to 'tut' when Zac came out of the shop and grabbed one.

'Oh, hello, Mrs Simmonds,' he said as he hauled it off the heap.

'Not at school?' she said.

'Next week. We go back later than state schools.'

He hefted the bag off into the shop and his place was taken by Olivia.

'Afternoon, Olivia.' Heather gestured to the mound of bags. 'The fruits of our labours?'

'Indeed. And I was coming to see you later.'

'Really?'

'I've got some good news.'

Zac returned from the shop empty handed and grabbed another bag.

'Yes,' said Olivia. 'I've got a job – well, I might have.'

'That's great but I didn't know you'd applied for one.'

Olivia recounted the nub of the story.

'Only you,' said Heather, 'would have that sort of nerve.'

Zac come out of the shop again, cast a baleful look at his mother and removed yet another bag which he dragged over the pavement and into the shop.

'Well, it's not completely a done deal. I have to prove myself.'

'You will but I have to say I think you're bonkers starting a new job with everything else you've got going on in your life right now.'

49

'Mum, are you helping or are you going to let me do this on my own?' said Zac on his return.

'I know, I know and I must go and help Zac. But wish me luck. I start Monday.' Olivia picked up another bag and said over her shoulder, 'I might have to give up on some committees.'

Heather continued on her way to the Co-op. Woodford Priors' gain would be the town's loss. Olivia might be a bit of a busybody but she was a dynamo who got things done. She wasn't everyone's cup of tea but she was a force for good and while Heather was happy for Olivia, she'd been assuming that, once Olivia had moved, she'd be able to rely on her to help with the fundraising. That hope now seemed to be shattered. Heather's new-found determination was already wavering.

Zac sat slumped in the passenger seat as Olivia drove the car back to their house.

'What's that about a job?' he asked.

'Well,' said Olivia, 'it isn't totally in the bag but I may be getting a full-time job at Woodford Priors.'

'Cool.'

'I'll be starting on Monday, on a trial basis and, if they give me the post on a permanent contract, I'll be starting for real the following week. But,' she glanced across at Zac, 'it'll mean some changes.'

'Oh, yeah.'

'I'll be working shifts so you and Dad will have to fend for yourselves some evenings.'

Zac stared at her. 'You mean Dad'll be cooking?' He sounded incredulous.

'And you might have to too.'

'Me?' His voice went up an octave.

'Yes.' Olivia turned the car into the drive.

'But I can't.'

'Then you'd better think about learning. It's not hard.'

'But... but...'

Olivia hauled on the handbrake. 'But nothing.' She turned and faced him. 'It's up to you but if you don't want to go hungry you and your dad are going to have to get a grip.' She got out of the car.

It was all very well taking a firm line with Zac – Nigel might be a whole other issue. She felt there might have to be a lot of compromise if he wasn't going to have a serious strop about having to do a load more around the house. And she didn't think, knowing Nigel as she did, that reminding him if he hadn't lost all that money none of this would be necessary would help matters either.

Olivia hadn't been wrong about the need to compromise. Nigel had been adamant that he couldn't be expected to leave for his office at six thirty in the morning, not get home till gone seven at the earliest and then be expected to cook his own dinner. Nor was he prepared to consider that Zac might be taught to produce anything edible. All he did agree to was to help with keeping their new place clean and tidy – which was something, Olivia supposed, gloomily.

The first week wouldn't be too bad – she'd be working nine to five while she learnt the ropes – but if she got taken on permanently she would be working shifts; early morning to mid-afternoon, afternoon to late evening, or, very occasionally, overnight. Nigel's argument had been that she had plenty of time to cook them supper if she just planned ahead and stockpiled the freezer with meals against the occasions when she wouldn't be around in the evenings.

On her first morning Olivia could feel her heart hammering as she arrived at the hotel and she knew it wasn't just from the exertion of the bike ride – she was excited and scared in almost equal measure. She put her problems about feeding the family and the impending move out of her head as she rode to the front door. She was about to dismount when she realised that she wasn't a guest but an employee – she needed to find the staff entrance. She hitched herself back onto the saddle and pedalled around to the rear. A sign on a door said 'Staff Only' – that'd be it, she thought. And even if it wasn't the staff entrance, logically the only people she'd meet on the other side of it would be employees and they could point her in the right direction.

She parked and locked her bike and pushed open the door. Unsurprisingly there were no sofas, no Persian rugs, no roaring fire but a stark white corridor with functional strip lighting and a lino floor – how different was this place when you went behind the scenes. Olivia smoothed her skirt down, took a comb out of her handbag and ran it through her hair. Without a mirror this was the best she could do before she met her employers. Feeling a little nervous she made her way along the length of the passage. She heard footsteps behind her and turned.

'Can I help you?' asked a young woman with a heavily accented voice. Polish?

'Mr Jameson told me to report for duty.'

'Oh, yes.'

'Yes. I'm the new receptionist.'

'Really?'

'Yes, really,' said Olivia firmly.

'I'll show you to his office.'

The woman led the way through a number of doors, taking several turnings until Olivia was sure she'd never be able to find her way back to her bike. She understood why Theseus had needed his ball of thread. At least she was only meeting Mr Jameson and not a minotaur...

The woman opened a last door and they were in the hotel proper. Instantly their footsteps became silent as they crossed onto luxurious carpet. Olivia's guide led her up the main stairs to the first floor and then opened a door marked 'Private'. She stood beside it as she let Olivia pass. Instead of a sumptuous bedroom Olivia found herself in a modern office with functional furniture, steel filing cabinets and a desktop computer, behind which sat a man wearing thick-framed glasses and a black business suit.

'Mr Jameson, this is the new receptionist,' said the woman. She shut the door.

'Ah, Mrs Laithwaite.'

'Olivia, please.'

Her new boss stared at her. 'I wasn't sure what to expect,' he said after a pause.

Olivia was nonplussed.

'But,' he added, 'if first impressions count for anything I don't think you'll be out of place behind our reception desk.'

'I'll take that as a compliment.'

'Have you done this sort of work before?'

'No, but I am good with people, bright and quick to learn. I am also punctual, tactful and reliable.' No point in *not* blowing her own trumpet, she thought. There was no one else to do it for her.

'As I think you said as much to Mrs Timms.'

Olivia nodded.

'Right, we'll get housekeeping to kit you out in the hotel blazer and then I'll introduce you to today's team at reception – our duty receptionist and the duty manager.'

Fifteen minutes later Olivia was in her uniform blazer with a lapel badge that announced she was a trainee and behind the desk in the hotel's entrance hall.

'I'll leave you in Amanda's capable hands,' said Mr Jameson.

Olivia recognised Amanda as the young lady who'd been on duty the previous week when she'd demanded to see the duty manager. Today's duty manager wasn't Mrs Timms but a young lad with a degree in hospitality, a chippy attitude and who was called Simon. Olivia thought he looked more like a kid who was bunking off school than a manager.

'Right,' said Amanda. 'I see you got the job.'

Olivia nodded. 'It's not definite yet. If I don't measure up this week, I'll be on my bike.' Literally, she thought.

'I suppose it all goes to show where being pushy will get you.' Amanda sounded deeply disapproving.

'I know what I did wasn't British, but I wanted this job very much.'

'Really?'

'Really.' And there was no way Olivia was going to elaborate.

Amanda sniffed. 'OK – so let's start with the basics. This is the computer terminal and this programme here...' she moved the cursor over a tab on a spreadsheet and clicked the mouse, 'is the list of all our current guests. Obviously, as new ones check in – which will begin after about two this afternoon – the list will grow. Now then...' Amanda clicked on a guest's name, 'this shows what their bill is so far.'

Olivia felt herself boggle at the figure.

Amanda must have sensed Olivia's reaction. 'They've been here a week. They're visiting from America.'

That was as may be – they were still racking up a bill that resembled the national debt. Olivia hoped they didn't do a flit.

By the time lunchtime came around Olivia felt reasonably competent with the computer system, she could print off a bill and she could programme a key card. There was probably a lot more to learn but she could at least be trusted to book in a guest. At three Amanda handed over to Susan who was told that Olivia was 'getting there'.

Damned with faint praise, thought Olivia. But then the last couple of hours of Olivia's first day coincided with a rush of guests wanting to book in, which left her feeling that she'd rather earned her stripes as she coped, more than efficiently, with their registration.

When she finally clocked off she felt completely drained and her head was buzzing with everything she'd learnt. She was also grateful that her journey home was downhill and the wind was behind her.

7

The next day, after Amy finished her shift at the post office, she popped into the pub.

She nodded to the old boys sitting in the window seat. 'Hi, Bert, Harry,' she said. Other than them the pub was empty.

'Morning, Amy,' they chorused back.

'Is Belinda around?'

'You'd better ask young Bex,' said Harry. 'She'll know.'

Amy walked over to the bar, which was unmanned, and waited for Bex to appear. Where was she? Amy drummed her fingers on the counter. A few seconds later Bex appeared at the cellar door with a tray of fruit juices under her arm.

'Hi, Amy, what can I get you?'

'Not here to drink,' said Amy. 'When do I have time of a lunchtime to bunk off?'

'So what can I do for you?'

'Is Belinda around?'

'Sure, she's upstairs.'

'Can you get her for me? I'd talk to you but you won't be on duty this evening.'

'OK.' Intrigued, Bex went to fetch her boss and returned with her a minute or so later.

'Hi, Amy, how can I help?' said Belinda.

Amy leaned over the counter and lowered her voice. 'The thing is...'

'Yes?' Belinda leaned forward too.

Bex began putting the fruit juices on the shelf, her ears straining to hear.

'I'm meeting someone here tonight,' muttered Amy.

'So?'

'It's a date.'

'That's nice.'

'Yeah, but it may not be. This is someone I've met on the internet. We've emailed and we had a quick chat on the phone but for all I know he may be a real creep or a sleaze.'

'Oh.'

'So can I ask you to do something for me?'

'If it's in my power.'

'If I rub my nose like this' – Amy scratched the side of her nose vigorously – 'can you tell me you've had a phone call from Ash and I need to get home?'

'I suppose. But, I mean, why would Ash ring the pub? Wouldn't he ring your mobile?'

'I've thought of that... no signal,' said Amy. 'This is the country – stands to reason, don't it? And this guy won't know what our mobile reception is like, will he?'

'Or you could pretend Ashley has texted you.'

'I could, but if you pass a message it'll look much more real. I mean anyone could pretend they've had a text.'

'I suppose.'

'Look, if you don't want to do it, say so.'

Belinda shrugged. 'No, it's OK. So what do you know about the guy?'

'Only what he's told me. And if it's anything like what I told him then it mightn't be the truth.'

'But, Amy,' said Bex, butting in, 'isn't the whole point of the process to find a match? If you're less than honest how will it work, how on earth will you find someone who is compatible? Someone like you?'

'But I don't want someone like me. I don't want someone with a string of dead-end jobs and who lives in a council house.'

Bex and Belinda laughed. Amy was always so refreshingly honest.

'And,' she continued, 'it'll work because, if he's not a complete tosser, he'll buy me a drink and I'll get a night out. If he is a complete tosser I'll still get a drink and I never have to see him again.'

Belinda and Bex exchanged a glance.

'What's wrong with that?' asked Amy.

Later that day, Amy pushed open the door of the pub. She was early but she wanted to bag a table near the bar so she could be sure that Belinda would be able to see her if she needed to make the emergency signal.

'Glass of tonic, please,' she asked Belinda.

'Ice and a slice?'

'Please. I can pretend it's the real McCoy then.'

Belinda put the glass under the gin optic and put in a shot of the spirit.

'Oi, I can't afford the gin.'

'On the house. Dutch courage.'

'You're a lege, Belinda.'

Amy took her drink and found a suitable table and then looked around at the other customers. She was pretty certain she'd got here way ahead of her date – a feeling that was confirmed when she didn't see any solitary men nursing a drink and looking apprehensive.

She took a nervous sip of her own drink and then pushed it away from her. She had to make this drink last until Dave... Dave-the-Date... turned up. She fiddled with her phone.

'Hello?'

Amy glanced up. 'Dave?' Bloody hell, he was early.

'You must be Amy.' He glanced at her glass. 'I see you've got a drink. I'll get a pint and then join you.'

Well, that wasn't in the plan... but he could buy her the next one.

Dave returned and sat down. 'Nice to meet you, Amy. I expect you want to know a bit about me.'

'A bit.'

'Well, as you know from the site I am thirty-seven and single and, if I say so myself, I am a bit of a catch.'

Amy looked at him. Really? His shirt collar was frayed, there was a mark on his fleece and dandruff on his shoulders. Jeez – if this was a catch she didn't want to contemplate the sort that got chucked back into the pond.

'Now then, I am a rep for a company that makes heating supplies. The things I could tell you about boilers...'

Amy took a slug of her gin and waited for the 'And what about yourself?' cue. And waited. She had another slurp and then another as Dave-the-date droned on about his job. Oh lordy, now he was on about micro-bore pipes. That was rich coming from a mega-bore.

'So, that's enough about work. You know what they say, "all work and no play makes Dave a dull boy".' Dave laughed at his joke while Amy opened her mouth to tell him something about herself.

'I know what you're about to say,' he said, nudging Amy so hard she nearly spilt what was left of her drink. 'You're about to ask me what I do in my spare time?'

Amy gazed at him in horror, but he completely failed to notice her expression as he launched into a monologue about the benefits of Nordic walking.

Amy began to lose the will to live. She drained her drink and looked at it pointedly. Dave knocked back his pint. 'Excellent. Your round, as I bought the last one.'

What the actual fuck? Amy rubbed her nose vigorously but Belinda was busy with other customers. Bollocks.

Stuff the plan. 'Actually, Dave, I don't think this evening is working out. I've just remembered that I've got some paint drying that needs watching.' She stood up.

'But... but we were getting on so well.'

'If that's what you want to think.' She grabbed her bag.

'But I came all this way...'

'Tough.' Amy began to make her way towards the door.

Belinda called to Amy. 'You off, hon?'

She went over to the bar. 'Yeah – turns out I didn't need that message from Ashley after all.'

Belinda glanced over at Dave. 'That bad?'

'Desperate.'

'Better luck next time.'

'If I can face a next time.'

Heather picked the letters off the doormat and began to sort them into the ones for her, the ones for Brian and the junk. The last she chucked straight in the recycling bin.

'Anything in the post, dear?' said Brian, emerging from his study.

Heather handed over a couple of envelopes and began to open the ones addressed to her. The electricity bill. She glanced at the figure. How much? Dear God – and they were careful to the point of frugality but at least their provider was assuring them that their direct debit would remain the same for the coming year. She sighed and opened her other letter which was the bank statement. She checked the balance and saw they were in credit... just. So their heads were staying above water; they had a roof, a living wage, food on the table and they could pay their bills. The basics were all OK. It would be nice, though, thought Heather, if, occasionally, she and Brian could have *more* than the basics. Once again the thought of taking on more paid work at the school flitted through her mind and once again she dismissed it, knowing that it would put more of a burden on Brian. All those little jobs that she did for the parish would fall on his shoulders and he had quite enough on his plate as it stood. And she was still cognisant that only six months previously he'd been unwell – she was still unsure about exactly what had gone on but he'd been deeply unhappy and troubled and she didn't want to do anything that might cause a recurrence. No, they would cope with *basics* if that meant Brian's sanity was secure.

Beside her she saw Brian rub his face and then run his hand through his hair.

'Something the matter?' she asked, recognising the body language as a sign of unhappiness.

'It's Graham's initial report.' He flapped the letter.

'Graham?'

'The bell man.'

'Oh... and?'

'It's not good.'

'And how bad is "not good"?'

Brian sighed. 'I suppose it could be worse – the bell frame is dodgy. The joints are in a shocking condition. He's going to come back and do a proper survey.'

'So we're definitely going to have to do some major fundraising.'

Brian nodded. 'Yes, he thinks the bell frames need an enhanced level of support and strengthening.'

'But it could have been a lot worse,' said Heather.

'I should give thanks for small mercies, I suppose.'

'You should.'

'It's still going to be a shedload of money we're going to have to raise.'

'There may be grants or charities we can approach. I'll have to have a look.'

Brian sighed again. 'Maybe, but I'll bet my bottom dollar the brunt of the costs will still have to be borne by the parish.'

'And Olivia is hoping to go back to work so that's probably my chief fundraiser and committee member out of the loop.'

'Really?'

Heather nodded.

'I'll pray for help.'

'Jolly good,' said Heather although in her heart she wasn't entirely sure that she had quite the faith that her husband had. She felt that leafleting the town might prove to be more productive.

8

On the Friday morning, Amy was busy getting her cleaning gear out of the kitchen cupboard at The Beeches when Bex came into the utility room toting the laundry basket. 'I've got to ask,' said Bex, dumping the basket on the floor in front of the washing machine, 'how did the date go?'

'Didn't Belinda tell you?'

'No. I meant to ask her yesterday but I forgot.'

'It was a total disaster. The git didn't even buy me a drink.'

'No! The rotter.'

'And boring. Honestly, Bex, he's the dullest bloke on the planet and he didn't shut up. Not once.'

'No? You're well out of that one.'

'Yeah but it's an hour I'll never get back.'

'You stuck him for an hour?' Bex was incredulous. She didn't have Amy down as the tolerant type.

'No, about thirty minutes but I'm counting the time to walk to the pub and back too.'

'That bad.'

'Awful,' said Amy gloomily.

'Are you going to try again?'

'Dunno.'

'There have to be some good blokes out there. They can't all be dreary bores, can they?'

'They'd better not be. If they are, I'll be having words with the dating site. Hey, before I forget, has your Megan said anything to you about a school panto? Ash says he wants to be in it.'

'She's mentioned it – said she might try out for it. She said a new teacher's formed a drama group and she and Ash have signed up.'

'And you're OK with that?'

'Why not?'

'They've got exams this year; they ought to be concentrating on those not poncing about on stage. Do you know what's involved?'

'Not much. The drama group is going to meet after school on a Wednesday and they're going to be performing *Cinderella* some time at the end of the term.'

'*Cinderella*? As long as they don't cast my Ash as an ugly sister.'

'Why not? It's a great part, lots of humour and one-liners.'

'And getting the piss ripped out of him for dressing up as a girl.'

Bex slammed shut the washing machine and straightened up. 'But isn't dressing up all part and parcel of acting?' She pressed the button to start the cycle. 'Besides, the school wouldn't allow the kids to be mean to him.'

'Like they didn't allow Lily Breckenridge to have a right go at your Megan.'

'That was different.'

Amy raised her eyebrows and stared at Bex. 'Really – and I'm still not sure I want my Ash getting all arty-farty. And if they make him drag up I don't want no one thinking he's gay.'

'They won't. As I said, dressing up is all part of it.'

Amy sighed. 'I suppose. And I suppose I can't stop him. Kids, eh?' She tucked the tin of spray polish under one arm, picked up the glass cleaner and some cloths with one hand and the vacuum with the other and headed through the kitchen to the stairs.

*

Olivia was standing behind the reception desk at the hotel trying to look calm but inside she was a mass of nerves. This was the day – she'd worked a whole week and at some point she would find out if the job was hers or if they were going to let her go. Her head told her that if she'd been useless she'd have already been shown the door, but her heart said that, useless or not, she'd provided an extra pair of hands for no extra cost beyond supplying her with a free lunch each day.

And over and above being apprehensive about her job, her mind was buzzing with everything she had to do before the process of moving into their new house began the next day. God, she wondered. What on *earth* had possessed her to think she could cope with a move and a new job? She must have been off her trolley.

The reception was quiet. The guests who were booking out had gone, the phone was silent, Amanda was in the back office cross-checking room service and minibar bills and Olivia was at a loose end. She tried to put out of her mind all the things she might be getting on with if she were at home but then gave up the unequal struggle, pulled a sheet of hotel notepaper towards her and started making a list.

Put freezer bag ice blocks in freezer – she didn't want anything to defrost between getting it out of one freezer and transferring it to the new one.

Check new freezer is plugged in and switched on – there was an integrated one in her new kitchen but was it working?

First van load, beds, bedding, food, essential kitchen equipment.

Make up beds.

Olivia tapped her teeth with the end of the pen. This wasn't rocket science. Did she really need a list at all? Was she being over-controlling, over-organised? The boxes she'd packed so far were all clearly labelled with the contents, and which room they were destined for in the new house. Her kids could read, they were grown-ups… why was she worrying that it would all go horribly wrong? She ought to trust them and delegate. If she got this job, she told herself, she was going to have to learn to delegate the running of the house a whole lot more. She crumpled up her list and chucked it in the bin.

She saw Mr Jameson walking down the hotel's main staircase. Her heart rate hit the roof. Was this crunch time? Was he coming to hand her her cards or the job? He approached the desk.

'Olivia.'

'Yes, Mr Jameson.'

'Would you come to my office? Ask Amanda to man the desk for a moment.'

'Yes, Mr Jameson.'

Feeling almost faint with nerves, Olivia did as she was told then followed her boss up the wide, shallow stairs to his office.

'Sit down,' he said.

Olivia took a seat. Surely if it was going to be good news he'd have just told her outright? Shaken her hand, said *welcome to the team* or something along those lines? What was all this about? She made up her mind she was about to be shown the door. And maybe it was for the best given everything else she had to cope with at the moment. She'd look for another job when she'd got the move sorted.

Mr Jameson pushed a piece of paper across his desk. What was this – a P45?

'If you'd like to sign this, please.'

'What?'

'It's a contract.'

'What for?'

Mr Jameson frowned and stared at her. 'You do want the job, don't you? You haven't changed your mind about working for us?'

'The job? I've got it?'

'Yes, of course. Do you honestly think we'd have kept you for the full week if you weren't an asset to the hotel? Especially in a front-of-house post?'

Olivia felt utterly foolish – her face flared. 'I'm sorry. I was assuming the worst.'

'Well, don't. I have to say I doubted your self-confidence when you demanded a trial but your faith in yourself wasn't misplaced.'

'I had doubts too. But I decided I had nothing to lose.'

'And quite a lot to gain.'

Olivia nodded.

Mr Jameson stretched across the desk and handed her a pen. 'If you sign in the places marked with a cross.'

Olivia shuffled her chair forward a few inches so she could lean on the desk, scanned the contract – all straightforward at first glance – and signed and dated in the relevant boxes.

She handed the pen and the contract back and Mr Jameson scribbled his signature on the pages too. Then he picked up a name tag with 'Olivia' written on it. 'Welcome to the team,' he said as he handed it to her. 'First shift, flying solo, Monday afternoon. And you'll get back pay from when you started.'

That was good about the back pay – the extra money would be useful. But… Monday afternoon. She decided she'd make supper for Nigel and Zac before she left for work – then they'd only have to heat it up. But what were the chances that they'd carry on sorting out the house without her and if they did, what, she wondered, were the chances of that all going smoothly? Now Zac was off drugs he was far less of a nightmare to live with – his mood swings had largely settled down, he was much less of a git but he was still a teenager and he and his father were still circling each other working out who was the alpha male. Some days Olivia almost expected them to clash antlers.

She shoved her worries about her domestic arrangements away. Mr Jameson didn't need to have the least inkling about her home life. 'Thank you, Mr Jameson. I can't wait to start. However, before I do, can I make a suggestion?'

Mr Jameson steepled his fingers. 'About what?'

'The music you subject people to when they get put on hold.'

'What about it?'

'Have you listened to it?'

'Er... no.'

'Then I suggest you do. It is appalling.'

A smile twitched on her boss's lips. 'And in its place – if it's so bad? Please, not the Four Seasons.'

'Lord, no. Maybe some Elgar, or another British composer? Frankly, anything would be better that what is on offer presently.'

'Thank you, Olivia. I'll have a think.'

9

Olivia waited until Nigel had poured himself a large gin and had sat down before she broke the news.

'I got the job. I start on Monday.'

'Huh?' He was reaching for the remote when the implications of what she'd just said hit him. 'But we're moving house tomorrow! You can't have forgotten.' He switched on the news.

Olivia glanced at the twenty-odd boxes stacked in the corner of the sitting room, the twenty-odd boxes she'd packed as opposed to the two boxes in the garage that had been filled by Nigel. She thought about the countless trips to the dump, to local charity shops, about the endless sorting and decisions made – what to keep, what to chuck... No, she hadn't forgotten about the move.

'So? We've got the weekend.'

'And what about the unpacking, the getting straight?' Nigel took a gulp of his gin.

'We,' she emphasised the word deliberately, 'will have to do it in our free time – evenings and weekends.'

Nigel sighed heavily. 'You don't have to work, Ol. Olivia,' he corrected hastily. He'd called her Ol for over thirty years and hadn't realised how much she hated the diminutive until she'd completely lost her temper when the truth about his gambling had come out. It was proving to be a hard habit to break – almost as hard as quitting gambling.

'It's nineteen grand a year, Nigel.'

'Is that all?'

Olivia felt deflated. She thought he'd be more pleased. She whipped the remote out of his hand and muted the TV.

'Hey.'

'It's nineteen grand a year, Nigel. Nineteen grand that *isn't* already accounted for like every penny you earn *is*, what with the rest of your debts, trying to sort out a pension, Zac's fees...'

'But I'm worried about you taking too much on. A full-time job on top of everything else is a big commitment.'

'Then you and Zac will have to help out around the house and help lighten my load.'

'But, Ol... Olivia, I work crucifying hours and it's not fair.'

Olivia thought that other men managed to help. She wouldn't expect him to do much regularly but even *a bit* would make a big difference. She sighed.

'And if it gets too much, you can always jack it in. I mean, it's not a massive wage, is it?'

Not compared to what Nigel earned, no. But it would make a big difference to them, to those *life's little luxuries* that she so missed.

But she didn't have time to argue the toss with Nigel; she had the rest of the kitchen to sort before Nigel went to the station to collect Jade and before her other two children arrived in their cars. Once that had happened, Olivia promptly despatched Mike, her eldest, back into town to collect fish and chips for everyone so she didn't have to worry about catering for her tribe. While he was doing that, and with the kitchen cupboards now empty, she and Tamsin began to take all the curtains down which Zac folded up and shoved into packing cases. Nigel was detailed to cart other boxes down from upstairs and stack them by the front door but with every journey Olivia became increasingly aware of the worried looks he was giving her. What she didn't know was whether he was worried she was taking on too much, or if he was worried about the impact on his own cushy home life.

Much as Olivia wanted to believe the former, she suspected it was the latter.

'Don't the new people want these?' said Tamsin as she balanced precariously on a chair and unhooked another pair of curtains from their gliders. Beneath her Olivia supported the weight of the fabric.

'They said they don't want anything – no lampshades, no fittings, nothing.'

'Carpets?' asked Tamsin.

'If they don't *they* can deal with them.'

Tamsin took out the last hook and let the curtain fall into her mother's waiting arms.

'Oof,' said Olivia.

'What are the new people like?'

'No idea – the estate agent has dealt with them. I've been right out of the loop. But they're moving here from London; that's all I know.'

'They're going to find this place quiet.'

'Maybe that's what they want.'

Tamsin looked down at her mother from her perch on the chair. 'Mum, we haven't even got a cinema.'

'There's one in Cattebury.'

'This place is a dump,' agreed Zac.

'No, it's not,' said Olivia.

But the debate on the pros and cons of Little Woodford was curtailed by the arrival of Mike with a pile of steaming white paper parcels smelling strongly of fish and vinegar. Oscar, aware that something odd was going on, had been cowering under the kitchen table but the smell of the food was enough to lure him out, tail wagging and a hopeful expression on his face. He was immediately made a fuss of as the family gathered in the kitchen and ate directly off the paper to save on washing up. Everyone talked at once, catching up on each other's news, commenting on the state of the world, arguing about politics, religion... everything. It was just like old times, thought Olivia, but then a sob threatened to erupt. She stood up and went to the sink so that she had her back to everyone as she brought herself under control. At the new house they might just squeeze everyone into the ground floor but she wouldn't be able to have them all to stay. No more big family parties, no big family Christmas... Moving out of The Grange was going to mean more than the end of an era, it was going to mean the fragmentation of her family.

At ten thirty, Olivia insisted everyone went to bed to get an early night.

'Tomorrow is going to be a long day,' she reminded them.

And so it proved to be.

Olivia was up and making tea for herself at six as she was worried about everything that had to be done before the van had to be returned to the hire company by the Sunday afternoon deadline.

As she made a pot of tea Mike stumbled into the kitchen, bleary-eyed.

'Pour me a cup too, please, Mum,' he said, dropping a kiss on the crown of her head.

'Sleep well?' she asked as she got another mug out of the cupboard.

Mike nodded. 'And I am planning on being so dog-tired tonight that I won't worry that my bed will be a mattress on the floor here.'

'I'm sorry you'll be stuck here on your own, but I think the sitting room is going to be so full of boxes it'll be impossible to even try to squeeze you in to the new place. And that reminds me,' said Olivia. 'I need to make sure we keep a set of Allen keys out to dismantle and reassemble all the beds.'

'What are we doing with the ones you can't take with you?'

Olivia handed her eldest child his tea. 'They're being stored in the garage here till Monday when a charity is picking up all the furniture we haven't got room for.'

'So, most of it then.'

Olivia stared at him. 'It's not funny.'

By ten o'clock the first of the van loads had been delivered to the new house and there were piles of boxes in the kitchen-diner, the sitting room and in all three bedrooms upstairs. Tamsin and Jade were busy unpacking the bedding while Zac and his mother wrestled with bed frames, the Allen keys and mattresses and made two double beds and a single, for Olivia and Nigel, the two girls and Zac to sleep in that night. As planned, Mike would be on a mattress on the floor of the old house. By lunchtime the beds had been made, and made up, and Olivia was busy trying to find places – and failing – for the contents of the first box of kitchen equipment, while Zac had been co-opted by his father and Mike to help with the heavy gear still to be transported, and Tamsin and Jade were rehanging some of the curtains. Most of them were in desperate need of altering, or being cut down to fit, but they would provide some privacy in the immediate future because, as they all had noted, with the houses on the estate being so close together, there was precious little of that particular commodity to be had. There was hardly a room in the house that didn't seem to be overlooked by a neighbour's window.

As fast as Olivia's team emptied the boxes and flattened them, Nigel and the boys arrived with more and more belongings.

'How are we doing?' asked Olivia as the men carried in the sofa to the sitting room. In the old house it had looked quite normal, but in this house it looked ridiculously large and, Olivia wondered, with a certain amount of desperation, if the other, matching sofa would be able to fit in too. She put her back against one of the arms and shoved it right against the wall of the sitting room. Maybe… maybe there was enough space for the other one. And if not…?

'Coo-ee.'

'Hello,' called Olivia. Who on earth could this be? 'In here,' she yelled.

'I brought these,' said Heather coming through the door carrying a huge tray of sandwiches. 'I was going to bring you a nice pot plant or something, as a housewarming present, but then I thought you'd prefer something practical.'

'Heather! You angel.' For the second time in twenty-four hours Olivia felt close to tears. 'You shouldn't have.'

'It's what friends do. Where's the kitchen?'

Olivia led the way and Heather followed. She pushed the heavy tray onto a yet-to-be-unpacked carton – the counters being covered in possessions that still had to be found homes.

'Got any plates?' she asked.

'Not that we've unpacked.'

'I am prepared for that. I've got a whole pile of paper plates in the car. Back in two ticks.'

Olivia followed Heather out of the kitchen but stopped at the bottom of the stairs. 'Lunch, girls,' she yelled.

A few seconds later her daughters came crashing down them. The noise of two pairs of feet on the treads was deafening.

Everything about this house, noted Olivia and not for the first time, was hollow and tacky and, consequently, all sounds reverberated. The stud walls, the stairwell, the pressed plywood doors that were designed to look as if they were solid, carved oak but had about as much substance as a flyscreen… everything was flimsy. She'd even noticed that the sound of someone peeing in the upstairs loo could be heard in the kitchen. She shuddered. The Grange had been all about quality, about high-end finishes, but this place… Even the garden was little more than a square of grass, a few paving slabs and a dreary fence on three sides. *Uninspiring* didn't even come close as a description. Olivia *wanted* to be positive about her new home but it was almost impossible. The only thing in its favour was the fact that it had allowed them to clear Nigel's debts.

Be grateful, she told herself. Be grateful that you still have a roof. She clamped down on the anger that it had been her husband's reckless addiction that had brought this circumstance about. He'd been ill. His addiction had been an illness. It hadn't been his fault. But deep down she wanted to rail, to shout, to throw things... especially at Nigel.

Heather returned with the plates and distributed them to the family while the Laithwaites, locust-like, fell on the food.

'There's veggie on the left and meaty on the right. Well, I say *meaty* – some of them are tuna.'

'Brilliant,' said Olivia picking out a cheese and pickle one. 'And so thoughtful to think of dietary stuff, though none of my kids have gone vegetarian – yet.'

'I'm trying to eat less meat,' said Tamsin. 'But – you know... bacon.' As she said this she picked a bit of ham out of her sandwich and threw it to Oscar who caught the morsel in midair and swallowed it whole.

'And roast chicken,' said Mike.

Heather watched them all tucking in for a few seconds before she said, 'Right, I'm going to get out of your hair. There's no hurry to return the tray – I have others.' She slid off, leaving the family munching.

By the evening most of the furniture had been transferred, as had boxes full of everything else from Olivia's kitchen and some of the family's clothes. Books, ornaments, spare bedding and towels, the contents of their home office, rugs, soft furnishings and anything that wasn't totally necessary for survival over the coming days and weeks were still in cartons which were stacked in the new garage or in the sitting room.

Olivia looked at the chaos that was her new kitchen and remembered the advice she'd given to Bex when she'd helped her with her unpacking – the advice about putting kit away in places where you planned for it to live for ever. Huh... fat chance of doing that here, not with the lack of cupboard space she now realised the kitchen suffered from. Yet another example of how the house looked superficially well-appointed but the instant you dug under the glossy surface you found it was an illusion. Fur coat, no knickers, she thought crossly.

At around six she slumped, tired out, on the sofa. Nigel collapsed on the other one and put his feet on a packing case.

'That's enough for today. I am bushed,' she announced.

'What's for supper?' asked Jade coming into the sitting room.

'It's either fish and chips again or the pub.'

'Mum! I can't have chips twice in two days – just think what it'll do to my skin,' protested Jade.

'Then find something else to eat,' said Olivia, refusing to be drawn.

'Like what?' Jade sat on the edge of the other sofa and eyeballed her mother.

'I don't know. There's a tin of beans somewhere, I think.'

'You're not going to cook?'

'No.'

'But, Mum... I'm tired and hungry and I really want to eat something healthy – not, you know, chips or pub rubbish.'

Nigel snapped. 'Jeez, Jade, we're all tired and hungry. Stop being so needy and spoilt. If you want home-cooked food, why don't you cook it?' He glared at his daughter.

Blimey, thought Olivia, that was a turn-up for the books. But she noticed *he* wasn't offering to cook. Baby steps, she thought, baby steps.

'But...' Jade lapsed into silence for a few seconds before she muttered, 'I thought you were broke. How come we can afford to eat out?'

Nigel shook his head in disappointment. 'I had a vague hope that some of you kids might fancy chipping in – you know, considering, Zac excepted, that you're all earning.'

'Un-fucking-believable,' said Jade standing up. 'We come here, we work our socks off and all the thanks we get is to be told to pay for our own supper. Like we *owe you* or something.'

'I think you'll find you wanted for precisely *nothing* when you were growing up. Is a bit of payback too much to ask?'

Apparently it was, thought Olivia, tiredly.

Outside the house, Olivia heard the van draw up. This would be Mike and Zac with the final load of the day. Olivia was tempted to tell them to leave it on the van – that they'd deal with it in the morning, but it was only kicking the can down the road. Tonight… tomorrow… the boxes needed unloading. Better to get it over and done with now. Wearily she stood up again and twenty minutes later the van was empty, the kitchen had even more boxes piled in it and Olivia got her phone out.

'We're going to have supper at the pub,' she told them. 'I'll book a table for thirty minutes' time.' She looked about at her family. 'It should give us time to have a wash and brush up.' Then she noticed Jade wasn't there. Maybe she'd gone to the loo.

'Sounds like a plan,' said Tamsin.

'Go and find Jade and tell her,' said Olivia. Olivia rang the pub and booked a table. She was just disconnecting when Tamsin returned.

'I couldn't find her so I texted her. She's at the station. She says she's going back to London. She says you've had your pound of flesh – whatever that means.'

Olivia didn't know what made her feel more disappointed: that her older daughter didn't get the Shylock reference or that her younger daughter was such a selfish spoilt little madam. She made light of it. 'One less meal to pay for then, and more room for you in the spare room tonight.'

10

The next morning Heather walked down the path from the vicarage to the church, wrapped up against a brisk autumn wind. She could hear a magpie's staccato call, like machine gun fire, coming from a tree in the churchyard and over to her right came the faint hum of cars on the ring road. The breeze rustled the leaves in the ancient oaks but here and there a leaf fell onto the outfield of the cricket pitch. Soon, thought Heather, there would be drifts of russet leaves and the local squirrel population would be bouncing around in them, hunting for acorns. The squirrels might be classed as vermin but she couldn't help loving them with their ostrich-plume tails, bright boot-button eyes and clever, dextrous paws. Whatever the weather or the season, Heather loved this view. A bit of English rural perfection.

Except today it wasn't perfect. Something was missing and ruining the scene. The bells were missing. The silence wasn't right. She stared at the church tower and wondered how long it might be before the bell frame got fixed and the congregation would, once again, be summoned by bells. Brian was already planning to exhort his flock to start fundraising. They had yet to have the problem properly assessed or to be given a proper estimate of the cost, but Brian had put out feelers to other parishes who had suffered similar problems and the sums involved were invariably eye-watering.

Heather reached the Norman porch and walked into the gloom, over the huge coir mat. Just ahead of her a familiar figure was picking up a hymn book and a prayer book.

'Olivia! What on earth are you doing here? Aren't you moving house?'

'I am, but I need an hour or so to gird my loins. I was up at six this morning to put a stew in the slow cooker so everyone will get fed later. I then did a couple of hours of unpacking before anyone stirred. I think I am entitled to some time off now.'

'I think you are too.'

'I need the peace, I need the strength...'

Heather put her hand on Olivia's arm. 'I understand.'

The pair made their way to the pews at the front.

'I didn't tell you,' said Olivia after they had prayed and slid back on the hard wooden seats. 'I got the job at the hotel – on a permanent basis.'

'That's brilliant.' But Heather's heart sank. No Olivia to help fundraise. She gave herself a slap for being selfish.

'I start on Monday afternoon – a late shift which finishes at about ten. I've told Zac and Nigel they need to start to learn how to fend for themselves. It hasn't been greeted with unalloyed enthusiasm.'

Heather could imagine.

'But Nigel was a trouper with the move and he *says* he'll do his best to help out a bit and he does work hideous hours...'

Heather put her hand on Olivia's. 'It'll be all right. If anyone can make it work, you can.'

At school the next morning, Lewis was still the centre of attention in the school playground because of the snake in his garden. Small boys were queuing up to be asked to his house for play dates which was great, in some respects, but Bex felt that it would be quite nice if *her* boys got invited back. She didn't resent feeding extra mouths – far from it – she was thrilled her boys were popular, but it would be quite nice to have a bit more peace and quiet after school, a bit more time to read with them, find out about their day before they hit the supper-bath-bed-story routine. Maybe she ought to ration play dates.

Bex was still thinking about this conundrum when she left the playground and began to walk down the hill. Out of habit she glanced across at Olivia's house and saw her friend's bike parked on the drive. She must be finishing off the last bits of the move. On an impulse, Bex crossed the road, trudged up the drive and rang the bell.

'Oh.' Olivia sounded surprised to see her. Then she added, 'Sorry. That wasn't very welcoming. I was expecting it to be the people from the charity to take away our unwanted furniture, but it's lovely to see you. Come in.'

She led the way into the cavernous room that looked even bigger now it was stripped of everything that had made it homely, with the exception of a mattress lying in a corner.

'We couldn't fit everyone into the new house so Mike slept here,' explained Olivia. The place echoed as they walked over the polished floorboards. 'I'd offer you tea but, as you can see, everything's gone.'

'How did the move go?'

'Not too bad; Nigel worked like a Trojan and cracked the whip with the kids too.'

Bex felt her eyebrows shooting into her hairline.

'I know,' said Olivia. 'I was a bit shocked too but as a result we got pretty much everything done. Of course the downside was one of my children had a monumental sense of humour failure and flounced off.'

'Oh, Olivia. That wasn't what you needed.'

'Kids, eh? Jade couldn't take being read the riot act by Nigel. It's my fault – I spoilt her. Well, I spoilt them all, truth be told, but the others seem to have worked out that their sense of entitlement is completely misplaced nowadays.'

'And how's it going at the other end?'

'Why don't you come and see? I can offer you tea there and everything – even a biscuit or two – that is, if you can bear to wait till after the charity people have been and collected the stuff we've no more use for.' Olivia said it lightly but Bex could see that the downsizing was tearing her apart.

'You don't want me cluttering up your morning, surely.' Although Bex was itching to see Olivia's new house.

'To be honest, I'd love an excuse to take a break from the endless business of getting straight.'

The doorbell rang again.

'This'll be them,' said Olivia as she headed across the room to open it. Bex heard her giving the men from the charity instructions before they came in, removed the mattress and then she heard the clatter of the garage door opening.

Twenty minutes later, their van had driven off and Bex walked beside Olivia as she wheeled her bike down the hill to Beeching Rise. Olivia parked her bike, got her key out and opened the door.

'Here we are.'

Bex thought her bright tone sounded more than a little forced. 'Gosh, you look almost straight.'

'Total illusion. But we are getting there,' said Olivia. She bustled into the kitchen and put on the kettle.

Bex followed her.

'How about a guided tour while we wait for it to boil. It won't take long,' she added with a wry smile.

She led the way up the stairs. The contrast between this place and the huge barn conversion couldn't have been starker.

'Poky, isn't it?' said Olivia, as she led Bex back to the kitchen and made the tea.

'Compact,' offered Bex.

'But, on the positive side, I have a job, full-time and everything.'

'Olivia, that's brilliant.'

'I'm quite pleased.' She looked it. The doorbell rang. 'Excuse me.' She left Bex sipping her tea.

There was the sound of voices and then some thumping. Curiosity got the better of Bex and she stuck her head round the kitchen door. There on the doorstep was a young woman with three suitcases by her feet, sobbing loudly onto Olivia's shoulder.

'This is Jade, my daughter,' said Olivia. 'She's a bit upset.'

No shit, Sherlock. 'I'll get out of your hair,' said Bex, putting her mug on the counter and then squeezing past the pair in the narrow hall.

'I'll catch up with you later,' said Olivia stroking her daughter's hair.

As Bex walked away she heard Olivia say, 'Of course you can stay – for as long as you want. It's not a problem.'

But Bex had seen the space available in the house and she rather thought that it might be.

Olivia installed her daughter on the sofa, made her a cup of tea and then dragged in the suitcases from the doorstep.

Dear God, where the hell were they going to store all Jade's stuff? The garage was full of boxes, the spare room had almost no storage space in it at all and the other two bedrooms were full of her, Nigel's and Zac's clothes and possessions. She piled the cases in the hall and went to talk to her daughter.

'Do you want to tell me what happened?'

'It's Luke,' said Jade, between sobs.

'Luke?'

'My boyfriend.'

'Sorry, darling, of course.' Olivia could have sworn Jade was dating Ryan. And she had to make a desperate effort not to glance at the clock. She had so much to do before she went to work.

Jade's sobs stopped and she glared at her mother. 'I've been with him for three months now. I told you I was moving into his flat.' Jade's irritation with her mother's failure to remember all the details seemed to suppress her misery.

'Yes, darling, of course you did.' Had she?

'Well, it's like – my phone dies on me when I was on my way back home yesterday so I couldn't call Luke to say I was coming home. And when I let myself into the flat...' Jade gave an anguished wail, 'he was shagging another woman.'

'Oh, Jade.' Olivia put her arms around her daughter as the crying started again. She glanced at her watch. Shit – she still had to shop and cook supper before work. There was time but it was getting shorter and shorter in supply.

By eleven Olivia decided it was time to get tough. She had heard, several times, what a rat Luke was, how Jade was better off without him and how her daughter ought to have seen the signs, how she'd gone to a friend's house and got wasted on vodka, how she'd spent Sunday alternately throwing up and crying, how her mobile wasn't just out of battery but now completely lost, how her life was ruined...

'But what about your job?' said Olivia, while thinking about her own.

'I'll phone in sick,' she said. Olivia wondered how, since she didn't have a phone. 'Anyway, I'm not going back,' added Jade. 'They can sack me for all I care. The job is awful and I only stuck it so I could afford my half of Luke's rent.'

Olivia's heart sank. 'But... your career?' She didn't think there'd be many job opportunities in a place like Little Woodford that would need an MA.

'It's only a job, Mum,' wailed Jade. 'There'll be another. Anyway, how can I think about that at a time like this?'

'But... but...'

'You don't want me here, that's it, isn't it?'

'Darling, this is your home, of course I want you here,' lied Olivia, thinking about the lack of space, the inconvenience, the

83

way her planned new routine was already being thrown into turmoil. She had to bite the bullet and pull some sort of order back into her disrupted morning. 'But I *am* going to have to go out. I need to shop and then cook supper for this evening, unless...' She paused and looked at her daughter. 'I mean, I find cooking very therapeutic and calming.'

'Well, I find it completely stressful.' Jade glowered at her mother. 'Unless you want to make things worse than they already are.'

Olivia backed down. 'No, no. But I must get on. You'll be all right on your own for a little while.'

'I suppose I'll have to be.'

Olivia got up from the sofa and Jade instantly put her feet up on the covers and her head on the arm. Olivia wanted to tell her to take her feet off the upholstery but didn't quite have the nerve.

'Right, back in a bit.'

She tiptoed out of the room and gathered up a couple of shopping bags and her list before she let herself out of the house and walked to the Co-op. She had planned to go to the supermarket in Cattebury but there wasn't time for that – not and be able to cobble together a meal too. One of the very few advantages of living in Beeching Rise was the town centre was on her doorstep.

Olivia whizzed round the Co-op shelves and got enough to feed her family that night and to fill the fridge with essentials. She could do a proper shop tomorrow.

On her return home Jade was still lying on the sofa like a distressed Victorian heroine, staring at the ceiling and sniffing occasionally. Her cases were still in the hall and her dirty mug on the coffee table.

Olivia took her shopping into the kitchen and began to unpack it.

'Mum?' came a plaintive wail from the sitting room. 'Could I have some more tea?'

Olivia stopped putting away groceries. 'Give me strength,' she muttered, before she put the kettle on. She made a pact with herself. She'd indulge Jade today, but tomorrow her daughter would have to brace up and pull her weight if she was going to stay.

11

Megan stood at her desk, her backpack in front of her as she loaded books into it ready to move off to the canteen for lunch. Miss Watkins, her new English and drama teacher, was busy wiping down the board. Miss Watkins looked barely older than some of the sixth formers and dressed like most of the female ones in jeans and T-shirts.

'Megan, Ashley, could you stay behind for a second?' she said.

The pair glanced at each other as Megan's mind trawled through anything which might have got her into some sort of trouble. Miss Watkins must have guessed she'd worried them. 'It's all right,' she told them. 'You're not in trouble.'

She picked a couple of slim books up off her desk. 'I'd like you to look at these.' She handed one to each of them.

Megan read the cover... *Cinderella*. 'Is this the script, miss?'

Miss Watkins nodded. 'I'd like you both to read it through before drama club on Wednesday if you can.' Megan and Ashley exchanged another glance. 'Or as much as you can. I realise this is GCSE year and you have other demands on your time.'

'I'll do my best, miss,' promised Megan. She flicked open the cover and spun the pages. There was quite a lot of white space – no dense text. It shouldn't take too long to read.

'I want you and Ashley to try out for parts in the play – I'd really like you to play Cinders, Megan. I think you'd be perfect.

Your part, Ashley, will be a bit more challenging – I want you to be an ugly sister. What do you think?'

The pair exchanged glances. Ashley looked distinctly downcast as Megan jumped at the part she'd been offered.

'Did you fancy being Prince Charming?' said Miss Watkins.

Ashley shuffled. 'Well…'

'This is a much better part. Honest. The prince just struts around and poses. He gets none of the laughs, none of the really good lines. Trust me – this needs someone who can act, someone like you.'

Ashley blushed and beamed. 'Really?'

Miss Watkins nodded. 'So?'

'I'll have a go, miss,' said Ash. 'Who's the other sister?'

'Dan Maitland in year ten. I'll want you to read some of it on Wednesday – so maybe you'd like to sort out a couple of scenes each to perform. I can read other parts in for you if necessary. Anyway, I won't keep you. I expect you want your lunch.' Miss Watkins bustled off leaving the two teenagers alone.

Megan pointed to the cast list. 'Looks like she wants us to play two of the biggest parts,' she said.

Ashley looked at her and nodded. 'What do you think? Do you want to have a go?'

Megan shrugged. 'Maybe. It'll be a lot of lines to learn.'

'Yeah, but it'd be cool.'

'You reckon?'

Ashley's eyes were bright with excitement. 'I do. It'll be brilliant. Just think about it, we'd be on stage, people will applaud.'

Megan looked sceptical. 'Only if we're any good. We might end up looking totally lame.'

'We won't. Come on, Megs, we can do this.'

Megan sighed.

'I won't do it if you don't,' said Ashley. 'Please.'

'OK then.'

'Ace.'

Amy was finishing off cleaning for Bex when her employer got back from her shift at the pub.

'Just had a text from my Ash,' she said as Bex took her coat off. 'Seems him and your Megan have been asked to try out for the main parts in the school play.' She sounded gloomy.

'But that's great.'

'It ain't. Miss Watkins wants him to be an ugly sister. He is so going to get the piss ripped out of him.'

'I'm sure he won't.'

'Huh. Everyone's going to think he's gay or a tranny or whatever they call blokes who wear dresses. My Ash – I ask you.' She stopped mopping down the kitchen counters and threw the cloth into the sink. 'Besides, he ought to concentrate on his schoolwork. They said he's university material. I want him to get some good qualifications.' Amy's pride was palpable. 'I don't want him to get sidetracked with some dressing up.'

'But universities like their students to be more than just brainboxes.'

'I suppose. Unis want a lot from students, don't they – and I don't just mean book-learning neither. It's all about money, ain't it, these days? All those fees.'

'It is expensive, yes.'

'I hope it'll be worth it. I worry about all that debt kids get themselves into.'

'Yeah, but if he gets a really great job as a result...'

'Billy said he ought to sack plans of uni and get a proper job. Billy said that way he'd earn decent money and not have a chuffing great debt to pay back.'

Bex raised her eyebrows. 'I think,' she said, 'that given Billy's idea of a successful career involved robbing half this town blind, I'd take his opinions with a pinch of salt.'

Amy ignored Bex's jibe about her ex. 'What I want to know is... where has my Ash got his ideas about acting from?'

'It's not a crime, Amy,' said Bex with a laugh. 'Nothing wrong with it in my opinion. I think it's great if kids have interests outside school. You don't mind him skateboarding, do you?'

'That's different.'

Bex didn't see how. She glanced at the kitchen clock. 'And this isn't getting me to the Co-op to pick up some bits and pieces before I go and get the boys from school.' She grabbed her handbag and took out a couple of notes. 'Here you go, Amy.' She handed the money over. 'I'll see you on Friday – make sure you leave the house locked.'

'Of course, Bex, and thanks for the dosh.'

And Bex went off to do her shopping feeling quite chuffed about Megan's possible inclusion in the school production. All was well, she thought. Megan wasn't being bullied and had joined a club, the boys were popular and she herself was involved in the PTA, the book club and the WI and had a bunch of new friends. Yup – they were all becoming part of the community. It was exactly as she'd hoped things would pan out when they'd moved here.

Megan and Sophie linked arms as they walked out of the school gates at the end of the day.

'That's great about Miss Watkins wanting you to be in the play,' said Sophie. She sighed enviously. 'And Cinders.' She sighed again. 'You'll get such a lovely costume. I wish I could have a go too – but what with Mum...'

Poor Sophie, thought Megan. Being her mother's carer meant she had to make some huge sacrifices. Lizzie might have a nurse who came in twice a day to make sure she was OK, but evenings and weekends were Sophie's responsibility. Extra-curricular activities on a regular basis were tricky.

'It's well unfair that you can't,' said Megan.

'Yeah, well...'

A yell from behind made the girls turn around.

'Hey, hey, Megan, wait for me.'

'Hi, Ash,' she said.

'Can I walk with you?'

'I suppose.'

'We need to arrange to go through our lines,' said Ash, ignoring Sophie.

Megan felt irritated. Ashley banging on about the panto was making things worse for her friend. How could he be so insensitive? 'Leave it, Ash.'

'But we've only got till Wednesday.'

'Read them with someone else if you're so keen.'

'No,' said Sophie. 'You mustn't blow your chances on my account. There's no point in both of us being miserable.'

'There, you see,' said Ashley. 'Sophie understands.'

Megan wouldn't have put it as strongly as that.

'Tell you what,' said Sophie, 'why don't you both come back to mine and have a run-through? My mum used to do some acting, before she got ill. She once had a bit part in the West End. Maybe she could give you some tips while I get our supper on.'

Megan looked at Ashley. 'I suppose.'

'But that'd be amazing,' said Ashley. 'It's perfect.'

'But you haven't asked your mum,' said Megan.

'Oh, she'll be cool.'

Megan and Ashley both texted their respective mothers as they walked to Sophie's house where she opened the front door to let them all in.

'I've brought some friends home, Mum,' she called as she took her shoes off in the hall. Megan and Ashley followed suit. She ushered her friends into the sitting room.

'Hi, Megan,' said Lizzie. 'Lovely to see you again. I told Soph to leave the spare bed made up after your sleepover – you're welcome back any time. Soph loved having you to stay.'

Megan felt her face colour at the compliment. 'It was good – we had fun.'

'And this is Ashley – Ash,' said Sophie. 'He's in our tutor group, too.'

'Hello, Ashley.'

'Hello, Mrs Smith.'

'It's Lizzie.' She smiled up at Ashley from her wheelchair.

'Ash and Megan have been asked to try out for the school play,' said Sophie.

'That's nice,' said Lizzie.

'And I thought you could help them while I get some supper fixed.'

'It's been a long time since I did any acting,' protested Lizzie. 'Sit down, you two. I'm getting a crick in my neck.' Megan and Ashley perched on the sofa while Sophie hovered by the door.

'Come on, Mum. You must remember how it's done.'

Well, yes. But it's different knowing how to do it yourself and telling someone else how.'

'Look,' said Megan, 'we don't want to be a bother…'

Ashley glared at her. He obviously didn't share her sentiment.

'It's no bother – I'm not going anywhere else, am I?' Lizzie laughed while Megan looked embarrassed.

'We're doing *Cinderella*,' said Ashley, jumping in before Megan could muck things up.

'That sounds like fun,' said Lizzie. 'So, which parts are you going for?'

'Miss Watkins wants me to be an ugly sister,' said Ashley.

'And she's asked me to try out for Cinders herself,' added Megan.

'So, big parts which means big commitments.'

'We'll be stars,' said Ashley.

'It's not all about the roar of the greasepaint and the smell of the crowd,' said Lizzie with a laugh. 'It's much more about lots and lots of hard graft.'

'We don't mind that, do we, Megs?'

Megan wondered just how much hard graft was going to be involved but she saw the look on Ashley's face and realised how much this meant to him. And maybe this wasn't going to be such a bad project – after all, it was going to provide an excuse to spend time with her two best mates in the class. It couldn't be all bad.

At ten o'clock that evening Olivia finished her shift, got her bike from where she'd parked it, switched on its lights and cycled down the hill back into the town and her new house. It hadn't been an arduous shift but it had been a long day and she was beat. As she cycled she passed her old place. Earlier in the day, when she'd been cycling the other way, there had been a fleet of white vans drawn up outside. Now they were gone and all that remained of the evidence that the new people were having a vast amount of work done on the place was a skip outside the front door. And the windows were blank and no lights were on, so whatever the new owners were having done was, presumably, happening before they moved in. For the life of her Olivia couldn't think what on earth there was to do to the place. The bathrooms and kitchens were only a few years old and had been bespoke and top-of-the-range when they'd been fitted, plus the decor was immaculate and the carpets spotless. In Olivia's opinion, all the new owners needed to do was unpack and put their stuff away, like she was doing. Still, each to their own.

As she cycled over the railway bridge and into Beeching Rise she saw the downstairs lights were still on at home. No great surprise there; despite his early commute to London every morning Nigel rarely went to bed before the evening news was over and, of course, Jade was back home now. Olivia dismounted at the end of the garden path and wheeled the bike up to the front door. Once they'd got the boxes in the garage unpacked it could live there but until then it had to be locked and hidden behind one of the shrubs in the front garden in the hope no one would spot it and nick it.

Olivia's key clicked in the lock.

'I'm home,' she called. And as soon as she opened the door she saw all of Jade's cases still piled in the hall where she'd left them. Olivia sighed. The girl could have taken them upstairs at the very least.

'Hi, Mum,' called Jade.

Olivia went into the sitting room. The dirty mug was still on the coffee table but now a couple of wine glasses had been added to the mix along with three trays, each with used plates and cutlery piled on them. Hadn't any of her family thought to clear up after their supper?

In the corner the TV was on and Nigel waved an acknowledging hand.

'How was the shift?' he asked.

'Exhausting.'

'Welcome to my world.'

Yes, but when he came home it was to rest and relaxation not more work. She eyed the dirty plates and full trays.

'You seem to have enjoyed supper.'

'Lovely, thanks.'

So much for the family doing their best to help out. Not a finger lifted and her hint that maybe they could have tidied up afterwards was falling on deaf ears.

'I think I'm going to have a cup of tea before I go to bed,' she announced. She stamped into the kitchen, angry that her family couldn't be bothered to help. The kitchen was an even worse mess. Olivia grabbed the kettle and banged it under the tap before she plugged it in. Then she leaned against the counter and blinked back the tears. Was it too much to ask that they cleared up after themselves? Two adults and a teenager… She sighed and pulled herself together. Of course they didn't get it. For thirty years no one had had to do a hand's turn around the house. It was her fault for never making them shift for themselves. But things were going to have to change.

As the kettle boiled she returned to the sitting room, took the remote control off the arm of the sofa and switched off the TV.

'I was watching...' Then Nigel saw the look on his wife's face.

'I have come home after a long day at work. I cooked your supper before I went out, and I have come home to this.' She swept her hand around the room and the mess. 'I am tired and I want to go to bed before I repeat it all again tomorrow. We don't have a "housework fairy" any more so I suggest that you two sort it out before breakfast – otherwise it's going to stay this way until you do.'

'I had a long day too, Ol...Olivia.'

'I expect you have. But Jade hasn't.'

'But, Mum...'

'You haven't even taken your cases upstairs.'

'I've been upset.'

'Not too upset to eat and drink.' Olivia glared at her daughter. 'I know you've had a rotten couple of days but I've had a rotten few months and I haven't had the luxury of sacking *real life* and taking to my bed with a fit of the vapours. I've had to get on, keep everything going, juggle moving with looking after everyone while keeping things as normal as possible—'

'Stop it, the pair of you,' shouted Nigel. He stood up, crashed the trays into a messy pile and slammed out into the kitchen where there was another bang as he thumped them onto a work surface. Olivia wondered how much china had just got broken. She didn't want to face Nigel and his wrath over being made to help around the house so she shelved the idea of tea and went to bed.

She didn't think she had the energy to face this sort of scene every time she returned from work. Was the extra money going to be worth it? She doubted it.

12

Brian was slathering marmalade onto a slice of toast as Heather poured the tea out of the pot.

'You haven't forgotten that chap, Graham, is coming to see us again tomorrow,' said Brian, his knife hovering about his toast.

'Graham?'

'The bell chappie.'

'Oh, him. Ummm…' Actually, Heather wasn't sure she knew anything about this return visit but it didn't really matter. Much as she supported Brian, the minutiae of running the church on a day-to-day basis really wasn't her concern. 'He won't need feeding or anything, will he?' She put the teapot down and picked up the milk carton.

'I think some tea and biscuits when he gets here might be welcome.'

Heather sloshed milk into both mugs and then got up to check the cupboard where she kept the 'best' biscuits. There never seemed to be quite as many there as she remembered. She opened the tin and surprise, surprise, the packet she'd thought almost full was almost empty.

'Have you been helping yourself to the biscuits again?' she asked Brian.

He looked pained. 'No. I only eat the digestives and the rich tea in the other tin.'

Well, someone was eating them and it wasn't her – maybe Brian gave more to his visitors than she would be inclined to. Heather sighed and put the tin back. She'd have to find time to get some more decent ones. And she was working at the school today as a teaching assistant – maybe she'd call into the Co-op on the way there.

'So, after his visit he'll be able to give us the low-down on the final cost,' she said, leaning against the counter.

Brian bit into his toast and nodded. 'Hnn-hnn.' He chewed and swallowed. 'That's right,' he repeated more distinctly. 'And we have to be grateful that Sarah—'

'Sarah?'

'Our injured bell-ringer.'

'Of course.'

'—is healing nicely with no complications and has absolutely no intention of taking any sort of action.'

Heather's eyes widened. 'Was that on the cards?'

'It might have been. You know what people are like these days.'

'But Sarah?'

'To be honest I never thought that it *was* a real possibility but… Anyway, it's one less thing to worry about.'

'So when will the foundry start work?'

'Just as soon as we can pay them.'

'But it could take months to raise the funds. Years! And then they've got to be repaired.' Heather was aghast.

'It's how it goes.'

'Couldn't we get a loan?'

'I think you'll find,' said Brian with a smile, 'that the Church has rather strong views about being involved with moneylenders.'

'But this is different. It's not the same thing at all. We're not inviting usurers to set up their stalls in the nave.'

'Even so.'

Heather sighed. 'What about the Church? Won't they fund this?'

'I have made a few tentative enquiries. It seems the general feeling is that bells are non-essential. An expensive luxury...'

'Oh, for heaven's sake!' She snorted to emphasise her displeasure before she picked up her laptop and returned to the table and her tea. She flipped open the lid and waited for it to boot up then she clicked on the icon labelled 'bells' and looked at the list of ideas that Olivia had given her.

'I think,' she said to Brian, 'we need to set up a dedicated bank account for the bell fund.'

'Yes, I suppose.'

'If people are going to subscribe to donate on a regular basis we can't have their money mixed up with the other general funds.'

'No, dear.'

'So will you organise that?'

'I suppose.'

'When?'

Brian looked at his wife and saw her expression. Given how cross she already was it might be better not to antagonise her further. 'Today?'

'Correct answer.' She drained her mug and began to clear the table.

The next day, when Amy arrived to clean for Heather she found her at the kitchen table typing away on her laptop. Also on the table were about a dozen boxes which, to judge by the contents of the one that was open, were filled with leaflets about the church bells.

'Blimey, you've been busy,' said Amy, slipping off her jacket.

'I got the print shop in Cattebury to run these off for me.' She picked a pamphlet out of the open box and handed it to Amy.

'*An Appeal for A Peal*,' read Amy. 'That's quite clever.'

'It seems,' said Heather, 'that if Brian and I don't raise the funds to sort out the bells, no one is going to.'

'That's a bit harsh, ain't it?' She handed the leaflet back.

'My sentiments exactly. Anyway, I've had these flyers printed and I am going to leaflet-drop the whole town in the hope that some people might feel inclined to respond – or even help.'

'The whole town?! Good luck with that.'

'Well, I am hoping that there will be some kind souls who will volunteer to do the area where they live for me. I mean, I think I can rely on Olivia to do Beeching Rise. And if I could find someone to do the council estate...' She gave Amy a significant look.

'Dunno if there's anyone from round me who goes to church.'

'I don't think they have to be churchgoers to want to offer to help,' said Heather, pointedly.

'No? So what needs doing today?'

Heather sighed and gave Amy a list of cleaning priorities. There's none so deaf as those that will not hear, she told herself. But, if she was going to be fair, Amy was hardly a slacker and 'volunteering' tended to be the province of the time-rich.

As Amy got going with the dusting Heather armed herself with a map of the town and a packet of leaflets and set off to do a couple of the roads near her. As she was leaving the vicarage a large blue van pulled up at the gate and two men got out. She recognised the driver.

'Hello,' she said. 'It's Graham, isn't it?'

'Hi, Mrs Simmonds. This is Trev, by the way.' Heather shook his hand. 'He's the guy with the technical know-how. I do the sums. Is your husband in?'

'In and expecting you,' she said. She retrieved her key out of her purse and let them in to the house. As she opened the door she saw straight down the hall and into the kitchen – and spotted Amy, who was in the act of putting back the tin where she kept the posh biscuits.

'Ah, Amy.' She saw Amy leap out of her skin. 'These two gentlemen have come to see Brian. Could you sort out tea and biscuits for them – the nice biscuits, please.' She walked into the kitchen. 'Yes, those ones,' she said, looking at the tin in Amy's hand. 'How clever, you must have read my mind.'

She returned to her visitors, showed them into Brian's study and then carried on with her leafleting, smiling to herself. That explained about the missing biscuits, she thought. She'd have to find a new hiding place for the good ones and put the dreary ones in the tin in the cupboard. In theory, she didn't mind Amy helping herself to a biscuit or two – she just rather resented that Amy was tucking into the biscuits she denied herself on the grounds that they were extravagant and a luxury. She stuffed the first leaflet through a letter box. One down, one thousand, four hundred and ninety-nine to go.

'Bex, Bex, Bex... I got the part,' squealed Megan as she burst into the kitchen that evening.

'Darling, that's brilliant,' said Bex as she stirred a cheese sauce on the stove.

'It's an awful lot to learn though.' Megan dropped her backpack onto a chair. 'It's going to be so much hard work.'

'But you can do it, I know you can. How did Ashley get on?'

'Yeah, he got what he was going for too. Isn't it great? Mind you, he already thinks he's going to be the next Benedict Cumberbatch.'

'Really?'

'Yeah. I thought he'd walk back from school with me but he said he wanted to talk to Miss Watkins about his part. He needs to know about the Ugly Sisters' motivation. I mean...'

'Blimey.' Bex switched off the gas under her saucepan and took it off the stove. 'That sounds a bit keen. Mind you, all great actors have to start somewhere.' She poured the sauce over some cooked pasta.

'Ash, a great actor?'

'You never know.'

'Anyway, the other thing is...'

'What?'

'Can I go and stay with Soph again? On Friday?'

'Friday?' Bex's heart did a massive skip of delight. Friday! On Friday Alfie and Lewis had both been invited to sleepovers too.

'Please.'

'If it's OK with Lizzie.' Please, *please* let it be OK with Lizzie. It wasn't that Bex wanted shot of her kids but the thought that she could have an entire evening to herself, where she could kick back, do something entirely selfish and for pleasure... She might even go to the pub and experience being on the other side of the bar for a change. And she knew she got out now and again – there was the book club, she went to PTA meetings, and she even went to the WI most months – but she was always aware that she'd left Megan in charge of the boys and she was scrupulous about scurrying back as soon as she could.

'Of course it's OK with Lizzie. She likes Soph to have friends round. And she wants to help me with the play. Did I tell you she used to act?'

13

On Friday, when Bex had finished her shift at the pub, she returned home to a house that had been cleaned by Amy that morning, and which was going to stay neat and tidy till the next day because all three of her children were going away for the night. She drifted into the kitchen and put the kettle on and then realised she felt oddly bereft. What the hell was she going to do with herself between now and bedtime?

She made herself tea and then sat at the kitchen table and considered her options – which seemed rather thin. She could take herself off to the cinema in Cattebury, she could go for a drink at the pub, or she could slob on the sofa with trash TV and a glass of wine. There really wasn't much else on offer. Did she really want to flog into Cattebury on her own to see a film for the sake of something to do? Going to the pub by herself didn't appeal either. She pulled the paper towards her and glanced at the TV listings pages; soaps, a documentary about the state of the planet, a bunch of cosy-crime dramas... She sighed and pushed the paper away again. If Olivia didn't have a job and hadn't just moved house she'd have suggested her friend might have fancied coming over for a drink... And there was Heather. But she was also a busy woman and Bex wasn't quite sure they were on close enough terms for such an invitation. And pretty much everyone one else she knew had kids and probably couldn't just light out. No, it looked like it was going to be a night in with the remote.

She picked up her mug and went through to the sitting room. Might as well start as she meant to go on. She switched on the TV and found a programme about house buying which she watched *faute de mieux*. She nodded off.

The doorbell woke her. For a second she was disorientated then she remembered – she was having an evening off. She glanced at the clock; it was gone five and, to judge by the scum on it, her tea was stone cold.

She got up and answered the door. It was Miles.

'Hiya,' she said happily, opening the door wider. 'Come in.'

'No, I won't stop. A little bird told me you're childless tonight.'

'A little bird called Belinda?' Just as she'd been leaving the pub earlier that afternoon, she'd mentioned to her boss that she only had herself to cook for that night. 'But I hate cooking only for me,' she'd added.

'Buy yourself a ready meal,' Belinda had suggested. 'Prick and ping.'

But Bex had dismissed that idea – it always smacked of being on the slippery slope to slutdom.

'It might have been,' admitted Miles. 'Was she right?'

Bex nodded. 'All three kids have been invited for sleepovers.'

'So what have you got planned?'

Bex shrugged. 'A night in with the box and a glass of something chilled and white.'

'You know how to live,' said Miles.

'Hey, don't knock it.'

'Look, I've got Jamie helping out in the kitchen tonight but he is perfectly capable of finishing off the last orders on his own. Why don't you meet me at, say, eight in the pub and we can have a drink together?'

'Really?'

'Unless there's something on TV that you'd prefer to watch.'

'No, absolutely nothing. Trust me.'

'Great. It's a date. See you later.' And Miles dipped in through the open door and planted a kiss on her cheek. 'Bye.' He bounced off down the drive leaving Bex feeling slightly flustered.

Did he mean a date – as in an 'arrangement' – or a *date*? she wondered.

Time dragged after Miles had left; rather ridiculously, she felt. Three whole hours. She had more tea, she cooked herself some supper, she watched the news... still an hour and a half. She decided to take a bath. As she went up to run it she told herself that she was doing this to kill time. And, anyway, when did she get a whole tank of hot water to herself and the luxury of time to pamper herself? Besides, this was taking advantage of the empty house and had *nothing* to do with seeing Miles. She ran a bath right up to the overflow, added some very expensive Jo Malone bath oil she'd been given ages previously and sank into the almost too-hot water. She shut her eyes. Bliss.

She let her mind drift and, once again, she found herself wondering about where, exactly, her relationship with Miles might be going. She realised with a bit of a jolt that it only mattered because she was keen to know. She knew she liked him, but was it rather more than she wanted to admit? But, and she had to admit this too, she wasn't sure she was ready for a proper relationship. Her husband had been killed only the previous year. But, on the other hand, she was frightened someone else might snaffle Miles before she was ready. She sploshed the water around with her hands. Was she being dog-in-the-manger?

Bex stayed in the bath until the water cooled and her skin went wrinkly and then got out and dressed with more care and thought than she'd done in years. She wanted to look casual but attractive. She finally settled on a pair of expensive jeans and a floaty blouse. She put on a hint of make-up and surveyed the result. She'd do. No... no... She slipped off her customary comfy loafers and rummaged in her wardrobe for a pair of heels. She hadn't worn heels for weeks, maybe months. She put them on. *Now* she'd do.

She checked her watch for the umpteenth time. She still had fifteen minutes – actually longer. She didn't want to be too prompt. That would look overly keen and that would never do. She went back into the sitting room and killed the time by channel hopping and checking the clock. Finally, at ten past eight she stopped checking the clock and checked her make-up instead, before locking up and going next door to the pub.

'There you are,' said Miles. 'I was afraid you were standing me up.' He smiled at her. 'You've changed.' He raised a quizzical eyebrow.

'Oh… I found a mark on my top,' lied Bex.

'And your jeans?'

He'd noticed this pair wasn't the same as the other pair? 'Well…' She blushed. Busted.

'What are you drinking?' said Miles moving off the subject.

'A white Rioja, please.'

Miles ordered their drinks and steered her to a table in the corner which, surprisingly on a Friday evening, was empty.

Bex sat down and twiddled the stem of her glass. 'I haven't done this much.' She took a sip.

'What?'

'Gone out for a drink – not since Richard died. For one, I haven't been invited and two it's taken a while to feel like I want to.' She looked directly at him. 'Not that I've been a complete recluse but… well, for a while it was all too soon, then we moved…'

'Then I'm glad that you feel like you can again. In fact I am more than glad, I feel quite honoured.'

'Don't be daft.' She stared at her wine again.

'I'm not being. Tell me about Richard.'

Bex looked up and then took another sip. How much did he want to know? Did he want the complete book or the synopsis? She decided to give him the short version but it still took a while. She told him what a funny bloke he'd been, how he could talk to dukes and dustmen with the same ease, what a great dad he'd been...

'He sounds as if he was very special.'

Bex nodded. 'I thought so.'

'You must miss him.'

'It's getting easier.' She smiled at Miles. 'It's been well over a year now and being somewhere new has helped. I wasn't sure at first that it would but it definitely has.' She decided to move the focus off herself. 'What about you? Did you ever have a significant other?'

Miles nodded. 'Several. You know about Belinda. To be honest she and I were never a proper item, more...'

'Friends with benefits?'

'Yup, that about sums it up.'

'And?'

'And there was Anna – that lasted several years and I had hopes... well, I thought marriage, parenthood... I'd have liked that.'

Bex studied him. He looked quite bereft. 'I think you'd make a great dad.'

'Maybe. Getting less and less likely.'

'You're not old. And it's not the same for blokes. Your biological clock has got donkey's years to run yet. Look at Mick Jagger!'

Miles sighed. 'I don't know. And I've yet to find Miss Right.'

'You will. You're a nice guy, good sense of humour, *terrific* cook. You're quite a catch, I'd say.' And he was. But did she want to go fishing? And if she didn't, was she being fair to Miles? Was she stringing him along? Perhaps in a few years... but then, would she want another child herself? In a few years Megan would be at uni and the boys would be heading for secondary school.

'Thanks. But it's not as simple as that; there's the negatives too. When you're a chef, the hours are antisocial and, Belinda will tell you, I'm not the easiest guy to live with.'

'Really?' He didn't seem so tricky.

Miles nodded. 'Yeah, I'm a bit OCD about things like folding up sweaters right, and how things are stored in drawers and cupboards.'

'And that's a problem?'

'Apparently.'

'Want to come and sort mine out?'

'I'd be delighted to.'

Bex notice that Miles's Guinness glass was almost empty. 'Another drink?' she offered.

'Why not?' He drained the dregs and passed it to her. Bex picked up her glass and went over to the bar where she handed them both to Belinda.

'Same again, please.'

'I'm so glad you turned up,' said Belinda as she turned on the Guinness tap. 'When you were a couple of minutes late, Miles got really stressy. I think he thought you might have stood him up, changed your mind.'

'No one wants to be stood up, do they? I mean, you always end up feeling such a fool.'

'I suppose. Nine pounds eighty, please. Anyway, I'm glad you're here.'

'Hey, the kids are all staying over with friends and I'm footloose and fancy-free. I was *not* going to turn down the offer of a night out.'

Belinda rang up the sale on the till and handed the change to Bex who stuffed the money in her purse, picked up the drinks and returned to the table.

'Here you go,' she said putting Miles's drink down in front of him. 'It's weird,' she continued, 'I'm not used to being this side of the bar unless I'm collecting dirty glasses.'

'Can't say I do this very often either. If I'm working, I'm in the kitchen and on my day off I always seem to have other stuff to do.'

'Like?'

'All the domestic stuff – shopping, cooking, cleaning...'

'Folding sweaters...?'

Miles smiled at her. 'I asked for that. So, what do you do in your free time?'

Bex almost splurted her drink. 'Free time – with three kids and a job?'

'OK, what would you *like* to do?'

'I keep meaning to make the cellar into a den for the kids. They'd love to have a hidey-hole – just for them. Every time I go into the cellar in the pub I get a guilty conscience about mine.'

'What needs doing?'

Bex had a slurp of wine before she said, 'What doesn't need doing? It's got a beaten earth floor and it smells of damp although, as far as I can tell, it's dry. But the lighting is pretty dreadful and the stairs are almost vertical and with no banister at all on one side and it's quite cold.'

Miles took a gulp of Guinness. 'If it's any comfort to you I can tell you the pub cellar has never had the least problem with damp as a result of the weather or the water table.'

'Really?'

'Dry as a bone. And since Belinda and I have been here we've had some shocking winters and torrential storms. I think the natural drainage around us is quite good.'

'That's nice to hear. I wasn't planning on doing very much; maybe putting down a proper floor and make the stairs better and then getting some old sofas or bean bags down there, maybe get some uplighters installed... oh, and a heater.'

'Sounds like heaven on earth. I'd have loved somewhere like that to hang out when I was a kid.'

'I thought as they got older, if they want to play music or anything, it's less likely to disturb the neighbours if they're below ground.'

'How big is it?'

'About the size of the pub cellar, I suppose.'

The pub door crashed open and about a dozen young men thundered in. It was the local rugby team who trained on a Friday evening and always went to the pub afterwards.

The noise in the bar went through the roof. Bex could hardly hear herself think. She saw Miles' mouth move but she couldn't make out what he was saying. She leaned across the table.

'What?' she almost shouted.

'I said,' bellowed back Miles, 'shall we go somewhere quieter?'

Bex nodded and drained her drink. The pair put their glasses back on the bar and escaped out into cooler and quieter air.

14

Bex looked at her watch. It was still early, she'd been enjoying herself and she really didn't want the evening to end. She made a decision.

'Look,' she said a bit diffidently, 'you could come back to mine if you like. I can't offer you Guinness but I have wine or coffee. And,' she added as an afterthought, 'you could give me your opinion about my cellar.'

'Why not.'

They nipped next door and Bex let them both in, flipping on the light switches as she pushed the front door shut. She led the way into the kitchen.

'What can I get you?'

'What are you having?'

'I'm going to stick with wine.'

'That'll be fine with me. Where's this cellar?'

Bex opened a door in the corner of the kitchen and switched on the light. 'You go and have a look and I'll open a bottle. And go carefully, the stairs are really rickety.'

Miles disappeared into the basement and Bex got a bottle out of the fridge. By the time she'd got the top off the bottle and had poured two glasses Miles was back in the kitchen.

'It wouldn't need that much work in my opinion.'

'You think?'

'I reckon. Look, I'll show you.'

Bex handed him a glass and picked up her own before she followed him carefully down the cellar steps, hanging on to the grimy handrail because she felt distinctly unsafe on the uneven steps in her heels. The handrail didn't feel any too safe either, she thought. Another job to be done before the cellar could be used regularly.

'Looks pretty grim to me,' she said as she reached the floor.

'OK, there's plenty of headroom,' said Miles, 'so you could put down a waterproof membrane, lay some underfloor heating pipes and then put a concrete floor on the top. I reckon that would sort out the damp and the heating in one fell swoop. There's leccy down here so no problem with the lighting – anything would be better than that single bulb but some recessed LEDs would transform the ambience of this place. Add a dimmer switch, some comfy seats, a TV and a sound system and your kids will have the perfect den.'

'You think?' Bex was trying to visualise it as Miles had projected it. 'I suppose. Maybe I should get a builder in to give me a quote.'

'At least then you'd know if you were looking at five hundred or five grand.'

Bex headed back towards the stairs and gripped the handrail again. She was about three steps up when she caught her heel, tripped and all her weight hung off the rail which pulled away from the wall. Her free hand flailed, sending her glass flying as she tried to keep her balance before she crashed off the unprotected side of the steps, a section of handrail in her right hand. She almost managed to land on her feet but because of her heels she instantly lost her balance and fell heavily on one side. She hit the beaten earth floor with a sickening thump and her glass splintered beside her a split second later.

'Bex!'

She lay there, winded and shocked.

In a second Miles was by her side. 'Don't move,' he commanded. 'Are you hurt?'

'I... I don't know. Bruised. My leg really hurts.' She breathed slowly and carefully, trying to assess which bits hurt the most and if the 'hurt' might be indicative of something serious.

Miles bent to look closer. 'Nothing looks like it's broken. Nothing obvious anyway.'

'I think it was my bum and my arm that took most of the fall.' Bex flexed her wrist. 'That seems to be working.' She was still holding a piece of handrail in her right hand. She jammed it onto the floor and levered herself up till she was kneeling.

'Jeez, I am going to have some bruises.' Slowly she got one foot under her, and then, using the handrail as a crutch and Miles's proffered hand she staggered upright. Something was far from right, then she realised that the heel of one of her shoes had broken off. She thought about slipping the shoes off but then she looked at the broken glass. She didn't want cut feet on top of everything else. 'What a waste of good wine.'

'Are you sure you are all right?'

Bex nodded. 'I think so. I'm going to be sore for a day or two but I'm going to live. Anyway, one thing is certain; either I get this cellar sorted properly, so it isn't a complete deathtrap, or I've got to put it out of bounds.'

'Let's get you back to the kitchen.'

Bex turned to head for the step but pain shot up her leg. She winced.

'You're not all right, are you?' said Miles.

'It's nothing. I've twisted my ankle,' she admitted. 'But nothing a cold compress and tubular bandage won't fix.'

'Here, put your arm round my shoulder so I can take some of the weight.'

Bex did as she was told and Miles held her close so that his left arm was also taking some of her weight but the steps then proved too narrow for the pair to go up side by side.

Bex removed her arm again. 'I'll be fine. I'll manage,' she said, not knowing how, especially as there was no handrail now to offer support.

'Desperate times demand desperate remedies,' muttered Miles and suddenly he'd half crouched beside Bex, swept one arm behind her knees, curved the other under her right arm and around her shoulders and before she knew it she was in the air and pressed against his chest.

'What the...?' she shrieked.

'Just stay still. I don't want to drop you,' said Miles through clenched teeth as he almost staggered under her weight.

Oh, God, she thought. Now he knew *exactly* how heavy she was. Too heavy. Too heavy by far.

He clutched her tight to him as he began to climb up the dozen or so steps. Bex found herself tempted to lean her head on his shoulder but felt that on one level it might be fundamentally wrong although, on another level, it might be so fundamentally right. She inhaled the scent of him, she held onto his shoulder – for support and balance... She could feel his heart hammering against his ribs and saw the sweat starting to bead on his brow.

Her mind flashed back to the time when Miles had comforted her after Alfie had briefly run away from home and scared the daylights out of her. He'd held her then... and she'd pushed him away because she'd thought that when he and Belinda had told her they were 'partners' that's what they were. Not *business* partners. And when she'd found the truth, although she liked him – A Lot – she still hadn't encouraged him. And as Bex lay in his arms and he laboured up the steps, she wasn't sure she had the courage to try and move things on. What if he rejected her?

By the time they got into the kitchen his breath was rasping in her ear. With a groan he lowered her onto the kitchen table and then slumped onto a chair, his chest heaving, his mouth open to maximise his air intake.

'Thank you,' she said. 'I'd have probably managed, though.'

'It's…' he drew a breath, 'it's… no… problem.'

Bex looked down at her floaty blouse. It was filthy down one side. She suspected the seat of her jeans might be too and she was already aware that she'd ruined her shoes. She must look a complete sight.

She toed off her shoes and they fell to the floor beside Miles. Gently he took her left foot in his hand.

'It's the right one I've buggered,' Bex advised.

Miles looked up at her and grinned and then started to examine her other foot. He rested it on his lap. 'It doesn't look too bad.' Slowly and gently he flexed and stretched the joint. 'Does that hurt?'

'Not really.'

He rotated it.

She jumped involuntarily at the pain. 'Ouch.'

'Sorry.'

'As I said, some decent strapping and it'll be as right as ninepence.'

'Where do you keep the bandages?'

'I think the most I can run to is some Calpol or Elastoplast.' Miles rolled his eyes. 'Wait here.'

'Where are you going?'

'The pub. There's a proper first aid kit there. Back in a jiffy.'

As soon as he'd gone, Bex slid off the table onto her good foot, hopped across the kitchen, got out two more glasses – their previous ones being still down in the cellar, hers in smithereens – and the bottle of white out of the fridge. She sat back on the chair and poured the drinks.

'I'm back,' called Miles a minute or so later. He tutted. 'What have you been up to?'

'Miles, I've got a slightly sore ankle. The other leg is working fine. I admit that getting up from the cellar would have been tricky, but I'm OK. Honestly.'

Miles raised his eyebrows in response and flourished a crêpe bandage and a safety pin. 'Let's get this ankle bandaged.'

With remarkable skill, dexterity and neatness, he had her ankle strapped in a couple of minutes and the loose end of the bandage pinned securely. 'How's that?'

Bex stood and gingerly put her weight on it. 'Pretty good. Where did you learn to do that?'

'Scouts.'

'Dib-dib-dib,' teased Bex.

'Don't knock it.'

'I'm not. I bet you were a cracking scout.'

'I was. I got loads of badges – including first aid.'

'Well, now I'm all fixed up, let's go and sit somewhere more comfortable.' Bex picked up her glass and led the way, limping only very slightly, into the sitting room. She switched on the lights and drew the curtains.

'This is very cosy,' said Miles, settling into an armchair. 'I love this house.'

'So do I.' Bex sat on the sofa, next to Miles's chair. She half-wished he'd sat on the sofa too. After all, just a matter of minutes previously she'd been in his arms and wondering how to move their relationship on. She made her mind up. With her heart hammering like Miles's had done earlier, she patted the cushion beside her.

'You could always sit here,' she said. 'If you'd like to.'

'I think,' said Miles, uncrossing his legs and standing up, 'I'd like that very much.'

15

Olivia hauled herself out of bed the next morning at six thirty and pottered downstairs to make tea. Nigel snored on. She could have really relished a lie-in, like Nigel was indulging in, rather than getting up at this ridiculously early hour because she had a mountain of tasks before her shift started that afternoon. That was the trouble with working in the hospitality business – someone had to be around to cater for guests' needs twenty-four seven. She was only expected to work ten days a fortnight but her days off, like her shift pattern, varied from week to week. She imagined she'd get used to it but at the moment she was having a problem getting her head round the fact that her 'weekend' wasn't necessarily going to coincide with her family's. As the kettle boiled she zipped around the downstairs, opening curtains, picking up dirty crockery and the previous day's papers, plumping up a couple of cushions and restoring order to the living area. The kettle clicked off and she made herself a cuppa which she left on the counter to cool while she returned to the bedroom and got her and Nigel's laundry from their en suite. The weather forecast for the day was fine and sunny so if she got the washing on first thing she might be able to get it to dry on the line before she had to go to work. She'd been told that this week her day off was on Sunday, so tomorrow, while she cooked the joint, she could iron it ready for the following week. Huh – some day off.

She stuffed the dirty clothes in the machine, dosed it, pressed the start button and then returned to the kitchen to make some lists – urgent things to do, less urgent things, shopping... She had limited time before she had to go to work and she needed to maximise it.

Half an hour later, while her family slumbered on, she was washed, dressed and had her shopping list in hand as she headed for the car and a trip to the twenty-four-hour supermarket in Cattebury. She was banking on the fact that at seven thirty on a Saturday morning she'd have the place to herself and would be able to whisk round in minimum time. She turned into the car park and saw it was practically empty. Sometimes, she thought, being organised was a definite asset.

She was back home and unpacking the shopping by half past eight. As she did so, Jade staggered into the kitchen.

'Bloody hell, Mum, do you have to make such a racket?'

Olivia, who had been bending down to pull boxes of cereal out of her shopping bag, straightened up. She stared at her daughter.

'And could you put the kettle on?' added Jade who was sitting at the table checking her new phone, one purchased to replace the lost one, and oblivious of the danger she was in.

Olivia reached forward and plucked the phone from her daughter's hand.

'Hey!' protested Jade.

'I'll give you *hey*,' snapped her mother. She slammed the phone down on the table. Jade jumped. 'I have had it up to here with you and the rest of the family. I am working round the clock and yet I have still to see anyone else do a hand's turn around the house. This morning I came down to find that, *yet again*, no one had managed to put their mugs and plates in the dishwasher. Is it too much to ask? It's not difficult.' She stopped. She was so angry she was afraid she might lose it. She turned away and looked out the window. She took a deep, calming breath. 'I have been up for two hours. I have tidied up, I have shopped for the week, I have got the washing on... and what have you done?'

'But it's the weekend,' protested Jade.

Olivia turned around and slammed her hands down on the table, causing her daughter to jump out of her skin yet again. 'The whole of last week was a weekend as far as you were concerned.'

'But—'

'There's no "but"! Either you *help* out or you can *move* out.'

'But I've got nowhere to go.'

Olivia drew an imaginary circle with her forefinger round her face and leaned in towards her daughter. 'Bovvered?' she said.

'But, *Mum*.'

What's going on?' said Nigel strolling into her kitchen in his dressing gown. 'You two sound like a pair of fishwives. We'll have the neighbours complaining next.'

Olivia rounded on him. 'And you're no better.'

Nigel took a step back and put his hands up. 'Hang on a sec—'

'No, I bloody won't. You're almost as bad. You promised you'd help out around the house a bit but you don't seem to be able to put anything in the dishwasher, pick up your clothes off the bathroom floor, cook for yourself, tidy up—'

'I work!' shouted Nigel.

'So do I.'

'You don't have to. I earn enough to pay the bills.'

Olivia shook her head. 'Yeah, yes you do,' she said in a quieter voice. 'And that's it. There's nothing left at the end of each month for anything else. No frivolities, no luxuries, nothing nice to look forward to. That's not living, Nigel, that's existing.'

Nigel chewed his lip and then said stiffly, 'I'm sorry I'm such a disappointment.'

'You're not.' Olivia sighed. 'All I'm asking is that everyone helps out a bit. And at the moment, none of you are.' She grabbed some more things from the shopping baskets and stuffed them on shelves while, behind her back, Jade and Nigel exchanged looks.

'You, Jade, need to sort yourself out. You need to find digs in London if you're set on leaving Luke. And go back to your old job. But you can't loaf on the sofa any longer and freeload off us.'

'Aren't you being a bit harsh, Ol?' said Nigel. 'Jade's had a tough time recently.'

'She dumped a boyfriend who was obviously a dud,' said Olivia. 'Compared to what half the world has to cope with that comes nowhere close to being "a tough time". And don't call me *Ol*.'

'Mum!'

'No.' Olivia rounded on Jade. 'I agree you are upset, but life goes on and you need to grow up, stand on your own two feet and start supporting yourself. If I was in a position like yours I wouldn't dream of throwing everything up and lying around like some wilting heroine in a Gothic melodrama. You're barely out of bed before ten, you do nothing all day, you've done nothing about your job... frankly, at the moment you're a waste of oxygen.' There, she'd said it.

'I'm not.'

'Yes, you bloody are. And I am fed up with waiting on you when you could have cooked the evening meal all of this last week instead of me having to do it on top of everything else.'

'But... but I can't cook.'

'Then *learn*!'

A taut silence descended as Olivia glared at her daughter, Jade looked close to tears and Nigel shuffled nervously.

In the utility room the washing machine beeped to indicate it had finished the cycle. Olivia grabbed the laundry basket off the counter and stomped off to unload it.

'And while I'm doing this you two can finish unpacking the shopping.'

As Olivia pegged out the washing in the garden in the thin lemony, autumn sunshine, she began to calm down. Was she being so unreasonable? she wondered. She wouldn't mind so much racing round, looking after Nigel and Zac – they both had demands on their time and work to do. But Jade?

Picking up the empty basket Olivia returned to the kitchen to find the shopping had all been dealt with, the bags and baskets cleared off the floor and no sign of Jade and Nigel. Olivia thought they'd probably gone to find flak jackets and tin hats. She sighed. Why, she wondered, why did she have to completely lose her temper to get a result? Why couldn't her family *see* which way the wind was blowing and do something about it before things got to such a pitch?

It's my fault, she admitted to herself. They'd none of them ever had to shift for themselves. No wonder it had left them all incapable of surviving unaided. Maybe she owed Jade an apology. She'd said some pretty horrible things – even if they had been true. She trudged up the stairs and knocked on the door to the spare room.

'Go away.'

Regardless, Olivia opened the door and went in. 'I'm sorry.'

Jade raised her tear-stained face out of her pillow. 'No, you're not.'

'I shouldn't have said those things.'

Jade buried her face back in her pillow.

Olivia, carefully avoiding Jade's feet, perched on the end of the bed. 'So,' she said, hoping she sounded more conciliatory, 'I imagine your job will be expecting you back soon anyway.'

'What job?' Her voice was muffled by feathers.

'I'm not with you.'

'They sacked me.'

'But you went sick. They can't do that.'

Jade rolled over and propped herself up on one elbow. 'They can if you were on a final warning *and* on probation.'

Olivia's mood and sense of despair deepened. A final warning? What had Jade been up to? How could her daughter be so irresponsible as to get herself into that position?

'It was a crap job and I hated it. I was looking for something else anyway.'

But it had been a job... 'Even so.' Olivia resisted the urge to shake her daughter. 'What are you planning to do now?'

Jade flopped back against the pillow and stared at the ceiling. 'I don't know. I haven't got a home, I haven't got a boyfriend, I haven't got a job, my parents hate me...' Tears of self-pity began to slide down her temples.

Olivia wasn't having this. 'Don't be ridiculous. You are not a refugee – of course you've got a home. Having a boyfriend isn't the be-all and end-all and, if you made an effort, a bright kid like you with a masters degree ought to be able to walk into a job in a heartbeat.'

Jade switched her eyes from the ceiling to her mother. 'Huh, you didn't say you and Dad don't hate me.'

Olivia rolled her eyes. 'Of course we don't hate you. I might be annoyed with you – but that's not the same thing at all. Now then, dry your eyes, get up, have a shower and start sorting things out.'

'How?'

'You can look for a job for a start. Listen, Jade, I'll be honest, you living here isn't ideal. This house really isn't designed for four adults but we'll cope. Of course we will. But at some point you need to find a place of your own again and if you *are* going to stay here for the time being I'm going to have to ask you to help with the bills. Your father and I really can't afford the extra cost of having a fourth mouth to feed plus the other costs of having another adult living here.'

'But—'

'If you're planning on living here for the foreseeable it's only fair. You have to get a job and pull your weight.'

'But it's the weekend.'

'Jade, as far as I am aware the internet still works on a Saturday. Look for a job there. It's how I found mine. Or go into town and go into every shop and ask if they need staff. And try the pub. Belinda is often after part-timers to cover shifts.'

'But that's so demeaning – begging for work.'

Olivia thought about telling her daughter about how she'd got her job; she'd virtually grovelled.

'No one has ever died of being rejected. And I don't know how much you've got in your bank account but, when that runs out, your father and I are in no position to start offering handouts. If you don't start earning you are going to find life very difficult indeed.' Olivia got up from the end of the bed. 'And I mean it about paying your way.'

She left the room and shut the door behind her. She stood at the top of the stairs and shook her head. Was she being too harsh – or was it tough love?

16

The following week Mags Pullen, Amy's mum, Ashley's gran and the town's ex-hairdresser, left her solicitor's office clutching a bunch of keys and walked to Beeching Rise. Selling her business had given her the wherewithal to become a house owner and today was the day she took possession. It had taken longer than she'd have liked to sort out the deal with the developers but, finally, all the Ts had been crossed and the Is dotted and the tiny two-bedroom terrace was hers. Her hand was shaking slightly as she slipped the key into the lock and opened the door to her new home. She almost skipped over the threshold. It smelt so clean and it was so bright! Excitedly she raced through the downstairs; it was as good as she remembered it from when she'd last been in, telling the builders what she wanted in the way of tiles in her bathroom and kitchen, and which floor coverings to lay. The walls were painted cream which she didn't much like – but she could get Ashley to help her with something brighter and nicer. Mags puffed her way up the stairs and opened the doors off the landing. She hugged herself as she took in her new bedroom. Fitted wardrobes – what luxury. She walked over to the window and looked across the road. The view wasn't so different from the one from her council flat – houses. But these weren't council houses. This was a private estate! My, how she'd gone up in the world.

Who'd have thought that Mags Pullen would be a property owner?

She wondered what her neighbours were going to be like. She hoped they wouldn't be snobby – that was the one good thing about the council estate; everyone had been proper friendly. People were always popping in and out of each other's houses. And it had been nice having her Amy just round the corner. Not that Beeching Rise was any distance away from her now but it was just too far to nip round on spec. They'd have to ring first to check the other wasn't out. Mags leaned her elbows on the windowsill and looked at the house opposite – a much bigger one than her little terrace. And they'd been in for a bit... there were ornaments on their sitting room window sill and their curtains were up. Sunshine glinted off something in the garden. Mags peered. A bicycle bell. She recognised the bike it was attached to. It was Mrs L's. Fancy that, Mrs L living opposite her.

Olivia was nearing the end of her shift – the breakfast to mid-afternoon one – when two new guests approached the reception desk pulling their Louis Vuitton bags behind them. She smiled as she made an instant assessment; wealthy professionals, she judged. The woman was tall, slim, immaculately groomed blonde hair in an up-do and elegant in her white jeans, heels and beautifully tailored jacket. Possibly a second wife considering the man she was with had to be at least twenty years her senior. He was wearing red cords and a black guernsey with a cravat at his neck. High court judge, surgeon, media type? wondered Olivia. The woman stalked towards the desk but was looking at her surroundings, rather than at the receptionist – appraising the decor which, if her expression was anything to go by, wasn't meeting with approval. Instantly Olivia knew that this couple were not going to be a pushover.

'Osborne,' said the man.

Olivia nodded and clicked the mouse. 'Of course,' she said. 'And welcome to Woodford Priors.'

The woman sniffed as Olivia pushed a registration form and a pen across the counter. 'If you could just fill this in.'

While Mr Osborne got busy with the paperwork, Olivia programmed two key cards and Mrs Osborne went over to the fireplace and warmed her hands.

Olivia took back the completed form and handed over the cards. 'And if I could just swipe your credit card...?'

'Don't you trust us?'

'Implicitly, but it's hotel policy,' responded Olivia smoothly.

The card was handed over with a sigh and Olivia put it into the machine and asked for the PIN. She handed back the card, the slip showing the transaction had been voided and a brochure about the hotel, its facilities and information about the local area.

'We don't need that,' said Mr Osborne dropping it back on the desk. 'We're not here to enjoy ourselves.'

Olivia was about to say that surely they could indulge themselves for just a couple of hours in the hotel's pool and spa but decided she couldn't be bothered. There was something about them that struck her as a bit 'puritan'. She wondered what they *did* do when they wanted to kick back. Cold baths? Self-flagellation? Hair shirts?

'If you'd like to leave your cases here I'll get them sent up to your room directly. And you're in room twenty-two. Up the stairs, turn right and it's on the left side of the corridor. You've got a lovely view over the gardens.'

Mrs Osborne's sneer suggested she'd be the judge as to whether the view was lovely or not.

They headed for the stairs and Olivia gazed after them before she rang the bell for a porter and gave him his instructions.

A few minutes later he was back down in the hall. 'Good luck with them,' he muttered to Olivia.

'Why?'

'I don't think she's happy.'

'But that's a lovely room – one of our nicest.'

'She was busy chucking the cushions and the bedspread out into the corridor when I arrived.'

'What?'

'She told me to call housekeeping and get it all taken away.'

Olivia sighed. Her instincts were going to be proved correct. Half an hour later she was busy in the office adding room service and bar tabs to various bills when she heard an imperious 'You there'.

She knew, without looking up, who it was going to be. She rose out of her chair, nailed on a smile and went to the desk.

'Mrs Osborne. What can I do for you?'

'I've got a complaint.'

There's a surprise. 'Really?'

'Yes. The room is full of trip hazards and dust traps – I am amazed you haven't been sued from here to kingdom come by people who must have had falls or allergy attacks.'

'Well, I haven't been here long but as far as I am aware we've never had a complaint before – or any accidents or illness.'

'If you say so. Anyway, housekeeping have removed some of the offending articles but they won't take down the curtains.'

Olivia fought to keep control of her face as she actually boggled at this.

Mrs Osborne tapped the desk with a pillar-box red fingernail. 'So… what are you going to do about this?'

Olivia made an instant judgement that this was way outside her pay grade. 'I'll get the duty manager,' she said. She picked up the phone and dialled Mrs Timms. 'Could you come to the front desk?' she asked. 'Now.'

'I'll be with you in two ticks,' was the response.

'And another thing,' said Mrs Osborne. 'The water in our bathroom is too hot.'

'Too hot?'

'Yes, I could have easily been scalded.'

'I've not had any other complaints.'

'You're getting one now.'

Mrs Timms arrived. 'Thank you, Olivia,' she said. Olivia retired to the office but earwigged the rest of the conversation.

'The floor is uneven, the whole room is a health hazard, the furniture is antediluvian, I dread to think what state the wiring is in – that's probably a death trap too – and as for your receptionist…'

Olivia had to restrain herself from marching back into the reception and challenging the Osborne woman. How *dare* she?

'… sullen, verging on obstructive…'

Sullen?! She'd been perfectly polite and friendly.

She heard Mrs Timms murmur platitudes and offer a massive discount.

'I suppose if that's the best you can do… Fine.'

Olivia waited for the sound of Mrs Osborne's footsteps to disappear before she ventured out of the office.

'In my defence, I wasn't sullen.'

'No, I don't suppose you were.'

'Or obstructive.'

'No. Luckily, we don't get many like the Osbornes.'

'Thank God for that. And I'm going to make sure I'm not around when they check out.'

'I don't blame you. I'll warn tomorrow's staff.'

Olivia felt drained when she got home and allowed herself the bliss of a cup of tea and a five-minute sit-down before she made a start on supper. The house was quiet; Zac was still at school, Nigel at work and Jade was presumably loafing in town or watching Netflix on her iPad. If Olivia hadn't felt so tired she might have suggested to Jade that she might like to help with the cooking but the thought of a row with her daughter was more exhausting than the thought of preparing supper unaided. Olivia cradled her tea and put her feet up. Just five minutes.

*

Mags saw Olivia return, put her front door on the latch and pottered over the road. She leaned on the doorbell of her new neighbour's house.

Olivia opened the door.

'Hello, Mrs L. Fancy you living opposite. That's mine, there.' Mags swung round and pointed to her own home. 'I'm moving in to my new place tomorrow. Now we're neighbours you must call me Mags and I'll call you Olivia. Wouldn't be right to be formal now we live so close, would it?'

'Er, no.'

'My Amy said you were moving in here. Not that I believed her at first. I mean, why would you want to move away from the lovely grand house you had at the posh end of town? Mind you, it must have been a bugger to heat. Amy told me all about it; great high ceilings and all those rooms. Much cosier here, isn't it?'

'A bit.'

'So, how are you getting on with the move? Aren't the kitchens lovely? All fitted units and everything. When I first saw my place I thought they'd forgotten the fridge – but no, there it was behind a door. I expect your kitchen must be a sight bigger than mine. Can I have a look?' And before Olivia could say anything Mags had pushed past her and was heading down the hall.

'Oooh, just like the one in the show house.' Mags opened cupboards and drawers. 'So much space.'

'Well, actually—'

'And three beds? I've only got two but with Amy so close what would I do with another one? Of course you've got Zac still at home, haven't you?'

'Yes.' Olivia's tone was quite sharp. 'Look, Mags, much as I'd love to chat I've only just got back from work and I've got a mass of stuff to do so…'

Mags felt herself being shepherded towards the front door. 'Yes, well…' She'd have to call round another day. She fancied a nose round Olivia's gaff. When her Amy had worked for her she was always getting told about some of the nice things Mrs L had. And, what's more, that story about the Laithwaites wanting to downsize had never quite rung true. And Mrs L had said she'd got in from work. Work? That woman had never done a hand's turn when Amy had cleaned for her. Mags longed to know if there was more to the decision than met the eye. Maybe if she got pally with Mrs L she'd get to find out.

'Nice to see you, Mags. Catch you another day.'

And before Mags could say 'goodbye' she was out on the path and the door was firmly shut.

Well!

The next day, an hour or so after Olivia had cycled past The Grange to start her early shift at the hotel, two massive removal vans drew up outside her old house. Miranda Osborne stood by the door and watched the removal men get out of the cabs and open up the lorries' huge back doors. She looked ready to spend a day lunching with girlfriends rather than about to move into a new house. Out of habit she fingered one of her emerald earrings – a present from her husband to celebrate their tenth wedding anniversary. She'd protested at the time that they were a ridiculous extravagance while rather hoping she might get a necklace to match when they got to their fifteenth.

'Roderick,' she called back into the house. 'Roddy, they're here.'

Roderick, a man who was the wrong side of sixty, with the hint of a paunch and thick glossy pepper and salt hair, dressed in mustard yellow chinos and a dark green V-necked sweater, clattered down the stairs. He looked at his Rolex. 'I'll give them their due, Miranda, they're punctual.'

Miranda arched a perfectly plucked eyebrow. 'As they bloody well should be.' Her accent was pure cut-glass. 'We're paying them enough. Besides, I told them you're a barrister and that we'd take them to the cleaners if the job wasn't finished today and done properly.'

Roddy Osborne laughed. 'I'd have thought you could have scared them into doing *exactly* as you wanted without bringing the threat of a lawsuit into it. And anyway, why mention me when you've got a perfectly good legal qualification of your own?'

Miranda bridled slightly. 'But I've been out of the loop for years now.'

'The removal men don't know that. Besides, there's nothing to stop you from getting back in the groove.'

She stared at her husband. Nothing to stop her...? OK, so it had been six years since she had lost the baby *and* almost lost her life in the process, but the mental scar was still there, the pain still caught her unawares on occasion, she still found herself gazing at prams in town and being reduced to tears... No, there was no way she could go back to work. Supposing she found herself dealing with a similar medical negligence case to the one she'd had to fight on her own behalf? Because if that happened there was no way she could be certain she'd be able to maintain any sort of professional detachment in court and what if she didn't? No, it would be too ghastly to even contemplate.

Except Roderick didn't see the issue like she did. He'd got over it, accepted they'd never have children and thought she should too. But he hadn't been carrying the baby, hadn't formed that bond, he hadn't experienced the guilt she'd felt. What had she done wrong? And while her insane workload during her pregnancy had been an excuse, it didn't absolve her of blame. Why hadn't she cut down on work, why hadn't she insisted that the health professionals were missing something when she felt under the weather...? Dear God, if only she had.

Miranda took a deep breath. Picking over the past wasn't going to bring little Emily back. She squared her shoulders, stepped over the threshold and went to greet the removal men.

'Well done,' she said. 'Bang on time. If you get started I'll make a pot of tea. Which would you prefer, Earl Grey or English breakfast?'

'Got any builders' tea, missus?'

Miranda narrowed her eyes as she considered correcting the foreman's familiarity. 'I imagine English breakfast tea is what you are referring to so, yes.'

'Good.'

'I'll bring a tray out in a few minutes.'

'Right, lads, let's get going.'

The men gathered at the ramp at the back of one van and began to unload boxes.

'Mr Osborne will give you direction,' said Miranda as she left the men to work and headed to the kitchen. The place, she noticed, still smelt faintly of paint. They'd had the whole interior redecorated in white as soon as they'd completed on the deal. The previous owners had had, she'd thought, quite a dubious taste in colour and wallpaper – especially in the bedrooms. She'd also had a wall of white fitted cupboards with push-to-open mechanisms built along the gable end wall under the mezzanine. To all intents and purposes the wall looked almost blank – as it should do – but behind was concealed a mass of shelves and drawers ready to hide their possessions from view. Less was, indeed, so much more.

The bathrooms and the kitchen were going to get the same treatment in due course but, for the time being, they would have to wait. She could live with them in the short term – just – but the sooner these awful faux-cottage cream kitchen units went along with their naff wooden handles the happier she'd be. White units, white tiles on the floor, white marble work surfaces and stainless steel appliances. Perfect.

Stacked on the counter were a few basics from their Kensington apartment, including a kettle and a box of identical white mugs. The milk, sugar and a couple of packets of biscuits, she'd bought that morning at the local Co-op. She'd dithered with the idea of giving the removal men soya milk because, as everyone knew, dairy farming was an abomination – just think what happened to the poor veal calves. However, Roddy had warned her that the movers might be difficult without a regular supply of tea with full-fat milk so, for the sake of their possessions, it might be worth abandoning her principles in the short term for a long-term gain. So, even though she could barely force herself to handle the plastic bottle, Miranda had conceded that her husband might have a point. As she'd proceeded to the checkout with her purchases she looked at the shop floor and concluded that, as a supermarket, it was a complete joke but it would just about do in an emergency. In London, for everyday groceries, she'd used a local Waitrose and she thanked God for online shopping, because there wasn't one close now they'd moved. For those decadent little luxuries that made life bliss, Harvey Nicks' food hall, or Fortnum's had been wonderful but that would have to be a thing of the past unless she could persuade Roddy to pop in when he went up to Town.

As she sorted out the men's tea, they hauled a steady stream of boxes and packing cases into the house and were directed by Roderick as to which room they should be taken.

Having delivered a tray of tea and biscuits to the workers, Miranda began to tear the tape off the crates and start unpacking various bits and pieces. She wasn't expecting the process of getting straight to take overly long. She didn't believe in clutter. When she'd viewed the house she'd been appalled at the amount of furniture the previous occupants had – such a waste of the vast airiness of the building. Surely, she'd thought, the whole point of living in a place like a barn conversion was to celebrate the space, not to try and make it cosy! What were they thinking of?

Several huge chrome and white leather sofas were hauled in, followed by a glass and polished stainless steel dining table, the fragile top swathed in acres of bubble wrap and heavy grey blankets. Miranda swooped on it as soon as the removal men had positioned it to her satisfaction. She dragged off the blankets and then tore off the rest of the protection. Once the table top was revealed she examined it minutely.

'If this has been damaged...' she muttered as she ran the tips of her fingers right around the bevelled edge, checking for the tiniest chip.

'OK?' queried Roderick.

'I think so,' said Miranda. 'By the way, Roddy, when is the chappy coming to look at the bathrooms and the kitchen?'

'He said later today.' Roderick got out his iPhone and checked his diary. 'Three o'clock.'

'Good. The sooner the better.' She cast a glance at the hideous kitchen. 'At least the decorators have finished.'

'Where do you want this, guv?' said one of the men. He was carrying a massive flat package.

Through the swathes of protective plastic Miranda could see a picture of stylised poppies.

'Prop it against that wall there,' she directed. Once again she had to bite her tongue. Why couldn't these oiks manage to call them Mr or Mrs Osborne and not resort to 'guv' and 'missus'? Pick your battles, she told herself. Once again she got busy removing the packaging so she could check for damage. She looked at a corner... was that a chip on the frame? She crouched beside the oil painting and rubbed the mark. No – just as well.

'Oi, missus.'

For God's sake... 'Yes,' she hissed.

'Visitor.'

'Visitor?'

She stood up in a fluid movement and walked to the door. Standing there was a short dumpy blonde with far too much cleavage showing. Dear God, this better hadn't be a neighbour. She hadn't paid such a vast sum for this house to have riff-raff like this on the doorstep.

'Yes?'

'Hiya. This is a bit of a cheek—'

'Mind ya back,' said a burly bloke hefting a stainless steel and white leather dining chair.

Miranda pulled her visitor out of the way and into the house.

'Blimey,' said the woman. 'This is a bit bright, ain't it?'

'Isn't it,' corrected Miranda. 'And no, it's not; it's called style.'

'What?' The blonde looked bemused. Well, what would a woman like that know about style? 'Anyway, bit of a cheek,' she continued, 'but I used to clean for the last people. I was wondering if you'd already got yourself fixed up or if you were looking for a char.'

Miranda stared at her. She had to admire her enterprise but she was similarly shocked by the brass neck.

'I've got a bunch of references and everything.'

'I'm sure you have.' And from other riff-raff, no doubt.

'I clean for lots of people; the vicar's wife and the doctor's.' The woman beamed at her.

'Really?' Good heavens – so not *all* riff-raff.

'Yeah, honest.' She rummaged in her bag and produced some rather dog-eared envelopes. 'Have a look.' She proffered the letters.

'Look, this isn't convenient. As you can see I'm quite busy.'

'I can come back tomorrow.' She beamed even more eagerly at Miranda.

Oh God, this woman was persistent but part of Miranda still quite admired her and she *would* need a cleaner. She'd employed a commercial firm in London but she'd never been entirely happy about the arrangement. And they'd been ruinously expensive. Not that that had mattered but she'd always worried that they'd hiked their prices because of her postcode.

'What do you charge?'

'A tenner an hour,' was the cheerful answer.

'A *tenner*?'

A worried frown creased the blonde's forehead. 'It's what my other ladies pay.'

'No… no that's fine.' Ten pounds an hour? Good God, could anyone live on those sort of wages? And a bit of a price change from the iniquitous sum she'd paid to get her apartment cleaned before.

'So I've got the job.'

'You've got a *trial*.'

'Oh.'

'If you meet my standards, *then* you'll have a job.'

'I did for Mrs L on Tuesday afternoon and Thursday morning. Is that OK for you, cos if it's not I've not got much other free time?'

'I suppose it'll have to be.'

'Good.' The blonde looked about her. 'I like your stuff. Bet that table shows the marks something dreadful though.' She stared at the big glass dining table. 'How many can you get round that? A dozen? Sixteen?' Miranda nodded. 'That's going to be a bugger to polish.'

'It just needs elbow grease,' advised Miranda. 'Now then, if that's everything…?'

'Yup. So, seeing as it's Thursday tomorrow shall I pop over in the morning to give this place a once-over?'

'I…'

'Only all this coming and going is bound to drag muck into the house.'

'Well…'

'Right, see you then. I'll be over around nine.' The woman bounced out of the door and down the drive leaving Miranda feeling slightly, and unaccustomedly, shell-shocked.

17

'Coo-ee,' yodelled Amy as she let herself into the vicarage. 'Sorry I'm a bit late – had to do something on my way to work.' She shrugged off her coat and hung it on the newel post.

'Morning, Amy.' Heather glanced at the kitchen clock. Nine fifteen.

'I'll make it up at the end.'

'Amy, a few minutes really don't matter. Tea?'

'Please. Gasping, I am.'

As Heather got out mugs and milk Amy put on the pinny she kept hanging behind the kitchen door and took her box of cleaning materials out of the cupboard.

'Meant to say last week – you're getting low on polish.'

'But you've got enough for today?'

Amy shook the aerosol. 'Probably. I've just been up at Olivia's old gaff.'

'Really?' Heather switched on the kettle.

'Yeah. Had a call from a mate of mine off the estate telling me the new people were moving in. She saw the vans there when she was dropping her kid off at school. So I thought I'd go up there on my way here and see if they want a char.'

'Very enterprising of you.'

'Yeah, I thought so and all. If you don't ask you don't get, that's what I say.'

'And did you? *Get*, that is?'

'Might of. She said she'd give me a trial.'

Heather dropped teabags in the mugs. 'So… what's she like?'

'Dead posh. And she'd painted the whole of the inside of the house white. And all her stuff is white and shiny. I tell you it don't half hurt your eyes just looking at it. She got this massive dining table – glass. I wouldn't give it house room, me. You'd only have to look at it and it'd be all smears. That's going to be a bugger to clean – I told her that, too.'

Heather didn't doubt it.

'I reckon they're loaded. I mean it stands to reason they've got a fair old wedge, given they've bought Olivia's place… but Mrs L only ever looked normal, if you know what I mean. This new woman looks like she's stepped out of a fashion mag. And her earrings… well, they might have come from Accessorize but if they were real emeralds they must have cost a mint. Honest, they were massive. Huge.'

'In which case,' said Heather as the kettle clicked off, 'I might have to approach her to help out with the bell fund.'

'Good luck with that one,' said Amy. 'When I told her what I charge for cleaning she looked like she'd swallowed a wasp. I mean, a tenner an hour is fair, ain't it?'

'It is.'

'I reckon she's as tight as a duck's arse. But a job is a job and I don't have to like her to work for her.'

Brian pushed the study door shut because Amy's conversation with his wife was distracting and looked at the report from the bell foundry, rereading, for the umpteenth time, the final amount. Thirty-six thousand pounds. Brian took his glasses off and polished them. He supposed he had to be grateful for small mercies; the tower itself was sound. Graham had regaled him with a number of horror stories of actual towers becoming unstable because of the weight of bells swinging in them over the years. It seemed that the fact it was just chunks of wood that had to be replaced and girders installed to underpin the work – but no repairs to the stonework and masonry or the bells themselves – meant they'd got off remarkably lightly. But the parishioners were already moaning about the lack of bells at services and several brides who had booked them for their weddings had had to be disappointed. He'd tried explaining about the dangers to the ringers if the damaged bell frame failed but it hadn't seemed to have cut much mustard. Huh! It'd be a different story if it happened.

He pressed a key on his computer and the screen saver which had been revolving mesmerically and gently on the screen disappeared to be replaced by a couple of dozen icons. He hit the one for the internet and then clicked through to access the church's bell-fund bank account. He gazed at the sum on the statement. Just over a couple of hundred pounds – the result of his exhortations from the pulpit. At this rate it was going to take years and years to get the bells ringing again.

He pulled a sheet of paper out of his filing tray – it was covered in Heather's handwriting; her notes from her fundraising brainstorming session with Olivia. One of the things mentioned was sponsorship by wealthy residents and successful local businesses. And the only way to approach them was in person... and the only person who could be expected to do that was himself.

Brian had drawn up a list of possibilities from the business community and now he needed to pick up the phone and start asking for appointments to see the CEOs or MDs or head honchos or whatever the bosses were called.

'Give me strength,' he prayed. He loathed this sort of thing but it was, he supposed, a necessary evil if he managed to add to the coffers but, seriously, was this really what he'd trained for when he'd followed his calling?

With a deep and heartfelt sigh he picked up the phone and began dialling the number at the top of his list.

'Good morning,' he said when the phone was answered. 'I'm Brian Simmonds, vicar of St Catherine's and I was wondering if I might make an appointment to see your managing director sometime in the near future.'

'I'll put you through to his PA,' said a female voice.

'Thank you.'

Ghastly tinny music came over the line as Brian waited. He started to lose the will to live. He switched from the computerised bank statement to a game of patience and began to move the cards on the screen. The game was resolved; he started another and the music played on.

'Hello.'

Brian jumped. 'Oh, hello.'

'So sorry to keep you waiting.' The woman sounded indifferent.

'No, that's fine.'

'I'm Mr Milward's PA. I gather you want an appointment to see him.'

'Please.'

'May I ask what it's about?'

Brian was tempted to say no, she couldn't. 'I would like to ask him if, as a valued member of our local business community, he might be prepared to donate to the restoration of the church bells.'

There was a second's silence. 'Mr Milward isn't a churchgoer.'

'Attending church isn't a prerequisite for wanting to help the local community.'

'As I said, Mr Milward isn't a churchgoer.'

'Maybe you would like to ask Mr Milward himself if he might find a minute or two in his schedule to see me?'

'Please hold.'

Once again the tinny music started but Brian had only heard about two bars of it when the PA came back on the line. 'I'm afraid Mr Milward's diary is full for the foreseeable future.'

'Thank you.' Brian put the phone down knowing that Mr

Milward hadn't even been consulted. 'Thank you very much indeed,' he hissed to no one.

This exercise was going to be even more depressing and dispiriting than he'd feared.

'That was brilliant,' said Miss Watkins, clapping her hands and beaming at the children sitting in a circle in the school's drama studio. 'Ashley, I am thrilled that you are so nearly off-book. And so early on.'

'Only the first act, miss. I haven't learnt the rest yet,' said Ashley, glowing with the praise.

'Even so. He's an example to the rest of you,' said Miss Watkins to her after-school drama group. 'Now then, I have printed off a further rehearsal schedule, if you'd like to pass them around, Megan.' She handed sheets of A4 to her and Megan walked around the room handing one to each pupil. 'So, as you can see, Wednesdays will continue to be a full-cast rehearsal but I want to go through specific scenes in the lunch hours.' One or two of the pupils exchanged looks which were intercepted by Miss Watkins. 'Yes, I know this means you lose some free time but if we're going to be ready to perform this in December then we're all going to have to make sacrifices.'

'It's fine with me, miss,' said Ashley.

'Licker,' someone said in a barely audible whisper.

If Miss Watkins heard the comment she ignored it but to judge by the scowl on Ashley's face he'd not missed it.

'So, if you make a note of the new schedule, some of you I'll see tomorrow and Friday – the rest of you, I'll see you next week. Oh, and don't forget to stack your chairs,' she added over the increasing hubbub as the drama club kids gathered up their bags and coats and got ready to go home.

Ashley and Megan put their chairs on one of the piles by the door and walked out into bright autumn sunshine.

'How come you've learnt so much?' asked Megan as they headed across the school grounds to the gate.

'I dunno. I just love this whole acting thing, don't you?'

'Well… I mean it's fun and the drama group has some nice people in and Miss Watkins is great…'

Ashley stopped and stared at her. 'But it's so much more than that.'

'Is it?'

'Yes!' The passion in his voice startled Megan. 'I can be… It's…' Ashley threw his hands in the air in frustration at not being able to vocalise exactly what he meant. 'It's so liberating.'

'Liberating? You're weird.'

'You don't get it. You're not really serious about it.'

'And you are? It's a school panto, Ash, get a grip.'

'How was drama club?' asked Amy as her son banged into the house. She was sitting on the sofa filing her nails.

'All right.' He slung his bag on the floor at the bottom of the stairs.

'Good. And I got a new job today. Well, it's more like an old one because I'll be working up at Olivia's old place but for the new people. Mind you, I might've thought that Mrs L was up herself but she's got nothing on this new woman. I mean, talk about humourless. If you told me she'd swallowed a poker I wouldn't be the least bit surprised.'

'Hmm.'

'You all right, Ash? Cat got your tongue?'

'Hmm.'

'You could at least be pleased for me.' She stretched her hand in front of her and admired her work.

'Yeah.'

'Something the matter?'

Ash shook his head. 'They don't get it.'

'Who? Who doesn't get what?'

'The drama club. They're just playing at it. They're not serious about acting, they're just playing at it. '

'But ain't that what it's about – *play* acting?'

'God, no, Mum.'

'Pardon me for being such an ignoramus. Anyway, what's with this sudden obsession? You spend every moment with your nose in that book, you hardly talk to me...' Amy stopped and stared at her son. 'Are you sweet on that Miss Watkins? I've been hearing about her. Someone told Gran that her husband had his eyes out on stalks at the last parents' evening and she looked young enough to be his daughter.'

'God, no, Mum. How can you suggest such a thing?' He sounded utterly disgusted then he turned and stamped off to his room muttering about going over his lines.

Amy stared after her son. He was really upset about being asked if he fancied Miss Watkins. When she'd been at school loads of the boys had the hots for some of the younger female teachers – so why not her Ash? And all this acting and dressing up and stuff... Supposing her Ash was gay? She'd worried that people might *think* he was gay because of this acting palaver but supposing he really was?

18

A couple of days later Amy was walking through town on her way to work at Bex's house. As she passed the pub she saw Belinda up a stepladder watering her hanging baskets.

'Hi, Belinda,' she called.

Belinda turned and wobbled. She clutched the top of the ladder.

'Careful,' exhorted Amy.

'Morning, Amy.' She put the can down on the top step and climbed down before lifting it off. 'How's the dating game going?'

'Not brilliantly. To be honest, that last one made me wonder if it's worth it.'

'Not all men are tight-fisted bores.'

'Yeah, well.'

'You should have another go. What have you got to lose?'

'If I get another date like the last one, the answer is an evening at home with the telly.'

Belinda laughed. 'Go on, have a go.'

'Maybe. Anyway, I'd better get on. Don't want to be late for Bex.'

Amy turned into the drive to The Beeches and let herself in the front door.

'Morning!' she called as she clacked across the tiled hall.

'Morning, Amy.'

Bex's voice came from the utility room. As Amy headed towards the kitchen she saw something lying on the floor. She picked up the item – a sock. A man's sock.

'I found this,' said Amy going into the utility room and handing it over.

'Oh.' Bex coloured before she added, 'One of my bed socks.'

Yeah, right. Amy had changed the sheets on Bex's bed more than enough times to know that Bex didn't wear bed socks. And if she did she wouldn't wear size twelves. So whose was it?

'The usual?' asked Amy as her mind whirled as to who might have left some laundry. Fancy old Bex snaffling a bloke. Not that she was 'old' and she was still quite a looker but, thought Amy, Bex was older than she was and had a load more kids so if someone fancied Bex, maybe there was hope for her. Maybe she shouldn't give up on finding someone just yet.

Bex nodded and slammed the washing machine shut. 'Please. I'm going to have to love you and leave you. We seem to have run out of almost everything and I need to hit the supermarket.'

'I'll still be here when you get back – unless you're going to be doing other stuff after.'

'No, just a shop. I'll be back by eleven unless something drastic happens.'

Bex whizzed around, gathering up shopping bags, her coat, her keys and her handbag before she left, while Amy went upstairs to make a start on the kids' bedrooms. She watched out of the window to see the car pull out of the drive before she went into Bex's bedroom and picked up the laptop from her dressing table. She sat on the bed and flipped it open and then logged into her dating site.

'Let's have a look at what's on offer,' she muttered as she scrolled down the page. After all, if Bex could find a date she should be able to; besides, she had much better tits than her boss and everyone knew that's what blokes liked.

At the end of the afternoon, Zac got off the school bus in the middle of town and looked up the road towards Beeching Rise and his home. He dreaded going home. The atmosphere was toxic, his mother was always stressed, Jade was a pain – either snapping and snarling or crying – and the place was a tip. He had to admit the irony of hating living in a mess. Six months previously, when he'd been heavily into drugs, his room had been vile. But getting Oscar and cleaning his act up had changed all that. Besides, now his room was the size of a shoebox, if he didn't keep it organised he'd never find anything.

Zac glanced the other way down the street – towards The Beeches. He wondered if Megan was in. He hadn't seen her for an age.

They'd started out as friends but they'd fallen out over his drug habit. It had all been his fault; he'd been a git, a total arse and, in retrospect, he was ashamed of his behaviour. They'd made up eventually but that easy familiarity that they'd first enjoyed hadn't been quite the same.

Zac made his mind up and headed towards Megan's house. He rang the doorbell and waited on the step.

'Hello, stranger,' said Bex, when she opened the door. 'How was the move?'

'Grim,' said Zac. 'The house is the pits.' He smiled at Bex. 'Sorry, but that's the truth.'

'I saw it the day after you'd moved there. It's not quite what you're used to, is it?'

Zac shook his head. 'Is Megan in?'

'Yeah, of course.' Bex moved to the bottom of the stairwell and yelled up two floors. 'Megan! Visitor.'

There was a pause before Megan appeared on the first floor, looking over the banister. 'Hi, Zac.' She pattered down the remaining stairs.

Bex slid off to the kitchen.

'I wondered if you fancied taking Oscar for a walk,' said Zac.

'I suppose. Why?'

'Well...' Zac shrugged. 'I haven't seen you for a while. You've not been down the skatepark.'

'Been busy. I'm in the school panto.'

'Hey, well done. What are you in?'

'*Cinderella*. I'm Cinders.'

'Good for you.'

'It's a lot of work... lines to learn, rehearsals.'

Zac nodded. 'So, do you want to go on this walk?'

'Yeah, why not? I'll just grab my coat and tell Bex I'm off out.'

A couple of minutes later the pair was heading towards Zac's to collect Oscar.

'I keep forgetting you've moved,' said Megan.

'I wish I could.'

'That sounded heartfelt.'

'The new house is a dump. And Jade's moved back in so we're really squashed. And she's being a total pain; always crying, rowing with Mum...' Zac gave Megan the low-down on recent events in his family. 'And, to cap it all, Mum's got a job.'

'Your mum has?'

'Yeah, I know. It's awful.'

'Why?'

'Why do you think? I'm having to do housework.'

Megan started to laugh. 'Ooh – boys do, you know.'

'It's not funny.'

'I dunno – the thought of you in a frilly apron and a feather duster...'

They reached Zac's new home and Megan took in the exterior. 'It doesn't look too bad.'

'Huh.' Zac let them both in and called to Oscar who came bounding over from his basket in the kitchen. 'Hello, boy. You pleased to see me? And I bet Jade didn't take you out, did she?'

Oscar's response was to wriggle round Zac's legs, his tail wagging like it was possessed.

'Come on then, walkies.'

Oscar barked joyously as Zac took the lead off the hook and clipped it onto Oscar's collar. Upstairs a door slammed.

'Zac?' said female voice.

'Yeah. Just taking Oscar out.'

Footsteps clattered on the stairs. A languorous brunette came into the kitchen.

'Oh,' she said, seeing Megan.

'Megan, Jade. Jade, Megan,' said Zac.

'Hi,' they said to each other in unison.

'You going to be long?' Jade asked her bother.

'Why?'

'Because I'm cooking supper and I don't want it ruined.'

'You're *cooking*?'

'Yeah. And?'

'Nothing,' mumbled Zac.

'Good. So be back by seven thirty, latest. Dad's promised to be back by then, too.'

'OK, whatever.'

Zac, Megan and an overexcited Oscar headed out and towards the nature reserve.

'How's Ash?' asked Zac. 'I've not seen him this term.'

'Hasn't he been down the skatepark?'

Zac shook his head.

'That's probably because he's in the school play too and he seems obsessed by it all. I mean, don't get me wrong, everyone in the drama group is taking it seriously and learning our lines and everything, but Ashley is going a bit bonkers about it all. He said he feels "liberated".'

Zac hooted. 'Liberated? What's a twat like him got to be *liberated* about?'

Megan put her hand on Zac's arm. 'Don't tell him I said that. And don't tease him.'

'Whatever.'

'Please?'

'I said I won't, didn't I?'

Mags watched Zac and Megan leave Olivia's house. She narrowed her eyes; she didn't like that boy. If half of what Amy had told her about him was true he was a right handful. He and Ash had once been mates, which had worried her and she was glad it seemed to have fizzled out – once a druggie, always a druggie in her book – but she wasn't sure Ashley's obsession with acting was much of an improvement. Which reminded her… she wanted to see her grandson and she had the perfect excuse to ask him over. She picked up her phone and dialled his mobile.

'Yeah, hi, Gran,' he said on answering.

'Hello, Ash. Can you come round?'

'What, now?'

'If you're not busy.'

'Not really.'

'Good, I need you to go up a ladder for me. I've got curtains that need hanging in the spare room.'

'I suppose. I'll be round in a minute.'

'You're a good boy, Ash. I'll put the kettle on.'

It had barely boiled when she heard the noise of a skateboard zipping up the pavement. Then the doorbell rang.

'Ta for this, Ash. The kettle's just boiled and I've got some Jaffa Cakes in.'

'Great.'

Mags got the packet out of a cupboard and handed it to Ashley then began to fill the teapot. 'I've just seen your mate, Megan.'

'Oh, yeah.'

'She was walking out with Zac and that dog of his.'

'Oh, yeah. You said his parents live opposite.' Ashley sounded uninterested in her bit of gossip.

'I though you liked her.'

'She's all right; we're mates, that's all.'

Mags sniffed. If he made a bit of an effort she was sure Megan would notice him and Mags would like that. After all, now his gran was a property owner there was no reason why he shouldn't set his sights on girls like Megan. Except he didn't seem to be interested. Instead she said, 'Your mum says you're very busy with the play.'

That wasn't what Amy had said. She'd said Ashley was obsessed by it. She'd also said he seemed much too interested in the dressing up and make-up for her liking.

'You don't think…? You're not suggesting…?' Mags had said. 'Your Ash…?'

'I dunno what to think, Mum,' had been Amy's response. 'I can hardly ask him, can I? He'll either have a go at me or he'll lie.'

Ashley's face lit up. 'It's great. Miss Watkins taught us about stage make-up the other day. It was brilliant. The things you can do if you know how. She's lent me a book on it.'

'A book on make-up? To you?' Gawd, maybe Amy was right.

'Why not? Actors have to know how to do their own make-up.'

'You? Wearing make-up!'

'God, Gran, it's what actors do. And some blokes do… all the time. Look at Russell Brand and Boy George.'

'You're not thinking of doing that, are you? Wearing make-up?'

'Course not, Gran. Except on stage, obviously. Now – these curtains.'

19

September slipped into October and the leaves on the trees were shades of russet and gold. The rehearsals for the panto continued, Olivia started to get to grips with juggling work and running a house, Jade grudgingly took on more of the cooking and began to job hunt seriously and Nigel learnt how to stack and run the dishwasher – unloading it seemed to be outside his skill set but Olivia kept reminding herself that some progress was better than no progress. Across on the other side of town, Brian's bank account for the bells began to grow. And Bex woke up one Saturday morning feeling sick. She lay in bed and waited for the nausea to pass while hoping that she'd not picked up a bug. The last thing she wanted was to be ill over a weekend. After a few minutes she felt better and went downstairs to make herself a cup of tea. The boys were already up and watching CBeebies.

'Hi, guys,' she said as she passed the sitting room door.

'Hi, Mum,' they replied in unison.

'Sleep all right?'

Two tousled blond heads nodded, their eyes fixed to the screen and the antics of the Octonauts.

Bex left them to it and went to make herself tea. As she turned on the tap she felt sick and dizzy again. She put the kettle on the draining board, leant against the sink and breathed slowly. The ringing in her ears faded as the queasiness went away. Bex pulled a chair over with her foot and sat down. She leaned her head against the cold china of the Belfast sink.

What's this all about? she wondered. Low blood sugar? It was a possibility – her supper the previous evening had been stuffed potato and not a very big one. Of course there was another possibility that came with feeling sick in the morning. That thought made her feel even worse. She couldn't be, could she?

'You all right, Bex?'

Bex jumped. 'Yeah, yeah, I'm fine.'

Megan stared at her. 'Really?'

'Just a dizzy spell. Head rush... you know.'

'I hate it when that happens. Did you stand up too quickly?'

'Must have done.' Bex stood up and picked up the kettle again. 'Tea?'

Megan nodded.

'Got any plans for today?'

Megan sighed. 'Ash wants to go through a couple of scenes.'

'He's very keen on this play, isn't he?'

Megan nodded. 'Tell me about it. But, I suppose it'll only take an hour or so. I think this afternoon Zac and I may go into Cattebury.'

'Zac?'

'I'd go with Soph but she can't get away and Zac says being at home is awful. His sister is still living with them and driving him spare.'

'It must be tricky.'

Megan sat down as she waited for her promised mug of tea and Bex went to the fridge to get the milk out. As she did a waft of leftover prawns from the previous night's stuffed spuds caught her and she gagged. Luckily Megan was busy looking at her iPhone and was oblivious to her stepmother's discomfort.

Which begged the question, thought Bex, as she swallowed bile – what the hell was she going to do if it turned out she *was* pregnant? She'd just got her life back now that the boys were both at school. She loved having time to herself during the day. Did she really want to go back to nappies and sleepless nights? No, no she didn't. And she didn't dare contemplate what Megan's reaction might be.

On the other hand this was Miles's baby too and he'd hinted how he wanted to be a father. When they'd slept together – and those occasions could still be counted on the fingers of one hand – they'd been very careful. Maybe her falling pregnant, if she was, was karma. Meant to be, not for her sake, but for his.

Bex took her tea and went back up to her room. She lay on her bed and stared at the ceiling. She liked Miles – she really did. And she liked lot of things about him, even his obsession with folding things up neatly. He was great with the kids, he was kind, he was a fabulous cook and, if she was honest, he was pretty good in bed. So... so if this was morning sickness did she want to contemplate a real commitment to Miles? Was she ready for that? Having a fling was one thing but this...? This was something else.

Bex sighed. She hadn't looked at this relationship beyond the here and now; a bit of fun, some companionship, someone to confide in, to share an evening with... And right up to this morning it had seemed completely simple and now – now, if her suspicion was right, it was a God-awful mess. A nightmare. She had to hope she wasn't pregnant, that was all, because if she was... How could she face Miles if she got rid of the one thing he really wanted and which was, if she was brutally honest, the last thing she did?

Brian looked, yet again, at the bell-fund bank account. His cold calls to local businesses had paid off to a certain extent and the total was creeping towards five figures. It was nice to see it grow; he gained a certain amount of satisfaction every time there was a deposit. He began to understand Scrooge and Harpagon's love of seeing large sums of money safely stashed. And, if all went well, the Heritage Lottery Fund might come through with a hefty grant – the promise of opening up the bell tower to teach youth groups, schools, the U3A... anyone... about change-ringing, plus the fact that bell-ringing was considered to be a heritage craft meant that their request for funds might be looked on favourably. Or so he'd been reliably informed.

Heather came into his study and looked at the spreadsheet over her husband's shoulder.

'We're getting there,' she observed.

'Not fast enough, though. I've had so many complaints now about the bells. People don't like them being silent.'

'No, but there isn't any choice. By the way, have you made an approach to the Osbornes?'

'Who?'

'The new people at The Grange. Amy says they're, and I quote, "stinking rich".'

'Richer than the Laithwaites before, er, Nigel's problem?'

'According to Amy, yes. Apparently the work that is being done on the inside of that house beggars belief. It's all to do with minimalism, says Amy. Just about everything that can be hidden behind an almost invisible door is. Apart from some huge great pieces of art.'

'Well, if Amy says it is so, it must be true.'

'Amy also says it is a pain in the arse because she can never find the hoover. She says the cupboards in the kitchen all look the same and she has to open them all to find anything she wants.'

'I can't see Amy complaining about having an excuse to have a good rootle around.'

'No... well...' Heather smiled. She was pretty sure that Amy needed no excuse to have a good rootle around. Not that she cared. There was nothing to hide at the vicarage – except the good biscuits and she didn't think Amy had found those yet.

'What about you going to see these people?' said Brian.

'Me?'

'Don't you want to see what they're up to?'

Heather couldn't lie. 'Yes, of course, only wouldn't it be better if you did – more official?'

'As these people are incomers and more than likely haven't formed a bond with the town, *and* given that we haven't seen them in church, I think the chance of either of us persuading them to make a donation is vanishingly small. So, bearing that in mind, it might as well be you who goes up there and gets a chance for a bit of a snoop round.'

'Put like that… I'll take a walk up that way now.'

Miranda Osborne placed an antique bronze figurine of a dancer in the centre of her dining table. While she didn't like clutter, she liked objets d'art, especially when she knew how much they had cost. This piece was by Marcel Bouraine and had cost an absolute mint. She loved it.

She stood back to admire it as the doorbell rang. She wasn't expecting visitors or a delivery and the builders wouldn't be back till Monday. She crossed the vast empty expanse of floor to the door and saw a woman in appallingly unfashionable clothes and bad hair standing there.

'Yes?'

'Hello, I'm Heather Simmonds and welcome to Little Woodford.'

The name rang a faint bell but Miranda dismissed it. Why would she have had anything to do with a country mouse like this? 'I'm Miranda Osborne.'

The woman looked at her, expectantly. Oh God, she wanted to be invited in. Miranda made a quick decision. She had no idea how influential or otherwise this person was but maybe it wasn't a wonderful idea to piss off the residents from the get-go. For all Miranda knew she might be the town mayor and, as she had ideas for this house that would involve getting planning consent, maybe she ought to be polite – for now.

'Lovely to meet you,' she said, turning on the charm. 'Come in.'

She threw the door wide and her visitor stepped over the threshold.

'Goodness, this is... airy.'

'Wonderful, isn't it? The previous owners really didn't maximise the potential of the space.'

'Didn't they?' The woman looked about her. 'Yes... very – um – minimalist.'

'Isn't it perfect?'

'Yes.'

'Coffee?'

'I'd love one.'

Heather followed Miranda into the kitchen area. 'Ooh, new units.'

'Ah – you knew the previous owners?'

'Oh, yes. Olivia and I are good friends.'

'My cleaner says she and her husband downsized.'

'Amy? Yes, they did. And Amy cleans for me too.'

So that's why she knew the name. 'Ah – you're one of the people who wrote a reference for Amy.'

Heather smiled happily. 'Yes, yes I did. She's a good cleaner.'

'She's a gossip.'

'Only if you encourage her.'

'I don't.' Miranda stood in front of a coffee machine that looked as if it would be more at home in a large branch of Costa. 'What would you like?'

'A filter coffee with milk?'

'OK. Except I only have almond milk.'

'Oh... well, yes, that's fine.'

'Dairies are concentration camps for cows.' She pressed some buttons. 'I take it you're a resident here?'

'Yes, my husband's the vicar.'

Which explained the clothes. 'Really? Roderick and I subscribe to the New Labour policy about the church.'

'Which is?'

'We don't do God.'

'No, people don't. Still, there's plenty who do.'

Behind Miranda the machine burped, steamed and gurgled and coffee dripped into a glass mug with a chrome handle while she bit back a comment about deluded fools.

'Anyway, I always think,' continued Heather, 'whether you are religious or not, one can appreciate the wonderful architecture of our ancient churches.'

'Hmm.'

'St Catherine's is Norman – well, quite a lot of it is. When this town got rich on the wool trade they added bits to it in the Middle Ages. And put in stained glass although some of that didn't survive the Reformation.'

Oh God, not a history lesson, please. 'Fascinating.' Miranda suppressed a yawn. The coffee machine finished making Heather's coffee and she handed her the mug and passed her the milk jug. 'Sugar?'

'Just milk. Actually, it's about the church I came – well, not the church exactly, but the bells.'

'The church has bells? I've not heard them.'

'Exactly.' Heather beamed at her. 'Isn't it awful without them? We've had to silence them because they're in a parlous state. We're having to raise thousands to get them fixed and I thought maybe, as you've chosen to live in this wonderful little town, you'd like to help us reach our total.'

'Donate to the bells?'

Heather nodded eagerly.

'So they can ring again? And shatter the peace?'

Her guest's face fell.

'We moved here to get away from din and racket.'

'But it's not din and racket – they're beautiful.'

'That's your opinion; one I don't share. Besides, there are laws about noise and I think you should know that my husband is a barrister. If your bells wreck the peace and quiet of this town we'll take action.'

Heather stared at her open-mouthed. Then she put her mug down on the counter.

'Well!' she said, and stalked out. She shut the door rather more forcefully than was necessary.

20

Olivia sat next to Heather in the front pew of the church, fuming. She was livid, incandescent. She hadn't felt this angry since Nigel had told her about his debts. She couldn't believe what Heather had just told her about what the new inhabitant had said about the bells.

'She said *what*?'

Beside her Heather whispered, 'Her exact words... "din and racket". She also told me her husband is a barrister.'

Olivia snorted. 'So all this fundraising may be in vain if we can't ring the bells at the end of it.'

'That's the size of it. Or we can block up the louvres in the bell chamber to muffle the sound; other churches have done that as a compromise, but if we do that'll be even more expense.'

The organist began the introit and Heather and Olivia stood.

'We must talk over coffee,' said Olivia. 'I don't need to rush back; I'm not working till later.'

At the end of the service, Heather and Olivia rehung their kneelers, gathered up their hymn books and Books of Common Prayer, their handbags and their gloves, and then made their way to the back of the church where the Friends of St Catherine's were dishing out coffee and cake. Small children, released from Sunday School in the community centre on the next-door cricket pitch, streamed into the building to be reunited with their parents and then run around in the big space by the font. Some of the old biddies looked disapprovingly at the children.

'Anyway, tell me more about the new people?' said Olivia as they reached the head of the queue for coffee. She took two cups and handed one to Heather and then Heather relayed all the details she could remember about the makeover that had been given to Olivia's old house.

'Honestly, it's bare and echoey. I mean, don't get me wrong, you can tell she's thrown a mint of money at it and there are some socking great pieces of art in it which I expect might be worth as much as a small country's GDP, but I wouldn't want to live there. There's no sense of comfort or personality. It's not a place to kick back and loaf in front of the TV. Not that I care,' said Heather. 'I can't see Brian and me getting an invitation to supper there any time soon.'

'Or ever.'

'No. Still, no loss. Although it would have been useful if she'd found it in her heart to give us a fat donation.'

'How's the fundraising going?'

'The Heritage Lottery Fund looks like it's going to come good and Brian's done well with the local businesses.'

'I feel so guilty about not being able to help more.'

'Don't. You've done plenty over the years. Did you know Belinda has promised to run a pudding evening at the pub?'

'Is she? Good for her.'

'Yup, £20 gets you all the puds you can eat. She says Miles is going to have about fifteen on offer.'

'Sounds lush. If I'm not working I might have to give it a go. Not that I should, of course.' She looked down at her stomach which was perfectly flat but, like many middle-aged women, she worried about middle-aged spread.

'Sadly, I don't think I will be able to go.'

'That's a shame.'

'Strictly between you, me and the gatepost, Brian and I need to tighten our belts – our expenses keep going up and our salaries don't. I am seriously thinking of putting one of our spare rooms on Airbnb.'

'Really?'

Heather nodded. 'Of course the problem is that I can't offer a room with an en suite. But I imagine, if I reflected the fact that we can only offer shared facilities in the price, we might get a taker or two. And a few extra quid each month would be a real help.'

'That bad?'

Heather nodded. 'We're the proverbial church mice.'

Olivia put her hand on Heather's arm. 'I wish I was in a position to help but...'

'I know.'

Olivia's brow wrinkled. 'But... would it be allowed – I mean, are you allowed to sublet the vicarage?'

'Not sublet, no, but I had a word with the bishop's office and they don't have a particular objection to us running a B and B. We'd have to give the diocese a proportion of our income but frankly we'd still make a healthy profit. I'm just not sure I've got the energy – it'd be a lot of work and I'd have to make a real effort to keep the place clean and tidy.' She sighed. 'Changing the subject, how's Jade?'

'Ah, well...' Olivia brightened. 'She's finally got a job. She's working as an office manager for a company on the industrial estate on the Cattebury road. I suspect she's probably overqualified for the role but at least she's employed now and not kicking her heels at home.'

'That's good.'

'Yes and no. She and I had words about her helping with running the house and, to give her her due, she did take on some of the chores and helped with the cooking. Of course now she works too, she can't possibly be expected to shoulder that burden as well.'

'But of course, you can.'

Olivia nodded. 'Obviously.' She drained her coffee. 'Time I got going. I ought to do the ironing before I go to work.' She sighed.

'No rest for the wicked.' She gave Heather a farewell kiss on the cheek. 'See you next week – shifts permitting.'

'Bye.'

Olivia walked out of the church and up the road past the cricket club onto the high street.

'Hiya, Mrs L,' called a familiar voice.

'Amy? How are you? I haven't seen you in an age.'

'Not too bad, Mrs L. I got my old job back at your house but she's a piece of work and no mistake.'

'Heather has just been saying something similar.'

'I tell you, if I didn't need the money I'd tell that Mrs Osborne where she could shove it.'

'Mrs Osborne?'

'Yeah, why, do you know her?'

'Tall, slim, hair in a French pleat?'

'That's her.'

'She stayed at the hotel.'

'Oh, yeah, you work up at the Priors, don't you? How are you getting on?'

'Mostly very well, when we don't have guests like her staying. She was a nightmare.'

'I can believe it. And you should see what she's done to your place. It's all white and shiny. And none of the cupboards have no knobs on them. She doesn't like knobs. Huh, well in that case she shouldn't have married one. Her old man is the biggest knob in Little Woodford, if you ask me.' Amy guffawed at her own joke. 'Anyway, mustn't keep you. Bye.' She went on her way leaving Olivia thinking about the awfulness of the Osbornes. Somehow she didn't think they were going to be an asset to the community.

She could hear the row before she opened the door to her house. Zac and Jade were going at it hammer and tongs and it seemed that Nigel had gone out. She was very tempted to turn around and go back out herself.

'Stop it!' she yelled in a nanosecond of silence.

'She started it,' Zac shouted.

'Quiet.' Silence fell. 'I could hear the pair of you out in the street. What on *earth* is going on?'

'Zac used all the hot water and I wanted to wash my hair,' whined Jade.

'For heaven's sake, is that all?' said Olivia. She stamped into the kitchen and hit the override button on the boiler. 'The water will be hot again in an hour.'

'Zac shouldn't have had such a long shower.'

'Maybe if you'd got up earlier, you could have washed your hair before Zac hogged the bathroom.'

'Why should I? It's the weekend and if he hadn't been so selfish—'

'I wasn't selfish.'

'Stop it,' said Olivia again.

'I pay to live here,' said Jade. 'That's more than he does.'

'It's a peppercorn rent,' said Olivia. 'It isn't enough to give you special treatment.'

'God, I hate this family.'

'Then move out.'

Jade scowled at her mother. 'Like that's affordable around here.'

'Then I suggest you shut up and put up,' said Olivia as calmly as she could.

Jade stormed out of the kitchen.

'I wish she *would* move out,' said Zac. 'I'm going to take Oscar out.'

'What about lunch?'

'I'm not hungry.' He called the dog and crashed out of the house.

Olivia pulled a chair out from under the dining table and sank down onto it, feeling exhausted. Was it wrong to long for the day when she had an empty nest? More to the point, was it too early for a stiff drink?

Bex felt worse the next morning and had a real struggle to get the children off to school. When the bell went and the kids disappeared into their classrooms she sagged down onto a bench at the edge of the playground and shut her eyes, willing the feeling of nausea to go away. Finally she felt well enough to totter down the hill and let herself back into her house. She shut the door behind her, flopped onto the sofa and closed her eyes. She still hadn't made her mind up about what she was going to do and her worry, about which course of action to take, really wasn't helping her physical symptoms. Thank God she didn't have to do anything this morning. She groaned and curled up. Just five minutes.

She woke with a start and a vile taste in her mouth over an hour later. She swung her legs off the sofa and headed into the kitchen to get a drink of water. As she passed the hall mirror she caught a glimpse of her reflection; yuck. She rinsed her mouth out and then went up to her bedroom. If she didn't want more people asking awkward questions she needed to slap up. Ten minutes later and with foundation and blusher applied, she stared into her dressing-table mirror – a definite improvement. At least she could venture out without fear of frightening the horses.

She made a shopping list and went to the big supermarket in Cattebury to stock up after the weekend and where she also picked up a pregnancy testing kit at the pharmacy section – having first checked there wasn't a soul about who could possibly recognise her – then she returned home. She unpacked the shopping and took the kit up to her en suite. She sat on the loo and read the instructions – it had been a while since she'd last done this.

Bugger – a solid blue line ran across the middle of the stick. *Ninety-nine per cent accurate* the packaging had boasted. Time was, Bex would have been delighted. She put the stick back in its box and went to the kitchen where she buried it at the bottom of the bin.

Feeling completely distracted and worried she carried on with mundane household tasks; putting the washing on, tidying up the boys' toys from the bedroom floors, checking her emails. And as she worked she chewed over the implications and her options.

When the time came to go next door to start her shift at the pub she was no closer to an answer. She walked to the pub feeling slightly sick, not just from the ebbing morning sickness, but with dread. She would see Miles, knowing what she knew, hiding her news from him... Would she be able to dissemble, to lie?

She knocked on the front door of the pub. Belinda unlocked it and let her in.

'Hi there, Glamour-puss. What's with the slap?'

'Oh, you know, I just felt like it. You get those days when you feel you want that lift, don't you?'

'Some days, when I look in the mirror, I see my mother staring back at me. In my head I am twenty-six, so to see this forty-year-old frump comes as a shock I can tell you!'

'You're not a frump.'

'You don't see me first thing.'

Bex took off her jacket and hung it on a peg before she grabbed a cloth from behind the bar and began polishing the tables and tidying up the beer mats.

'And when you've done that if you could bottle up. I'm going to change the mild.'

Belinda went off to the cellar as Bex worked her way around the bar. By the time she'd finished Belinda had changed the barrel and had brought up two trays of mixers.

'I'm going to leave you to it today – the dreaded VAT return beckons.'

Bex worked on getting the bar ready for opening time. Behind the kitchen door she could hear the sounds of Miles prepping for the lunch service. Part of her knew she ought to go and say hello but part of her couldn't face it. What if he guessed she was hiding something from him? She'd always been a shit liar.

The door banged open and she jumped.

'Morning, Bex,' said Miles cheerfully. He checked the bar was empty except for the pair of them before he kissed her on the cheek.

'Stop it,' she protested.

'Why? I'm sure Belinda knows I've spent a few nights at yours. Let's face it, she's only got to look out of her window first thing to see me sneaking off before your kids stir.'

'Except, given that Belinda is rarely in bed before one most days, I doubt if she is up when you leave.'

'Well... Maybe. But I don't know why we're keeping things a secret. Are you ashamed of me? Am I your guilty bit of rough?' He gave Bex a lecherous grin.

'Don't be silly. It's just...'

'I know, Megan. And I completely get it. I do. So we'll keep things quiet a bit longer.'

Bex glanced at the bar clock. 'Time to open up. And yes, let's not tell the world just yet.'

'Indeed. Although, as we both know, keeping any sort of secret in a place like this is bloody difficult.'

Bex felt her face flare.

21

Z ac texted Megan... you going down the sk8 park

    Got a rehearsal

    Another 1

    Yes

    Forget it

He threw his phone onto the bed and sighed. He could go to the skatepark on his own and hang out, but the trouble was most of the kids down there were just that... kids. He'd look a bit of a sad loner if he was there on his own. But he didn't want to stay in the house; he hated the place and, now his mum worked and Jade had got a job, it was lonely at home on his own.

He decided to take Oscar for a walk. He pottered down the stairs, got the lead off the hook on the back of the front door and Oscar, a dog with the hearing of a bat, was beside him in a moment.

Zac grinned down at the dog, sitting at his feet, tail wagging vigorously to and fro across the carpet leaving several clumps of black fur.

Zac clipped on the lead, made sure he had his keys in his pocket and a ball for Oscar and let himself out. With Oscar walking beautifully to heel, he trailed up the high street and past the shop windows now full of orange and black decorations, spiders and witches' hats. Not so very long till Hallowe'en, he thought. And, on an even brighter note, half-term first. Zac continued on his way up the road and wound up near his old house. He crossed the street and stood at the end of the drive. He'd always assumed this was going to be the family's forever home – not that trashy little box they'd wound up in. His mum had explained his dad had been ill but he still found it hard to forgive him for what he'd done to the family. He'd said as much to him mum once and had got a lecture about drugs, and what they would have done to them all if he'd carried on taking them, and how he and his dad were as bad as each other, and all addictions were evil... In a way he knew she was right but he still couldn't help feeling resentful.

He walked on past the house to the field beyond it. He climbed over the gate and let Oscar off the lead before throwing the ball as hard as he could. Oscar zipped off across the tussocky grass like a high-speed train. The ball bounced awkwardly but with a leap and a twist Oscar caught it in his mouth and then hurtled back to Zac. Zac walked around the edge of the field, throwing the ball every now and again.

After about a hundred yards he came to a gap in the hawthorn and bramble hedge which allowed him to see into the garden of The Grange. Something large and white was lying on the grass at the back of the house. Zac stared. It looked like a flagpole – how very weird. Why on earth would anyone put a flagpole that big up in their garden? But then he noticed several huge blades lying behind the pole. Blooming heck – it was a wind turbine and a monstrous one at that. He reckoned his mum would have something to say about a turbine at a point in the town where everyone, pretty much, would be able to see it.

Eventually Oscar looked worn out and Zac's arm was aching from throwing the ball so the pair plodded back through the town. When he got in he could hear someone moving about in the kitchen – unlikely to be Jade, he thought. Now she'd got a job she'd reverted to type and expected everyone else to wait on her hand and foot. Zac wondered if her ex-boyfriend had deliberately engineered Jade finding out about his infidelity to get rid of her. He wouldn't have blamed him if he had. She was a royal pain to live with.

He walked into the kitchen and found his mum cooking supper.

'Hi, Mum.' He shrugged off his jacket and let Oscar off the lead before going to one of the cupboards and getting out the dog food. He tipped it into Oscar's bowl and told the dog to sit. Patiently, Oscar sat in front of his bowl, drooling at his supper until Zac said 'go'. Oscar fell on his meal as if he had been starved for a week.

'You'll never guess what I saw,' said Zac.

'What?'

'They're putting up a massive wind turbine at our old house.'

His mum stopped stirring the sauce she was making, put the wooden spoon down and turned. 'Are you sure?'

'Pretty certain – I saw a blooming great mast lying on the ground and what looked like three helicopter blades. What else could it be?'

'How big?'

'I don't know, Mum. Funnily enough, I left my tape measure at home.'

'Roughly.'

Zac shrugged. 'Ten metres, maybe more. It was *huge*. Why?'

'Because there are rules about this sort of thing – planning regulations.'

And Zac knew his mum knew about this stuff – what with being on the town council up till recently.

'So you think they won't be allowed to build it?' he asked.

'They might be. It depends. On the other hand, given the way Mrs Osborne has already hacked me off *and* the way she spoke to Heather Simmonds the other day, it would give me a lot of pleasure to find out that she is in breach of planning regulations and she can't put it up.'

'OK,' said Zac, slowly. 'I kinda wish I hadn't told you. Not if it's got her into trouble.'

'I don't think Mrs Osborne is the sort of woman who cares about trouble.'

'And I thought you liked *green* stuff.'

'I do, mostly.'

'But you don't like the new people in our house.'

'No,' admitted Olivia. 'Apart from the fact she was horrible to the hotel staff she's been horrid to Heather too. So, I really don't.'

Zac returned to his bedroom and got on with his homework – or tried to. He'd just made a proper start on his science when Jade retuned from her job and started playing music. The bass thumped through the walls into his room clashing with the music Zac was listening to through his headphones. He leaned over his desk and thumped on the wall.

'Cut it out, Jade.'

Expletives followed by a return thump was the response.

Zac threw his pen down and thundered down the stairs.

'Mum, Mum, tell Jade to turn her music down. I can't hear myself think.'

'Hmm – and all those times I put up with your music.'

'That was different. And I'm trying to work.'

'OK.' Olivia climbed the stairs and opened Jade's door. Zac followed her and, over the music heard Jade yelling the words *unreasonable*, *unfair*, *snitch* and a few other less than complimentary words about her family followed by silence as the music was switched off and then, 'I hate you all.'

Zac went into his room and shut the door but he could still

hear the row going on in the next bedroom through the thin stud walls.

'And another thing,' said his mother, 'I really don't mind you doing your washing, really I don't, but you could at least fill the machine up. Today I took out three T-shirts, a couple of pairs of pants and a skirt and I had a load of whites that could have been done at the same time.'

'Oh, so you want me to do your washing, as well, now.'

'That's not what I said.'

'Sounded like it to me.'

And so the row continued for another five minutes with Jade railing against the awfulness of home life and his mother trying to be reasonable until finally he heard the bedroom door open and slam shut and silence fell.

Tentatively Zac stuck his head out of his door and saw his mother go downstairs.

He followed her. 'I didn't mean to cause such trouble,' he said quietly.

'You didn't. Not specifically. It's been brewing for a while. The bottom line is this house is too small for four adults.' Olivia sighed. 'But we're stuck with the situation, so we'll just have to do what we can to rub along.'

'Or Jade could move out.'

'Don't be silly, Zac, have you seen the rents around here? Jade couldn't afford her own flat – not on what she earns.' Olivia paused, her mouth agape. 'Hang on a sec...'

'What?'

'Never mind. I might have an idea.'

Olivia picked up the phone and dialled Heather's number from memory. What she had in mind mightn't be a done deal – it all depended on all parties agreeing to her proposed solution. On the other hand, if it worked out...

'Hello, the vicarage.'

'Heather, hello... It's Olivia here, is this a good time to call?'

'Fine. What can I do for you?'

'Look, you know you wanted to let out your spare room now and again; well, would you be prepared to rent it out on a slightly longer-term basis?'

'I suppose. I might have to run it past Brian, to say nothing of the bishop. Why?'

'Would you let it out to Jade?'

'Jade? Yes, I suppose so. I mean, I don't have any objection in principle but how long are we talking about and how much can she afford to pay in rent?'

'That's the thing, I can't say how long – how long is a piece of string – and as for rent...? At the moment she pays me sixty quid a week for bed and board. Given that she doesn't eat breakfast and she has lunch at work, the money probably more than covers the cost of having her around. But, to be honest, I'd rather have the spare room than the cash. I'll be frank with you, Heather – if she stays here I might just kill her – or her, me. And I appreciate that sixty quid is a ridiculously low rent.'

'No... no... I think I might suggest that if I feed her it might have to go up a bit but, even a couple of hundred quid extra a month would make all the difference. Truly.'

'I haven't even run this idea past Jade yet.'

'She might be appalled at the idea of sharing a bathroom with the vicar,' said Heather drily.

'Yes, there's that. And I think you and Brian ought to do some serious sums about what a realistic rent might be, given that your utility bills are bound to go up. And Jade might baulk at paying more. Her job isn't the best paid on the planet.'

'Welcome to my world,' said Heather with a laugh. 'You suggest it to Jade and come back to me with her reaction. I won't be offended if it's one of horror. I can't think there would be many young people who would think that moving into the vicarage would be cool.'

'But she might find it a deal more attractive than living here with her family.'

'Indeed. If Jade's up for it, I'll suggest a rent and we can then see if she thinks it's reasonable. Does that sound like a plan?'

'It does. And I shall keep everything crossed that it works out. I really, *really*, don't want to wind up in Holloway on a murder charge.'

22

On Tuesday morning, when she awoke, Bex felt worse than ever. She dragged herself out of bed and into her bathroom, retched for several minutes and then sat on the edge of her bath and wondered how she'd find the strength to get the kids' breakfasts sorted and then do the school run. And Megan wasn't stupid – she was bound to notice that all wasn't well sooner rather than later. Which led to another train of thought: she was going to have to make a decision about her pregnancy and she still didn't have a clue what was for the best. What she really wanted to do was confide in someone, but whom?

Her mother? No way. Her mother wasn't going to accept for one second that an abortion might be an option.

Belinda? Hmmm… But Belinda probably knew how much Miles would want this baby so would encourage Bex to make his dream come true.

Olivia? Possibly. But she had enough on her plate and it mightn't be fair.

Heather? No, she'd probably have set views too. Bex wanted someone who would look at the two possible choices dispassionately.

Someone she knew from the book club or the WI? But she didn't know anyone well enough to burden them with this.

Amy? God, no, not unless she wanted the entire country to know what was going on.

Feeling weak and rough Bex went to wake up the kids before she put her own clothes on and crawled down to the kitchen to make tea and toast and lay the table. The kettle boiled and the toaster popped but Bex suddenly went off the idea of either. A few minutes later her boys thundered into the kitchen, grabbed their choice of cereal and began to shovel down milk and flakes as fast as they could. At least they were of an age when they rarely noticed anything that didn't have a direct impact on their own lives.

'Morning,' she said to Megan, feigning a brightness she certainly didn't feel, when her stepdaughter made an appearance some ten minutes later. Megan grabbed the toast that Bex had ignored as the boys finished scraping out their bowls.

'Can we watch telly now? asked Lewis.

'Lewis, how often do I have to say this – not till you've cleaned your teeth, got your book bags and tidied your rooms.'

'Aww,' whined Lewis.

'Just do as you're told,' snapped Bex. Her tone was much harsher than she'd meant it to be and there was a shocked silence.

'All right, Bex, they were only trying it on,' said Megan, giving her stepmother a worried look.

Bex shut her eyes and sat on a chair. 'I'm sorry. I had a rough night.' She smiled at the boys. 'Go and clean your teeth and get ready for school and we'll see, eh?'

Silently the two boys slid out of the kitchen.

'You all right, Bex?' asked Megan. 'You look as white as a sheet.'

'As I said, I had a bad night. I'll be fine.'

'If you say so.'

'I do.'

Megan slathered her cold toast thickly with butter and marmalade before she took a big bite. Bex saw the topping smear Megan's teeth and lips with sugar and grease. She felt her gorge rising again and knew she wasn't going to have time to reach the downstairs loo. She darted for the sink and hung over it as her stomach heaved.

'Eugh, Bex. I'm eating,' said Megan.

Bex ran the tap, swirled water around the sink and then scooped a couple of handfuls up to rinse her mouth. 'Sorry,' she said turning but hanging onto the porcelain as she still felt shaky.

'I hope you're not going to give that to me and the boys,' said Megan, chomping another big mouthful.

'I'll try not to,' said Bex, through gritted teeth. She wanted to snap at Megan for being more concerned about her own health than her stepmother's, for eating buttery toast, for witnessing her hurling... but none of that was Megan's fault.

Megan finished her toast and went to get herself ready for school, leaving her plate on the table. Bex wanted to call her back and tell her to put it in the dishwasher but didn't have the energy. Five minutes later she'd left, banging the front door behind her, and Bex was able to collapse onto a kitchen chair and stop pretending she felt anything other than dreadful. As she sat there she heard the boys creep downstairs and into the sitting room where she heard the TV go on. Five minutes, she thought, glancing at the clock. I still have five minutes. She folded her arms on the table and rested her head on them.

'Mum, Mum, aren't we going to school today?'

Bex was awake in a trice and looked at the clock. Five past nine?! Fuck!

'Boys, I'm so sorry. Grab your things. We'll go in the car.' She flew into the hall, picked up her keys, then raced into the garden, plipped open the car and threw open the big five-bar gate. The boys were piling into the back seat as she shut the front door behind them. A few minutes later she'd parked outside the school – no problem finding a space at this time! – and she escorted them to their respective classes, apologising profusely to their teachers.

'I overslept,' she told Lewis's teacher.

'No, you didn't, Mummy. You fell asleep after breakfast.'

Bex forced a grin. 'Miss Dickson doesn't need to know the details.' But the look on Miss Dickson's face suggested otherwise. 'I had a shocking night,' lied Bex, trying not to look at her in case her fib was obvious. 'I'm not feeling one hundred per cent.'

'You don't look well,' conceded the teacher. 'Let's hope it isn't something catching. We don't want everyone to go down with it, do we?'

'Yes, well…'

'So, if Lewis or Alfie show similar symptoms we'd all appreciate it if they didn't come to school.'

Bex was tempted to laugh. If only Miss Dickson knew…

She dragged herself back to her car and drove home. She swung her car into her drive and killed the engine then shut her eyes and leaned her head on the steering wheel. This had to stop; people would notice, people would talk, and then what? Maybe she ought to go and see Dr Connolly, make arrangements.

A tap on the driver's window made her leap out of her skin. She turned.

'Miles.' She pressed the button to lower the window.

'Are you all right? God, you're not, are you? You look awful.'

'Thanks, Miles.'

'I saw you drive in and I thought I'd come and beg a cuppa but then, when you didn't get out of the car…' He smiled at her but worry lines creased his forehead. 'What's the matter?'

'Nothing,' she said automatically.

Miles shook his head. 'Really?' He raised his eyebrows, his disbelief annoyingly obvious. 'I may only be a chef with a vague knowledge of first aid but this isn't *nothing*.' He opened the car door. 'Come on, let's get you indoors.'

Bex unclipped her safety belt and hauled herself out of the car. Miles put his hand under her arm and took the keys off her. A minute later she was back in the kitchen, sitting where she'd been when Lewis had awoken her and with Miles bustling about making tea.

'Where do you keep the biscuits?' he asked.

'No... no... I couldn't eat one.'

'Have you had breakfast?' He looked at the detritus on the table and saw only the remains of three meals and then began opening and shutting cupboards looking for the biscuits. 'You haven't, have you?'

Bex shook her head.

'No wonder you look wobbly. You can't expect to function on an empty stomach.'

'Please... no.'

'Ah, here they are.' He pulled out a packet and tipped the biscuits onto a plate. 'No, sorry, Bex, but you need fuel.'

He slapped down a mug of sweet tea in front of her followed by a plate of digestives. Bex swallowed bile.

'I'm not taking no for an answer.' He plonked down on a seat beside her and looked at her.

Bex took a biscuit and nibbled a few crumbs off an edge. She forced them down as Miles nudged the tea closer to her. Bex looked at it. You can do this, she told herself. She took a tentative sip and swallowed that too.

She sat there, willing herself to keep everything down, to hold it together, but then her ears rang and the dizziness started and her stomach heaved... For the second time that morning she was sick in the sink.

She tottered back to her chair and collapsed with her eyes shut.

'So what was that all about?' said Miles.

'I think I've got a bug.'

Again he raised his eyebrows in his annoying way. 'A bug?'

Bex couldn't look at him.

'Look,' he said gently, 'I've worked in hospitality a long time and I've seen most things... and this is none of my business—'

'No, it isn't.' Fear and nausea made the sentence come out with a much harsher edge than she intended. Miles recoiled. 'Please, Miles, it's just a bug. I'll be better in a day or two.'

'Fine.' It obviously wasn't. 'Shall I tell Belinda you're taking a sick day?'

Bex knew that if she was going to keep the 'it's just a bug' lie going she couldn't possibly go into work, even if she felt better by lunchtime. 'Yes, please.'

'And I think you ought to go back to bed.'

'I'll be fine.'

Again those raised eyebrows. 'Then go and lie down on the sofa at the very least. Come on.' Miles stood up and picked up her tea. He glanced at Bex sitting on the kitchen chair before he marched through to the sitting room where Bex heard him plonk the mug on the table. A few seconds later he was back in the kitchen. 'Can you walk or shall I carry you?'

'I'll walk. Honest, I'll be fine.'

'Really.' His eyebrows rose yet again.

Olivia was behind the desk at the hotel when her mobile vibrated in her pocket. The reception was like a morgue but even so she moved right away from the duty manager's office. Taking private phone calls at work wasn't encouraged. She glanced at the caller ID before she accepted the call.

'Heather. What can I do for you? I have to say it's not totally convenient – I'm at work.'

'Sorry, only I thought you ought to know what that woman—'

'The Osborne woman?'

'The very person. Anyway, I thought you ought to know what she's done.'

'And?'

'And she's set up an online petition to stop the bells being rung after they've been repaired.'

'She's *what*?' screeched Olivia. She glanced around the hotel lobby to see if her outburst had been noticed but was relieved to hear the murmur of voices and clatter of office machinery coming from the back office remained steady.

'Exactly. That was pretty much my reaction.'

'She's got to be stopped.'

'Sadly, there's no law against it.'

'No. Look, if it's convenient I'll drop in to yours on my way home. We must have a council of war.'

'What time?'

'Three thirty-ish. Is that OK?'

'Perfect.'

When Olivia finished her shift she whizzed down the hill towards the town on her bike and peeled off the main road to Heather's. At three twenty she parked her bike and rang the vicarage doorbell.

'Come in, come in,' said Heather as she opened the door and stepped back to let Olivia in.

'That bloody woman,' said Olivia. 'I can't believe it.'

'Well, it's true.' Heather shut the door and led Olivia into the kitchen where she plugged in the kettle. 'What can we do?'

'Start a counter-petition to begin with,' said Olivia. 'That woman obviously doesn't care who she upsets. I mean, why move to a town – which you must surely *like* when you elect to live there – and then try and change the very fabric of the place as soon as you arrive? I mean, if she doesn't like church bells why the hell did she come and live somewhere that's got them?'

'Search me.' Heather got out the mugs.

'And I'll tell you something else.'

'What?'

'Zac told me about it so I checked for myself on my way to work. She's going to put up a bloody great wind turbine in her garden. Zac said he saw it when he was out on a dog walk so I went into the field behind the house and had a snoop through the hedge.' She saw Heather suppress a grin. 'Anyway, there it was, lying on her lawn, presumably waiting for the contractors.'

'But there are planning regulations, surely.'

'There are, but this'll probably come under the "permitted development" umbrella. I bet she's the sort of woman who has checked that out. I'm not against renewable power – obviously not – but the trouble is, where the house is, on the hill, I should think it'll be visible to almost everyone in the town. It'll be a real eyesore.'

'That's awful.' Heather poured the boiling water onto the teabags and added milk.

'Like she'll care. But I tell you something, I shall check out the spec and if she's a millimetre over any of the allowable dimensions, I'll make sure it has to be demolished.'

Heather grinned. 'Good on you. Right, now, about this counter-petition...'

'We're going to have to strong-arm everyone in the book club and the WI to sign it. We have to convince them that *not* signing isn't an option. No one must be allowed to assume the status quo will prevail.'

'Right... plan of action.' Heather drew a notebook towards her ready to take notes.

It was getting late when Olivia got home. The downstairs of her house was in darkness but she could tell both children were home by the clashing music blaring from both bedrooms.

'Give me strength,' she muttered as she shrugged off her coat and headed for the kitchen.

Even though she was tired after her shift at work and her discussion with Heather she had to get supper on the go. It was Nigel's day for his Gamblers Anonymous meeting and he was due home early and would expect supper to be ready so he could go straight out again. Olivia got the ingredients for the meal out of the fridge and began to chop onions.

Jade slid into the kitchen. 'Oh, you're back. I was beginning to wonder when supper was going to be.'

'You could have made something,' said Olivia.

'Mum! I've been at work all day. I'm tired.'

Olivia continued to chop onions as she counted to ten, not trusting herself to answer.

'Anyway,' continued Jade, 'I thought your shift finished at teatime.'

'It did. I had to go and see Heather.' Olivia got a pan out of a cupboard, drizzled some oil in and put it on the hob to heat. Then she swept the onions into it. 'Look, Jade, you know how small this house it?'

'Yeah.' Her daughter sounded wary.

'Well, supposing I found you somewhere to live that was bigger – much bigger.'

'And?'

'Would you move out?'

'Doubt it – the rent would be mahoosive.'

'But what if it wasn't?'

'Then the place would probably be a dive. What's this about, Mum?'

'I've got a friend with a room available – a big room, I've seen it. And the rent would be not much more than I'm asking you to pay me. And, as it would be a proper business arrangement, you wouldn't be expected to do anything except keep your own bit clean and tidy – or not, if you didn't want to.'

'Where is it?'

Olivia took a breath. 'The vicarage.'

'The *vicarage*? You're expecting me to live with the vicar?'

'It's a really lovely room.'

'In case you hadn't noticed, Mum, I don't do God or religion or shit like that.'

'Heather wouldn't expect you to. She gets that.'

'Yeah, right.'

'And she'd cook for you – unless you'd rather cook for yourself, in which case she'd take something off the rent.'

'How much?'

'I don't know exactly, but she's planning on asking three fifty a month all found.'

'Three fifty? What's the catch?'

'There isn't one. Which means you'd probably be able to save enough to put down a deposit on a place of your own in the not too distant future. '

'I suppose. And I'd get my own bathroom.'

'No – but you have to share with Zac here.'

'He's my brother. It wouldn't be like sharing – Jeez – sharing with the vicar.' Her lip curled.

'There's a separate loo upstairs as well as the one in the bathroom. Heather said that loo would be yours, exclusively.'

'It's still gross.'

'But you won't find cheaper.' Jade shrugged. Olivia felt she wasn't completely dismissive. She pressed the point. 'So can I tell her you'll think about it?'

'Whatever.'

'Only I need to tell her soon because she'd like to put it on Airbnb if it's a no.'

'God, Mum, give me a break. OK, I'll think about it.'

'So... when?'

Jade let out a yell of frustration. 'Can you get off my back and stop hassling me? I'll tell you when I've made a decision.' She stormed out of the kitchen and thumped up the stairs to her bedroom where she slammed the door. The whole house shook.

'God, I hate this place,' said Olivia.

23

The following evening, Amy walked into the pub and smelt the scent of wood smoke overlaid with beer.

'Hi, Belinda,' she said as she approached the bar. 'It's a bit quiet, isn't it?'

'It wasn't twenty minutes ago. You've hit the lull between the people who want a drink before their supper and the people who have one afterwards. What can I get you?'

'A glass of white wine, ta.' Amy got out a fiver and put it on the bar.

Belinda got the bottle out of the chiller and began to measure the wine out. 'Do you know what's up with Bex?'

'Bex, no, why?'

'She's called in sick the last couple of mornings.'

'Really? I've not seen her since Monday afternoon when I cleaned her place. She seemed OK then.'

'Miles saw her early yesterday and he said she was as sick as a parrot.'

'Sick – in the morning…?'

'Don't be daft, Amy. It's a bug.' Belinda put Amy's drink on the bar and picked up the note.

'I wouldn't be so sure. The other day a man's sock fell out of her laundry. Of course *she* said it was a bed sock. Yeah, right. I can tell when someone is lying.'

'Don't be daft,' repeated Belinda. 'It probably *was* a bed sock.'

'If that's what you want to believe. I mean, Miles is round there quite a lot, ain't he?'

'Miles? No, they're just mates. Anyway,' said Belinda moving away from the subject, 'what are you doing here? You're not normally in on a Wednesday. Another date?'

'Might be.' Amy took a slug of her wine. 'Actually, can I ask you something?'

'You can try,' said Belinda. 'What do you want to know?'

Amy lowered her voice and checked no one was close enough to eavesdrop. 'It's about my Ash.'

'Why – what's he done? I thought he was all wrapped up in this school panto he's in with Megan.'

'That's it – that's the problem. It strikes me he's getting a sight too interested in all that arty stuff. And the other day he was getting all excited about make-up.'

'Stage make-up?'

Amy shrugged. 'Make-up is make-up if you ask me, and I'd have thought a normal teenage boy would run a mile from that sort of thing.'

'So what are you saying?'

Amy armed herself with more wine. 'I'm worried he's gay.'

Belinda cocked her head on one side as she thought about it. 'I don't think it follows. Surely he's just interested in all aspects of acting – the costumes, the make-up, the wigs... well, that's a part of it, isn't it? Besides, would it be so terrible if he was?'

Amy, mid-sip, nearly choked. 'You're joking me, right?'

'But he's still your son.'

'Not if he's gay, he won't be. And as for what his gran will have to say about it...'

'Look, I don't know much about this sort of stuff and I know diddly-squat about kids but all I can say is that you fretting and worrying won't change how Ashley is going to turn out. He's a nice kid with nice friends and as long as he's happy – well, isn't that all that matters at the end of the day?'

'I suppose,' said Amy, gloomily. 'Anyway, let's not talk about Ash.'

There was silence for a second or two before Belinda said, 'This date of yours… do you want the same arrangement as before – me giving you a message from Ash if you rub your nose?'

'Nah. If this guy is as bad as the last one I'm not going to worry about hurting his feelings; I'll just bugger off. And if I'd known how crap the last guy was going to be I wouldn't have bothered making that plan.'

'Amy,' said Belinda ringing up Amy's bill and getting out the change, 'if you'd known how crap the last guy was going to be, you wouldn't have bothered coming to meet him at all.' She handed over the coins.

'Good point.'

'So what's this one like?'

'His profile looks OK. You know, the usual.'

'Tell me.'

'Single, good sense of humour.'

'Which means he hasn't got one. People who've got one don't make a song and dance about it.'

'He said he's honest,' countered Amy.

'Pathological liar.'

'Athletic.'

'Watches sport on TV.'

Amy started to giggle and got her phone out to give Belinda the benefit of the full profile. She scrolled to the app with her thumb. 'Attractive.'

'Arrogant.'

'Likes pubs and clubs.'

'An alcoholic.'

Amy was shaking with laughter. 'Outgoing.'

'Thinks he's funny when drunk – see previous answer,' added Belinda. 'Oh, hang on, customer.'

A bloke with bad posture, a massive beerbelly, thinning red hair and a wispy beard came through the door.

'What can I get you, sir?' said Belinda.

'Actually I'm looking for someone,' he said. His voice was a Brummie nasal whine

'Oh, yeah. Who might that be?'

'A lady called Amy.'

Belinda caught the look on Amy's face. She frowned, as if in deep thought. 'Are you sure you've got the right place?' she said to the man.

'Oh, yes.'

'Can't help you, I'm afraid. Never heard of an *Amy*.' She looked straight at Amy. 'Have you, ducks?'

Amy bit the inside of her cheeks as she shook her head. 'Nope.'

The man looked as if he might cry. 'Oh, well. Sorry to have bothered you.'

'No worries,' Belinda called after him as he shut the door.

The pair dissolved.

Next morning, after Belinda had cashed up, taken the takings to the bank and hoovered the pub carpet, she popped next door to see Bex. The car was parked on the drive so there was every possibility her neighbour was in. She rang the doorbell and waited... and waited. A chill breeze nipped at her legs under her skirt and Belinda began to wish she'd slung on a coat. Maybe Bex was in town running some errands – or doing PTA business...

The door opened and there was Bex looking grey and ill.

'Oh, hi, Belinda.'

'Hell's teeth, Bex, what on earth is the matter?'

Bex let Belinda in and closed the door behind her. 'Just some rotten bug.'

'Have you seen the doc?'

'It'll pass.'

'I'll take it that means "no".'

Bex led Belinda into the kitchen and slumped onto a chair. She looked done-in. Belinda sat opposite her.

'Bex, you've been ill for three days. This can't be some twenty-four-hour sick bug.'

'So, it's a seventy-two-hour bug. Look, I'm sorry I've let you down this week.'

'I'm not here about you going sick. I'm here because I'm worried about you. And so is Miles.'

'You shouldn't be.'

'How are you coping?'

'Honestly, don't fuss.' She sounded tetchy.

'But seriously, what about cooking?'

'I manage.'

'Miles could help. He could rustle up some stuff so all you have to do is heat it through.'

'No!'

Belinda stared at her friend. She was tempted to tell her to keep her hair on but stopped herself. She stayed silent, hoping to force Bex into talking. The silence stretched on.

'I'm sorry,' said Bex eventually.

'I'm not asking for an apology.'

'Then what?'

'Look, tell me to mind my own business but is it something more than a bug?'

A tear slid down one of Bex's cheeks. She dashed it away.

'Honey, tell me,' implored Belinda.

'I can't.'

'Oh, God, you're not... I mean... not... not cancer.'

Bex gave her a weak smile. 'No, it's nothing terminal. Nothing life-threatening.'

'Then what?'

'Don't judge me.' There was a long pause. 'I'm pregnant.'

'Bloo... dy... hell,' whispered Belinda.

'Yup, pretty much my reaction.'

'Are you sure?'

Bex nodded. 'I've done the test – there's no doubt. I mean, I was pretty sure anyway. I've done this twice before so I kind of know the symptoms.'

Belinda stared at her and blinked. She didn't know what to say.

'I'm not sure if I can cope with it, though, this time,' admitted Bex.

'What? You mean...'

Bex nodded and shrugged. 'Belinda, I don't know. I've been over and over it. I can't bear the idea of a termination but I can't bear the idea of nappies and sleepless nights either. And then there's Megan. I mean, she mightn't react as badly as I think she might, but why wouldn't she go bat-shit? Her dad died only last year and she might be horrified. What I've done isn't against any law, but Megan mightn't see it like that. I wouldn't blame her if she felt as though I'd betrayed Richard. And if she does... well, it might destroy her relationship with me.' She gazed at Belinda. 'You're the only person I've told so far and please, *please* don't breathe a word.'

'No, no of course not. Shit, I'd *never* do that. It's your body, your life; you must do what's best for you.'

'I suppose.' Bex still looked miserable. 'I wish I knew what that was.'

'Would you like tea?' offered Belinda.

Bex shook her head. 'But you make a cup – I'm not sure mine'll stay down.'

'The morning sickness is that bad?'

'Worse. I can function by the afternoon but the mornings are the pits. It'll pass.'

'If you keep the baby.'

Bex rubbed her face with her hands. 'Yes. God, this is a mess.'

'Does the father know?' asked Belinda, getting up to fill the kettle.

Bex sighed. 'Not yet.'

'Are you going to tell him?'

Bex looked close to tears again. 'I don't know. If I do, it'll complicate everything all the more.' She looked up at Belinda. 'And don't tell me I should.'

'Sweetie, I wouldn't dream of it.'

'At least you haven't asked me who the father is.'

'Believe me, I'm dying to but… well… very occasionally, I do know how to behave properly and tactfully.'

Bex smiled for the first time. 'God, you're such a great friend.'

'It doesn't mean I'm not still gagging to know.'

'Megan, *Megan*,' called Ashley across the school playground.

Megan turned, her heart sinking. She'd been avoiding him on purpose because, if she was honest, she was getting a bit sick of him wanting to rehearse all the time.

'Yeah?'

'What you doing after school?'

'I'm going round to Soph's.'

'Can I come?'

'Er… why would you want to? Soph and I have got things we want to talk about – *girl* things.'

'Oh.' Ashley looked crestfallen.

'Anyway, won't you want to be going over your lines or something?'

'I know my part backwards.'

Which was undeniably true and which was a boast Megan couldn't share. 'Yeah, well.'

'Besides, I'd really like to see Soph's mum.'

Megan frowned. 'Then why don't you ask Sophie if you can? Although you must have got every last shred of info about acting out of Lizzie.'

'I doubt it,' said Ashley. 'I mean, there's so much to know. I bet actors like Benedict Cumberbatch never stop learning.'

'But you're not an actor, you're a kid in a school panto.'

Ashley looked devastated and Megan regretted her hurtful words instantly. 'I'm sorry, Ash, I didn't mean it like that.'

'You don't get it, do you?'

'I don't get what?'

'You don't get acting. To you it's just an after-school thing. But to me… to me it's… Oh, you just don't understand. No one does.' He strode off.

Megan stared after him. This acting thing was really changing him. Maybe he was really serious about it after all – like he was going to wind up doing it for a living. People did, she supposed, she just never thought she'd be friends with someone who did. Wouldn't it be cool to be mates with a film star?

24

Amy let herself into Bex's house.

'Coo-ee.'

A weak 'hello' was the response from the sitting room. Amy crossed the hall and saw Bex sitting on the sofa – she had dark shadows under her eyes and she looked far from well.

'You still poorly? Belinda said you weren't well when I saw her the other evening.'

'It's just a bug,' said Bex.

'Dragging on a bit, ain't it? Belinda said you've been off a couple of days and that was on Wednesday.'

'Yes, well... I'm sure I'm going to be better soon.'

'The usual, then?'

'Please.'

'I'll shut the door so you don't get disturbed. You look like you could do with a rest. Thought I'd make meself a cuppa – you want one?'

Bex shook her head.

Amy pottered off into the kitchen. While the kettle boiled she decided to empty the bin. She flipped open the lid and began to haul out the plastic bag. Jeez, what was in it? It was full to bursting and weighed a bloody ton. She gave it a yank and the bag ripped.

'Oh, for gawd's sake,' she sniped. She sighed and got a fresh bag out of the drawer where Bex kept them. She returned to the bin and wondered how best to go about dealing with the mess. She opened up the new bag and rolled it down so she could dump the torn one straight into it once she'd extracted it. Well, that was the plan. As she hauled the old one out it gave way completely and rubbish cascaded over the floor.

'Bollocks!' Amy shook her head in frustration, grabbed the rubber gloves and began to pick up soggy bits of kitchen towel, non-recyclable plastics, used tissues – ugh – a pair of socks with holes in, cling film, a Clear Blue pregnancy test box… A what?!

Amy rocked back on her heels and looked at the box. Blimey. She glanced at the door then rattled the box. Yup, the result was in there although she really didn't think she needed to check – not with the way Bex was looking – but she did anyway. Well, well, well.

Later, when she'd finished at Bex's, Amy thought she'd call in on her mum.

'Wotcha,' she said, when Mags opened the door.

'Hiya, Ames. Cuppa?'

'Love one. Gasping, I am.' Amy closed the door behind her and peered into her mum's sitting room. 'You look nearly straight.'

'Yeah, pretty much. The spare room's still got stuff in it but I ain't in no hurry to get that sorted. Can't see loads of people queuing up to visit all of a sudden.' Mags filled the kettle.

'It didn't take you long, did it?'

'It's amazing how much time you've got when you don't work. What do people on the dole do with themselves all day?'

'Watch daytime TV, I suppose. Although that Mrs Osborne up at Mrs L's old place ain't straight yet and she don't work, and I can't see her watching Jeremy Kyle – right snooty she is. Mind you, when you're hell-bent on having every last thing you own hidden in a cupboard, I suppose it takes longer.'

'What's the point in having stuff if it's all shoved out of sight?'

'Lord knows. But she's going to have to get most of it out again soon – she's got builders coming in to rip half the house out – new bathrooms this time... I dunno, more money than sense, if you ask me. There was nothing wrong with the old bathrooms. Anyway, that's not why I've come round.'

'What's up?'

'Guess what I found out today.'

'Dunno, tell me.'

'Bex is up the duff.'

'Get away.'

'Straight up. I found a positive pregnancy test in the bin.'

'It could be her daughter's.'

'Megan? Give over.'

'It's not such a daft idea, she's been knocking around with that Zac lad again.'

'I used to hope that her and Ash might get friendly but even with the panto and everything they don't seem to want to walk out together.'

'If you're right, that he's ... you know... that's not going to happen, is it?'

Amy sighed. 'I suppose. On the other hand I wouldn't have to worry about him getting some girl up the duff like his dad did to me. Or someone did to Bex. She was on the sofa when I went round this morning, looking like death warmed over.'

The kettle boiled noisily and clicked off.

'Who do you reckon the dad is?' asked Mags as she chucked teabags into two mugs.

'I reckon it's Miles. I've seen him round there a few times. Besides, I don't think Bex knows any other men – well, not single ones.'

'Being single's never mattered.' Mags fished out the bags and added milk.

'I think it would to Bex,' said Amy. 'She's a really nice lady and as she's lost her husband I don't think she'd nick someone else's.'

'If you say so,' said Mags.

Bex clicked off the website on her laptop. She'd been looking at ideas to combat morning sickness. When she'd been pregnant with the boys it hadn't really bothered her; she'd felt ropy first thing but then she'd been pretty OK for the rest of the day. This sickness was something else and while she didn't want to take medication – knowing about thalidomide meant that she didn't trust anything pharmaceutical – she was happy to have a go at some natural remedies. Ginger and lemon tea seemed to be a popular one, along with nibbling on crackers before getting up. She'd give it a whirl over the weekend. She really wanted to go back to work and the kids needed a proper mother, not a semi-invalid.

She dragged herself to the Co-op and got a packet of water biscuits, a few lemons and a large piece of ginger root. As she paid for her purchases at the till she saw Belinda enter the shop. Putting on a brave face she waved across the shop floor.

'How are you doing?' said Belinda as she approached.

'Oh, you know...'

'Still feeling crap?'

Bex indicated the objects on the conveyor waiting to be paid for. 'I've read that this lot might help and I am willing to try anything – well, within reason. It can't do any harm.' The cashier rang up her shopping and Bex handed over a fiver, stuffed her shopping in a carrier and took her change.

'I don't know anything about this,' said Belinda, 'but isn't it going to get worse before it gets better?'

'Not necessarily and I need to come up with strategies so I can cope. I can't lie around all day. Apart from anything I'm going stir-crazy.'

'Look, I've got a part-timer filling in for you, but she knows her stuff and the pub is like a graveyard at the mo; frankly I am surplus to requirements. Why don't I come round to yours when I've done my shopping and we can have a bit of a chat? What time do you have to get the boys?'

Bex consulted her watch. 'Not for another hour. Yes, that'd be lovely.'

Ten minutes later the pair were both in Bex's kitchen; Bex sipping water with a slice of lemon floating in it and nibbling on a cracker while Belinda tucked into tea and Hobnobs.

'You must be poorly if you can't eat a Hobnob,' observed Belinda.

'Actually, while I don't want to eat one, I don't feel sick at the thought of *you* eating one, which is how I felt earlier this week. I have to be able to function if Megan isn't going to start asking awkward questions.'

'You haven't made your mind up what to do, I take it.'

Bex shook her head and took another sip of water. 'I think if it were just me and the boys I wouldn't hesitate about keeping it. My first reaction was horror at the thought of nappies and broken nights but... well... it might be a girl and, while I loved looking after Megan when she was little, I didn't come into her life till she was gone two.' She sighed. 'And I don't think the boys would judge me, not being as young as they are, nor knowing how babies are made.' She gave Belinda a lopsided grin. 'But Megan...'

'Yes, I understand.'

'I've got to consider her too and I think, in fairness to her, I can't keep the baby. Except a part of me wants to. Belinda, I am so torn.' Bex felt close to tears. Hormones, she told herself. She sniffed and sat up straighter.

'Oh, Bex.' Belinda put her hand over her friend's. 'You can't keep putting off this decision, though. To be honest, I'm surprised Megan hasn't noticed.'

'She's all wrapped up in the play she's in and I was careful she never saw M... I was very discreet.'

'Even so.'

'I've promised myself to go and see Dr Connolly next week.'

'Good.'

'He can refer me to a clinic and I can talk to a counsellor. The trouble is, I can talk it through till the cows come home – I still have to make a decision at the end of it. One way or the other.'

Over the weekend, at Beeching Rise, tensions in the Laithwaite household finally came to a head. On Saturday, Nigel lost his temper with Jade, who slammed a door so hard a lump of plaster fell off the ceiling on the landing.

Jade was unapologetic and blamed everyone else for not understanding her before she ran, sobbing, out of the house. There was silence after her departure.

'This can't go on,' said Olivia. 'If that child doesn't move down to the vicarage, I think I will.'

'If that child,' snarled Nigel, still almost apoplectic, 'doesn't move out, I will personally pack her bags and put them on the road. I will not be spoken to like that.'

Olivia conceded that Nigel had a point. She would never have dared tell her parents that they were emotionally retarded fuckwits.

She left Nigel in their tiny sitting room with the Saturday paper, while she got out the hoover and swept up the evidence of Jade's tantrum. The damage to the ceiling was probably simple to repair, the builders were still on site and she had every intention of telling them that she'd awoken one morning to find the plaster had somehow and inexplicably become detached. Given how shoddy some of the work was in the house, she didn't think they'd be the least bit surprised. But the fact that she could probably get the evidence of Jade's temper repaired for free didn't excuse her daughter's behaviour and nor would it mean there mightn't be a repeat performance. And frankly,

Olivia didn't think she could take much more of the tensions within the house.

She moved around the house doing a few tasks while Nigel calmed down, trying to make as little noise as possible so as not to disturb Zac in his bedroom who seemed to be doing his homework. Actually, she thought, she was being unfair to Zac. He probably *was* doing his homework; his reports from his teachers for this term had all waxed almost lyrical at the change in his behaviour and his projected grades. It seemed there was every chance he was going to salvage his education and get some decent GCSEs – and that wasn't something that had been on the cards when he'd been in the Lower Fifth.

After a couple of hours Olivia texted Jade and asked her where she was and if she planned to come home for lunch.

None of your business and no, was the terse reply.

Your row wasn't with me, texted back Olivia. I could bring you a sandwich when I head off to work.

Not hungry.

You will be later.

I'm in the coffee shop.

Olivia quickly made up a couple of rounds of ham and pickle sandwiches.

'Just popping out for a few minutes,' she told Nigel. The reply was a grunt from behind the paper.

Olivia banged the door behind her and walked the few hundred yards to the town centre. Jade was sitting at a table in the corner of the little café with her phone in one hand and a tissue in the other.

Olivia slid into a seat beside her and handed over the packet of food. 'Not that you can eat it here.' She spotted that her daughter's cup was empty. 'Can I get you another one?'

'Yeah, a cappu would be nice.'

Olivia went to the counter and ordered two coffees and returned with them a few minutes later. She also brought with her two blueberry muffins.

She was rewarded with a faint smile before Jade scooped up some cocoa-powdered froth with her teaspoon and ate it.

'I'm not going to say sorry,' said Jade belligerently.

'That is between you and your father.'

'He started it,' said Jade.

'I'm not going to take sides.'

'Then why are you here?'

Olivia looked at her daughter and decided that while she loved Jade – of course she did – she didn't actually *like* her daughter very much. 'I just want you to be aware that your father is getting to the end of his tether.'

'Him and me both.'

'But I think you are forgetting it is his house.'

Jade raised her eyes and stared at her mum. 'Are you threatening to throw me out?'

'I'm not, but your father might, and I want to remind you there is a solution.'

Jade shook her head. 'I am not living with the fucking vicar.'

'Language,' said Olivia mildly. 'And, if I were you, I would give it serious consideration. Heather is lovely – actually Heather *and* Brian are lovely. They'd let you come and go as you please, you'd have far more space and you wouldn't have your father on your case.'

'No.'

'Fine.' Olivia bit a big chunk out of her cake.

'It's all bluff, isn't it? Dad wouldn't really throw me out?'

'If you want to think that, go ahead and be my guest, but I think there is a considerable chance that he might.'

Jade stared at her mother wide-eyed. 'But he couldn't. Where would I go?'

'The vicarage.'

Jade sagged and rolled her eyes. 'You've got it all planned, haven't you? One way or another you're going to make me go there.'

'Don't be ridiculous. No one at home has made you row with your father. You could have done as you've been asked. You could have kept your music down, you could have tidied up after yourself, you could have helped more—'

'OK!' yelled Jade. 'I get it. I'll go. Happy?' She glared at her mother.

'Not especially,' lied Olivia. 'I'll tell Heather. When can she expect you?'

25

Bex's home remedies didn't solve her problem but they did help. She still felt washed out and nauseous but, by Monday, she wasn't being sick except first thing in the morning and she was able to keep food down as long as it was bland and tasteless. She got back from dropping the boys up at their school and didn't want to crawl back into bed. I can cope, she thought. Just about.

Bex was wary about overdoing things and didn't bother with what she usually did on a Monday, which was shop for the week and then tidy the house ready for Amy's visit after lunch. She had enough in the way of leftovers to make supper for everyone that evening and, if Amy didn't manage to finish in her allotted three hours because she had to pick up the boys' toys before she hoovered, well, so be it. Instead she rang Belinda.

'I think I feel better. Do you want me or have you got cover?'

'Sweetie, I am so pleased for you! Hurrah. And yes, I'd love you to come in but only if you feel OK. My part-timer was a kid who was home from uni on her reading week – whatever that is—'

'I think it's like half-term.'

'Anyway, she's gone back so I'd love you to if you're sure you're up to it.'

'Let's give it a go, shall we?'

'See you later.'

Bex put the phone down to Belinda, took a deep breath, and rang the surgery.

Later that morning she walked next door and rapped on the pub door.

'Come in, come in,' said Belinda. She examined her employee's face. 'I'd like to say you're looking a lot better but...'

'I'm *feeling* better, that's the main thing. And,' Bex lowered her voice, 'I've phoned the doc. I've got an appointment for Thursday.'

'Good.'

Bex stepped into the pub. 'I've missed this place. I've missed the grumbling of Harry and Bert and the other regulars, I've missed the buzz when it's busy, the peacefulness when it's not.'

'Steady on, you were only off a week.'

'I know but I was so bored. Or I was bored when I didn't have my head down the lav. Right.' Bex took off her jacket, and grabbed a cloth. 'Tables, then bottling up?'

'Sounds fine to me. I'll leave you to it. I've a mountain of ordering to do.' Belinda went through the door that led to her upstairs flat.

Within a few seconds, Bex was back into her old routine, humming happily as she polished the tables and piled up the beer mats in the centre.

'Hey, stranger.'

She looked up. 'Miles.' He was standing in the open door to the kitchen.

'You feeling better?'

'A lot better, thank you.' She walked over to the bar.

'You still look a bit peaky.'

'I'm fine,' said Bex firmly. A whiff of the day's special – chicken korma – wafted out of the kitchen. Bex's gorge rose. She grabbed the water jug off the bar, poured herself a glass of water and sipped it. The nausea passed.

As Bex was getting back into her routine, Joan Makepiece, Bert the churchwarden's wife, walked through the town to the Co-op.

'Hello, Joan,' called out a voice from behind her.

She turned. 'Mags! Good to see you. How's retirement? How's the new house?'

'I miss working, truth be told. And have you seen what she's done to my salon? I mean, I know it's nothing to do with me now but really.'

'I don't like it much either. All too bright. I mean, yellow walls. And the lights. My eyes ache after I've been there five minutes. I think next time I go in I'll have to take sunglasses.'

Mags stared at her old customer. 'And, if you don't mind me saying so, Joan, what's she done to your hair?'

Self-consciously, Joan lifted her hand to her curls. She shook her head. 'It's not right, is it? I don't think Bert likes it either – not that he'd say anything but I see him staring at it.'

Joan's traditional 'set' had been replaced by something much more modern – all spiky and tousled. 'Mimi – I mean what sort of name is that? – says it's taken years off me. If you ask me it makes me look like I don't know how to brush my own hair.'

'I suppose it's on-trend,' said Mags.

'But I don't want to be "on trend",' sniffed Joan. 'Mutton dressed as lamb and that's not me.'

'Do want me to have a go at it for you?'

Joan's eyes widened in gratitude. 'Would you?'

'Course – that's what friends do.'

'When?'

Mags shrugged. 'Anytime. Come round to mine on your way home, if you like – I mean, if that suits.'

'Suits? Of course it does.'

Twenty minutes later, Joan was banging on the door of Mags's little home in Beeching Rise.

'Come in, come in,' exhorted Mags as she opened the door.

'Ain't this nice,' said Joan as she stepped inside.

'And it still smells of new carpets. I love that smell,' said Mags.

Joan sniffed and nodded. She moved along the hall and peered around a door. 'Ooh, lovely kitchen, too.'

'Come on, I'll show you round. Well, this is the kitchen-diner…'

They finally made it upstairs, after Joan had exclaimed over the fitted kitchen and the bi-fold doors that led out into the tiny garden, the little sitting room with the faux-coal gas fire and the recessed ceiling lights and, even, the understairs cupboard.

'And that's Olivia's place,' said Mags pointing out of her bedroom window.

'Lovely,' said Joan.

'She doesn't think so, I can tell.'

'It's a bit smaller than her old house.'

Mags turned and leaned against the window sill. 'Do you believe that story about them wanting to downsize?'

Joan thought about it. 'Well, their place was big…'

'Huge. Amy said half of it was never used.'

'And this must be cosier – cheaper to run.'

'Yeah, but she never struck me as someone who'd care about *cosy* when she could lord it over the rest of us from that blooming great place on the hill. And she certainly never cared what she spent.'

'No.'

Both women considered the assessment.

'Still, this ain't getting your hair done.' Mags led Joan through to the bathroom where she settled her client on the stool by the bath and got out a couple of clean towels. 'No backwash unit, so hold a bit of the towel over your eyes to stop any soap getting in.' She tucked a towel round Joan's shoulders. 'Right, lean over the bath. This isn't great but it's the best I can do. I'll try not to get you too wet.' She ran the taps and checked the temperature of the water coming out of the shower head as Joan leaned over the bath.

'This reminds me of when I was a nipper,' said Joan. 'Only we didn't have no shower so my mum washed our hair with hot water in a jug. Most of it always ended up going down our necks.' She chuckled at the memory.

'Oooh, talking of nippers...'

'Yes.'

'Amy says that Bex-woman—'

'The one at the pub?'

That's the one – well, Amy says she's up the duff.'

'Really? But she ain't got a husband.'

Mags started lathering Joan's hair. 'We both know that doesn't matter – not these days. It didn't bother my Amy.'

'True. But that was fast work. She hasn't been here five minutes.'

'Easter she arrived.'

'Even so.'

There was silence as they both considered Bex's situation.

'Who's the father?' asked Joan.

'Amy reckons it's Miles.'

'Get away.'

'Straight up. Stands to reason,' added Mags. 'They see a lot of each other when she's working and they're both single.'

'I suppose. Well, if that's the case, Miles must be as pleased as a dog with two tails. He'll make a good dad, he will – and not before time. He's not getting any younger, is he?'

Olivia dropped Jade at the vicarage and helped her unload her suitcases.

Jade stared at the house from the end of the garden path. 'If they make me say grace or go to church I'll not stay,' she muttered to her mum.

'They won't. Heather understands that this is a commercial transaction and has nothing to do with them trying to convert you.'

'Good.'

Olivia stood one of the cases upright and pulled out the handle. 'Come on then.'

Leaving Jade to bring the other two cases she led the way to the front door and rang the bell.

'Hello!' said Heather warmly. She looked past Olivia to Jade. 'Your room is all ready. I hope you like it. Bring your bags in and then I'll show you around.' Jade and Olivia dragged the cases over the doorstep and the big coir mat and into the hall. Jade let go of her cases — one of which fell over. Olivia laid the case she was in charge of on the floor, then followed Heather and her daughter up the stairs.

'Here.' Heather threw open the door to a room at the end of the landing. The bedroom was big and square with a massive, old-fashioned, dark-wood wardrobe, a matching chest and a dressing table with a mirror. The walls were primrose yellow and the carpet was pale green and the soft furnishings, which seemed to feature spring flowers, toned beautifully. Heather had put a big vase of flowers on the dressing table and there was a pile of glossy magazines on the bedside table. A small portable TV stood on the chest, a Wi-Fi router blinked in the corner and there was a kettle next to it. Despite the furniture, it was bright, light, cheerful and spacious and seemed to have almost everything to make it as self-sufficient for Jade as possible.

Jade walked into the middle of the room and stood by the bed as she looked around it.

'Yeah, it's nice,' she said.

'I told you so,' said Olivia.

'Let me show you the bathroom,' said Heather.

The bathroom was dated but clean and had the same hideous green tiles as Heather's kitchen. The shower was the old-fashioned sort, attached to the wall above an enormous bath with a curtain to stop the water splashing everywhere, but it would do. Olivia saw Jade sneer at it.

'But so much bigger than the bathroom you share with Zac.'

Olivia's statement was undeniably true. The family bathroom at Beeching Rise was more of a glorified shower room and the bath was minute – not like this monster.

'I suppose,' said Jade.

'We have a basin in our bedroom,' said Heather, 'so we only use this for showering and Brian is an early riser. To all intents and purposes this is your bathroom and we'll borrow it if we need to.'

'OK,' said Jade.

Olivia and Heather exchanged a look behind her back

'Three fifty a month, you said.'

'Bed, breakfast and evening meal,' agreed Heather.

'Fine.'

'Let's get your cases,' said Olivia before her daughter could possibly change her mind.

Five minutes later, she and Heather sat in the kitchen drinking tea while, in the background, came the sounds of drawers opening and shutting as Jade unpacked.

'I owe you for this. Honestly, I think if you hadn't offered to rent your room to her either Nigel or I would have killed her.'

'It's my pleasure. And it's nice to have a young person around here again.'

'You may not say that when she starts playing her music.'

'I doubt she'll have it up too loud. It's one thing to have it blaring when it's your parents you are pissing off. It's something else to do it to strangers.'

'I wish I had your faith.'

Heather reached across the table and touched Olivia's hand. 'It's all going to be fine. Trust me.'

26

A couple of days later, Miles was walking to work at the pub from the little flat he rented behind the town hall. He was striding along the high street, avoiding shoppers heading for the market and vaguely thinking about the possibility of doing a Hallowe'en menu or whether he'd be better concentrating on Bonfire Night. The kids loved Hallowe'en, that was for sure, but their regular customers, who it would be tricky to describe as 'kids', were probably more the sort who thought Hallowe'en was a nasty American import which only encouraged the youths of the town to indulge in legalised begging. So, he thought, rather than pumpkin soup and pumpkin pie, would he be better with bonfire-type recipes – bangers, hot dogs, apple turnovers…?

'Hi, Miles. Congratulations,' said a woman who was familiar as a pub regular but whose name escaped Miles.

'Oh, hi,' responded Miles, automatically as she passed. Congratulations? What the heck was that about? Maybe he'd misheard. The woman was now several paces away and Miles couldn't be bothered to chase after her and ask what she was on about. He walked on. He was nearing the pub when he saw Bert, on the other pavement, wave at him followed by a thumbs up.

What the fuck was going on? Had he won the lottery?

Unlikely, given he hadn't bought a ticket in months. He ferreted in his pocket, found the pub key and let himself in.

He stood at the bottom of the stairs that led to Belinda's flat. 'Only me,' he called.

'Hi, Miles. I'll be down in a minute.'

Miles pushed open the kitchen door, took his coat off, grabbed a sparkling white chef's jacket from behind the door and buttoned it up. Then he went into the pantry and began to gather together the salads and vegetables that he'd need to prep ready for the lunch service. A few minutes later he was slicing and dicing at a counter and sweeping the results into stainless steel bowls which he dumped in one of the big industrial fridges ready for use.

Belinda appeared in the kitchen. 'Morning, Miles. All OK?'

'It's good thanks. Are you putting in an order to the wholesaler sometime soon?'

'This afternoon. Why?'

'I've got a list of stuff we're going to need.'

'Let me have it later.'

'Sure thing.'

'I'm going to make myself a coffee,' said Belinda. 'You want one?'

'Please.' Miles returned to his chopping. 'Hey, Belinda,' he said after about a minute.

'Yeah?'

'Bert gave me a big thumbs up when I was on my way here and I swear someone else said "congratulations".'

'Congratulations? Why?' Then she added, 'Who?'

Miles shrugged. 'Can't remember her name, but she drops in here now and again.'

'So she might have got the wrong person.'

'I suppose. But Bert? Why would he be pleased for me? And what about?'

'Search me,' mumbled Belinda.

'I'll ask him later.'

'You do that.'

Miles carried on chopping and slicing and missed the worried look on Belinda's face.

Miranda Osborne picked up a box of leaflets and dropped them into her sisal shopping bag. She might be against the church spreading the message about its services via the medium of bells and change-ringing but she had a message of her own that she felt the townsfolk of Little Woodford ought to hear – whether they liked it or not. She suspected that "not" was probably going to be the case and she was steeling herself for some unpleasantness but, she told herself, it would only be an exchange of words, nothing physical. Or, at least, she hoped that was all it might amount to. Today's terrorist is tomorrow's freedom fighter... not that she was a terrorist, of course.

Feeling purposeful, she walked down to the market place. The weather was overcast but dry and she hoped that there would be plenty of people thronging the stalls of the market – people she could try and convert to her way of thinking.

She found the spot that she'd scoped out the previous week – between the fishmonger's van and the butcher's stall – and put her shopping bag down by her feet. She reached down, opened the box of leaflets and picked out a handful.

'Meat is murder,' she shouted, pressing one of her flyers into the hand of a surprised passer-by. 'Meat is murder!'

Some shoppers managed to scuttle past her, unaccosted, but Miranda was ruthless in her attacks. One after another she managed to skewer unsuspecting market-goers with her gimlet stare and then force upon them a leaflet.

'You don't need to eat meat,' she told people. 'Think of the suffering you'll be sparing the poor dumb animals.'

One or two people, so intimidated by her, shied away from the butcher's and the fishmonger and headed towards the Co-op where they could buy their protein without a side-order of guilt.

'Oi!' said one of the guys behind the meat counter, waving a massive knife. 'You can't do that. You're ruining my trade.'

'I can do whatever I like,' riposted Miranda, firmly. 'This is a free country with freedom of speech as one of our key tenets.'

The butcher came round to the front of his stall still clutching the huge blade. He rather pointedly stuck his knife into his chopping block before he turned and spoke to Miranda. 'And I've got a right to trade.'

'In the dead bodies of poor suffering beasts.'

'They never suffered and I resent your implication that they did.'

'Executed in cold blood? Of course they suffered.'

Several people gathered nearby to watch the exchange. This was the most action that Little Woodford had seen in months.

'These animals were humanely slaughtered.'

'Huh. And what sort of life did they have before? Intensively reared in vile conditions, caged, force-fed—'

'Now you listen here, I know the farms these animals came off and they had the best conditions.'

'Of course you'd say that. Do you take me for a fool?'

'And why shouldn't I? Bloody townie, interfering in matters you don't understand.'

'I understand about the indiscriminate use of unnecessary antibiotics, of overcrowding—'

'Not on the farms I use.'

But Miranda didn't want to listen to the counter-arguments and turned her back on him to press her leaflets into the hands of the gathering onlookers. 'Meat is murder,' she cried as she did so. 'Meat is murder.'

'And you're committing a breach of the peace,' said Leanne Knowles, the local police community support officer.

Miranda spun round. 'Don't be ridiculous. I am carrying out a perfectly lawful protest.'

'And I'll be carrying out a perfectly lawful citizen's arrest unless you move on.'

'You can't do that, you have no powers.'

Leanne raised her eyebrows and reached for her handcuffs. 'I can restrain you until back-up arrives.'

Miranda eyed the handcuffs warily.

Heather, who was in the market doing a spot of shopping for fruit and veg chuckled with schadenfreude. She couldn't wait to tell Olivia about Miranda Osborne's latest exploit.

Because of the market the pub was pretty busy – even by market-day standards. Miles was rushed off his feet in the kitchen and, in the bar, Bex had to call upon Belinda to lend a hand on several occasions.

After about two, things began to calm down and, while Belinda went upstairs to sort out the wholesaler's order, Bex used the last half hour, before she knocked off her shift and went to get the boys, to repair some of the damage done to the stock levels by going down to the cellar to get some trays of mixers. She did several journeys with shrink-wrapped packages, stacking them on the side of the bar ready to load them onto the shelves.

'How's it going?' asked Miles, coming out of the kitchen, his chef's whites now spattered and stained.

'That's it. Just Statler and Waldorf in the corner left now,' said Bex, nodding at Bert and Harry who were two thirds the way down their second lunchtime pint. It never ceased to amaze Bex that the pair could make two pints last as long as they did. Miles was about to return to the kitchen as Bex picked up a tray of ginger beers.

'Oi,' said Bert.

Bex turned.

'You shouldn't be lifting heavy things, not in your condition.'

Bex froze.

'What's that?' asked Miles, his hand on the door to the kitchen.

'You oughtn't let your lady friend risk the baby. Ain't it bad for women in the family way to lift heavy things?'

Bex felt rooted to the spot. Her gaze flicked between Bert and Miles. Then she found her voice. 'Don't be silly, Bert,' she said firmly. 'I don't know what you're on about.'

'So Mags Pullen's got it all arse about face, has she?' Bert chuckled. 'Wouldn't be the first time, though, neither.'

'Mags has got *what* arse about face?' said Miles. He was staring at Bex.

'About Bex expecting a baby. And there was me thinking what lovely news it was. Oh well. Sorry I got it so wrong,' said Bert, draining the dregs of his pint and heaving himself out of his seat. 'Still, no harm done.' He walked over to the bar and put his glass down. 'See yer, Harry. Bye, you two,' he said cheerily to Miles and Bex, oblivious of the look of horror on Bex's face and the stunned one on Miles's.

Bex turned and fled, banging the bar flap down behind her to block Miles's way – even if only for a second or two. She grabbed her coat from the peg and barged past Bert to reach the front door ahead of him. A minute later, panting with exertion she had her own front door slammed shut behind her and was leaning against it, her heart hammering and feeling sick.

'Shit,' she breathed. The dring of the door bell a couple of seconds later made her jump out of her skin and she felt the vibration of the hammering of the old door knocker rattle down her spine.

'Bex, Bex! We've got to talk.'

For a couple of seconds Bex considered pretending she wasn't at home but she knew it would be useless. Sooner or later she was going to have to have it out with Miles – she was postponing the inevitable. Feeling suddenly bone-weary she opened the door.

'Well?' he said.

Bex sighed heavily. How could she continue to lie? 'I know what you want to know, and I probably know what you're going to say, but this isn't the time. I've got to pick up the boys in a few minutes and then Megan will be home.'

'Is it true?' Miles's face was contorted with anxiety.

Bex nodded.

'And it's mine?'

'Jesus, Miles, who else's?'

There was a pause. 'Sorry, that was crass.'

Bex nodded and pursed her mouth. Yes it was – and rather insulting, but he hadn't meant it like that – at least, she didn't think he had. 'Look, why don't you come round after you've finished the evening service. We can talk then.'

'No, not tonight. I've arranged to meet someone who wants me to do some catering for a function. I don't suppose I'll be finished till late.'

'OK – then tomorrow morning, after I've done the school run. Nine-ish.'

'That's fine. And you're all right?'

'Miles, I'm pregnant, not ill. I've pretty much got the morning sickness under control and let's face it, I've done this before. I've managed to live through two pregnancies so I think it's safe to assume that this one won't be life-threatening either. '

'Yes… yes, of course.' He hovered in the hall looking uneasy. 'And you've seen the doc?'

'Not yet. I've got an appointment at eleven tomorrow.'

'Good. And you're looking after yourself?'

'Yes,' she snapped. Miles looked crestfallen. She breathed and counted to five. 'Miles, I've got to go and get the boys. You and I can talk tomorrow but, please, don't fuss.'

'Of course. It's just…' He dipped in and gave her a swift kiss. 'This is such wonderful news.'

Bex's heart sank at his reaction but, hoping her face didn't betray her feelings, she opened the front door to give him the hint to go. 'Tomorrow – nine o'clock,' she said, firmly.

'Yes, yes, bye.' Miles slid off looking like he'd won the lottery.

Bex shut the door again and felt a wave of exhaustion weigh her down. No, Miles, she said to herself, this isn't wonderful news.

Bex went to fetch the boys and found that, once again, she seemed to be playing the Pied Piper as Alfie and Lewis both wanted to bring friends home on a spontaneous play date. Megan, she reasoned, had drama club after school and, as having friends over would probably keep her lads occupied, it wasn't such a bad idea. She herded four small boys down the hill to her place, checked she had more than enough fish fingers, beans and potato waffles to feed them and then slumped on a kitchen chair while the boys played a game in the sitting room that involved a lot of Lego and shouting.

After about half an hour she felt energised enough to offer them orange juice and biscuits and to see what damage had been wrought to her soft furnishings. Apart from a mountain of plastic bricks on the carpet the boys seemed to have been well-behaved and the sitting room still intact even if they had made enough noise to raise most of the occupants of St Catherine's graveyard.

Bex returned to the kitchen and turned over the problem of Miles, Megan and the baby again and again in her head. If there was a way of finding out Megan's reaction without *actually* telling her the news, everything might be hunky-dory. Megan didn't seem to dislike Miles, she might welcome the idea of another sibling, she might feel that enough time had passed since her dad had died not to feel betrayed by what her stepmother had done... or she might not. God, if ever she needed a crystal ball.

27

The next morning Bex got back from the school run and flopped onto a chair feeling utterly beat. And it wasn't, she knew, the tiredness that pregnancy caused, this was mostly the exhaustion of not having slept the night before. She'd gone over her options time and time again – which was ridiculous considering there were only two – keep the baby or not. Shit, if only she could turn back the clock and refuse to have sex with Miles until she got her own contraception sorted out, instead of relying on his. But that would have taken ages and they'd both wanted sex right then. And condoms were almost one hundred per cent reliable... except *almost* one hundred per cent wasn't good enough. Not in the cold light of the situation right now.

The doorbell rang and Bex jumped. She glanced at the kitchen clock – he was bang on time. Feeling anxious she went to the door.

'Hi, Miles.'

He stepped inside and took her in his arms, kissing the top of her head. Bex pushed him away.

'Don't.'

'What's the matter? Don't you feel well?'

'Not really. Apart from still feeling shit in the mornings there is a lot else to worry about.' Bex led Miles into the kitchen and pulled out a chair for him to sit on. 'Tea? Coffee?'

'Coffee, please.'

'It'll have to be instant.' Bex bustled about making Miles his drink, more to put off the impending discussion than in a spirit of hospitality. She put the steaming mug in front of him and took her seat again.

'Look... Miles... this isn't easy.'

'No, I understand. Being pregnant is a huge responsibility.'

Bex rolled her eyes and shook her head. 'You don't understand. This isn't *just* about me and it certainly mightn't be about you.' She outlined her fears about Megan's possible reaction.

'But you don't *know*. She may be fine. She may be delighted.'

Bex stared at him. 'She's already been betrayed by her birth mother who ran away; abandoned her. Her father was killed in a traffic accident and now I – the only bit of stability in her life – am having a baby. She may see it as a betrayal of her father, she may see the baby as usurping her place in the family... or she may just be disgusted that I had casual sex.'

Miles stared at her. 'So what are you saying? You're going to have an abortion?' He got to his feet. 'But it's my baby too. You can't do that.' He was almost shouting, pleading. 'I'd support you, I'd help you. You wouldn't have to do this on your own. I know four kids would take a lot of looking after but I'll be right here. And I'd support you financially.'

Bex got to her feet too so he wasn't looming over her, intimidating her. 'This isn't about me coping or not coping, this isn't about money or anything like that. This is about a family dynamic that you know precious little about and which, if you'd been just a little bit more careful, wouldn't be about to go tits up because I've got the most unplanned pregnancy since Mary had to break the news to Joseph.'

'Unplanned pregnancy?' said Megan from the door.

The pair were shocked into silence.

Bex felt the colour leech from her face. She felt sick and dizzy with horror. 'Megan.' She gazed at her stepdaughter, trying to think of something to say but she had no words. Nothing.

'I thought having a banging headache made it a shit day,' said Megan. 'That's why I got sent home. But, no... this is the shittiest day on record. Ever!' She turned and headed for the stairs.

'Megan,' called Bex after her. 'Megan, I'm sorry.'

'Fuck off,' screeched Megan from the landing.

There was silence for a few seconds. 'Maybe I'd better go,' said Miles. He twisted his hands. 'You said you're seeing the doctor this morning.'

Bex nodded.

'Do you want me to come with you?'

'I think you've done quite enough, don't you?'

Bex followed her daughter up the stairs as Miles let himself out of the front door. She got to the bottom of the attic stairs and called softly.

'Megan? Megan, may I come up?'

'Go away,' was the reply which was almost subsumed by a hiccupping sob.

It was an improvement on 'fuck off'.

Bex crept up the stairs to her stepdaughter's bedroom. She stopped at the top. 'Megan?'

Megan was curled up in a foetal position, facing the wall. 'I said *go away.*'

'I know, but we need to talk.' She took a couple of paces into the room. There was silence. 'Megan?'

Megan rolled over, her face blotchy and wet as she glared at Bex. 'You mean, *you* want to talk. Justify to me what you've done... How could you?'

'I didn't plan it.'

'What?' said Megan, real anger in her voice. 'Having sex or getting pregnant? Not that it really matters; either way it's disgusting,' she spat. She flopped onto her back and stared at the ceiling as she dashed away her tears from her cheeks with the palms of both hands.

'Well, that makes things easier,' said Bex. There was no response from Megan. 'I've got an appointment with the doctor later this morning. I'm going to ask to be referred for a termination.'

Megan's head whipped round. 'You what?'

'It's the only way if it's going to make you so unhappy.'

'Like killing a baby is going to make things better.'

'It's not a baby – not yet.'

'It is. I don't care what you say, I've read stuff in magazines, I've seen pictures and you can't.' Megan's voice was getting shrill.

Bex was tempted to tell Megan that she could; that it wasn't Megan's decision to make, but maybe now wasn't the moment to have the conversation when things were all too raw. She wished she hadn't put off making an appointment for so long. She wished she'd gone to see Dr Connolly as soon as she had a suspicion of what was going on – before Miles and Megan had found out; when it was only her decision to make. If only... if only...

Bex crossed the room and sat on the end of Megan's bed. 'I don't have to see the doctor today,' she said, quietly. 'I can cancel the appointment. I... I thought...' She shook her head. 'I don't know what I thought.'

'You thought you could get away with it, without me finding out,' said Megan.

'Maybe.'

Megan curled up and looked at the wall again. 'I don't know how you can live with yourself.' She whipped her head round. 'How could you have done that to Dad? How *could* you have done?'

'It doesn't mean I don't love your father any the less. You can love more than one person at a time – just like I love you and the boys.'

'Huh.' There was silence for a few seconds. 'So, do you love Miles?'

Bex was startled. It was a question she hadn't even really asked herself. 'He's a good man. I'm very fond of him.'

'Well, that's obvious given that you slept with him.'

Bex wanted to tell Megan that it hadn't been like that and nor was she a nun. Being a widow didn't mean an automatic vow of celibacy; Richard was only a memory now and she couldn't have sex with a memory, be held by a memory, be kissed by a memory…

'Look,' she said. 'If you'd like, I can cancel today's appointment and maybe, when we've both had a chance to calm down, we can talk about it. There's no desperate urgency – I'm only about six or seven weeks pregnant.'

'But you've made your mind up, haven't you? You want rid of it.'

'I thought it would be better for you… in the long run. And you're right, I didn't want you to find out. I thought I could sort all of this by myself except, somehow, someone blabbed my news all over the town. Until then I thought it was going to be my body, my decision.'

'And the baby? Doesn't the baby get a vote?'

'I think there are quite enough people with a vote already,' said Bex. She changed the subject. 'Do you want something for your headache?'

'Yeah, please.'

Bex went down to her bathroom, got a couple of ibuprofen out of her medicine cabinet and filled a glass with water. She returned to Megan's room and put them on the bedside table. 'I'll go and ring the doctor; postpone seeing him until we've had time to talk.'

'Whatever,' said Megan who was back facing the wall again.

Wearily, Bex returned downstairs and rang the surgery. The receptionist didn't sound best pleased that Bex didn't want her appointment. 'But at least you've had the common courtesy to let us know,' she said. 'Precious few do.'

Bex ended the call and mulled over her conversation with Megan and tried to decide which would upset her stepdaughter the least: to carry on with the pregnancy or to have a termination? Talk about being on the horns of a dilemma. She made herself a cup of tea and had a desultory tidy-up of the downstairs which mostly involved collecting up all the Lego bricks from the four corners of the sitting room and beyond, after the boys' rumbustious game with their friends the previous evening.

She was killing time making a shopping list, before her shift at the pub, when she heard footsteps coming down the stairs.

'Oh,' said Megan. 'You're still here.'

'I don't start till eleven thirty,' said Bex. 'Can I get you anything?'

Megan shook her head.

'How's the headache?'

'A bit better.'

'I'm glad.' An awkward silence followed. 'Do you feel better enough to go back to school?'

'Not really.'

'OK. Are you missing anything important?'

'Nothing I can't catch up with off Soph.'

'Look... about what's happened...'

'What?' Megan's voice was sullen.

'I never meant for anyone to find out.'

'Really.'

'Yes, really.'

'So you didn't think about, like, the morning-after pill.'

'I thought Miles and I had been careful.'

Megan rolled her eyes. 'Shit, Bex, you're a grown-up. Didn't you even think it might be a good idea – you know, just in case?'

Bex was aware of a growing resentment about being lectured by her stepdaughter about contraception but she battened it down. 'Maybe in hindsight... But we are where we are.'

'Up shit creek.'

Well, they agreed on something. Bex nodded. 'Look, Megan, the reason I didn't want you to find out was because I knew you'd be hurt... and probably angry.'

'You're not wrong there.' Her tone of voice underlined her emotion.

'And that's why I thought that maybe… well, a termination would be for the best.'

'For you, you mean.'

'And you.'

'Don't you use me as an excuse. If you want to kill a baby, you go right ahead, but I'm having no part in this decision.'

'You'd rather I kept it?' Bex was confused.

'As an alternative to what you've got planned – yes.'

Heather rang the bell of Olivia's new house. She had no idea if Olivia would be in or not, not now her friend worked shifts up at the hotel. The door opened – good.

'Hi, Olivia, is this a good time?' said Heather.

'Perfect. Come in. Lovely to see you. Apart from at church, our paths never seem to cross these days.'

'I know. And I miss you on my committees.' Six months ago, Heather wouldn't have ever believed that she would say such a thing, but it was true. Olivia could be opinionated and stubborn but, boy, she got things done.

'How's the bell fund?' said Olivia as she led the way through to the kitchen-diner.

'Getting there. The Heritage Lottery Fund is looking very hopeful. Brian and I have to work out how we can involve the community but the schools and groups like the Scouts and Guides seem to be keen to learn about change-ringing and we're planning on producing a booklet about the history of our bells so it's all coming together.'

'As long,' said Olivia, 'as you're allowed to teach kids about change-ringing because, if that Osborne woman gets her way, your plans will go belly up.'

'Don't,' groaned Heather. 'But… talking of that Osborne woman, I thought she was going to wind up in the clink yesterday.'

'No! Tell.'

Heather related the incident at the market. 'She certainly knows how to make herself popular. First the bells, then the wind turbine, now making waves at the market... And what is happening about the turbine?'

'It's all legal,' said Olivia, gloomily. 'I guessed it would be and, as far as the council knows, the contractors will be arriving in the next few days to erect it. I'm rather hoping they'll get it monumentally wrong and the whole thing falls on her roof in the first winter storm.'

'Hmmm,' said Heather. 'It's an idea. I'm not sure I can ask Brian to intercede on your behalf, though.'

'I don't want anyone killed,' added Olivia.

'Absolutely not.' Heather grinned.

'And how's my daughter?'

There was a momentary pause before Heather said, a bit too brightly, 'Fine.'

'Don't lie,' said Olivia. 'Truthfully...?'

'Challenging. She's not the tidiest tenant.'

'I'm sorry,' said Olivia.

'Don't be.'

'I'll have a word.'

'No. She's our problem now. Brian is going to talk to her, set down some house rules. We should have done it from the start.'

'Good luck with that.'

'You're not to worry. We get the rent, it's up to us to make it work.'

'Kids, eh?'

'And talking of kids, have you heard anything about Bex?'

'Like what?'

'I heard it from Amy that she's expecting a baby.'

Olivia's eyes popped. 'No!'

'Well... according to Amy...'

'Even so, that's not the sort of thing even Amy would come out with, without there being *some* basis of truth. Although, she *did* confide in Belinda that she thinks Ash might be gay because he's so keen on acting.'

'Ash? Not if I'm any judge,' said Heather.

'No, I don't think so either but you know what Amy's like. If she can add up two and two and make seven and three quarters, she will. But even *I* don't think Amy would make it up about Bex. And I saw Belinda the other morning and she said Bex hadn't been well – a sick bug.' She gave Heather a knowing look.

'Goodness. And the thing is,' said Heather, slowly, 'what we don't know is whether it's a cause for celebration or not.'

'No,' said Olivia.

'I was wondering... do you think I ought to pop round?'

'On what pretext?'

'Same as I used on you this morning – that I haven't seen her for an age.'

'I suppose. If she wants to talk she will, if not, you can blag a cuppa off her and have a bit of a chat. Go for it, I say.'

Bex banged on the door to the pub which was opened after a few seconds by Belinda.

'So,' said Bex, without preamble, stamping in with a scowl on her face, 'Who did you tell?'

'You've lost me,' said Belinda, closing and locking the door.

'About me being pregnant? Bert knew, he'd heard it off Mags and now both Miles and Megan know. And, knowing this town like I do, probably everyone else does.' Her anger threatened to turn into tears.

Belinda's forehead creased as she put her hands up. 'Not me. I didn't breathe a word, honest, and I *certainly* didn't tell Mags.'

'Well, someone did and as you are the only person on the planet who knew besides me...'

'I don't know how to make it any clearer, but I didn't tell a soul. I wouldn't. It's not what friends do to each other.'

'OK, I believe you.' Although she wasn't sure she did, because if it wasn't Belinda, who the hell else was it?

'And I'm sorry.'

'Not as sorry as I am.' Bex explained about the reaction of Miles and Megan.

'Jeez,' breathed Belinda. 'Messy.'

'That's one word for it,' agreed Bex. '"Absolute fucking disaster" are three more.'

28

Megan heard her stepmother go out to work and came downstairs again. The analgesics had worked, her headache had almost disappeared and she was peckish. She mooched into the kitchen and opened the fridge door. She considered the contents – nothing much that didn't need cooking. She picked out a lump of cheddar and then rummaged in the bread bin. A cheese and pickle sandwich would have to do. Not bothering with a plate or a chopping board she made her snack and, oblivious of the trail of crumbs that followed her, she went into the sitting room, flopped on the sofa and switched on the TV. Idly she flicked through the channels as she ate her sandwich – Jeez, the dross. She switched the TV off again, tossed the remote onto the table and slumped back on the cushions.

Her phone pinged. A text from Ashley.

Watkins wants 2 no if u feel well enough 2 come in after school.
Wants 2 see us 2 discuss costumes.

If Megan were totally truthful with herself, she probably felt well enough to go back into school right now. Besides, there was nothing to do at home and the lessons timetabled for the afternoon were English and history – both of which she quite liked. She made her mind up, found her school bag and let herself back out of the house.

She signed back in at reception fifteen minutes later and went to the library to wait for the school bell to signal the start of the lunch break. She drifted over to the reference side of the library and looked at the books about child development. It wasn't a subject she'd opted to take – choosing drama instead – but some of her friends were studying it. Megan had always argued that, with two much younger brothers, she'd seen quite enough of it at first hand to want to do it at school too. She'd been seven when Lewis had been born and, while it had been fun to have a proper 'living doll' to play with and help change and feed, the novelty had worn off quite fast – especially when his crying woke her up in the night. And now that almost six years had passed since Alfie's arrival, her recollections of what it was like to have a baby in the house were a bit fuzzy. She picked a book off the shelf and flicked through it. The babies in the pictures were quite cute, she decided, before she slapped the book shut and shoved it back on the shelf. It didn't matter how cute babies were – it didn't alter the fact her stepmother had slept with Miles. Ugh.

The bell rang and Megan went off to meet her classmates as they exited from maths.

'You feeling better?' said Ashley as they walked along a corridor and headed for the canteen.

'A bit. It was only a headache.'

'Miss Watkins is well excited about the designs for the costumes the art department has come up with. She wants an extra meeting of the drama group tonight to get us measured up.'

Megan shrugged.

'Aren't you keen to see what we've got to wear?' asked Ashley.

'Not really.'

Ashley looked at her. 'I don't get you. Don't you want to be in the panto, because you're behaving like a right old wet weekend.'

Megan rounded on him. 'I do! You're just so self-obsessed

with your part and being *liberated* and all arty and poncy you can't see that everyone else's lives aren't all hunky-dory.'

Other kids streaming along the passageway stared at the pair in curiosity.

'Me? Self-obsessed?' shouted Ashley back at Megan.

'You so are!' she countered.

Sophie appeared at Megan's elbow. 'Come on, Megs, leave him.' She tugged on Megan's arm.

Megan gave Ashley a parting snarl and followed her friend.

'Come on,' repeated Sophie. 'Let's go and get some lunch.'

'I'm not hungry.'

'Well, I am.'

As they reached the canteen the hubbub of voices became louder. The two girls joined the queue to be served.

'So what was all that about?' said Sophie as she pushed her tray along the counter.

'Nothing.'

Sophie grabbed a plate of quiche and salad. 'Nothing?' She headed for the queue to pay. 'You sure you're not hungry?'

Megan shook her head. 'I'll bag a table.'

A few minutes later Sophie joined her and sat down next to her. 'Look,' she said, shovelling in a mouthful of cheese and onion tart, 'I get that this panto is a shedload of work but you've got to look at the bigger picture. It's going to be such fun to be up on that stage – performing to everyone.' Sophie sighed enviously. 'And you're going to be the star. God, Megs, what I'd give to be in your shoes.'

'You wouldn't think that if you knew.'

'I'm not with you.'

'It doesn't matter.' Morosely Megan picked a bit of tomato off Sophie's plate.

'So, it's not the panto.'

Megan shook her head.

Sophie ate another mouthful. 'You're not getting bullied again, are you?'

'No.'

'Come on, Megs. I can't help if I don't know what the matter is.'

'You wouldn't be able to help if you did know.'

'Suit yourself.' Sophie ate another mouthful and another. The silence stretched.

Megan could bear it no more. 'It's just…'

'Just what?'

'It's Bex.'

Sophie put her fork down. 'Shit, Megan, she's not ill, is she?'

'God, if only.'

Sophie glared at Megan. 'Don't say that. If you only knew… I mean, you know how hard it is for me and my mum.'

'Sorry, I didn't mean it like that.'

Sophie shook her head. 'So?'

Megan leaned in towards Sophie and lowered her voice. 'She's expecting a baby.'

Sophie almost choked. 'What?'

Megan nodded. 'Which means she and Miles must have…' She shuddered. 'I mean, how could she? How could she go with someone? I thought she loved Dad.' Megan's eyes filled and she blinked back the tears.

Sophie didn't know what to say so she put an arm around Megan and gave her a hug.

Across the room Ashley watched and wondered what was upsetting her so much.

The designs for the costumes that Miss Watkins presented to the cast after school were, they all agreed, pretty lush.

'And the A-level textiles group have agreed to make them,' she told her performers.

The children pored over the sheets of A4 cartridge paper, trying to imagine what they'd look like in them. Megan had three changes: the rags in the opening scenes, the ballgown and a wedding dress for the finale. Ashley and Dan, the other ugly sister, only had two costumes but both so outrageously over-the-top that they would be likely to steal any scene they appeared in. The other costumes, in comparison, were positively subfusc.

Ashley held the two designs that were destined for him and wandered over to where Megan was. 'Sorry I shouted at you earlier,' he offered.

Megan looked at him and sighed. 'And sorry I shouted back.'

'I'm not self-obsessed, am I?'

'A bit. You're no fun any more. All you want to talk about is this blooming panto.'

'Yeah, but it's such a big deal.'

Megan raised her eyebrows. 'In the grand scheme of things, it isn't.'

'I suppose. But it is to me.'

'In which case, Ash, you need to grow up.' She swept off leaving Ash looking miserable. Their reconciliation had been stillborn.

'And where the hell were you?' ranted Bex when Megan got home.

'At school.'

'Then why didn't you leave a note or something? You didn't even answer my text. I was worried sick.'

'Really?'

'Yes, *really*. I thought... well, never mind what I thought.'

'I bet you thought I'd run away. You'd have liked that, wouldn't you?'

'How can you say such a thing?'

'Because you don't care about me. If you did you wouldn't have...'

Bex felt as if she'd been kicked. She gasped. 'Megan, you don't really believe that, do you?'

Megan dropped her gaze.

'Megan, I love you, I always have.'

'That didn't stop you… you know.' Megan shuddered.

'No, no it didn't.'

'So why did you?'

'It's complicated.'

'Yeah, right.'

'Like I said, this isn't about me loving your dad any less. I'm not betraying him, or being unfaithful, honest. Do you really think he'd want me to be lonely and miserable?'

Megan shrugged. 'I dunno,' she mumbled.

'Daddy would want us all to be happy.'

'But we are.'

'Yes, we are, mostly.'

'Mostly?'

'Look, you and the boys have your friends, people you can have a laugh with, hang out with… don't you think I might want that too?'

'But you've got Zac's mum and Heather and… well, the book club lot, the PTA.'

'And they've got their own lives, their own families, other calls on their time. Sure, they're nice people but I want more than just a bit of a gossip and a laugh.'

'I suppose.'

'And I like Miles, a lot, and I think he likes me.'

'Yeah, well, that's obvious. What if I don't?'

'But you do, don't you?'

Megan shrugged. 'Would it have made a difference if I didn't?'

'Yes, yes, of course.'

'Says you.'

'I do. And I also mean it when I say that I want to hear what you really want… about what happens next.'

'You mean about the baby?'

Bex nodded.

'I dunno.'

'It's a really important decision. And now you're involved I need to know your views too.'

Megan stared at Bex, her forehead creased. 'I don't know. Why are you asking me? I can't make this decision. This is your problem – you sort it.' She turned and ran out of the house.

When she got a hundred yards from her home she stopped and texted Sophie.

Can I come round

Of course

Five minutes later Megan was ringing the bell to her friend's house.

'Hi, Megs. You'll have to come into the kitchen – I'm cooking our tea.'

Megan put her head round the sitting room door and said hello to Lizzie before following Sophie into the tiny kitchen at the back of the house. She pulled a stool out from under the counter and plonked herself down on it while Sophie carried on peeling potatoes.

'So?' said Sophie over her shoulder.

'So Bex wants me to tell her what to do.'

Sophie dropped a peeled spud back into the water. 'Huh?'

'About whether to keep the baby or not.'

'You're kidding me.'

Megan shook her head.

'That's well unfair.'

'What's this?' The girls spun round and saw Lizzie in the doorway. Her wheels had allowed her to approach in silence.

'Nothing,' said Megan.

'Sweetie, it didn't sound like nothing to me.'

Megan glanced between Lizzie and Sophie. 'If I tell you,' she said, 'you mustn't breathe a word.'

'Cross my heart.'

'Bex is pregnant.'

'Oh.' There was a pause, then Lizzie added, 'It's not the end of the world.'

'It's gross,' said Megan.

'It's life.' There was another pause. 'Is Bex happy about it?'

'I don't know. She said she thought about getting rid of it till me and Miles – that's her bloke – found out.'

'I expect,' said Lizzie, 'that was what she planned when she thought she could restore the status quo with no one being any the wiser.'

'You think?'

Lizzie nodded. 'But, if I'm any judge of human nature, I don't think Bex would *want* to have a termination. Not that I know her that well but I don't think it's what any woman wants. But she'd do it if she felt she had no choice – like if it was going to make you very unhappy.'

Megan thought about it. 'I think I'd be unhappier if she did.'

'Then I think you have your answer. I don't expect Bex planned this – it's just one of those things.'

'Maybe.'

'We all make mistakes. None of us is perfect.'

'I suppose. And Miles is OK. The boys like him.'

'Do you?'

'He's all right.'

Lizzie smiled at her. 'Your mum thinks so.'

'Stepmum. And yeah, I suppose.'

'She's got a life too. She's only young – she's fit, she's healthy, she's very pretty. Don't you think she deserves to have some fun?'

'Suppose.'

'I think you ought to go home and have a long chat with her.'

'Maybe.'

'She's been there for you all these years, maybe now she needs some support from you.'

Megan nodded. 'Yeah. Thanks.'

29

The following morning, feeling slightly apprehensive, Heather rang the bell of The Beeches. She had her excuse for her visit at the ready but, even so, she couldn't be certain that Bex wouldn't smell a rat.

The door was opened by Amy. Damn, she'd forgotten Amy did for Bex on a Friday.

'Oh... hello, Amy. Is Bex in?'

Amy nodded and yelled over her shoulder. 'It's Mrs S, Bex.' She opened the door wider. 'I'm sure Bex wouldn't want me to keep you waiting on the doorstep.'

Heather stepped over the threshold as Bex trotted down the stairs.

'Hi, Heather, what can I do for you?'

'I came to see how you are. I heard on the grapevine you haven't been well – some bug or other,' said Heather, avoiding looking directly at Amy although, out of the corner of her eye, she saw Amy's expression of astonishment at the lie.

'I'm much better now,' said Bex. She turned to Amy. 'Do you want to hoover the stairs first, rather than do the kitchen? That way Heather and I won't be getting in your way.'

'I *was* going to finish off downstairs but if that's what you want – you're the boss.'

Amy's tone was sullen. Heather reckoned she was unhappy

at being deprived of an eavesdropping opportunity but she grabbed the vacuum cleaner and lugged it upstairs. As Bex led Heather into the kitchen, the whine of the electric motor echoed around the stairwell. Even so, Bex shut the kitchen door behind them.

She picked up the kettle and, with her back to Heather as she filled it, she said, 'So, what did you *really* hear on the grapevine?'

'Ah.' There was a pause.

'Because the whole town seems to know my business.' Bex put the kettle on its stand and flicked the switch.

'Well...'

Bex turned and faced Heather. 'Bert knows, Mags knows and that means that probably everyone else does too, now. I'd hoped to sort out the situation in private. Fat chance of that.'

'Amy told me she'd found a positive pregnancy test in your bin.'

'She found a...' She sighed. 'So that's how the word got out. Bloody Amy.' Bex snorted angrily. 'I'll have to apologise to Belinda. I blamed her for telling everyone. I confided in her – I needed to talk to someone. It never crossed my mind for a second that Amy had gone through my rubbish.' Heather could see Bex's jaw working in anger. 'I've a good mind to sack her.'

'Isn't that rather shutting stable doors after the horse has run off?' said Heather, gently.

'Probably – but it would make me feel better.' Bex got out two mugs and dropped teabags into them.

'So what are you going to do?'

Bex shook her head. 'Honestly? I haven't a clue.' The kettle boiled and she turned her back on Heather to make the tea. 'I was going to ask for a termination – then I could pretend that nothing had happened. And that idea was just fine and dandy until both Miles and Megan found out.'

'Oh, my dear.'

Bex sloshed in milk and put the mugs on the table. 'No, that bit definitely wasn't in my plan. Miles is desperate to be a father and he'd be a great dad. He's lovely with my lot and they like him.' Bex shook her head. '*I* like him.'

Heather nodded. 'And Megan – how did she find out? Was it someone at school?'

'She got sent home from school yesterday morning with a headache and she overheard me and Miles talking. I think she hates me for what I've done. She's angry, hurt... It's awful.'

Heather reached across the table and took Bex's hands in hers.

'We had a long chat yesterday evening – a real heart-to-heart – and she's really unhappy but she'll be even more unhappy if I have an abortion.' Bex gave Heather a pinched smile. 'She'll hate me even more if I do that.'

'Oh.'

'It's a ghastly mess.' She pushed both hands through her short curls. 'I wish it had never happened.'

'Sadly, we can't turn the clock back.'

'More's the pity.'

The kitchen door banged open.

'Sorry to interrupt,' said Amy, who obviously wasn't to judge by the look on her face, 'but if you want the kitchen mopping...'

She sounded a bit belligerent, thought Heather, like the kids at school did when they knew they were in trouble and felt they needed to front it out. Amy glanced from one to the other and shifted from foot to foot. A guilty conscience if ever there was one.

'Thank you, Amy,' said Bex. 'Do you want to do that before or after you've gone through the bin?'

'You what?'

'You know exactly what I mean.'

Amy narrowed her eyes. 'I didn't go through it, the bag split. OK? Everything fell out.' She glared at Bex.

'Really. And then you took it upon yourself to tell all and sundry about what you'd found, because, as far as I can see, half of Little Woodford knows I am pregnant.'

'I never told no one – well, apart from Mum.' She glanced at Heather. 'It was only her. Cross my heart and hope to die.'

'In future,' said Bex, 'I would much rather you didn't discuss me or my family with *anyone*. Understand?'

'Whatever,' said Amy.

'I think,' said Heather, 'an apology wouldn't be out of order.'

Amy shot her a sulky look. 'Sorry,' she mumbled. 'How was I to know Mum'd tell people?'

Heather had to suppress a laugh. After Amy, Mags was the biggest gossip in the town. Of course Mags would have talked.

The two women took their mugs into the sitting room while Amy clattered around the kitchen.

'Anyway, the upshot is...' She paused and took a breath. 'I'm going to keep the baby.'

'I see.'

'I don't feel I've got a choice. Miles wants me to and Megan has made her views more than plain.'

'But what about you?'

'I don't suppose being a single mother with four kids is so very different to being a single mother with three kids.'

'That's not quite what I meant.'

Bex shrugged. 'My mess, my fault, my responsibility.'

Zac got off the school bus in the middle of town and looked towards the station and the houses behind. Beeching Rise was such a dump; he hated it there. It was marginally better now Jade was living with the vicar but the house was still gross. Besides, his mum always expected him to do stuff like clean the bathroom or take the bins out. It'd never been like that before.

He sloped off towards the skatepark. It wasn't very warm but he'd rather be cold than at home. And Ash or Megan might be hanging out there. Then he remembered the play – no, Ashley probably wouldn't. Since he'd got into acting he'd gone really weird, always talking bollocks about characterisation and motivation. Anyone would think he was playing Hamlet at the National, not an ugly sister in a school panto.

Zac mooched over to the ramps which were almost empty. A couple of young kids were mucking around on their BMXs and there were some teenage girls sitting on the roundabout in the kids' play park but other than that he had the place to himself, not surprising given that the weather was damp, dreary and decidedly chilly. Zac ran up one of the slopes, hitched himself onto the edge of a half-pipe and dangled his legs over the edge. He saw someone else come into the park and walk along the path towards him – he recognised the figure.

'Hi, Megan,' he yelled and waved at her. She waved back and headed towards him. 'Not rehearsing with Ashley?' asked Zac as she got closer.

She shook her head. 'Not today, and with any luck I'll be able to avoid him over the weekend too.' She ran up the half-pipe and sat down beside him.

'I thought you liked him.'

'I did, but now all he can talk about is bloody acting. I mean, don't get me wrong the panto is fun but...' She sighed deeply and shrugged. 'I'm not obsessed with it and he is.'

'I know what you mean. He's no fun any more.'

Megan nodded. She shivered and pulled the sleeves of her blazer down to cover her hands.

'Are you cold?'

'A bit,' she admitted.

'So why don't you go home?'

'Home sucks.'

'Yours too?'

Megan nodded morosely.

'At least,' said Zac, 'you've got space to get away from your family. The only place I've got in the shithole we live in now is my room and there's nowhere to rig up my computer and PlayStation. Mum says they've got to live in the conservatory but then she complains at me for playing games. I mean, what the fuck does she expect me to do on them?'

'Your homework.'

Zac rolled his eyes. 'Anyway, what's your problem? Fallen out with your brothers?'

'No.'

'With your mum?'

'Stepmum.' Megan sighed. 'Not really. It's just... oh, never mind. Look, I'm freezing. Want to come back to mine? Bex was making a cake when I left. It might be ready by now.'

'Lush.'

The pair wandered out of the park and along the road to The Beeches. Megan banged open the door, hung her blazer on a peg and trailed into the kitchen. Bex was standing by the table slathering strawberry jam onto one half of a Victoria sandwich.

'Hello, Zac,' she said. 'Long time no see.'

'Hello, Bex. Yeah, well, been busy moving and stuff like that.'

Megan made them both a cup of tea while Zac watched Bex assemble the cake, topping it off by sifting icing sugar over the surface.

'Fancy a slice?' she offered when it was done, just as Megan put their drinks on the table.

'It looks too good to cut,' said Zac.

'Then there was no point in me baking it,' said Bex, selecting a large knife. She cut a big wedge which she shoved on a plate and handed it to Zac. 'Megan?'

'Please, only about half what you gave Zac.' She accepted the plate. 'Come on, Zac, let's go up to my room.'

The pair disappeared out of the kitchen and took themselves up the stairs.

Bex watched them go thinking that now Zac had cleaned his act up Megan could do a lot worse. And maybe, if she had a boyfriend, she'd understand a bit more about her stepmother's need for that sort of companionship.

30

Autumn progressed with deteriorating weather, half-term came and went, everyone in Little Woodford turned their calendars to the November page, the local rugby club had a fireworks display, Bert harvested the last of his carrots and autumn raspberries down at his allotment and Olivia was now a key member of the front-of-house team at Woodford Priors. At the secondary school, the rehearsals continued and the first of the costumes had been produced and fitted while the coolness between Ashley and Megan continued. Bex, thankfully, had stopped feeling sick and had been for her first scan, accompanied by Miles. She'd dithered about inviting him but he was so ridiculously thrilled and excited about the baby she decided she had to let him be involved as much as possible. And his joyful reaction when he saw the pictures made it all worthwhile.

Down at the vicarage, Heather was feeling less joyful. For a start, having Jade as a paying guest was a cause of almost constant friction despite Brian's list of house rules which Jade seemed to mostly ignore. But the rent made a significant difference so she and Brian had privately decided that they would persevere – for the time being. And then there were the bells; her leafleting campaign had yielded a certain amount of money and Brian's strategy of cold-calling local businesses had also reaped rewards but the gap between the cost of the repairs and the balance in the bank was still considerable – thousands of pounds – even if the Heritage Lottery Grant came through, which wasn't a done deal. Frankly, thought Heather, they needed to make another push at the fundraising. Taking a cup of tea and a plain digestive she knocked on Brian's study door.

'Sorry to disturb you, darling, but I was wondering if you'd heard anything from Belinda about the pudding evening she promised to run.'

Brian looked up from what he was working on at his desk and ran his hands through his hair. 'Er, no,' he answered.

'Do you think I ought to give her a nudge?'

'I suppose.'

'Maybe I'll wander up to the pub later on this morning and have a word. I suspect that Miles might have forgotten about it in the excitement of discovering he's going to be a father.'

'Possibly. How's it all going?'

'Pretty well, I imagine. I haven't seen Bex to ask, to be honest. I know she was very worried that Megan might have issues coming to terms with such a momentous change to their little family but she seems to be coping reasonably well – or, at least, I've not seen anything to the contrary at school.'

'That's good.' Brian bit a chunk off his biscuit.

'Anyway, now we've got Jade's rent money I think we could afford to go to the pudding evening – that is, if Belinda puts it on.'

'Ah… so that's the reason you're keen for it not to be forgotten.' Brian smiled at his wife. 'It's nothing to do with the fundraising and everything to do with having an evening stuffing yourself with treats.'

'Busted,' said Heather. 'And I need some sort of reward for putting up with the tenant from hell. Only don't you dare tell Olivia I said that.'

Later that morning she walked briskly up the road wishing that her winter coat wasn't quite so threadbare while wondering about using some of their spare cash to nip into the Oxfam shop to buy one that would provide more protection against the bitter wind that whipped down the road. She got to the pub a few minutes after opening time and revelled in the warmth that greeted her when she stepped through the door.

'Hi, Heather,' said Bex who was busy putting new, clean beer mats on all the tables. 'We don't often see you in here.'

'No, well… actually, I've not come here to drink.'

'You sure? My treat,' said Bex.

'Well…'

'Oh, go on. Have something like a whisky mac – something nice and warming, it's perishing out there.'

'Tell me about it,' said Heather rubbing her hands together to restore the circulation. She smiled at Bex. 'And a whisky mac would be lovely. I haven't had one of those in years. I think the last time was when I was at uni.'

Bex poured her the drink and popped the money in the till. 'So, now I have tempted you down the path of degradation and depravity, what else can I do for you?'

Heather sniffed her drink. 'If this is degradation and depravity, bring it on.' She took an appreciative sip of her drink. 'Oooh, that's lovely. Takes me right back to my mis-spent youth. Actually, I didn't come here to scrounge a drink but to ask about the pudding evening.'

Bex shook her head. 'Pudding evening?'

'Yes, Belinda's and Miles's contribution to the bell fund.'

'Best you talk to Miles. Belinda's popped out to do the banking from last night.' Bex reached behind her and pushed open the kitchen door. 'Miles,' she called through it, 'if you've got a min, could you have a word with Heather? Something about a pudding evening.'

A muffled answer reached across the bar to Heather and a few seconds later Miles emerged.

'Ah, yes – the pudding evening,' he said. 'Maybe we should fix a date now.'

'That'd be good.'

'I'll have to check it's OK with Belinda when she gets back. And you'll want it sooner rather than later.'

'Please. The bells have already been silent for almost two months and the bell-ringers are finding other places to ring. We're in danger of them being poached permanently by other towers.'

'That doesn't sound very Christian.'

'I don't think that being Christian comes into bell-ringing that much. Half the time they don't even stay for the service because they've got to dash off to ring the bells somewhere else. It can be very disconcerting for poor Brian to have the whole team troop out of the back of the church just as he's getting into his stride.'

'How's the fundraising going?'

'As well as can be expected. The awful thing is that it might all be in vain.'

Miles looked perplexed so Heather told him about Miranda Osborne and her antipathy towards the bells.

'Can she really do that?' Miles was appalled.

'It's happened in other places. And she doesn't seem to be the sort who cares if she is making herself deeply unpopular. You've seen her protests at the market. The trouble is we've looked into it and, because the bells haven't been rung since she moved here, she can't apply for the environmental health people to come out and assess the problem till we've started ringing again. Can you imagine what people will say if we raise all that money only to have her ruin everything?'

'Is she barking mad?'

Heather suppressed a smile. 'You might say that – I couldn't possibly comment.'

'Very diplomatic,' said Miles. 'But she has to be; she moves into a community, which she's presumably chosen because she likes the look of it, and then proceeds to change the things at the very heart of it – like the market and the bells. I mean, where's the sense in that?'

'We have to hope that she doesn't succeed. Now then, let's get some dates fixed before this place gets busy.'

During the lunch break, Ashley made his way to the textiles department and opened the door. The instant he stepped through it he was assailed by memories of having to do sewing as part of Design and Technology when he'd been in year seven. They'd had to make a cushion, he recalled. His had been disastrous – mostly because he'd mucked about with the other boys instead of knuckling down. He still wouldn't be able to thread a sewing machine if his life depended on it.

'Come in, Ashley,' said Mrs Edwards. She smiled at him, which surprised Ashley slightly as, when they'd last encountered each other in this room, she'd mostly threatened him with detentions. 'I need you to slip your blazer and shirt off so we can try your costume on.'

'OK.' He began to unbutton them, feeling a bit self-conscious. He wasn't ashamed of his body, he knew he was pretty fit and toned, but having a teacher see him semi-naked… that was just plain weird.

She pulled aside a curtain and revealed a rail of clothes. He instantly spotted the ones that he and Dan were destined to wear – creations in orange, lime, purple and chrome yellow. Subtle they weren't. Next to them was Cinders' ball dress. She was going to look stunning in the creation in ashes-of-rose pink, spangled with silver stars and with a fishtail train at the back.

'Wow!'

'Do you like it? It is rather gorgeous, isn't it? Megan is going to steal the show, but then so are you,' said Mrs Edwards as she pulled a purple dress trimmed with orange and magenta fake fur off the clothes rail. She unzipped it and gathered the skirts up to the waistline. 'Step into this,' she ordered as she bent down so Ashley could do as he told.

She pulled the dress up over his hips and Ashley shoved his arms into the sleeves before she zipped it up again. 'There!'

Ashley turned to face the full-length mirror in the corner of the room. Jeez. 'Blimey, miss.' Well, it was bright. And big. And completely hideous.

'It'll look better with the wig and make-up.'

'Yeah, I know. And it'll raise a laugh.' And no one would forget him and his role, that was for sure.

'Job done then.' Mrs Edwards began to check the fit. 'Put your arms up,' she said.

Ashley raised them.

'Not too tight?'

'No, miss.'

Mrs Edwards took a pin from the pincushion that was strapped to her wrist and tugged at the fabric at his waist. 'Hmm...' she muttered as she pinned the fabric. 'Right – now the length. I'd like you to stand on this table.' Mrs Edwards pulled a chair out so Ashley could use it as a step to get onto the big cutting table. 'Now, you're going to be wearing heels but we want the audience to be able to see your shoes in all their glory so I'll make the dress shorter than I would normally.' She got busy with her pins again as Ashley slowly rotated on the spot.

'There, all done.'

She held her hand out to steady Ashley as he stepped down then unzipped him.

'Carefully does it,' she advised.

Ashley wriggled and the dress fell down, pooling around his ankles.

'Oh... sorry.' Megan stood in the door, blushing and staring at him.

Ashley bent down and grabbed the dress – hauling it back up to cover his chest, disregarding the fact that he was scattering pins over the floor.

'Ashley! Careful!' admonished Mrs Edwards.

'I'll come back later,' said Megan.

'You'll do nothing of the sort. Ashley, put your shirt on.' She picked it up from where it was dumped on a chair and handed it to him. 'Megan, you can get changed in my storeroom.' Mrs Edwards went to the rail and removed the sparkling gown. Megan's eyes widened.

'Wow – that's so lush.'

Mrs Edwards preened. 'Isn't it? My A-level group are very proud of it.' She opened the door to the storeroom and ushered Megan through. 'Let me know if you need a hand with the zip,' she said as she shut the door.

Ashley stepped out of his dress again and handed it to the teacher.

'I've just got to hope that my alterations are still in place,' she said as she took it.

'Sorry, miss.'

Ashley slipped his shirt on and began to button it up. He took his time – he wanted to see what Megan's dress looked like on.

'Come along, Ashley, chop-chop.'

But as he put on his blazer Megan appeared in the doorway. The dress was breathtaking. Megan was breathtaking. And Ashley felt downhearted. No one would remember him and his performance when they saw her in that dress.

31

'Miss, miss,' said Ashley, chasing after Miss Watkins.

His teacher heard him and stopped. 'Ashley, what can I do for you?'

'It's about acting, miss.'

'Yes?'

'It's… well… I really like it.'

'Yes, I know. You're by far and away the keenest in the drama group.'

Ashley was momentarily wrong-footed. He'd wanted to hear he was the *best* not the *keenest*. He took a breath and decided to ignore the remark. 'I think I want to do more of it.'

'Really? I'll be doing another production in due course.'

'Oh.'

'If you stay in the drama group I'll definitely consider you for a part.'

'That's not what I really meant.'

Miss Watkins raised an eyebrow. 'So?'

'Is there a theatre group I could join? And do you think I'd be good enough?'

'The answer to your second question is yes although you'd probably have to audition. As to the first – I only moved here in the summer and I don't know. I'll ask around in the staffroom. Someone is bound to know.'

'Thanks, miss.'

'Are you sure you want to take this on? It's a big commitment – especially when it's getting close to the actual performances. So...' she smiled, 'do you think you will find the time to do that and the work for your GCSEs?'

'I think so. Anyway, they probably wouldn't give me a part straight off, would they, miss? And that's if they'll even have me.'

'I wouldn't bank on them not wanting you. Local am-dram companies often have loads of grown-ups in them but precious few kids. It's relatively easy to make someone look old but it's a bit of a stretch for the poor old make-up artist to turn a pensioner into a teenager. Anyway, as I said, I'll ask around. Now, you'd better get going or you'll be late for your next lesson.'

Miss Watkins walked off along the corridor, her heels tip-tapping on the tiles as Ashley thought about what she'd said about auditions. Could he use a speech from the panto? No, he didn't think that would be suitable. Anyway, most of his dialogue consisted of swift repartee between him and his 'ugly sister'. Perhaps there were recommended pieces for actors to use? He glanced up and down the corridor to make sure there wasn't a member of staff around and pulled his phone out of his pocket. Pupils were permitted to bring phones into school but their use was strictly prohibited except in proper breaks. He quickly switched it on and tapped into Google. *Top ten choices for audition pieces,* he typed. *Hamlet... Macbeth... Love's Labour's Lost... The Seagull* by Chekhov... Who the hell was Chekhov?

'Pullen!'

Ashley jumped and almost dropped his phone. Shit. Old man Johnson had caught him.

'Hand it over,' said Mr Johnson.

'But, sir...'

'You know the rules perfectly well.'

'Yes, sir,' sulked Ashley. He passed his phone to his maths teacher.

'Detention. Lunchtime,' barked his nemesis. 'See me at the staffroom, twelve thirty.'

'Sir.'

Ashley turned and walked quickly away from Mr Johnson and into the classroom for his next lesson – maths with Mr Johnson. He took his seat, throwing his backpack onto the floor beside his desk before having to almost immediately stand up again as his teacher entered the room.

'Morning, class,' he said as he took his place behind the desk at the front.

'Morning, Mr Johnson,' chanted thirty-one pupils in unison.

'Sit.'

Chairs scraped as they all did as they were told.

'It seems I have to remind you that the use of mobile phones is not allowed between lessons. I will not tolerate blatant flouting of the school rules. Do I make myself clear?'

'Yes, sir.' The pupils looked around the class to determine who the culprit was, although it wasn't difficult to work it out as Ashley's sullen face flared red with guilt and embarrassment.

'That was harsh,' said Sophie to Ashley as they left the classroom an hour later. 'He didn't have to single you out like that.'

'I hate him,' said Ashley vehemently. 'The bastard gave me a lunchtime detention.'

Sophie gave him a sympathetic smile.

'He's such a twat-faced git,' said Ashley.

'Am I?' said a voice behind him.

Ashley froze as he realised who it was.

'I think,' said Mr Johnson, 'you've just earned yourself an after-school detention, as well. Insubordination, bad language, disrespect… I'll give you the slip for your mother to sign when I see you at lunchtime. Don't make any plans for tomorrow.' He gave Ashley a cold stare before he swept off.

'But there's a rehearsal tomorrow,' whispered Ashley, horrified. 'I'll miss it.'

'That won't cut any ice with him. Best you apologise to Miss Watkins.'

Ashley punched the wall next to him and then regretted it as he bruised his knuckles. 'Everything is so unfair.' He looked close to tears.

'It's only a rehearsal.'

'You don't get it. You don't understand anything.' He strode off.

At lunchtime, Ashley reported, as directed, to the staffroom door. He rang the bell, asked to see Mr Johnson and then waited.

'Ah – Ashley,' said Miss Watkins as she headed towards the room and her sandwiches.

'Miss.'

'I've got some good news; I've found there's a member of staff who is in the theatre group. It's Mr Johnson, he's their treasurer. I'm sure he'll be thrilled to hear you want to join the company.' Mr Johnson exited the staffroom, answering Ashley's request to see him. 'Oh... Malcolm. We were just talking about you.'

Mr Johnson looked from Miss Watkins to Ashley and back. 'If this is because I have given Pullen an after-school detention for tomorrow and he'll miss a rehearsal, let me inform you now that I am not prepared for an after-school activity to take precedence over a disciplinary matter.'

'I... no... that wasn't it,' said Miss Watkins, confused.

'Good.'

'No, Ashley wants to join the theatre company. I was telling him he should talk to you.'

Mr Johnson sneered at Ashley. 'Given his extreme disrespect towards his elders and betters I am not sure he is the sort of material the theatre company would want.'

'I'm sorry?' said Miss Watkins – even more confused.

'It doesn't matter,' mumbled Ashley.

'Thank you for your interest in doing our recruiting for us,' said Mr Johnson, 'but maybe it would be better if you stuck with your own drama group.'

Miss Watkins stared at him, hardly believing her ears before she sniffed in anger and stomped into the staffroom.

'And if you think,' said Mr Johnson, 'you can curry favour with me by pretending to be interested in real acting as opposed to larking about on the school stage, you can forget it. Right...' he handed a slip of paper to Ashley, 'your mother must sign this and return it by tomorrow or the punishment will be doubled. And for your lunchtime detention you are to clear all the litter from the main playing field.' He handed Ashley a black plastic sack and a litter-picker. 'No slacking; I'll come and check on your progress shortly.'

'Yes, Mr Johnson.' Ashley stuffed the paper in his pocket and took the other objects before slouching away to the playing field. As he went his head was filled with dark and uncharitable thoughts – mostly involving painful and lingering ways in which he hoped Mr Johnson would meet his end.

As December fast approached, the panto progressed, the coolness between Ashley and Megan continued, the Co-op began to stock chocolate advent calendars, a massive Christmas tree was delivered and erected outside the front of the town hall, the local radio station dusted off its collection of Christmas records and added them to the playlist, progress on the new wind turbine seemed to stall – much to Olivia's delight – Alfie was becoming completely hyper about his impending birthday *and* the fact that Christmas was on its way and Bex's pregnancy began to show.

'Are you all right?' asked Belinda as Bex eased her back and flexed her shoulders as she finished emptying the glass washer. It was five minutes to opening time and this was the last job on that morning's list before Belinda unlocked the door.

'Just fine.' Bex dumped the wire basket on the bar and began to put the glasses on the shelves.

'Are you sure you should be on your feet for half the day?'

'Belinda, I'm pregnant not ill.'

'I know but—'

'But nothing.'

'But Miles will never forgive me if you overdo things.'

'And how do you think I coped, racing around after a toddler when I was in the family way with Alfie? Honestly, Lewis weighed just as much as a crate of mixers and, when he made me carry him, he was wriggly to boot. Also, neither the stock nor the customers indulge in throwing tantrums.'

'I dunno,' muttered Belinda, 'we get the odd one at closing time.'

'And, these days, when I'm not working I can put my feet up on the sofa.'

'If you say so.' Belinda didn't sound convinced. 'Anyway, the schools will be breaking up for Christmas soon, so I suppose you can take it a bit easier. I've got your shifts covered, by the way – the usual crew, back from uni.'

'Great – but you're mistaken about taking it easy. I've got a birthday party to organise for Alfie the day school breaks up and I've got my mum and dad coming down from the Lakes; I finally persuaded them to get the train.' She sighed at the thought of all she had to do over the coming weeks. 'I'm going to have a houseful for the entire holiday. Don't get me wrong I am *so* looking forward to seeing them and everything else but sometimes it all seems a bit overwhelming and I can't expect Mum and Dad to flog all this way for just a few days so they're staying for a fortnight.'

'You know what they say about visitors?'

'What?'

'They're like fish – they stink after three days. Not that I'm saying your parents are difficult.'

'You haven't met them, have you?' said Bex with a wry grin. 'And they're not tricky, not really, but Dad is losing his sight so we're limited as to what we can all do. I think I'll run out of ideas way before we get to the end of the two weeks.'

'Will they be here in time for the school panto? There's a lot of people in the town talking about it. Did I hear it's on for four performances?'

Bex nodded. 'No, they're going to miss that. I think Megan will be on her knees by the time it's all over; Thursday, Friday *and* Saturday nights plus a matinée Saturday afternoon. That's the one I'll be taking the boys to. I kind of feel I ought to go to all of them but I think that'll be taking the "doting parent" bit a tad too far. Besides, where am I going to find a babysitter?'

'Olivia's Jade'll probably do it for you – if you asked nicely.'

'Actually the babysitting-card is what I've played so don't tell her about Jade. I really don't think I could sit through anything four times on the bounce. She's happy that the boys and I will be at the matinee and they are thrilled at the thought of having a special Christmas treat and seeing their big sister on stage. And Miles is going to the first night. I did think about getting tickets to the Saturday night performance but I think it would have been too much for Alfie. And for me, to be honest. These days I'm totally whacked by about nine and catatonic with exhaustion if I'm up much later than ten. I was the same with both my other pregnancies.'

Belinda walked across the carpet and drew back the bolt on the front door.

'Have you told your mum and dad about the baby?'

Bex stayed silent a little too long.

'Do I take that as a no?'

'I've told them I'm seeing someone. I thought it might be better to wait until I could break it to them in person rather than over the phone.'

'What about Richard's parents?'

Bex shook her head.

'You're putting that off too?'

Bex nodded. 'The thing is, I know they adore their grandchildren but I always kind of felt they didn't entirely approve of me. There was a phrase that one of Richard's work colleagues used to use about some of his golf shots. He'd call them daughter-in-law strokes.'

'Huh?'

'Not quite what he'd hoped for,' explained Bex.

Belinda hooted.

'I think my mother-in-law thought of me a bit like that.'

'Surely not.'

'Oh, she never said as much – but you know… I could tell.'

'Then she's mad. Absolutely bonkers. But I can see this isn't going to make things easier.'

Bex sighed. 'No, it's not.'

32

Megan stood on stage, dressed in rags, with a broom in her hand, in front of the plasterboard fireplace. Under the stage lights, as she looked down, she could see the hem of her costume was shaking in rhythm with her knees. She couldn't remember *ever* feeling this nervous. Would she remember her lines? Would she remember all the stage directions? Would the transformation scene work? Dear God, there was so much that might go wrong. On the other side of the heavy velour curtain she could hear the hubbub of the audience. She wished Bex was out there but she'd have to make do with Miles rooting for her. And she knew he would. He'd promised he'd be embarrassing he'd whoop and holler so loud.

'But, you won't hear me because everyone else will be doing that! It's going to be fab-u-lous.'

Over the last few weeks she'd realised how kind he was to Bex, how great he was with the boys, how attentive he was – doing little things to make life easier for everyone; a bit of cooking, playing with her half-brothers, fixing things, helping in the garden... And she rather liked it. She liked the fact he was becoming part of the family more and more. He'd even sent her a text telling her to *knock 'em dead*. She knew he wouldn't have wanted it to make her have a bit of a weep, but it had – the message should have been from her dad. It should have been him whooping and hollering and clapping. But then she'd dashed the tears away before they could spoil her stage make-up and been grateful that she should be lucky enough to have someone else who cared. Bex had sent her a big bunch of flowers – *Every leading lady needs flowers on her first night* – which had also made her well up and so, what with the audience in their seats and the expectations of her family weighing on her, there was no way she could do a runner now.

'Two minutes,' whispered Miss Watkins from the wings.

Megan's heart did a crazy backflip and her jelly-knees shook so much she had to lean on her broom for support.

The two minutes inched past and then the audience fell silent. The house lights must have dimmed. Any second now…

With a whoosh the curtain rose and Cinders was in the spotlight.

By the end of the first act Megan had overcome her nerves and was loving the limelight. She was thrilled as the audience laughed at the capers on stage, she adored the way they booed and hissed the wicked stepmother, the way they partook in all the cheesy 'behind you' and 'oh, no he isn't' routines. Her legs had long since stopped shaking and she felt relaxed and confident, now the adrenalin had been banished by a dopamine rush. She skipped off the stage at the end of the act and floated down the stairs from the wings and into the classroom that was being used as the girls' dressing room.

As she went through the door other cast members and the backstage team clapped which made Megan flush with pleasure and embarrassment. Miss Watkins gave her a big hug.

'Brilliant. Just brilliant.'

Megan flopped down onto a chair and smiled. 'Aren't the audience great?' she said.

'Of course they are but it's because they're having a fab time.' Miss Watkins clapped her hands for silence. 'Right, everyone.'

She looked round at the expectant faces. 'You've all got fifteen minutes in this interval while they change the set. Have a drink, check your make-up, go to the loo... I'm just going across the corridor to see how the boys are getting on. But everyone is doing wonderfully. Keep up the good work.'

The fifteen minutes raced by and it seemed to Megan that it had only been moments since she'd left the stage before she was back on it again with Ash and Dan, trying to lace them into their ballgowns. The audience was rocking with laughter at the boys' antics and despite the fact that the pair both had an equal number of gags and prat-falls there was no doubt that Ashley was the one who stole the limelight. Even Megan, who had seen his performance dozens of times in rehearsals and who knew his lines almost as well as her own, was taken aback by the way his performance soared now he was in front of an audience. He owned the stage and his timing was impeccable. Megan was hard-pressed to speak her own lines clearly and with a straight face because inside she was howling with laughter, especially when he produced a couple of tricks he'd kept hidden from the cast before and added several ad libs and asides to the audience.

Finally, the two boys swept off to the ball and she was left alone on the stage while the audience simmered down ready for the appearance of the fairy godmother who arrived with a puff of smoke and a shower of glitter dust from above. Pleasingly, the entire audience went 'oooh' right on cue.

The transformation scene went seamlessly and the team backstage had Megan out of her rags and into her ballgown in five seconds flat while the audience was distracted by the appearance of the pumpkin coach and six Year Sevens dressed as prancing ponies which effectively hid her from view as she changed. She then stepped out of the carriage door and into the middle of the stage in her beautiful dress to a huge round of applause which was only slightly less ear-splitting than the applause which erupted as the final curtain came down.

As the curtain lifted again for Megan, Ash and the rest to take their bow they were stunned to see they were the object of a standing ovation. They had three more curtain calls before they were allowed to leave the stage, all of the cast grinning from ear to ear. As she left the stage and the lights began to dim, Megan remembered sitting on the sofa on a wet Saturday afternoon with her dad and Bex watching *My Fair Lady* on the box and that scene when Eliza sang 'I could have danced all night'. She had an epiphany as to why Eliza had felt so wired, so hyper, so utterly, totally alive. She could dance all night too.

She went back to the dressing room and took off her beautiful gown, hung it up carefully and got back into her street clothes before she got busy with the wet-wipes, cotton wool and baby lotion and stripped off all the slap to get back to normal. She suspected she was going to find little patches of pancake for days to come. While she was doing that Miss Watkins came in.

'You were all stars,' she said. She stopped and swallowed. 'I couldn't have been more proud of all of you if you were my own kids.' Megan saw her eyes glistening. Were those real tears? 'When I planned this I thought it might be quite fun and we'd achieve a good show but it wasn't a good show.' She paused. 'It was a fabulous show. You worked so hard for this result and it has exceeded all of my dreams and hopes and aspirations.'

The girls in the classroom shuffled. Few had ever had such effusive praise from a staff member.

'And what's more, I know this is going to get better and better. I can't wait for the final performance. Today Little Woodford, tomorrow – Broadway!'

Everyone laughed and there was a chorus of 'we couldn't have done it without you, miss,' and 'thank you, but it was your idea,' and 'aww, too kind.' But despite the self-deprecatory remarks everyone stood a bit taller with their chins a little higher.

When Megan had got herself back to something that resembled her normal self she said goodbye to everyone and slipped round to the school entrance hall where she'd arranged to meet Miles. He was waiting for her along with a gaggle of other parents and friends of other members of the cast and crew.

As Megan approached Miles he began to applaud again.

'You were wonderful, sweetie. Just brilliant. I am so proud to know you. It was a terrific panto.'

Megan felt her face burning again. 'Thanks,' she mumbled. 'I was lucky to have such a good part.'

'And that friend of yours, Ashley. His comic timing was unbelievable.'

'He was good, wasn't he?' Megan felt more comfortable as the spotlight fell away from her. The two began to walk out of the school. 'I got arsey with him about being obsessive about his acting but he's got proper talent, hasn't he?'

Miles nodded. 'He has.'

'And you're not just saying it was good, you know… because…'

'Because I ought to? Absolutely not!'

They reached the end of the school drive and headed along the road that led to the town centre.

'Wait! Wait for me.'

They turned and saw Ashley racing to catch up.

'Hi,' said Miles. 'We haven't been introduced. I'm a friend of Megan's – Miles, Miles Patterson. But I know who *you* are – you're the star of the show.'

Even in the sodium street lights it was plain that Ashley was blushing furiously. 'Nah. I was just an ugly sister.'

It was time, thought Megan, to offer a proper olive branch to Ashley. 'Miles is right, everyone's saying how brill you were. Genius.' She didn't mind he'd stolen the show. She knew her role had been a bit like how Miss Watkins had described Prince Charming's one to Ashley – *he just struts around and poses*. All she'd had to do was remember her lines and look pretty. 'You were so funny. You even had me in stitches.'

'Really?'

Megan nodded. 'That scene where I was getting you and Dan into your dresses... I don't know how I kept going. I couldn't look at you half the time because if I had I'd have lost it. I was supposed to be feeling resentful and jealous and all I wanted to do was to cry with laughter. I mean, what a mad idea to have your bows wired up so they spun round.'

'Oh, that was ace,' agreed Miles.

'You never did that stuff in rehearsals,' said Megan. 'Nor the bit with the escaping helium balloon coming out of your cleavage.'

'No, I thought it would be better if I surprised everyone on the night. I thought it would have more impact.'

'It certainly had that,' said Miles. 'Touches of comic genius.'

'Thanks. Well, this is my turning,' said Ashley. 'See you at school tomorrow,' he said as he left.

'If I can get near you for crowds of adoring groupies,' Megan called after him. After they'd walked on a few paces she added, 'I think he's serious about his acting.'

'I think he should be,' said Miles. 'And he seems like such a nice lad too.'

Megan thought about him – how buff he was, how good-looking – and realised that she probably fell into the category of 'adoring groupie'. Or maybe it was more than that. Shame he didn't seem to reciprocate the feeling.

33

Ashley let himself into his mum's council house and went into the sitting room. His gran was there too.

'Hi, babe,' said Amy. 'How did it go?'

'Oh, Mum!'

'That good, eh?'

'It was… it was…' He shrugged but his face said it all.

'You remembered your lines, then,' said Mags.

Ashley nodded.

'We were just saying,' said Amy, 'we can't wait to see you on Saturday night.'

'It'll be even better by then,' said Ashley. 'We were all a bit nervous tonight, not sure how it would go, not sure it'd all work, but, oh, Mum…'

'Well, maybe I shouldn't… but there's a couple of beers left over from when Billy used to come round. Seeing as how you're over sixteen and seeing as how you're as high as a kite already I think you should crack one open while you tell us all about it.'

'Really, Mum?'

'I don't see why not. And the booze might help you get off to sleep because, looking at you, I can't see you calming down this side of the crack of doom. Ain't that right, Mum?'

Mags nodded.

'They're under the stairs,' said Amy.

Ash didn't need telling twice and a few seconds later he returned to the living room with a can of Stella and a glass.

'So... tell us all about it,' encouraged Amy.

'Well...' started Ashley before he took a sip of his drink. Ten minutes later he had got to his drama teacher's reaction: '... and Miss Watkins was almost crying she was so pleased.'

'Looks like we're in for a proper treat,' said Mags.

Ashley drained his glass. The drink emboldened him. 'Mum, Gran... I think... no, I'm sure...'

'What?' said Amy. 'Spit it out.'

'I want to go to drama school.'

'You what?' Amy almost choked. 'Don't be daft, Ash, why would you want to do that?'

'What?' Ash was genuinely bewildered.

'But drama school is for ... well, not people like us. Not *normal* people.'

'Shit, Mum, I've no idea what you're on about.'

'People like us don't do poncy stuff like that,' said Amy.

'What?' Ashley's voice was an octave higher than normal.

'And who ever heard of a council estate kid making a living from prancing about on a stage?' added his mother.

'Load of actors come from estates like this.'

'Yeah? Name one.'

Ashley struggled. His mind went blank, then he remembered a name. 'Cheryl Cole – or whatever she's called these days – did.'

'That's different, she won a talent show.'

Ashley was so bemused by the logic he couldn't find an answer.

Amy and Mags exchanged triumphant looks and Ashley's euphoric mood popped. He put his empty beer can and his dirty glass on the table and stood up. There was no point in arguing with them – they didn't get it and they never would.

'Night, Gran. Night, Mum.' He sloped up the stairs. They didn't understand. No one understood. But he clutched onto one little straw of hope. Miss Watkins had told him that old man Johnson had been in the audience and had told her in the interval that he was surprised how talented some of the cast were.

'He was talking about you,' she'd said. 'I know he was. I also know you and he have had a falling-out but why don't you try out for the Woodford Players? Mr Johnson is only the treasurer when all's said and done, not the director or the artistic director... Why don't you?'

Ashley made his mind up as he shut his bedroom door. The theatre group rehearsed on a Tuesday. In the New Year he'd be there and he didn't care what Mr Johnson said or did. He was going to join them.

'Oh, Megan,' said Bex as she walked her daughter home after the Saturday matinée, with Lewis and Alfie still squealing with laughter as they exchanged their recent memories of the panto. 'Megan, I thought I'd burst with pride. You were so brilliant, so lovely.'

'Thanks, Bex,' she mumbled.

'I have to say, I did think that Miles might have been exaggerating but he underplayed it if anything. And your pal Ashley... where did that come from?'

'Everyone is saying that.'

'With good reason. He had that audience in the palm of his hand.' They walked in silence for a few paces. 'You won't know what to do with yourself when this is all over.'

Megan shook her head. 'I do, I'm going to sleep and sleep.'

'You do that. Tomorrow you don't have to do anything so you can lie in as long as you like.'

'Until I have to get up to do my homework. And then it'll be Christmas in a couple of weeks. And then mocks.' She grimaced but then cheered up with, 'But there's a party tonight to look forward to.'

'I've asked Miles if he'll come and collect you from that.'

'Miles?'

'I can't come out at that time – who will stay with the boys?'

'I suppose.'

'You won't do anything silly at the party tonight, will you?'

'Bex!'

'Sorry, I know I can trust you.'

'Didn't sound like it.'

'Well… you just steer clear of any sex or drugs or rock and roll.'

Megan rolled her eyes and grinned. 'Yeah, promise, although I have it on good authority that there won't be *any* rock and roll going on. As for the rest…' She glanced at Bex who was also smiling. 'Anyway, Miss Watkins will be there, and Mrs Edwards, to say nothing of the teachers from IT who did the lighting and the ones from the art department. Trust me, there's no chance of anyone getting away with anything. Nothing at all.'

'OK, OK, I'm reassured. And Miles'll be there at midnight.'

'I won't be late. I know what happens to girls who stay at parties after midnight, remember.'

The curtain came down on the final performance and the noise in the auditorium went off the scale. Quite apart from clapping, people stamped their feet, whistled, whooped, shouted and, when the curtain went back up again for the walkdown, the wall of sound that burst onto the stage was ear-splitting. Megan, in the centre, thought she'd cry with happiness and pride and her smile was so broad her face ached. When the audience finally started to settle down, Mr Smithson, the headteacher, got up on the stage and thanked the cast and crew for everything they'd done.

'This was all quite remarkable,' he said. 'Not the least because I think you'll all agree that we have discovered some remarkable talent, not just in the drama department but also with our textiles group, in the young artists we have here who did the painting and set design and even in the IT and tech department with the effects they achieved through lighting and sound. But our especial thanks must go to Miss Watkins whose brainchild this was in the first place. Ashley? Dan?'

And with this cue, Ashley and Dan left their places in the line-up; Dan to drag Miss Watkins from one side of the wings into the centre of the stage and Ashley to collect a massive bouquet of flowers from the other wing and present it to her. The audience went mad once again and the curtain fell for a final time.

At the party afterwards, Ashley was the centre of attention and Megan found herself feeling a little resentful – even more so when she tried to catch his eye and he didn't respond; he was too busy hoovering up the praise. She'd been joking when she'd made the comment about adoring groupies but it now seemed that her glib remark had turned into reality. She remembered that after the first night, when she'd told him how good he'd been he hadn't reciprocated with compliments about her performance. She was right – he *was* self-obsessed. But, despite that, she still fancied him and she couldn't help it. But it was a one-way street. Megan's euphoria slowly trickled away and she was glad when midnight came and she could go home.

34

On the following Monday evening, Heather slicked on a coat of lipstick and pursed her lips in her dressing table mirror to check the effect. You'll do, she told herself. She grabbed her winter coat from the cupboard and pottered downstairs and into the kitchen.

'Evening, Jade,' said Heather, as she saw her lodger standing by the counter, making a cup of tea. How could anyone make such a mess while making a hot drink?

'Hi, Heather. Want one?' she asked as she lifted the kettle.

'No, thanks.' And risk further chaos? And did she risk a row and mention the mess? Heather bottled out. 'No, you're good. Brian and I are going out to the pudding evening at the pub.'

'Yes, you said, yesterday. And to judge by the posters it looks like a chocoholic's idea of heaven on earth.'

'Oh, yes indeedy!' Heather smacked her lips in anticipation. 'You didn't fancy it?'

'Heather, I'm going to get as fat as a pig over Christmas – I don't need to add to the damage by stuffing myself with puddings as well.'

Heather eyed Jade. 'You, fat? I'd like to see it. You can only be nine stone soaking wet.'

'I wish. Anyway, I hope you and Brian have a great time and raise a zillion pounds for the bells.'

'Thank you.' Heather walked out into the hall. 'Brian. Brian!'

The study door opened and Brian appeared. 'Yes, dear?'

'Time we were off.'

'Off where?'

'The pudding evening.'

'Oh. Is it tonight?'

Heather shook her head as she put her gloves on. 'Yes. And as it's in aid of your bells I suggest you get your skates on. You, of all people, should be there on time.'

'Righty-o, sweetie.' He disappeared again and re-emerged a minute later pulling on his tatty old jacket. Heather despaired. It was rare they went out in the evening to anything other than church-related events and she thought that it might be nice if, once in a while, he made an effort.

Brian must have caught the expression on her face. 'What? What's the matter?'

'Nothing.'

He looked down at his clothes. 'It's only the pub, Heather.'

'Yes, yes it is.'

Brian grabbed his mac off the hook in the porch and the pair let themselves out of the house. With their arms linked they made their way into the town.

'Jade was in the kitchen when we left,' she told Brian.

He sighed. 'How bad?'

'Like a bomb had gone off. And I said nothing because I didn't want to come out feeling angry – it would spoil the evening and I am so looking forward to it.'

'I'll have another word.'

'No, it's my turn. And we'll not say anything to Olivia. Deal?'

'Deal.'

They reached the pub, pushed open the door and a barrage of sound greeted them along with the waft of hot chocolate, beer and caramelised sugar. The place was rammed. Brian and Heather wove their way through the tables to where Olivia and Bex were sitting.

'Hello, you two. Thank goodness you saved us places,' said Heather as she took off her coat. She draped it over the back of her chair. She dipped over the table to give her friends a peck on the cheek. 'Brian, don't stand there, go and buy a bottle of something.'

'No need,' said Bex. 'We've got one on the go.' She picked up a bottle of Merlot. 'That is if you don't mind drinking red. And I took the liberty of buying you a pint, Brian. There's one in the barrel for you. I thought you might prefer that to start off with.'

'Oh, Bex, you shouldn't have done, but thank you, thank you very much.'

Brian went off to join the throng crowding round the bar to collect his drink and Olivia poured a glass for Heather.

'Well, I must say this is very well attended,' said Heather looking around.

'Good, isn't it? Miles said it's a sell-out,' said Bex.

'And how are you and Miles?' asked Heather.

'Good, thanks. He's even better with the boys – as if that's possible – and even Megan seems to have decided that he's not evil incarnate.' Heather laughed. 'OK, I exaggerate. And I think she's accepted that it's not morally unacceptable for a widow to think about having another relationship.'

Heather put her hand on Bex's. 'That's good. And how's the pregnancy going?'

'It's fine. All going swimmingly.'

'I'm glad.' Heather picked up the printed menu card that was lying on the table. 'So what has Miles got for our delectation?' She ran her eye down it. 'Hang on... what's with the steak and kidney pudding?'

'That's to start with,' said Bex. 'Miles thought that no one would have had supper before they came out so he's made some teeny little individual ones that he's going to serve up with petits pois and baby carrots before we get onto the main event. A sort of savoury *amuse bouche*.'

'What an ace idea.'

Brian returned with his beer just as the kitchen door opened and the staff brought in especially for the occasion appeared carrying the first of dozens of plates of food. The level of conversation quickly died as the guests were served and people concentrated on eating rather than talking.

The steak and kidney puddings were followed by the sweet variety; sticky toffee, bread and butter, spotted dick, chocolate sponge... all served with a choice of cream or custard. Brian began to flag.

'Stop, please,' he groaned, holding his stomach.

'Wimp,' said Heather cheerfully as she accepted a spoonful of apple crumble. 'Look, even Bex is managing another pud.'

'Yes, but I am eating for two.'

'I'm not,' said Olivia. 'I'm just being greedy!'

But even they had to admit defeat by the time they got to the chocolate fondant and decided that what they needed most was a cup of coffee to round things off.

Bex went to the bar to order them.

'Fab evening,' she told Belinda.

'And Miles reckons that once we've taken out our expenses we can donate over five hundred to the fund.'

'But that's brilliant. Does Brian know?'

'Not yet. Miles is going to make an announcement in a couple of minutes. Go and sit down. I'll get one of the girls to bring your coffees over.'

As the coffees arrived at their table so Miles came out of the kitchen. He was greeted with a round of applause and a rousing chorus of 'For he's a jolly good fellow!'

'Thank you, thank you.' He held up his hand for silence and people shushed each other loudly. The sound was like air being expelled from a dozen bike tyres. Silence gradually fell. 'Thank you. Thank you for supporting this event, thank you for eating the puddings but most of all thank for the contribution you have all made to the bell fund. Brian... If you'd like to come here please...'

Brian stood up and squeezed between the tables and chairs to reach Miles. He paused at a particularly narrow point. 'You know,' he said, turning to address his fellow diners, 'a couple of hours ago I slipped through this gap with no trouble at all. But now...' He looked around in mock despair as one guest had to move to let him through. Everyone laughed.

'Anyway,' said Miles as Brian reached him. 'I have here a cheque for five hundred and forty pounds, which is the profit from tonight.'

'But that's wonderful,' said Brian, beaming. 'Just wonderful. And the good news is that yesterday I heard that that the full amount that we applied for from the Heritage Lottery Fund has been approved. As a result of that and the generosity of the people of this fabulous town we can instruct the bell foundry to start work straight after Christmas.'

Everyone cheered and clapped and some people banged their pudding plates with their spoons. Heather sat there, looking as if she might cry.

As Brian came back to the table she stood up and hugged him. 'You didn't tell me!'

'I thought you'd enjoy the surprise.'

'I did, it was wonderful. What a fabulous Christmas present.'

'All we have to hope for now,' said Olivia, 'is that *that woman* doesn't mess things up with her petition to keep the bells silent.'

Heather's face darkened. 'Indeed. You know she's still down the market most Wednesdays, yelling about meat being murder.'

Olivia shook her head. 'I don't get why someone would move to a town and then try and change everything about the place when – presumably – they liked what they saw when they were thinking of buying a house.'

'Maybe, in her head, she thinks she's making it better.'

'If she consulted the locals she'd soon discover that we don't want *better* – we want it left alone.'

*

268

Two days later, up at The Grange, *that woman* picked up the local newspaper off the doormat and walked over to the kitchen to make herself a soya milk latte while she read it. Frankly, Miranda didn't give a toss about what the townspeople got up to in the course of their humdrum little lives – did anyone *really* care if Amelia Gutbucket (or whatever the chubby teenager, leering out of a picture on the back page was called) got a medal for swimming? God, if that was the best the neighbourhood newshounds could come up with then they must be suicidal about their career prospects. However, the local paper wasn't just about local news; she liked to keep abreast of the wider picture, to see what the council might be getting up to, whether the town was going to be subjected to further housing development, whether a new road or, heaven forefend, an airport might get proposed. And that last fear wasn't beyond the bounds of possibility – look at Luton and Stansted. She'd moved out of London to get away from gridlocked traffic, noise, pollution and ridiculous numbers of people, and she wasn't going to countenance those problems creeping into Little Woodford because the country bumpkins that made up the town council didn't know how to run a proper protest to nip such proposals in the bud.

She cast an eye over the front page. *Vicar Thrilled by Lottery Grant*. And there was a picture of the vicar and his mousy little wife, grinning like loons with the belfry in the background. She threw the paper onto the counter. Over her dead body. Her coffee forgotten, she sat on a stool and stared across the vast, mostly empty, expanse of her new home and at the white Christmas tree decorated with identical but graded silver baubles as she wondered how best she might stop the din that the bells would create. She did *not* want her weekends ruined by the endless clanging of tuneless bells for weddings and services. And that was before the bell-ringers practised... which presumably they did, despite the evidence to the contrary, which was bound to happen at least once a week. No, she wasn't having it.

Miranda put on her coat and let herself out of the house. She noticed the blades of her recently installed wind turbine were barely turning in the almost still air. Even so, they'd be generating the odd kilowatt hour. All grist to the environmental mill. She pressed the button on her key fob and opened the garage door to reveal her shiny hybrid Range Rover. A couple of minutes later she'd backed it out of the garage and was trawling along the high street, trying to find a parking space. Bugger – in her irritation at the news about the church bells she'd forgotten it was market day. Moreover, it was the last market day before Christmas. The town was teeming with locals, wrapped up against the bright, cold weather and cluttering up the pavements with their pushchairs and wheeled shopping baskets. Miranda sighed crossly as she drove past the town hall and then the rec and there was *still* no sign of a space. She turned the car round and retraced her route. Nothing. Really! Couldn't some of these people have walked into town? She passed the town hall a second time – still nothing – and decided to see if there might be a chance of a space in the station car park. But that was full too. She continued on into Beeching Rise. Now that was an estate that was going to go downhill, if she was any sort of judge. But at least there were no parking restrictions and it was close to the town centre. She just had to hope that if she parked on this ghastly development no one would vandalise her car. She drew up alongside the kerb and got out.

'You can't park there.'

Miranda spun round. 'I beg your pardon.'

'You can't park there, you're blocking my drive,' repeated the woman in a surprisingly educated and cultured voice for someone who lived in a place like this. She was apparently about to go somewhere because she was holding the handlebars of her bike. So if she was going out by bike, what was her problem?

Miranda said as much to the woman who looked vaguely familiar – she was sure she recognised her from somewhere. 'Besides, I'm only going to be a couple of minutes.' Even so, she checked where her car was in relation to the dropped kerb. She had to concede it was across about a foot of it but it was hardly *blocked*. Any driver with any nous would be able to get past if they needed to.

'It's Mrs Osborne, isn't it?'

Miranda was startled. 'Yes. How—'

'This is a small town, Mrs Osborne.'

'Yes but—'

'And I have lived here for a long time.'

That was a lie. This estate was brand new.

The woman put her foot on the pedal and prepared to mount her bike. 'Take it from me, it's a mistake to make yourself unpopular in a place like this. No one likes your protest at the market, or your petition against the bells, or your wind turbine. It's a total eyesore and it's causing a lot of resentment. People around here have long memories.' She pushed off on her bike and rode away. She turned and called over her shoulder, 'Very long.'

'Like I care,' muttered Miranda. She sniffed then made her way towards the town hall feeling unaccustomedly rattled.

However, her slight unease only made her more determined and she stamped into the town hall and marched up to the desk. Imperiously she pinged the bell. And why wasn't this place manned? she wondered.

'Yes,' said a woman who appeared from the back offices.

'I want to see your environmental health officer – I want to make a complaint about noise pollution.'

'I'm sorry, but we don't have one.'

'But you must.'

'This is a parish council. Environmental health is a district responsibility.'

Miranda stared at the woman to try and judge if she was being fobbed off. 'Then I'd like you to contact him.'

'*She* can be contacted through the district council website.'

'So you are refusing to help me.'

There was a tiny pause before the receptionist said, 'Not in the least. It would be easier all round if you fill out the appropriate forms via the website. Although, if the noise is coming from one of your neighbours, maybe a friendly word first…?'

'It's not *a neighbour*. And a "friendly word", as you so tweely put it, probably won't work. This is general noise pollution that affects the entire town.'

The receptionist gestured to the computer terminal sitting in the corner of the town hall's reception area. 'I can't think of anything of that nature in the town.' She looked perplexed. 'And, certainly, we've not had any other complaints from the residents.'

'Really?' Probably because they were all too stupid to know that they could.

'If you need to make a formal complaint, you can do it from here if you don't have a computer at home.'

'Of course I've got a computer,' snapped Miranda.

'Search for Cattebury District council and then environmental health and you'll find everything you need to know.'

Did this wretched woman think she was stupid? 'I know how to use a search engine.'

'Good. Then if that's everything?' The woman turned to go back into her hidey-hole.

'One more thing…'

'Yes.'

'I've heard a rumour that my very eco-friendly, micro-generation turbine is a cause of dissent in this town.'

'Ah – *your* turbine. You must live at The Grange. And, yes, we've had enquiries about it.'

'Really?'

'Mostly residents want to know if it's legal.'

'Of course it's legal.'

'Yes, so we understand.'

'Do you think I would be so irresponsible as to flout permitted development laws?'

'Mrs…?'

'Osborne.'

'Mrs Osborne, I believe you've also protested against some of the market traders.'

'I have been exercising my right to freedom of speech. Besides, eating meat is vile.'

'If you say so. It's just this is a small town in the heart of a farming community and people here are inclined to like the way things are. And I don't know what this noise is that you're so dead set against, but if you're in a minority I would imagine that the environmental health officer is unlikely to find in your favour. You might be wasting your time.'

'We'll see, won't we?'

'Indeed.'

The two women eyeballed each other until Miranda decided she had better things to do than try and stare down this jumped-up functionary. But she didn't like the fact that two people, in the space of just a few minutes, had made comment about her turbine and her protest. Then she told herself that these people just needed educating and to do that she needed to stick to her guns.

Cynthia, the town hall receptionist, blew out her cheeks in relief after Mrs Osborne had slammed out of the building. She opened her contacts book and reached for the telephone.

'Heather? I've just had Mrs Osborne from The Grange in here. A word in your ear but, you know she's got that petition about getting the bells stopped? Well, she was asking about environmental health and noise pollution... Yes, I think she's still going to take action... Indeed... Very unpopular... Yes... Having met her, I don't think she gives a damn.'

35

Amy was round at her mother's new house helping to put up the Christmas decorations. Every flat surface in the living room was covered in cards, and tinsel and streamers were draped over the pictures. Sprigs of holly were tucked behind ornaments and a large piece of mistletoe hung in the hall. Amy, balanced on the top of a set of folding steps, was hanging lametta over the lampshade in the sitting room. Her skirt had hitched up and the tops of her tights showed.

'Ash breaks up tomorrow,' she said as she leaned precariously to arrange the silvery strands.

'They're late this year, ain't they? It's only a few days to Christmas now.'

'But they don't go back straight after New Year. He's glad about that. He says he's got a ton of revision to do – he's got mocks starting the first day of term.'

'He's a good lad, your Ash. He works hard.'

Amy climbed down the steps and pulled at the hem of her skirt. 'Yeah, but all work and no play...' She picked up a box of multicoloured baubles. 'Mum, I'm worried about him.'

'Why?'

'He's barely said a word to me since that panto. He spends all his time in his room and when he does come downstairs he pretty much ignores me. Something's bothering him and I wish I knew what.'

'You did burst his bubble when he said he wanted to go to drama school.'

'Come off it, Mum. Acting's not a proper job. He needs to be told to go for something sensible and if I don't do it who will?'

'Maybe, but if it's what he wants to do… And he was good. He was the star in that panto and no mistake.'

'So? If I've told him once I've told him a thousand times he ought to get a degree and then have a proper career. Besides, I don't want him hanging around with all them arty types. They're all gay, you know.'

'Don't be daft, Ames.'

'Huh.'

'And what if he does? Your Ash isn't gay.'

'Really, Mum? I'm not so sure. He hasn't got a girlfriend; he's always talking about costumes and make-up. I swear he was jealous of Megan's frock in the panto…' Amy sighed and began to hang the baubles on the fake still-bare Christmas tree in the corner.

'No – leave that. I need to get the lights on it first. Actually,' Mags added as Amy began to put the little glass balls back in their box, 'send Ash round to help me with the lights. I want some to go up round the front door too – you know, those nice flashing ones we bought in the sales last year. I might need a hand to put some hooks up for them.'

'OK, Mum.' Amy looked around the sitting room which was now filled with a total mishmash of colourful Christmas decorations. It was garish and over-the-top, but bright and jolly. 'In that case, we're about done for today. I'll send Ash round later. You have a word with him and see what you think and I hope you find out I'm wrong, I really do.'

★

Over at The Beeches, Bex was also decorating but in her case she was busy decorating Alfie's cake, lovingly made in the shape of a bulldozer which was pushing a huge pile of M&Ms with its bucket. It was a masterpiece, but there was a bit of Bex that worried about what Alfie's reaction might be when it came to cutting it. The yellow earthmover was sitting on a big block of chocolate sponge on which she'd iced *Happy Birthday Alfie* and some markings to make it look like a piece of roadway. She supposed that if the worst came to the worst his guests could be fobbed off with the base rather than the digger itself. She finished the icing off with two big eyes on the bulldozer's windscreen and straightened up. Her back ached and she put a hand behind her to try and ease the dull pain.

'The joys of pregnancy,' she muttered as she picked up the empty bowl of icing and put it in the dishwasher before she put on the kettle. She glanced at the clock as she plugged it in. She had half an hour before she went to the pub to work her last shift before Christmas. As the kettle boiled she went over what had to be done before the Big Day. She grabbed a scrap of paper and began to make a list. Her first priority was the party the next day – she began with that.

Alfie's party
pass the parcel
goody bags
jellies
pin the tail on the donkey
musical bumps/chairs/statues
prizes...

But then she'd really need to pull her finger out about Christmas.

Decorate house – because it wasn't fair on Alfie to have his birthday overshadowed by Christmas.

Find and fill stockings...
Collect turkey
Collect parents
Collect Christmas tree
Make up spare room bed

Bex threw down her pencil. OK, so once Alfie's party was over the list would be a lot shorter but how on earth was she going to get all the rest of this done before Tuesday – Christmas Day? Especially as once her parents arrived on Saturday they would need a lot of attention and looking after. Tiredness washed over her as she got to her feet to make her cuppa. But, tired or not, she was going to have to cope. She could put her feet up on Boxing Day when the family could be fed on leftovers.

As she sipped her tea she reckoned that she had all day tomorrow to get the bulk of the shopping done and prepare for Alfie's party, then on Friday, while Amy cleaned she could decorate the house which, hopefully, would keep the kids occupied, and then on Saturday, when her parents arrived, at least she'd have two other adults in the house to play board games, read books and keep Lewis and Alfie occupied while she and Megan got on with everything else. As a plan, it was pretty scrappy... but it was the only one she had.

She finished her tea, cleared up the kitchen, hid the cake in the pantry on a high shelf and walked round to the pub where she knocked on the door and waited to be let in.

'Morning,' said Belinda, all bright and breezy. 'Want to know what I heard?'

Bex shrugged off her coat as she said 'Hi,' and 'What?'

'I bumped into Cynthia from the town hall.'

'Cynthia?'

'Nice woman – works on reception. She says that frightful piece of work who's moved into Olivia's old place has been stirring up all kinds of shit.'

'Really?'

'Well… she didn't say "all kinds of shit", she's much too PC, but you get my drift.'

Bex nodded – she did. 'Doesn't she do the protest at the market?'

Belinda nodded. 'Makes herself a proper laughing stock. I think when she first did it people got a bit intimidated but now she does it every week… well, they just ignore her. But she's the one who set up the petition against the church bells. And now Cynthia says she was asking about the environmental health officer and wanting to know about noise pollution.'

'She cannot be serious.' Bex hung up her coat and went behind the bar to get the dusters and polish ready to clean the tables.

'It seems she is.'

'She wants to watch upsetting too many people. I can imagine that she might find life becoming a bit tricky in a small place like this.'

'Not tricky enough, if you ask me,' muttered Belinda. 'Besides, from what I've heard she doesn't use local tradespeople *and* she gets her groceries delivered so she obviously does her shopping online so, as far as I can see, there's nothing we – the locals – *can* do. I suppose we could ask Amy to boycott cleaning for her and I could bar her from the pub, but, seeing as how Amy needs the cash and Mrs Osborne has never darkened this door, both of those ideas are total non-starters.'

'What's a non-starter?' said Harry, one of their lunchtime regulars coming in for his pint.

As Belinda pulled Harry's beer she explained the situation.

'Sounds like a right piece of work,' said Harry. 'We don't want that sort living here. And as for that ruddy windmill she's got… What's all that about?'

'She generates electricity with it,' said Belinda.

'She's too posh to get her leccy off the national grid like the rest of the country, is that it?'

'I think she's trying to be eco-friendly.'

'Oh, yeah,' said Harry. 'So why does she drive everywhere in that darn-great four-by-four? Pah. She's just full of bullshit – pardon my French.'

'That's as maybe, but I still can't see what we can do to stop her.'

'I expect she'll get her comeuppance,' said Harry. 'Mark my words. Someone round here will make it obvious how the town feels – and I don't suppose she'll like it when they do.'

If Bex had felt knackered at the prospect of Alfie's birthday party the reality was even more exhausting, but eventually fifteen five- and six-year-olds went home, having been entertained, fed and watered and given a thoroughly good time. Their mums and a few dads, who had been treated to soft drinks or wine when they came to pick up their little darlings, had helped keep a certain amount of control as the state of general overexcitement, sugar and additives began to take their toll. The digger birthday cake had stolen the show and several mums even asked Bex if she'd make cakes for their sons when the time came. Finally peace descended and all that was left were sticky floors, crumbs and a kitchen that looked like a bomb had hit it. At least, thought Bex as she flopped onto a kitchen chair, no one had to get up early in the morning as the Christmas holidays had now started. Just five minutes' peace would be nice, she thought, before she began the bedtime routine for Alfie. What would be even nicer would be a glass of wine, but that wasn't an option.

And tomorrow she'd have to start Christmas preparations in earnest. No peace for the wicked.

36

The next morning, Amy persuaded her son to go and help his grandmother to finish off her Christmas decorations while she went to work at Bex's. Twenty minutes after he arrived at Mags's house he finished tapping some nails into the tiny wooden porch outside her house and then wound the flex that connected the string of fairy lights around each one. He managed to make two circuits of the porch with the decorations and secured the free end with a small cable-tie. Then he tucked the battery pack onto a convenient ledge, switched it on, and eureka – it all worked. He reopened the door and called to Mags. Outside, the multicoloured lights were strutting their stuff. According to the instructions they could be programmed in a variety of ways: steady lights; slow flash; ripple flash; slow fade; quick fade… or what they seemed to be doing at the moment which was a bit of everything in succession.

'Gran, what do you think?'

Mags clapped her hands. 'Oh, these are perfect.'

Ashley explained about the different settings.

'No,' said Mags, 'no, I like them just like this. It's just what I want.'

She saw Olivia staring out of her window at the lights and Mags gave her a cheery wave.

'I bet she isn't happy,' she said out of the corner of her mouth to Ashley. 'I bet she hates my lights.' She chuckled wickedly. 'I think I might see if I can get some of those picture lights in the sales – you know, reindeers or snowmen or Santa – ready for next Christmas. Mrs L would do her nut over ones like that!'

They returned indoors and left the lights to flash garishly outside.

'Tea?' offered Mags.

'I thought you wanted me to put the lights on the tree as well,' said Ashley.

'You can do that while I'm making it.' She handed Ashley the carrier bag containing a tangle of wires and bulbs.

Ash looked in. 'Gran! This is a right old mess.' He sat down and put the lights in his lap as he picked at the scrambled wires in an attempt to make some sort of sense of them.

A few minutes later, while he was still trying to unravel the flex, Mags put a cup of tea on the table in front of him and sat down on the chair opposite with an audible 'oof'.

'You still set on going to drama school?'

He looked up. 'Why?'

'Your mum's worried about it.'

He returned his attention to the lights. 'It's what I want. And I don't see what the problem is.'

'She's worried about the types you'll be mixing with.'

'What? Because there'll be people who don't live on a council estate or went to comps? It'll be the same at uni.'

'It's not just that.'

Ashley snorted. 'She doesn't get it, does she? This is *my* life and *I* want to live it how *I* want. And you'll have to tell Mum that because she might listen to you. She sure as hell hasn't listened to me. She wants me to be something I'm not and I'm not going to change, not for her or anyone.'

'If you say so, dear,' said Mags, mildly. But inside she was wondering just what it was that Ashley wanted to be. Was it just being an actor or was it more than that? Was Amy right?

Ash gulped down his tea. 'Anything else you want me to do?'

'No. You're a good lad.' She fished in her handbag and handed him a fiver.

'Gran! No, I don't want any money.'

'But I want you to have it. Get yourself a treat. Go on.'

Diffidently Ash took it and then dipped down to kiss his gran on the cheek. 'Ta, Gran.' He slipped the note into his pocket. 'Right, I'll be off. Mum says you're coming to ours for Christmas lunch. Do you want me to come over and walk you round?'

'Don't be daft. It's only a hop, skip and a jump. I may be old but I'm not crocked. Not yet. See you Christmas Day.'

'Bye, Gran,' said Ashley firmly as he shut the front door behind him. He paused for a moment to take in the lights he'd put up. Blimey they were bling. He looked across at the Laithwaites' house opposite. All very boring with plain white lights. No, Mrs L would deffo be unhappy about his gran's lights.

He made his way down the road, past the station and onto the high street. He slipped his hand into the pocket of his jeans and felt the money he'd been given. Maybe he'd buy something for his mum – a surprise for Christmas. He felt bad that his mum and gran were worried about him. Was it because he wanted to act rather than go to uni? But she was his mum and he supposed worrying about their kids was what mums did. Maybe he'd treat her to some chocs, or nice flowers. He'd already bought her a proper present from the money he'd saved during the year from doing odd jobs for neighbours and the occasional fiver his mum gave him as pocket money, when she was feeling flush – which wasn't often – but another little gift would be nice. He wondered what she'd like.

He walked along the road which was rammed with pedestrians doing last bits of Christmas shopping. It wasn't actually raining and it seemed that every single resident of Little Woodford was out and about. He had to stop every few paces to let other people pass, or sidestep out into the road to avoid gaggles of other shoppers, and every now and again he saw people he recognised to whom he said hello or waved at. Progress was slow.

He reached Boots and dithered outside. Maybe there'd be something in this shop that his mum might like. He only had a fiver but that would be enough for some nice bubble bath or something, wouldn't it?

He pushed open the door and was assailed by a warm gust of air. He shouldered his way through the shoppers towards the back of the store to where he could see a sign dangling from the ceiling announcing 'bath, skin care, shampoo'. He trawled along the shelves but the trouble was there didn't seem to be much in his price range. There were quite a few '3 *for the price of* 2' offers but he didn't want three of anything.

'Hi, Ash.'

Startled, he looked up. 'Oh, hi, Sophie.'

'What you after?' she asked.

'Something for my mum.'

'Like?'

'I haven't a clue,' he said wearily. 'Something I can afford.'

'What's your budget?'

'Not much,' he admitted. He pulled the fiver from his pocket.

'There's these.' Sophie indicated some nice bath oils.

'I suppose.' His lack of enthusiasm was tangible.

Sophie drifted off and examined some of the other brands and offers. She glanced occasionally at the shopping list clutched in her hand as Ash dithered with the bath oil which was, frankly, unexciting. He was about to pick it up for want of anything better when Sophie bounced back.

'I've had an idea.'

'What?'

'So, if I buy these two things and you buy something like this,' she picked up a gift pack of toiletries which was way outside Ashley's budget, 'we'll get one of them for free.' She stared at the price tags. 'It'll be the cheapest so... this one. And the other two together come to under fifteen quid. You give me a fiver, I pay a tenner and Bob's your uncle.'

Ashley frowned as he thought about it. 'But you could buy three presents and keep all of them.'

'But I don't want three presents, I only want two.'

'Even so…'

Sophie shrugged. 'Take it or leave it.'

'I'm sorry; I sound like a right git.'

'You do,' she agreed. But she said it with a smile.

They grabbed their purchases and headed for the till.

'Why are you doing this?' asked Ashley.

'Why not? This way we both save a bit.'

'I suppose.'

The girl at the till rang up the bill. 'Want a bag?' she asked.

Sophie shook her head and pulled an old carrier out of her pocket. 'No, ta.'

'Fourteen ninety-eight,' said the checkout girl. The pair handed over the money and stuffed their presents into the bag.

'What you doing now?' asked Ashley as they stood outside the shop.

'Going home,' said Sophie. 'What about you?'

Ashley shrugged. 'Nothing. I'd take you for a coffee to say ta but I'm skint again.'

'Don't worry about that. As I said, we both saved on the deal.'

'You could have saved more if you hadn't done what you did for me.' Ashley saw the exasperated look on Sophie's face. 'OK – I'll shut up. But thank you.'

'If you want a coffee you could come back to mine.'

'Really?'

Sophie nodded. 'I expect Mum'd like to tell you how much she enjoyed the panto. We both did.'

'That'd be nice, I'd like to.'

They wandered along the high street to the turning to Sophie's house. She got her key out of her bag.

'Come on in,' she said as she opened the door before she called out, 'Mum, I'm back. I've got Ash with me.'

'Hi, sweetie. Hi, Ash.'

Sophie stuck her purchases on the stairs and went into the kitchen. 'I'm making a coffee, Mum. Do you want one?'

'Lovely.'

'Go and talk to Mum,' Sophie ordered as she filled the kettle.

Ashley went into the sitting room. It was decorated with pine garlands which looped along the cornice at the top of the walls and in the corner was a big tree. The tree and the garlands had hundreds of white lights wound round them and the effect was quite magical. So very different from his gran's bonkers decorations – although part of him liked the madness; it epitomised her.

'Hi, Lizzie. Love your decorations,' he said.

'Thank you. We do the same every year but we like it like this. I'm a sucker for fairy lights.'

Ashley nodded. 'So's my gran – only with her the more colourful and flashier they are the better.' He grinned. 'She doesn't do tasteful.'

'I bet they're lovely all the same. I don't think there's a wrong or right when it comes to Christmas.'

'You haven't seen them.'

'So,' said Lizzie, 'what are you going to do with that great big talent of yours?'

'Eh?'

'Acting.'

Ashley could feel his face flaring. He shrugged with embarrassment. 'I dunno. Except...' He paused.

'Yeah?'

'I'm going to go along to the theatre group after Christmas and see if they'll take me on.'

'Take you on?' squawked Lizzie. 'They'll bite your hand off.'

'You think?'

'I *know*.'

'I told my mum that I'd like to go to drama school rather than uni.'

'And?'

'She's not happy.'

'Neither were my mum and dad. It's a dodgy old existence once you graduate and auditions are hell on earth – but when you land that part... There's no feeling like it.'

Ashley's eyes shone. 'I think I know. When I stood on that stage and made people laugh...'

Sophie came in with a tray of coffees. 'I'm going to have to go back into town.'

'Why?'

'I've just used the last of the milk. I'll have this, and then shoot. You can stay here and keep my mum company, if you like.'

'Sure. If that's OK with you?' He looked at Lizzie.

'Of course.'

Lizzie turned to her daughter. 'Ash has told me he wants to go to drama school.'

'Cool!'

'You think?' said Ash.

'Totally.' Sophie nodded her head vigorously and then slurped at her coffee. She gulped it down. 'Back in a mo,' she said as she dumped her mug on the table and scooted out of the room.

'If it's any help, I think uni is overrated,' said Lizzie. 'Mind you, I didn't go, so I'm probably biased. But I did learn how to touch type and do basic accounting so I could always work as a temp between jobs.'

'My mum's ex-boyfriend said I should get a trade like being a plumber or a mechanic.'

'You'll need something to fall back on when you're resting – and something that earns a decent wedge. It's all very well doing bar work or waiting on tables but the pay is lousy and the hours are worse.'

'I'm used to being skint,' said Ashley.

'Aren't we all,' said Lizzie. 'Living on benefits is no laugh. If it wasn't for Soph's Sunday job at the filling station she wouldn't get no treats at all, poor kid.'

'I didn't know she had a job.'

'It's only a few hours but it helps.'

'I ought to get a job.'

'Well, if you're serious about joining the theatre group and you want to do well in your GCSEs you might be a bit stretched.'

'If I'm going to act I won't need exams.'

Lizzie scowled. 'Now, you listen to me... you can't apply for drama school till you're eighteen and supposing you don't get in? I am *sure* you will but what if you don't? You have to have other options.'

Ashley shrugged. 'You mean I've got to stay at school and do A levels?'

'Why not? Anyway, what's wrong with school? I'd have thought that after the panto you must be about the coolest guy in the class.'

If Ashley could have blushed redder he would have done. And the thought that he was one of the cool kids made him even more set on becoming an actor.

37

Christmas Eve, a Monday, dawned in Little Woodford much like any other Monday with the exception that, across the town, most small children were almost beside themselves with excitement. Alfie and Lewis were no exception and crashed into their grandparents' room at half past six with shrieks of, 'Is it Christmas yet?'

Granny May sat up in bed and put on her glasses while Grandpa Jack slumbered on beside her, his hearing aids on the bedside table, happily oblivious of almost all noise. They'd arrived from Cumbria the night before, shattered from all the travelling and the boys had both been allowed to stay up to meet them. They'd all expected – and hoped for – a bit of a lie-in the next morning as a payback. No such luck, it seemed.

'Goodness me, boys,' she said, 'if you're not careful you'll wake Grandpa and then he'll be grumpy all day.'

Lewis and Alfie looked at each other. 'Grumpy Grampy,' whooped Lewis, shrieking with laughter.

Granny May sighed and said, 'You two go downstairs. I'll be along directly.'

The two boys clattered down the stairs and Granny got out of bed, slipped on her dressing gown and slippers and followed them – much more decorously and almost silently. As she reached the ground floor she could hear them wrestling over the remote and then the sound of the TV switching on. Leaving them to it – they'd be quiet for a few minutes she went into the kitchen and was surprised to see Bex there, sitting at the table with a cup of tea, playing on her laptop.

'Hello, lamb,' said her mother. 'What are you doing up so early?'

'I was hoping to get some stuff done before the boys woke up.'

Granny May snorted. 'Fat chance of that.'

'The kettle's just boiled,' said Bex.

'Good.' She went over to the counter and made two mugs of tea. 'I'll take this up to Grandpa although he managed to sleep through the boys' invasion. Sometimes there are advantages to not being able to hear without hearing aids!'

When she returned Bex had her big Kenwood mixer out and was measuring fat and flour into the bowl.

'You can never have too many mince pies,' she said, switching on the big machine.

'But you can have too many cooks. How about I go and make sure the boys are OK. I'll see if they'd like a story reading to them, shall I, pet?'

'Oh, Mum, that'd be ace.'

As Granny May left the kitchen Bex's laptop pinged so she stopped watching the beaters turn flour and fat into tiny, breadcrumb-like particles and checked what the Facebook notification was all about. For a second she stared at the picture that popped up, unable to quite make head or tail of what she was seeing. Then she realised. It was Olivia's old house but at the top of the drive, where it joined the road up the hill, was an enormous, steaming pile of manure. The caption read – *It seems as if someone who is full of bullshit needs some more.*

Bex swallowed down the urge to laugh. On one level it was quite funny but on another a tiny bit of her felt sorry for Mrs Osborne. For a start, how the hell was she going to get the midden moved given that it was Christmas? It'd be days before she'd be able to get a contractor to come and shift it – and that was if there even *was* a contractor who'd take the job on. Plus, there was no way of getting a car in or out of the drive and, to cap it all, it must stink to high heaven.

Old Harry at the pub had said she'd get her comeuppance. Now she had. And he'd said she was full of bullshit… But the name at the head of the picture wasn't Harry's so maybe he was innocent, except… No, surely not Harry.

When Bex had got a batch of two dozen mince pies in the oven she went into the sitting room. The boys were transfixed by an episode of Octonauts and Granny May was half-asleep on the sofa.

'Mum,' said Bex.

Granny May's eyes snapped open. 'What is it, love?'

'Why don't you bring your tea into the kitchen where it's warmer? The boys are fine here.'

'If you're sure.' She picked up her mug and followed her daughter.

'Sit down,' said Bex.

Granny May frowned as she took a seat and put her mug down on the table. 'This sounds serious.'

'It is. Kind of.' There was a silence that stretched for a number of seconds.

'And…?'

'Mum… I'm pregnant.'

'So that's why you look a bit peaky. I did wonder why but I didn't like to ask. I have to say it's a bit of a relief that that's all it is. No… that came out wrong. I was worried it was something serious, something nasty. I am delighted for you, as long as you are delighted for yourself.'

'I am.'

'Then I'm really, really pleased. It'll be lovely to have another little baby in the family. They grow up so fast.'

Bex nodded.

'Who's the father – if you don't mind me asking?'

'It's Miles.'

Granny May nodded again. 'From what you've said he seems like a nice guy.'

Bex nodded and told her mum all about the new man in her and her family's life. 'You'll meet him tomorrow – he's coming over for Christmas lunch. Actually, he'll probably cook most of it.'

'That's good. What about Richard's folks?'

Bex shrugged and looked at the floor.

'You've not told them?' There was a pause. 'You can't *not*.'

'I'm going to FaceTime them tomorrow – so the kids can chat to them on Christmas Day. I'm going to break it to them then.'

Granny May raised her eyebrows. 'A Christmas present.'

'Something like that. It's been over eighteen months since Richard died...'

'You can't live in the past.'

'And it isn't as if I meant this to happen. And I honestly think Richard would be pleased for me – that I've found someone else.'

'Yes, I think he would. Whether his mum and dad will see it like that...' Granny May knew all about her daughter's tricky relationship with her in-laws.

'We'll find out tomorrow, won't we?'

Miranda, half-asleep, slowly became aware of a noxious smell. What on earth? What the hell had Roderick done in their en suite? She opened her eyes and as full consciousness returned she realised that whatever it was she could smell it probably had nothing to do with her husband.

Dear God, what were the locals up to now? And on Christmas Eve? Who on earth would be muck-spreading now? She glanced at the bedside alarm. Seven? Ridiculous!

Crossly she threw back her unbelievably expensive eider down duvet and sat up. Whoever was responsible had to be stopped.

This was outrageous. Even as she swung her legs out of her bed the wording of a letter to the council was starting to come together in her head. She appreciated this was the country and the local-yokels did things differently here but this was a step too far. In fact, given the awfulness and strength of the smell, might it not be hazardous – in which case ought she to ring the emergency services?

Still contemplating her letter and other possible courses of action Miranda hit the button on the remote to raise the electric blinds at the windows as she headed into the en suite for an early morning pee. After she'd finished and washed her hands she returned to her bed and glanced out the window – largely to see what the weather was doing.

She froze. What the…?

'Rod! Roddy.' She shook her husband's shoulder.

Roderick grunted and rolled over. 'What's the matter?' he slurred, sleepily.

'Roderick. It's a disaster,' she said as she slammed the vent shut.

'What is?' He sniffed. 'And what's that smell?'

'Exactly!' screeched his wife. 'Look!' She pointed out of the window as Roderick scrambled onto his knees and turned round to see what she was pointing at.

'Holy shit.'

'Are you trying to be funny?' she snapped.

'But… but why?'

'Because I ordered it for the garden.'

'You what?'

'Oh, don't be ridiculous, Roderick. Of course I didn't. This is probably from some small-minded farmer trying to dissuade me from protesting about the sale of disgusting meat products at the market. Well, it's not going to work.'

Roderick sighed. 'So what are we going to do about it?'

The pair got back under the covers as Miranda outlined her plans to contact the council and the emergency services on the grounds that it was a toxic health hazard and needed to be moved instantly.

'I think,' said Roderick, 'that it'll be entirely our problem. I'm pretty certain that if this constitutes fly-tipping, and I think it might, the council will wash their hands of any responsibility. The ball is in our court.'

'But we're the victims here. That can't be right. No, the council must do it.'

Roderick shook his head. 'Even if I'm wrong about whose responsibility it is, it's Christmas Eve.'

'So? It's not a bank holiday. As soon as the town hall is open I shall order them to sort this out.'

'Good luck with that,' murmured Roderick under his breath. In a louder voice he said, 'I expect the staff are off for the holiday now. And even if there's a skeleton team on duty they won't have the wherewithal to deal with that.'

Miranda's brow creased and a horrified expression crossed her face as she realised that her husband might have a point. She shuffled out from under the covers and leaned on the window sill again. Her husband followed suit. The pair stared at the steaming midden that blocked their drive. Miranda remembered the house guests they had invited to spend Christmas with them.

'And how are the Clifton-Prices going to get to the house?' said Miranda as another realisation struck her. With their drive comprehensively blocked no one would be able to get a car in or out.

Roderick sighed. 'They'll have to park on the road and try and walk past it.'

'But... but... But their first impression of this place will be ruined. Ruined!'

'I'm sure they'll understand.'

'Understand what? That we've been the butt of some vile local practical joke? Roderick, Valentine is a high court judge. We can't subject him or Candida to having to negotiate that.'

Miranda pointed dramatically at the manure. 'No, you're going to have to find someone – anyone – to shift it.'

'Who?'

'I don't know. A local farmer. A builder. Anyone.'

'Do you know any local farmers?'

Miranda looked close to tears. 'Of course I don't. Why on earth would I? But someone must. We must ask around.'

'Who?' said Roderick, reasonably. 'Who have you made friends with?'

'I... I... There's that woman from the vicarage. I've spoken to her. And Amy – the cleaner.'

'Then perhaps *you* ought to talk to them. It would be better coming from you. After all, I've never met either woman.'

Miranda contemplated the prospect of asking that frumpy mouse Heather or her cleaner – the *cleaner,* for God's sake – for help. Christ, how demeaning. But Roderick was right; he'd never spoken to them so it would have to be her.

'OK, I'll do it.' She gritted her teeth. 'But I need some tea first. I'm going to have a cup of hibiscus and mulberry; my blood pressure needs it. How about you?'

'I think I'll have a chai – I need the stimulation.'

She slipped on her dressing gown and slippers and went downstairs to make their tea. It only took seconds with the boiling water tap and she carried their drinks back into the bedroom where she picked up her phone off her dressing table. She settled back in bed before she accessed her contacts list and then hit the icon for Amy.

The phone rang and rang and went to voicemail. Miranda disconnected and rang again. This was an emergency. Why didn't the bloody woman answer? She had to repeat the procedure twice more before she finally got though.

'Wuh... Mrs Osborne?' came Amy's sleepy voice down the line.

'Amy. I need your help.'

'Wha... why? It's Christmas Eve.' She sounded a tad more alert.

'I don't care about that. I need a farmer.'

'Do you know what the time is?'

'I don't care about that either. I need a farmer. Or someone with earth-moving equipment. Do you know any?'

'Mrs Osborne, it's Christmas Eve, it's...' there was a pause while Amy obviously checked the time, 'it's seven fifteen and the answer is, no I don't. Goodbye.'

'Wait!' shrieked Miranda.

'What?' Amy's voice was unmistakably sullen.

'Amy, I'm sorry, but this is an emergency.'

'Really?'

'Someone's... someone has dumped tons of manure on my drive.'

Amy's gale of uncontrolled laughter exploded into Miranda's ear. She waited for it to subside. 'It's not funny.'

There was another snort then, 'No. No, it isn't.'

'So, can you help? I need to get it moved.'

'Yeah, I can see that. But the answer is still no. I don't know anyone that fits the bill.'

'Do you think the vicar's wife might?'

'Dunno. You'd have to ask her.'

'Yes, yes, I will. I just don't have her number. I don't suppose...'

'Yeah, yeah. I've got it.' Amy reeled it off. 'But I wouldn't ring her right now. She might have more Christian charity than me but I still wouldn't piss her off. Know what I mean? Leave it till later, eh?'

Miranda snorted in disgust as she threw her phone down on the bed. She'd sack Amy if she wasn't such a good cleaner. Dreadful, common little baggage.

38

Heather was making tea in the kitchen for herself and Brian when Jade appeared, tousle-haired and yawning.

'Morning, my dear. All set for tomorrow?'

Jade yawned. 'Kind of. Got a text from Mum yesterday wanting me over early tomorrow morning to help with the cooking. And I'm going round for supper tonight so I'll take all the pressies and put them under the tree then.'

'That'll be nice – you and your mum working together to produce a lovely family feast.' And good luck with that, Olivia. A bit of Heather longed to be a fly on the wall – she doubted if Jade would be a help... more of a hindrance if she was any judge.

Jade gave her a look that suggested she wasn't quite so enamoured with the idea of helping either.

'And as the kettle is on, can I make you tea too?' offered Heather.

'Please.' She got out her phone and looked at the screen while Heather bustled round with the mugs and the milk.

'Hey... have you seen this?' said Jade.

'Seen what?'

Jade passed over her phone in return for a steaming mug of tea.

Heather looked at the screen. 'Is that...? Oh my goodness.' She giggled as she read the caption. 'No, I mustn't laugh.'

'Why not?' asked Jade. 'I bet the rest of the town is. My mum hates her.' She saw the look of disapproval on Heather's face. 'Well, she doesn't hate her, but you know what I mean.'

Heather remembered her own encounter with Mrs Osborne. 'I do indeed. She's not a woman who is easy to actually like.'

The phone rang.

'Hello, the vicarage.'

'It's Miranda Osborne here.'

'Mrs Osborne?' Heather had to make an effort not to say 'talk of the devil'. Instead she winked at Jade who looked at her, curiosity writ large on her face.

'We met – when I first arrived here,' Miranda said.

'Yes, I remember. I remember it very well indeed.' And not for the right reasons.

'Amy Pullen thought you might be able to help me. She gave me your number – I hope you don't mind?'

'Mrs Osborne, this is a vicarage. We tend not to keep our number a secret.'

'Yes… well… I was wondering if you knew of any farmers.'

'Do I know any farmers?' repeated Heather for the benefit of Jade.

'Yes, I need… I need something moved. I need someone who might have a digger, or a bulldozer.'

Heather winked again. 'So what exactly do you need moving?'

'Some manure.'

'Manure? How much?'

Jade's shoulders stared to shake with laughter.

'Tons. It's been dumped in our drive. A prank, no doubt.' Miranda's voice was very clipped.

'Oh dear. How very unpleasant.'

Jade had tears rolling down her face.

'Well, the thing is, Mrs Osborne, I don't think I can help you. Not this side of Christmas. As you can imagine this is one of our busiest times of year and I really haven't time to put out feelers on your behalf. Not on top of everything else. But good luck with your search for a friendly farmer. Goodbye.'

Jade let her bottled up laughter out. As she calmed down she said, 'Oh, that was priceless. And even if she does find a farmer it'll probably be the same one that dumped it there in the first place. I hope he charges her a mint to sort out the mess.'

'Now, now, Jade... we mustn't gloat.'

'Really?'

Heather's mouth twitched. 'No, we really mustn't.' Then she burst out laughing too.

Zac, grasping Oscar's lead, let himself out of the front door and set off, down the road, over the railway bridge, towards the nature reserve. He breathed a sigh of relief as he got away from the house. His mum was getting all stressy about Christmas and was crashing around the house with the hoover. Like anyone would care if there was fluff on the carpets or a cobweb in the corner. OK, so things were going to be bonkers with the rest of the family arriving and the house would be completely overcrowded but Jade would go back to the vicarage to sleep and Mike had said he'd bring an airbed and sleep on the sitting room floor which left the spare room for Tamsin, so it wasn't going to be impossible to put everyone up. And then there was the way his mum banged on about doing Christmas *and* a job... It wasn't like millions of other people didn't manage both. Zac really didn't see what she was on about; how hard could it be to cook what was basically a big chicken and wrap a few presents?

He wandered along the high street which was manic with shoppers getting last-minute gifts or food and found himself wondering, even more, what all the fuss was about – surely Christmas couldn't be so hard to organise, and it wasn't as if it came as a surprise; same day every year, same meal, same people to buy presents for, same tree, same decorations...

Oscar kept tucked in close behind him, out of the way of the forest of legs, as they pushed their way through the crowds. As they reached the pub things thinned out considerably and Zac walked another few yards before he stopped on the pavement, outside The Beeches, and glanced over the gate. He hadn't seen Megan for ages. Maybe she'd like to go for a walk with him. On impulse he unbolted the gate and let himself into their garden. He pressed the doorbell.

'Oh…' he said to the elderly woman who answered the door. 'Er… I was hoping to see Megan.' From behind the half-open door he could hear the completely overexcited shrieks and squeals of Lewis and Alfie.

'Who shall I say it is?' said the woman, whom Zac assumed must be a relation of sorts.

'Zac. I'm a friend.'

She left Zac on the doorstep as she wandered back into the house. A minute later Bex appeared out of the kitchen wiping her floury hands on an apron. 'Hi, Zac. I think she's upstairs in her room. Want to go on up? It's chaos here.'

Zac nodded. 'It's the same at mine. Mum's going a bit bonkers so I thought I'd take Oscar out for a walk; get him out from under her feet.' He didn't add that it would also prevent him from getting roped in to any chores she might want to divvy up.

'Well, if you would like Megs *and* the boys for company… I'd completely understand if you'd rather not take the boys but anything which might either wear them out or calm them down would be welcome.' She smiled. 'See what Megan says. She might prefer to fry her own eyes.' Bex's eyes widened. 'Oh – I mean about taking the boys… not going for a walk with you.'

Zac chuckled. ''S all right, Bex. I knew what you meant.' He shortened Oscar's lead, wiped his feet and headed up the two flights of stairs. At the bottom of the second flight he stopped and called Megan's name.

She answered. 'Zac? Come on up.'

Zac emerged into Megan's attic. Megan was sitting on a bed with a pile of gifts and two rolls of wrapping paper.

'I'm escaping from my mother,' said Zac. 'She's going mental with Christmas arrangements and preparations. I thought I'd take Osc for a walk. Wanna come?'

Megan looked at her pile of presents. 'I meant to get this done this morning.'

'I could give you a hand.' At Zac's feet, Oscar yawned prodigiously and flopped onto his tummy.

'OK. That'd be nice. So much easier with two pairs of hands.'

So Megan cut the paper and Zac handed her lengths of sticky tape as she needed it and soon the pair had the presents wrapped and stacked in the corner of her bedroom.

'Right,' said Megan, looking at the result. 'Walk time now.' Oscar's ears pricked.

'Your mum asked if we'd take the boys with us.'

'I don't see why not, if you don't mind. But let's go to the reserve via the Cattebury road.'

'Why?'

'You'll see.'

Ten minutes later the four kids and the dog were walking up the hill on the Cattebury road. Alfie and Lewis were taking it in turns to hold Oscar's lead and were, for once, walking sensibly because they'd been told that if they made Oscar excited he might run into the road. Both Zac and Megan knew this was completely unlikely because Oscar was nothing if not well trained. But the boys didn't know that.

A waft of something strong and very agricultural hit them.

'What on earth is that smell?' said Zac as they neared one of the entrances into the nature reserve.

'So it really is true.'

'What?'

'Poo!' shrieked Alfie.

A few yards up the road they could see the pile of dung steam gently in the cold air.

'That's exactly what it is,' said Megan, her face wrinkled in disgust. 'Mum said it was on Facebook that someone had blocked the drive to your old house with a pile of manure.'

'When Mum was on the council,' said Zac, 'I know she put a few backs up.' He grinned. 'She probably still does, you know what she's like, but no one ever did this to her.' He stared again at the dung heap. 'These guys must have done something really bad.'

'I wonder what?' said Megan as they turned onto the path to the reserve.

Zac unclipped Oscar's lead and released the dog to bound off and the boys shot off too.

'Not too far,' shouted Megan at their retreating backs. 'So, how's things? I haven't seen you for ages.'

'No. You were busy with the play. How's Ashley?'

'Boring. Since the panto he'll only talk about acting and the stage and shit like that.'

'So he's gone all luvvie, has he?' Zac hooted.

'Kind of, only don't say I said so.'

'Why not? It'll be a laugh.'

'No, it wouldn't.'

'Just because you've got no sense of humour.'

'Just because you've got no sense of loyalty or decency.'

'Oh, don't be such a killjoy.'

'Just stop it. Stop being a git or I'll take the boys and go home.'

So Zac shut up. But he wasn't going to forget about the ammo he had against Ashley. He wondered when he might use it.

39

Christmas in the town came and went with varying degrees of excitement, quiet contemplation, overindulgence or loneliness depending on who was celebrating and whether or not children were involved.

At the vicarage, everything revolved around the services that Brian conducted, with an early breakfast before Holy Communion. Heather dashed back from that, got the turkey into the oven and the vegetables prepared before she was back in church with her two boys in time for the eleven o'clock family service. Once the family had returned from that she could think about roasting the potatoes and making the bread sauce so they could sit down to eat at two. It was only when lunch had been cleared away and everyone was feeling sleepy and sated that they got on to the business of distributing the presents from under the tree.

At The Beeches it was all anyone could do to keep Alfie and Lewis under control for the early part of the morning until everyone was ready to settle down after breakfast and open their gifts. Once the two boys had seen the huge pile of brightly coloured packages under the tree, the contents of their stockings lost their allure and they were almost beside themselves with excitement when everyone trooped into the sitting room and the boys were finally allowed to see what Santa had brought them.

Miles had arrived in time to join in the present-giving and to help cook the lunch and was introduced to Bex's parents, who took to him immediately.

While Miles was helping Lewis and Alfie build a huge Playmobile pirate ship – a present from their grandparents in Cyprus – Belinda opened up the pub at eleven thirty for a couple of hours for the diehard regulars, before toting two bottles of decent champagne over to Bert and Joan's who had invited not just Belinda, but a few other waifs, strays and singletons from the pub, to theirs for a slap-up feast.

Over at Amy's Mags arrived pushing a wheeled shopping basket containing her presents for Ashley and Amy and a bottle of sweet sherry which she and Amy managed to polish off before lunch, after which Amy cracked open the cava.

Across the road, at Olivia's house, the morning had been rather more decorous, sober and organised with carols playing on the radio as she, Jade and Tamsin prepared the vegetables to go with the turkey, and Mike, Zac and Nigel sat around in the living room discussing the state of the economy, the condition of the government and other non-festive subjects. Olivia, hot, flustered and certain she'd forgotten some vital ingredient or other and that Christmas lunch would be ruined, longed to ask them to lend a hand and do something useful, like lay the table, but didn't want to wreck a rare moment of harmony amongst the men in her life.

At Olivia's old house Miranda was handing around some spinach and cashew bites to her house guests while a parsnip and artichoke bake cooked in the oven. Luckily the main window in her huge barn conversion looked out over the garden and the countryside and not the massive pile of dung that still festered on her drive and which, despite Miranda deploying every method she could think of to freshen the air, still permeated the house with its smell. Prior to breakfast, Valentine and Candida had had a discussion in their room and had resolved to fake a text message about a plumbing emergency in their London mansion block which would necessitate them leaving shortly after lunch. They would have liked to have gone straight after breakfast, regardless of the fact that it would mean missing out on the Christmas feast entirely, but even they thought that would be too obvious.

Several hours later, the Clifton-Prices, followed by Miranda and Roderick, picked their way past the manure heap, lugging their suitcases to their car which was parked on the main road. Candida held a hanky to her nose with her free hand and tried to keep her feelings of guilt at bay as she ignored Miranda's suggestion that they should return once they'd sorted out an emergency plumber.

'No, we can't possibly muck you around any more than we have. We feel bad enough about leaving you in the lurch like this as it is,' lied Valentine smoothly as he plipped open the door to his Lexus.

'But we were so looking forward to showing you around the area tomorrow. The countryside is so pretty,' said Miranda. 'Such lovely walks.'

'And we're devastated to be missing such an opportunity,' responded Candida as she dropped her bag in the boot and then slid into the passenger seat. 'But thank you for a wonderful lunch. Such a treat to have a change from turkey.'

Valentine shook Roderick's hand before he got into the car. 'And good luck with your problem,' he said, nodding at the midden.

The Osbornes waved until their visitors were out of sight and then inched back to their front door, trying to avoid the worst of the muck.

'I think I might chuck these shoes,' said Miranda slipping her loafers off in the porch. 'They'll never be properly clean.' She shuddered. 'Do you think the Clifton-Prices really had a burst pipe in their apartment?'

Roderick looked at his wife. 'What do you think?'

Miranda sighed. 'This has been an unmitigated disaster.' She flopped onto a sofa and ran her fingers through her immaculate hair. 'I still can't believe the police were so inadequate. Good God, fly-tipping, criminal damage... and that's just to start with. And all they could offer us was a crime number for the insurance. God alone knows how much it'll cost us to get the drive cleared and to repair the damage.'

'But there hasn't been any damage – not really – and there were no witnesses, no evidence—'

'No *evidence*?' shrieked Miranda. She gesticulated in the general direction of the dung heap. 'What the hell do you call that?' She took a breath and calmed down. 'And all the food we're going to have left. A whole week's worth.'

'You can't blame them for going. Wouldn't you if the situation was reversed?'

There was a pause before Miranda answered, 'You're probably right. Maybe we should follow their lead. Find a hotel that might put us up for a few days till we can get this sorted. We're probably stuck here tonight but tomorrow... let's see if we can book into Woodford Priors. It's not ideal – all that fusty decor – but it would be better than here.'

At teatime Lewis and Alfie finished watching *Cars* for the umpteenth time and Bex decided that, with them now calmer, it was time to FaceTime Granny Helen and Grandpa Phil in Cyprus, so everyone could thank them for their generosity. Once that had been done and the children had had a chance to chat to them she planned to finish off the conversation in private and break the news to them about the baby. Miles followed her out of the sitting room when she went to fetch her iPad from the kitchen.

'Do you want me there too, when you do that?' asked Miles. 'So you can introduce them to the villain of the piece.'

'Not this time,' said Bex. 'But thanks for the offer. I can't say I'm looking forward to this call.' She returned to the sitting room and got the kids to sit with her on the big sofa and then she hit the FaceTime icon on the screen and pressed the dial-up for Megan and the boys' grandparents.

The ringtone warbled away for a few seconds before Granny Helen's face appeared and then Grandpa Phil's, beaming over her shoulder. 'Hello! Happy Christmas,' they said, before Helen continued, 'Did you have a good one?'

'Hi, Granny and Grandpa,' chorused the children.

Then Megan added, 'Yes, it was lovely thanks. A bit chilly, though. How was yours?'

'Quiet,' said Granny Helen. 'Maybe one year you could persuade your stepmum to come over at this time of year instead – then you could escape the cold.'

Already a dig, thought Bex. 'I'd love to, Helen. Maybe when Megan isn't facing mocks as soon as she gets back to school.'

'So next year, then.'

'Maybe.'

'Anyway, thank you for my pressie,' said Megan, jumping in and changing the subject.

'Did you like it? I never know what to get you – you're growing up so fast and we see you so rarely.'

Another dig, thought Bex. But she said, 'And the Playmobile for the boys was wonderful. They loved it.' She pointed the screen at them so their grandparents would see them nodding enthusiastically. Lewis jumped off the sofa and went to fetch the plastic pirate ship.

'Look,' he said showing her. 'It's even got cannons.'

'And they fire cannon balls,' added Alfie.

'And the boys loved their Transformers too and my Turkish Delight was such a treat.' She loathed Turkish Delight and she thought Granny Helen knew – had it been deliberate?

Megan gabbled on for a few more minutes, filling in Granny Helen about the panto and the end of term disco. The boys began to wriggle as their boredom threshold kicked in and Bex used this as an excuse for the children to say goodbye.

'I'll just take you through to the kitchen,' she said, carrying her tablet out of the sitting room and shutting the door. 'I think the boys want to watch a DVD.' She sat at the kitchen table and propped her iPad up in front of her. 'Anyway…' She paused as she felt her courage start to fail. 'I didn't just ring you to thank you for the presents. I've got some news.'

'Oh yes.' Granny Helen sounded wary.

'Yes. You're going to have another grandchild – well… step-grandchild.'

'What?' Granny Helen's eyes boggled.

'I'm pregnant. The baby is due in June.'

'June.' She'd managed to get her feelings under control and her voice was cold. 'And the father is?'

'It's Miles. You know, I've told you about him – he and I work together.'

'A publican.' The sneer was more than apparent. Even usually jovial Grandpa Phil's smile had gone.

'A chef,' countered Bex, firmly.

Granny Helen's disapproving sniff eloquently conveyed that she didn't think it was any better.

'He's very nice,' said Bex.

'Is he?'

'Lewis and Alfie adore him,' she added.

There was a pause. 'I see. And you're still working?'

Bex nodded.

'Is that quite wise?' Not that Granny Helen sounded as if she really cared.

'I feel fine.'

'But pub work?'

Was the implication that the baby was being exposed to undesirable influences… even in the womb? Bex didn't feel inclined to answer but forced a smile instead.

'Well, I hope you'll be very happy with this new,' another pause, another sneer, '*arrangement*. Now, if you'll forgive me, I've got things I must see to.' She watched as Granny

Helen's finger reached towards the screen and the call was killed.

'She'll come round,' said Bex to herself, knowing she was probably being totally over-optimistic.

Olivia spent the early part of the morning of Boxing Day carving the rest of the meat off the turkey and turning the carcass into soup.

She'd just finished piling the meat onto a plate when Nigel arrived in the kitchen, yawning widely.

'Anything I can do to help?'

Olivia smiled at him. 'You can put the kettle on and make tea and then turn some of that,' she nodded at the turkey slices, 'into sandwiches.'

'Sure.' Nigel bumbled around, filling the kettle, getting the bread out, finding some lettuce and the bread board while Olivia rammed the turkey bones into a huge saucepan with a bunch of other ingredients to produce a stock.

'Thank you for yesterday,' said Nigel. 'It was a lovely Christmas.'

Olivia paused her stirring. 'That's OK.' She couldn't remember the last time Nigel had said that to her.

'I mean it. I know it was tricky for you, what with this house being a squash and work and everything and I admire you for the way you still managed to give everyone a wonderful day.'

'I'm glad it all worked.' She smiled ruefully. 'Even Jade seemed to quite enjoy herself.'

'Although she bitched about having to walk back to the vicarage.'

'Like anyone was in a fit state to drive her.'

'I realise how much hard work it was too.'

'The same as it always is,' said Olivia, making light of her husband's unexpected compliments. 'Except this year it all had to be done at a less leisurely pace than I am used to.'

'Even so…'

Having felt for a number of years that her efforts – especially at Christmas – were taken for granted and under-appreciated, Olivia felt suddenly rather teary at Nigel's kind words. She cleared her throat as she got her emotions under control.

The pair worked in silence as the rest of the family appeared and helped themselves to breakfast. There were some quiet discussions about plans for the day but no one seemed to want to do anything very much except possibly go to the pub for a lunchtime drink.

'There,' said Olivia, as she switched off the gas under the huge saucepan. 'Can I ask one of you to put this in the garage to keep cool in a little while? The fridge is too full. I'll finish turning it into soup tomorrow.'

'You off somewhere?' said Mike from the sitting room where he was deflating his airbed.

'Work,' said Olivia.

'But it's a holiday,' said Tamsin, her mouth half-full of toast.

'Not in the hospitality industry, it isn't. Which is why your dad's made a stack of turkey sandwiches for lunch. I'm off at six so I should be back in time to make supper.'

'What is it?' asked Tamsin.

'Turkey fricassee.'

'Yum, I like that.'

'If you feel like making a start on it...' said Olivia, hopefully.

'Sorry,' said Tamsin. 'I've promised to meet some of my old school friends in the pub. I'll be back in time for supper though,' she promised.

Olivia managed to stop herself from rolling her eyes. 'Never mind.' She glanced at the kitchen clock. 'Right, I need to get going.'

As she picked up the car keys she asked the children to load the dishwasher and run it – and what are the chances they'll empty it when it's finished, she wondered – and then set out for Woodford Priors. Out of habit she glanced at The Grange as she drove past. What the...? She was the only car on the road so she jammed on the brakes and reversed a few yards to have a proper look. A bubble of laughter rose in her throat because somehow she didn't reckon that the Osbornes had actually ordered the manure for their garden. 'Oh dear,' murmured Olivia to herself. 'How very unfortunate.'

She was still smiling when she pulled into the staff car park at the hotel. As she walked through the brightly lit service corridors to the front-of-house area, she tried to tell herself that if she felt too much schadenfreude she'd get her comeuppance but it simply didn't work. It couldn't have happened to more deserving people was all she could think.

The morning passed quickly as she checked out those guests who had only opted to stay for Christmas Day itself and answered queries from others who were staying longer and needed activities to fill the oodles of time they now found they had, given that the hotel staff were picking up the household chores that would have fallen to them had they stayed at home. It being Boxing Day, Olivia knew that there were precious few local attractions open and so the most she could offer was a leaflet detailing a number of walks around the area and some suggestions of good local pubs. And, armed with local knowledge, she could suggest which walks would combine exercise with a decent meal.

At midday, she grabbed a lunch break of soup and a roll in the staffroom next to the kitchen before she returned to the reception desk. The hotel was deathly quiet as the guests seemed to be either enjoying a postprandial snooze in their rooms or in the lounge, or had taken note of Olivia's suggestion and were out and about.

The front door banged open and Olivia looked up from the computer terminal where she was updating guests' accounts, instantly recognising the woman who had come in – Miranda Osborne. Behind her trailed her husband in a pair of cherry-red trousers, pink shirt and cravat under a Barbour jacket. He was trying, she thought, to look as if he belonged to the country-landowner set. But he failed – he looked more like some escapee from a seventies fashion shoot. A wannabe James Bond with a paunch. She stood up and tried to look welcoming.

'Good afternoon,' said Olivia.

There was no returned greeting just a peremptory, 'I've booked a room.' Miranda stared at Olivia. 'You?'

'I'm sorry?'

'The woman with the bike.'

'Ah, yes… the car driver who blocked my drive.'

Miranda sniffed. 'Hardly *blocked*.' The pair stared at each other before Miranda dropped her gaze. 'So, my booking?'

Olivia clicked the mouse. 'Ah yes. Four nights – in the Lloyd-George suite.' She took a plastic key card out of the drawer and swiped it through a machine to programme it. 'And if I could just get you to fill in this form and give me a credit card for security.'

'Roderick,' ordered Miranda. Her husband meekly offered up a Visa card.

'Now, I believe you've stayed with us before…' said Olivia.

'Yes.'

'So you are aware of the hotel facilities.'

'Yes.'

'And that this is a listed building so please remember that some of the floors and stairs are uneven and we also have a few low beams.'

'Then you'd better hope I don't suffer any injury.'

'If,' said Olivia, as evenly as she could, 'if you think you won't be able to cope with the nature of this building, might I suggest the Premier Inn in Cattebury? That hotel is fully disabled friendly and very modern.'

'Don't be ridiculous,' snapped Miranda. She pushed the completed form over to Olivia.

Olivia glanced at it although she knew perfectly well what address had been written on it. She feigned surprise and gave her a fake smile. 'The Grange? Such a lovely house.'

'It is now.'

'I drove past it only this morning.'

Miranda narrowed her eyes and contemplated Olivia as Roderick shifted restlessly at her side. She gazed at Olivia's name badge. 'You said… when we last met… that you'd lived here a while. Have I remembered right, Olivia?'

'About twenty-five years.'

'Miranda—' said Roderick.

'In a minute, Roderick.' She turned back to Olivia. 'I… we have a problem. Which is why we're staying here. We've been the victims of some fly-tipping.'

'Really?'

'I need to find someone to move the… the… clear up the mess.'

'I see.'

'Would you know of anyone?'

'I can't say I do.' Which was kind of true, but with her contacts in the town Olivia knew she could have made a few enquiries and probably found a solution to Miranda's problem in a matter of a couple of hours.

Miranda blew down her nose and then turned to head for her room. Olivia half-expected her to shout 'heel' to her unfortunate husband who followed her, dragging the suitcase.

40

Over the next few days the townsfolk of Little Woodford who happened to travel up the Cattebury road were entertained by the sight of the Osbornes getting their hands dirty – literally – as they shovelled barrowload after barrowload to the side of their garden to create a passageway for their cars. They had managed to find a commercial company which was prepared to remove the heap, for a price – an eye-watering price – and their insurance company had agreed to pick up the tab, but nothing could be done until well into January. Miranda had tried everything to persuade the company otherwise but they refused to be budged so she and Roderick had come to the conclusion that unless they wanted to take taxis for every journey they had no choice but to clear a section of their drive themselves in order to get their cars out.

Miranda became increasingly tight-lipped as she realised that some of the passers-by had come specifically to gawp. And even more tight-lipped when she realised that, because they were on a public highway, there was nothing she could do. She considered telling them to clear off but even she realised that it was probably only going to give the local oiks even more satisfaction.

After a couple of days the novelty of watching the incomers shovel shit had worn off for the passers-by and anyway Miranda and Roderick had cleared most of their drive. Moving the midden had stirred up the smell again but once they stopped it seemed to settle down and, despite there still being a hideous eyesore in their garden, the worst of the problem seemed to be over. Finally they were able to move out of the hotel and back to their house where Miranda spent over an hour soaking in her bath into which she'd poured half a bottle of Jo Malone bath oil. She felt that the farmyard stink had got into her very bones and she was determined to eradicate it.

Later, wrapped in a luxurious towelling robe, she drifted downstairs, opened her laptop and began to write a vitriolic email of complaint to the local constabulary, copied to the county council and the parish council and, for good measure, the local paper. The service she'd received, she wrote, had fallen woefully short of expectations and the total lack of assistance to clear the mess had left her feeling traumatised. Her diatribe continued for two pages and by the time she'd finished writing she felt calmer. Her rant had been cathartic – whether it would achieve anything was almost incidental. With a sigh of satisfaction she pressed send. Should anyone come back to her, she thought, and ask if anything could be done retrospectively, she would demand heads on platters. But the reality, she knew, was that no one would care and her letter would probably end up in a digital waste-paper basket.

Business at the Talbot was brisk over the holidays and Belinda was run off her feet for a few days but, as the break went on, the novelty of having time off on a weekday wore off and trade dropped off too. Miles and James worked in tandem in the kitchen and Miles frequently wondered how he'd managed on his own before the arrival of his new assistant. He supposed people just had to wait longer for their food, or maybe, because the service had been slower, they had lost orders. Behind the bar Belinda had a number of students, back from their universities and in need of cash, to help her out on the busier shifts but she missed the quiet and efficient competence of Bex.

She wasn't the only one. ''T'ain't the same without Bex,' grumbled Harry as he stood at the bar one lunchtime and waited for Belinda to pour his pint. He was, as happened frequently, the first in after Belinda had opened the doors. Belinda wondered what the rest of the day's business would be like. Given that she was going to be on her own for the first hour she was rather hoping that it wouldn't be too busy.

'Sorry I'm not good enough,' she responded, handing over his drink and ringing up the bill on the till.

'Still,' said Harry cheering up, 'it's not all bad. Did you hear what happened up at Olivia Laithwaite's old gaff?'

Belinda grinned. 'I certainly did. Not that I've ever met the new people but from what I've heard from Amy she's not a woman to be messed with. If she finds out who dumped that manure I wouldn't want to be in their shoes.'

'Oh, she won't find out,' said Harry.

'I don't know how you can be so sure,' said Belinda.

Harry didn't say anything but raised an eyebrow and tapped the side of his nose.

'Harry?'

'Nope, I don't know nothing,' said Harry but he was chuckling as he took his drink and went over to his usual seat in the corner near the window. From his chair he called across the pub, 'But I tell you something, young Belinda, that woman has managed to upset more people since she moved here than anyone else in half a century. If she don't mend her ways there's folk here who'll make life miserable for her. Or should I say, *more* miserable for her.'

'Don't be like that, Harry. It makes it sounds as though the locals are going to lynch her. We don't want that sort of thing here; it's not our style.'

'She's upset a lot of people at the market and if she stops them bells ringing I reckon folks around here'll turn real nasty. Maybe not a lynching…' Harry paused and sipped his pint. 'Mind you, the Catte Witch got drownded back in the reign of old Queen Bess.'

'Yes, well,' said Belinda, 'let's hope there won't be a repeat of that sort of behaviour either.'

'What? Drownings or witchcraft?'

'Both.'

A few minutes later, Amy pushed open the door of the pub and found it to be much quieter than she expected. Behind her Ashley and Mags trooped in and made their way to an empty table.

'Refugees from turkey leftovers?' asked Belinda as Amy stood at the bar.

'What?' The penny dropped. 'Yeah, kind of. And Mum's had her winter fuel allowance but her new house is dead cheap to heat so she hasn't had to use it. She's treating us to lunch out.'

'That's nice.'

Amy ordered drinks and took the bar menu over to her mum and Ashley.

'Hey… Amy,' said Harry from his table.

'Harry?'

'You clean for that there Osborne woman, don't you?'

'What if I do?'

'What has she had to say about that pile of sh…' Harry glanced at Ashley, 'dung that got dumped there.'

'Dunno, Harry. I've not been up there since the week before Christmas. I start back again next week. She rang me just after it happened – asking me if I knew anyone who could move it. Even if I had, I wouldn't have told her – miserable bat.'

'I've heard she's a right piece of work.'

'Don't get me going. I mean, I know I shouldn't say anything but she's proper barking. She's all into being veggie and animal rights and meat is murder but you should see her shoe collection – honestly, how many Milano Blahniks can a woman want?'

'What's that got to do with the price of fish?' asked Harry.

Belinda butted in. 'And don't you mean Manolo Blahniks?' she asked, confused.

'Manolo... Milano... the shoes are still made of leather – you know, an animal product.'

'Well, that ain't right.'

'And then there's her being all environmental and yet she only ever drives anywhere in that ruddy great Range Rover. I mean, Olivia's a bit potty on that score but at least she puts her money where her mouth is; she never takes her car if she can ride her bike. Frankly, Harry, if Mrs O wasn't a good payer I'd sack her. There's no pleasure in working for her, I can tell you. If I knew who'd dumped that manure on her drive I'd buy them a drink.'

'Almost worth owning up then,' said Harry.

'So it was you,' said Belinda from the bar.

'Nope, I never said it was,' said Harry quickly. 'Besides, where would I get a load of manure from? I don't own no farm, do I?'

'All I can say,' said Amy, 'is that it couldn't have happened to a nicer woman. Only don't you go telling anyone I said that. You know as well as I do how people in this town gossip.'

41

On New Year's Eve Miranda drove into the centre of Little Woodford and parked her car in the market square. She had several errands she needed to run before everything shut down for yet another bank holiday. Ye gods, was another break really necessary? If people were more self-restrained and less overindulgent at New Year there wouldn't need to be a holiday while they recovered from their self-inflicted hangovers. Honestly, giving the proletariat the next day off was akin to the state actively encouraging people to get recklessly drunk. What was wrong with people that they thought that getting legless was acceptable behaviour? If she had her way, alcohol sales would be banned – well, apart from decent wines. She barely drank herself but she did enjoy a very occasional glass of vintage wine.

She got out of her car and looked at her fellow townsfolk. They were all shapes and sizes and some of them looked like unmade beds. No one was coiffed or manicured, no one had any idea about style or fashion and some of the shoes were a joke. But no one cared, no one judged and amazingly, despite their down-at-heel appearance, they all looked pretty happy as they smiled and nodded to acquaintances as their paths crossed, or stood in small huddles exchanging news and gossip. London had never been like this where ladies-who-lunched only made eye contact with themselves as they checked out their appearance in shop windows, where almost every pedestrian wore earbuds and existed in their own world or, if they were talking, it was to some invisible presence at the end of a phone line. It was a long time since she had noticed people actively seeking out and enjoying each other's company just on spec without complicated dinner arrangements or plans for long weekends. When, she wondered, had she last run into a friend and decided to stop and chat, or go for a coffee? How long ago? She sighed. Years. Years and years. Maybe as far back as uni. It certainly hadn't happened in chambers because everyone there was a potential rival. She hadn't wanted to get chummy with people she might have to clamber over to reach the top. And she did have acquaintances who she and Roddy saw socially but in their circle everyone knew that such friendships were based on mutual usefulness and not on actual camaraderie.

As she watched she saw a mother with a child hanging off each of her hands greet another mother pushing a buggy. They seemed genuinely pleased to see each other and Miranda felt an unaccustomed pang of jealousy as she wondered what it must be like to have a circle of friends whom you didn't have to try and impress, who just liked you for yourself. Or maybe it was the connection that having children gave them? Maybe if Emily had lived...? Maybe if she hadn't married someone so much older she might have had another chance of children? Maybe if she hadn't been so flattered that Roddy, a QC, had taken such an interest in her, a junior partner...? Maybe... maybe... Miranda gave herself a shake and told herself not to be so ridiculous and sentimental before picking up her basket and sweeping into the florist to buy some lilies.

The door pinged as she entered and she was assailed by the scent of a dozen different types of flowers. She examined the huge buckets of cut flowers that were ranked on the staging that ran down one side of the shop. Ranunculus, roses, freesias, gerberas, sweet William, carnations – how naff – daffodils...

And Miranda supposed if you liked that sort of thing then as a selection it might do – at a pinch. But no lilies.

She went to the counter and peered into the room behind it where the two florists were busy tying up bouquets.

'Excuse me!'

'With you in a moment, dearie.'

Miranda breathed in and out slowly in an effort to stop her blood pressure rising. Maybe expecting shop workers to show some deference was expecting too much in a backwater like this but *dearie*...?

A woman came out of the back room wiping her hands on her apron.

She smiled. 'Yes, dear, what can I do for you?'

'Good morning. And I am *not* your "dear".'

The smile vanished and her eyes hardened. 'As you wish. But that doesn't answer my question.'

'I want to buy some lilies.'

'Then you'll have to want, won't you? We're fresh out of lilies and we're not expecting a delivery until after the holiday.'

'Well, really.'

'If you'd ordered them earlier in the week I'd have kept some back. I can't be stocking expensive flowers on the off-chance that someone will want them, not with a bank holiday coming up. I'm running a business, not a charity.'

'Yes, yes, I understand that.'

'Good.'

'So what *have* you got?'

The woman looked at Miranda and... did she actually roll her eyes? No, surely not. But she pointed at the buckets.

'Is that it?' God, not much of a selection.

'If you want to know if I've got a secret stash the answer is, no I haven't.'

Miranda sighed. 'So be it. I'll have two dozen of the white roses, then.'

'Sorry, they're spoken for.'

'There's no indication of that.'

'There doesn't have to be. I know what's been ordered and what hasn't.'

Miranda examined the rest of the flowers. Everything else came in twee pastels or garish shades of red, or orange or yellow. Everything except the white carnations and she wasn't going to sink to *that*.

'I'll leave it, then.'

'As you wish.' The florist returned to the back room leaving Miranda to stalk out of the shop wondering if the roses really were on order or whether she'd been the victim of yet another example of how small-minded and petty this town could be. It might be a tight little community if you fitted in but it seemed that they had a way of closing ranks against incomers.

Feeling disgruntled and strangely irritated, Miranda strode to the bakery and pushed open the door. The smell of warm chocolate, baking bread and some sort of jam greeted her. Ahead of her, at the counter, was the vicar's mousy little wife – the woman who had refused to help her with the manure debacle. Miranda was sure Heather would have known someone who might have helped, but no… she'd almost certainly, deliberately, withheld such information. And her a Christian. Miranda stared at her back and hoped her conscience was really troubling her. It ought to be.

Heather finished buying some bread and a couple of cakes and carefully put her paper bag of purchases in the bottom of a wicker basket. She looked up as she turned.

'Ah… Mrs Osborne. Happy Christmas. Or at least I hope that's what you had. And did you manage to resolve your problem with the… manure?'

Did Miranda detect a suppressed smile? 'Yes, thank you.' She almost added *and no thanks to you*. 'Although the contractor can't come till next week.'

'I'm glad you found a solution. So sorry I was unable to help.' She didn't sound it.

'And,' Heather continued, 'I expect you heard our good news – about the bells? We've raised the money and work is going to start in the New Year. Isn't it exciting?'

'I think you know my views on noise pollution.'

'Then we'll have to agree to disagree.' Heather beamed at her. Miranda felt it was a smile of triumph – it certainly wasn't one of friendship. She stared after Heather as she left the shop.

What was it with this place? In London, she'd been able to voice her views, protest against things she vehemently disapproved of, belong to activist groups and while she hoped people paid attention to *what* she was saying, no one knew – or even cared about – *who* was saying it. It was the message that was important – not the messenger – but these people in this town didn't see it like that and seemed hell-bent on making it personal. And in scoring petty points – like Heather not helping with the manure and the florist refusing to sell her the roses.

She bought a sourdough loaf which she asked to be sliced. As the bread rattled through the slicer, she looked at the array of baked goods on display. She wouldn't dream of buying such things herself, filled as they were with fats and sugars and Lord only knew what other additives, but she supposed there was a market for them. You only had to look around for a few minutes to see chunky people who ought to know better, grazing on food and calories that they certainly didn't need. Miranda shook her head.

'Can I get you anything else?' said the shop assistant as she bagged up Miranda's loaf and put it on the counter.

'No, thank you.'

'One eighty, please.'

As Miranda got out her change purse and rummaged for the right money another customer entered the shop. It was a stocky bloke in paint-splattered coveralls.

'Two sausage rolls and an apple turnover, please,' the chap ordered.

Miranda gave up the search for the right money, got out her wallet instead and extracted a fiver. She watched as the shop girl picked up the sausage rolls and then the turnover with a pair of tongs and dropped them in a bag.

'Excuse me,' said Miranda tersely.

The girl looked over and put the bag down. 'Sorry, are you ready to pay?'

'Yes, but I am more concerned about contamination.'

'What?'

'Are those turnovers suitable for vegetarians?'

'Er, yes, I suppose so.'

'And yet you touched them with the tongs you used with the sausage rolls.'

'Look, missus,' said the bloke. 'I don't care, I'm eating all of it. It's all going to be touching once it's in my belly.'

'That is *not* the point.'

'For gawd's sake, lady, I'm in a hurry.'

'I've a good mind to report this shop to environmental health and trading standards.'

The girl behind the counter looked ready to cry. 'One eighty, please,' she repeated.

'Do you have other tongs?' asked Miranda.

The girl nodded.

'Bloody hell,' said the man. 'I want my lunch, so if you don't want your stuff at least let me pay for mine.'

Miranda glared at him. 'I don't think you realise the gravity of this.'

'Oh, for fuck's sake,' muttered the man. 'Forget it,' he said more loudly and stamped out of the bakery.

'Is the manager here?' said Miranda.

'She's on her break,' whispered the assistant.

'Then I suggest you call her.'

The girl, looking terrified, went out of the door at the back and Miranda could hear her pattering up the steps. A minute later, a much older woman returned.

'Mary's told me what the problem is and it was a mistake,' she said smoothly, as she entered the shop.

'And what would have happened if I hadn't been here? Hmm? How often has your employee already committed the same act this morning?'

'Well… I—'

'Exactly. You have no idea how many items have been contaminated. I demand that you dispose of everything on display and then educate your staff on correct procedures.'

'But… but this is our busy time. People rely on us for lunches.'

'That isn't my problem. Either you do as I suggest or the next people through that door will be representatives from the food standards authority.'

'But the food isn't unfit for consumption.'

'It is if you are a vegetarian.' Miranda glared at her opponent.

'Then supposing I put a notice on the counter, advising that today our goods are unsuitable for vegetarians?'

Miranda considered this option. 'That's far from ideal.'

'It's better than food waste.'

It was. 'I shall be back to check.'

'Be our guest.' The shop owner smiled but Miranda knew she wasn't being friendly. Well, tough. It wasn't as if she cared. Besides, if the town was set on making life difficult for her she was perfectly prepared to repay the favour.

Miranda drove home, parked her car at the front of the house and let herself in. She knew she ought to go and open the garage door and put the car away but what with one thing and another she felt devoid of energy. All she wanted was to sit down for a few minutes, in peace and quiet, and breath and meditate. She was sure her chakras were all out of kilter – and not surprisingly given the morning she'd just had.

'Roderick, I'm back,' she called.

Her husband got up from the sofa where he'd been reading the broadsheets.

'How was town?'

'Ghastly.' She sniffed. 'The flower shop didn't have any lilies and then wouldn't sell me the flowers they did have, the bakery was worse and I spotted some appalling food contamination issues which they really didn't seem to care about and, to cap it all, I met that awful woman from the vicarage who positively gloated when she confirmed the bells are going to get fixed.' She flopped dramatically onto the sofa. 'Honestly, I sometimes wonder if it was worth moving here.'

'Oh, darling, they just need educating. I'm sure everything will improve in time. And you've got to admit that it's so much better here in the country away from all that traffic and noise and pollution.'

The word traffic reminded Miranda of something. 'Roddy, would you be a sweetie and put my car back in the garage? I really don't have the energy.'

'Of course.' Dutifully, he trooped out to do his wife's bidding. He came back in a minute or so later. 'Miranda, did you have an accident in town?'

'Accident? No, of course I didn't. What *are* you on about?'

'Come and have a look.'

Miranda followed her husband out and round to the back of her car where he pointed to the damage. Right across the tailgate of her vehicle and all down the passenger side was a deep scratch. Someone had keyed her car – and badly.

Miranda felt like crying. First the manure, then the attitude of the townsfolk and now this. It begged the question, what next?

42

Z ac sat on his bed and texted Megan. Fancy a walk

No ta mtg soph @ playpark.

Can I come 2

There was a pause of several minutes. Zac guessed Megan was texting Soph to see if it was OK with her.

Yes if u want came back the reply eventually.

Zac trotted downstairs and slipped out of the house before Oscar could pick up on the fact that there might be the possibility of a walk in the offing. Dogs were banned from the play park and anyway, if he was going to hang out with Sophie and Megan, he didn't want Oscar yawning and whimpering and making it plain that he wanted to *walk* and generally being a distraction. It was only after he'd slammed the front door behind himself that he realised it might have been wise to grab a jacket. His sweat top, T-shirt and jeans weren't exactly suitable for the temperature.

Ignoring the cold, Zac strolled down the road, past the station and onto the high street. It was, he thought, surprisingly busy but then he supposed that people were stocking up for New Year's Eve parties and the impending bank holiday. Not that his family was doing anything for New Year. His mum was going to be working up at the hotel and his siblings were all going to parties or clubs up in London. He supposed he and his dad would watch the fireworks on the TV and then call it a night. Jeez – sometimes his life was the pits. Disconsolately he kicked at a stone on the pavement and sent it skittering into the road.

He turned into the park and looked about for the girls. It seemed they weren't here yet so he headed over to the skateboard ramps and ran up a half-pipe to sit at the top. From his vantage point he could see across the entire park and the allotments behind. In one direction was a bunch of bungalows and in the other was the council estate and behind that he could just see the roof of the comprehensive school hall. The skatepark itself was almost empty. A couple of kids were practising grinding on the kerb and another lad was trying to do wheelies on a shiny new BMX but other than that there was nothing much going on. Across at the play park there were a few mums and dads hanging about in groups, wrapped up in thick coats or jackets, watching while their kids amused themselves on the equipment. It was, realised Zac, quite more than a bit chilly – it was bloody freezing and it was made worse sitting on the cold steel of the half-pipe and in such an exposed position. He hauled himself to his feet, ran down the slope and ducked under it, intent on taking shelter out of the breeze.

A voice from the deep shadow greeted him. 'Hi, Zac.'

'Ash? What are you doing lurking here?' Zac hunkered down near his pal and leaned against one of the metal uprights.

'I'm not lurking.'

'Looks like it to me.'

'I wanted some space. You know what my mum's like.'

Zac nodded. 'Mums, eh? Actually, now mine works she's off my back a lot more.'

'Lucky you.' Ashley sounded properly pissed off. 'Mine's not working this week because none of her ladies want their houses cleaned over the holiday and she's always badgering me, asking me if I'm all right, or trying to tell me I don't want to do acting or... Jesus, questions, questions, questions.' Ashley kicked out and the metal of the skate ramp reverberated. 'I just wish she'd leave me alone.'

Zac sympathised. Time was when his own mum had been like that and he said as much. 'It's only cos mums care,' he added.

'Then I wish mine didn't.'

'Mine was worst when I was doing drugs. I think she knew something was wrong but she didn't have a clue what it was but she thought if she asked enough questions she'd get me to tell her. Like that was going to happen.'

'But she found out in the end.'

'Yeah, because your mum blabbed to Mrs Simmonds.' There was a short angry silence then Zac retracted his comment. 'Yeah, I know she didn't mean to.'

'She didn't. Anyway, what are you doing here?'

'Meeting Sophie and Megan.' Zac glanced over Ashley's shoulder. 'And here they are.' The two boys emerged from under the ramp.

'Hiya,' said Sophie and Megan.

'So what's the plan?' asked Zac.

'There's no plan,' said Sophie. 'Although as it's perishing it's daft us staying here.'

'If Dad was out I'd say we could go to mine – it's closest,' said Zac. 'But there's nowhere private downstairs for us to talk and my room's too small.'

'Same for me,' said Soph. 'What about you, Ash?'

'No chance – Mum's home.'

'Looks like it'll be yours, Megs,' said Sophie cheerfully.

The group arrived at The Beeches and Megan let them in.

'Bex? Bex!' called Megan as they trooped into the hall.

'In the kitchen.'

The children followed the source of the voice and a flurry of greetings and late Christmas wishes followed.

'We're going up to my room, if that's OK,' said Megan. 'It's too cold and miserable to hang about at the play park.'

'Of course that's fine,' said Bex. She eyed Zac. 'Did you go out without a coat? No wonder you're frozen. You could've caught your death!'

'Yeah, well. Blokes are hard – aren't we, Ash? Well, I am anyway.' He punched Ashley playfully on his arm.

'Ow!' Ashley scowled at Zac. 'What was that for?'

Zac shrugged. 'Don't make such a fuss – it wasn't hard.'

'You go on up,' said Bex. 'I made some butterfly cakes earlier – I don't know if any of you fancy one…'

The looks of expectancy and hope answered Bex's question.

'Good. I'll bring up some squash and cakes in a few minutes, then.'

The gang clattered out of the kitchen and up the stairs, up to the top of the house and Megan's attic.

Sophie and Megan sat on the bed and Zac claimed the armchair while Ashley sat on the floor and leaned against a wall.

'Anyone got any plans for tonight?' asked Zac.

They all looked morose and shook their heads.

'Coo-ee,' called Bex from the bottom of the attic stairs. A couple of seconds later she appeared carrying a large tray which she slid onto the dressing table. On it was a big jug of orange squash and a plate with about a dozen buns on it. 'Here you go. I wasn't sure how hungry you'd all be, so I brought quite a few.'

'Thanks, Bex,' they all said.

'Bex? Are we doing anything for New Year?' asked Megan.

Bex shrugged. 'Not really. The boys are too young, your grandparents are too old and I'm too knackered.'

'There's fireworks at the cricket club,' said Zac. 'We could go to that.'

'And who will go with you?' asked Bex. 'You're too young to go on your own at that time of night. I'm sorry, Megan, but you can't go unless there's an adult with you, and I imagine your friends' parents will feel the same.'

Zac, Megan and Sophie looked at each other and then at Bex.

'Not me,' said Bex. 'I'll be in bed way before then.'

'And my mum won't… can't,' said Sophie.

'And my mum's working,' said Zac.

Ashley stayed silent.

'Sorry, kids. Maybe next year – when you're all a bit older,' said Bex as she disappeared downstairs.

Megan hauled herself off the bed and handed out the cakes but even the delicious squidginess of the butter-cream filling didn't lift the gloom.

'What about your mum?' said Zac to Ashley. He was angry at the thought of missing out.

'What about her?'

'Wouldn't she have helped?'

Ashley shrugged.

'You didn't even offer to ask her,' continued Zac.

'Why should I? Anyway, she'd have probably said no.'

'She might not have done. Don't you want to go to the fireworks? Or would it upset your delicate sensibilities? All a bit much for a luvvie like you.'

Megan rounded on Zac. 'Shut up, Zac. It doesn't matter.'

'Why? I'm only repeating what you said.'

'I… I didn't.'

'Yes, you did. You said Ash had gone all weird and poncy since the panto.'

Megan flushed bright red. 'I didn't… that's not…'

'Yes, you did.'

'No, I just said he talked about acting a lot.'

'So? It's the same thing,' said Zac.

As the two rowed Ashley levered himself off the floor and ran down the stairs,

'Now look what you've done,' Megan shouted at Zac. 'You're the pits.'

'Well, if you're going to be like that…' And grabbing another cake, Zac left too. The front door banged again.

Sophie looked at Megan. 'Well, that went well. Not.'

'Bloody Zac,' snarled Megan.

'Text Ash. Tell him to come back.'

'No, he thinks I've been laughing about him behind his back. Why would he even want to see me again, let alone talk to me?'

'And you didn't?'

'Of course not.' Megan sighed. 'I *did* say he talked about acting all the time – but he does.'

'Then apologise. It can't make things worse, can it?'

Ashley stormed down the road, angry and hurt. Megan and Zac had been making fun of him behind his back. And he'd thought they were his mates. Moreover, he'd thought Megan understood. Ashley turned into the nature reserve and strode along the muddy paths, his fists clenching and unclenching. He kicked at a stone by the path. Rain began to fall, spattering him with cold drops intermittently. Ashley looked at the sky and saw that the high light cloud was being hidden by thick black banks rolling in from the west. He turned and began to jog back the way he'd come but the rain got worse along with the light and Ashley realised that if he headed for his own home he'd be drenched long before he reached it. He picked up his speed and raced back onto the high street and turned up the road to the station to his gran's. A couple of minutes later he stood under her little porch and hammered on the door.

'Come in, come in out of the wet,' she exhorted when she opened the door and stood aside to let Ashley past. He got into the hall and shook his head to get the worse of the drops out of his hair.

'Hey,' said Mags. 'I don't want to get wet too.'

Ashley slipped his coat off and hung it on the stairs.

'And what were you thinking of – being out in this weather?' said Mags. 'You'll catch your death.' She tutted as she bustled into the kitchen. 'Tea's what you need. Something wet and warm. Go and sit down in the sitting room and put the fire on while I boil the kettle.'

Ashley went into the sitting room and lit the gas.

'Now,' said his gran, bustling into the room. 'What's going on? You've come here looking like you've lost a fiver and found a tanner, your face is as black as thunder.'

'Nothing,' snapped Ashley.

Mags crossed her arms across her ample chest. 'Don't give me that. I wasn't born yesterday. If you ask me you've not been right since you took up that play-acting lark.'

'What do you expect with Mum telling me I shouldn't want to do it? You're against it, you don't understand – of course I'm not happy.'

'Are you sure that's all it is?'

Ashley hesitated. Did he tell Gran that even his best mates had turned against him?

'Come on, son. A problem shared is a problem halved.'

'Well… it's Megan.'

'Megan?'

'You know, Amy cleans for her mum.'

'I know who Megan is – what's she got to do with everything?'

'She said some horrid things about me to Zac. She said I've gone all luvvie.'

Mags blew out her cheeks. 'Ah.'

Ashley looked at her. '"*Ah*"? What's that supposed to mean?'

'Well, your mum and I did wonder…'

'Wonder what?'

'If… you know… if you're on the other bus. I mean, all this interesting in acting and make-up and dressing up…'

'You and Mum think…' Ashley's brow furrowed. 'What? That I'm gay?' His astonishment was tangible.

Mags nodded. 'Your mum'll get used to the idea. I mean, she still loves you. And everyone's told her that no one minds these days.'

Ashley's jaw slackened and his eyes narrowed. 'So… *everyone*. She's been talking about me. Who to?'

'Your mum was worried, she wanted advice.'

'Exactly who did she talk to?'

'How am I supposed to know? The ladies she cleans for, I expect.'

Things were getting worse and worse. 'Like Megan's mother? So Mum's told Bex I'm gay?'

Mags shrugged. 'Maybe. But I'm sure she's OK with it.'

'But... but...' Oh, God... How *could* his mum have done that? Blabbed to the whole town about him? 'Sorry, Gran, but I need some space. Forget the tea.'

And stuff the rain. Ashley grabbed his coat and ran out of the house. As he did so his phone pinged. He stopped under a tree to check the message.

Are u alright? Zacs a git. And I never called you a luvvie – honest.

Ashley stared at the text. A picture popped up on the screen. It was of the plate of butterfly cakes which still had half a dozen on it.

Help us with this lot

Another picture pinged in. This one was of Sophie and Megan, their cheeks blown out and both trying to look fat.

Save us from ourselves

Ashley found himself grinning involuntarily. Megan was apologising. And he knew what she was saying was the truth. And these weren't texts from someone who never wanted to see him again. Maybe the sensible thing would be to go back to the girls and make up. His relationship with his mum though... that was a whole other issue.

43

Miranda contemplated writing another stiff letter of complaint to the council with a copy to the local rag. The noise of the New Year's Eve fireworks had been a total abomination, even worse than the racket created by Bonfire Night but at least that firework display had been at the other end of the town. And as for the waste of money and the air pollution... Why on earth did normally sane people think it was OK to lob noxious chemicals into the sky and make them explode so the whole area got showered in poisons? And that was before anyone took into consideration the effect it had on wildlife and other animals. She assumed that the oiks were too stupid to understand the implications of such a display and what it did to the wider environment. And on another, more serious, level this was a country that seemed to pride itself on its anti-terrorist measures and yet there were times in the year when any Tom, Dick or Harriet could waltz into a shop and buy kilos upon kilos of high explosive. Where were the safety regulations regarding that?!

On the other hand, thought Miranda, if she took a stand, there was the distinct possibility it might lead to more unpleasantness. Her protests against eating meat had only elicited curious stares and a confrontation with the butcher – oh, and a threat of arrest. Not that the local constable had carried the threat out but it had been a nasty moment all the same. Since then she'd still protested but the shock of the new had been lost and no one, not *one* person had asked questions about veganism or interacted with her in any way, but it had obviously upset someone. There was a slight chance that the damage to her car might have been accidental, and the incident in the florist might have been a misunderstanding... but there was no doubt the manure had been dumped spitefully and deliberately. Nor was there doubt that the townsfolk had stood around and gloated as she and Roderick had cleared up the worst of it, nor was there doubt about the way no one had seemed the least prepared to help find someone to move it off their land. And there was no doubt she wasn't winning in the popularity stakes.

As if she cared.

Miranda stood up and went over to the window and stared at the view. Out of the corner of her eye she could see her wind turbine pirouetting in the breeze. And that was another issue... Amy had left her in no doubt that the locals didn't like *that* either. She'd tried explaining the good it would bring to the environment in general but Amy's eyes had glazed over. Well, no surprise there because if Miranda was any judge of character Amy might be able to follow a soap opera – well, the simpler plot lines – but that would be the limit of her intellectual capacity. Certainly the ins and outs of global warming and the benefits of sustainable energy were way outside her skill set.

For some reason her thoughts drifted back to her trip into town the day before and all the people she'd seen meeting and greeting each other and, inexplicably, she felt another tiny stab of jealousy. What would it be like to be a part of a community? She realised she didn't have a clue. At school and university she'd been too busy with her studies to bother with irrelevances like acting groups or choirs. Her entire focus had been on succeeding, on being the best, on having a career that would be the envy of her peers – peers who had sneered at her for being the poor kid in a rich kids' school. Admittedly she'd joined the debating society when she'd been studying for her degree but only because she'd felt that would hone skills she'd need in a courtroom. And then when she'd specialised in medical negligence law and had been called to the Bar she never cared a jot about being *liked* – it was all about *winning*. But then there had been Emily... And her breakdown... And her retirement from her chambers. And the start of her isolation.

She was, she admitted to herself, lonely. There were days, when Roderick was in court or at his chambers, when she didn't speak to a soul the whole day. As she stood by the window and gazed at the idyllic countryside she wrapped her arms around herself. Outwardly she had an enviably perfect life; the house, the clothes, the lifestyle. She fingered her emerald earrings – no, she didn't want for anything material, not now. But if anything desperate happened to her, who would run to her aid? And the answer was, besides Roderick, probably no one. Not even her mother, whom she had alienated when she'd refused to listen to her doubts about marrying a much older man.

'You're looking for a father figure,' her mother had counselled. 'Just because your father died when you were little doesn't mean he needs to be replaced by your fiancé. You'll regret it.'

'I won't.'

'He's stealing your youth.'

'For God's sake, Mother, I'm twenty-nine, not nineteen.'

'You're still young and he's fifty-five.'

'You just don't want me to be happy, that's it, isn't it?'

'I don't want you to be left a widow, like me.'

'At least I'll be a rich widow,' she'd spat back. 'At least Roderick will make sure of that. Not like Daddy who left us dirt poor.'

'Apologise for that,' her mother had hissed.

'Why? It's the truth.' Which it was because he'd been conned out of his savings and his pension scheme by some shyster who sold him a too-good-to-be-true, get-rich-quick scheme. The only person to get-rich-quick was the shyster.

'You're wrong, it wasn't his fault,' said her mother.

But Miranda had shaken her head, told her mother she was as deluded and foolish as her father and had walked out. And she wasn't going to back down, not till her mother told her she was right. Miranda went back to one of her cream sofas and curled up in a corner. The sobering reality was that she'd spent her entire adult life achieving, getting on, then creating a perfect home, a perfect marriage, a perfect lifestyle... but what did it all count for? Was she happy? Contented? A tear rolled down her cheek as she addressed the answer. It was all very well wanting to be better than everyone else but all it did was push them away – the people who couldn't or didn't match up, or who got fed up with competing in a race they weren't going to win. And that included her mother. And now it was too late because her mother was dead.

Maybe if she'd had Emily things would have been different. Before the miscarriage she had already made up her mind that Emily was to have lots of friends because being socially accomplished would always stand her in good stead. She'd had it all mapped out. Emily was destined for a nice little private nursery, maybe somewhere like Thomas's Battersea where she'd have met the right sort of child. And then maybe a private prep school followed by Benenden or Roedean or perhaps Cheltenham Ladies College? She would have met other mothers, made friends with them, had their children for play dates... It all promised to be so perfect. Another tear plopped onto her cashmere roll-neck.

Maybe being perfect wasn't the answer. Those people she'd seen the day before seemed quite content with their humdrum lives and they all looked far from perfect. And if she wanted friendship maybe she should become more accepting of the way this town did things. Maybe she ought to go with the flow and not try and swim against the tide.

She made a decision.

'Roderick,' she called.

From his study upstairs she heard him answer.

'I'm going out for a walk. I may be a while.'

'OK, dear.'

'I'll be back in time to cook dinner.'

'That's fine, dear. Enjoy your stroll.'

Miranda grabbed a notebook and pencil which she dropped in her handbag, picked up her coat and let herself out of the house. She flung a glance at the midden, which, thankfully, had stopped steaming and reeking and was now piled at the side of the drive. There was still an unmistakable agricultural tang in the air but, compared to what they'd endured over Christmas, it was nothing. And by next week it would be gone.

Miranda walked purposefully down the hill and then along the high street. The town was deathly quiet. Everyone sleeping off their hangovers, she thought. She passed a large Victorian villa and heard the sound of children shrieking and squealing. She slowed her step to look over the five-bar gate and saw two small boys being chased by a man pretending to be an ogre, to judge by the way he was acting, and being watched by a woman who was leaning against the porch, her hand resting on the little bump of her belly. Pregnant? A happy family, she thought, and about to get happier if she was right about the baby. The woman in the porch flashed her a smile and Miranda smiled back.

'Happy New Year,' she said tentatively to the stranger.

'And you,' came the hearty reply.

Feeling uplifted by this ridiculously small exchange, Miranda continued on her way. She passed the pub where the landlady was saying goodbye to the last of her lunchtime customers and was about to lock up. Once again there was a brief exchange of greetings and wishes for a Happy New Year. Maybe, thought Miranda, some of the locals weren't so bad after all.

She arrived at the town hall and extracted her notebook from her bag. She peered at the noticeboard and began to note down some of the long list of the various clubs and societies which seemed to abound in the town. She was reasonably selective in her choice – she didn't want to do gardening, nor did she want to join the Men's Shed, even though it promised it welcomed all for 'chat, coffee and tinkering'. But the book club looked promising, as did the running club – she'd run quite a bit in her youth but had given it up in London – and the Friends of the Earth group might be interesting. Oh, and Amnesty International. She jotted the details of that down too and snapped her notebook shut. A second later she reopened it to check her notes. The book club contact was down as Bex Millar, The Beeches, High Street. Wasn't The Beeches the house where the kids had been playing?

Miranda turned and retraced her steps and checked the plate attached to the five-bar gate. The Beeches. The garden was now quiet and deserted so she leaned over and unbolted the catch before pushing the gate open. She closed it carefully and crunched over the gravel to the front door.

After she rang the bell she had to wait a few seconds before it was opened by a black-haired beauty with smouldering eyes.

'Yes?'

'I was wondering if I might speak to Bex Millar. I've been led to believe she lives here…'

Languidly the teen opened the door fully and said, 'She's in the kitchen.'

Gales of laughter billowed from the room to the right of the door, the hall had pairs of shoes in a number of different sizes strewn across it, the newel post was lost beneath a mound of coats and somewhere a radio was blaring pop music. Miranda was part-appalled by the chaos and part-fascinated by this insight into family life.

The sultry teen pointed out the door to the kitchen before she shut the front door and drifted into the sitting room.

Miranda clacked across the tiles towards the sound of the radio which had now been joined by the high-pitched whine of a small electric motor. The noise was almost untenable.

She stood by the door and watched the blonde who had wished her a Happy New Year beat yellow goo in a bowl with a hand mixer. She switched the mixer off and the radio was able to reassert itself.

'Hello,' said Miranda.

The woman jumped.

'Sorry, I didn't mean to startle you. Your daughter let me in.'

'Hello.' The woman, Bex presumably, creased her brow. 'Although, didn't we say hello to each other just a few minutes ago?'

Miranda nodded. 'I'm Miranda Osborne. I moved into The Grange a little while ago.'

'Oh – so you're the new owner of Olivia's place.'

'Olivia? Olivia Laithwaite?' The woman who was on the reception at Woodford Priors, the woman with the bike, the woman who 'didn't know' of anyone who might be able to clear the manure. Olivia had owned The Grange? Well!

'You've met her? Well, no surprise there, Olivia is one of the main movers and shakers in this town.'

'I don't really know her. Our paths crossed when I stayed at the hotel.'

'Of course, she works there but that's not *really* meeting. Then I must introduce you properly. Olivia is the fount of all knowledge about what goes on around here.'

'Is she now?' And yet she didn't know anyone who could have helped with the manure. Hmmm.

'Anyway, I'm being terribly rude. I'm Bex Millar.' She stuck out her hand for Olivia to shake. 'Can I offer you tea? I'd offer you cake too but I haven't finished making it yet.'

'Um… no to either, thank you. I'm vegan.'

'Oh dear.' Bex looked nonplussed. 'Oh yes, of course you are, I'd forgotten. The protests…' Her voice petered out.

'I'm not here about that. Your name is down as the person to contact about the book club.'

'Yes, that's right. Would you like to join?'

'It depends. It depends what sort of books you read?'

'Anything and everything. To be honest it's not entirely about the books – it's much more of a friendship group, a get-together, you know with a glass of wine and a few nibbles. We meet on a Monday once a month, above the pub. It's great fun. You ought to come along.'

'I don't know...' It sounded awfully frivolous. Not at all what she was expecting. 'What's your current book?'

'This one.' Bex reached over to a work surface and picked up a paperback with a pastel cover and curly script. She tossed it across the kitchen table to Miranda who caught it deftly.

Dear God, did people actually read books like this? Chick lit? She saw the banner at the top of the book. *Sunday Times Number 1 Bestseller*. Really? Did tens, possibly hundreds of thousands of people buy books like this? Miranda despaired. What *was* the human race coming to? 'I... I don't think...'

'It's a great read. Honestly. I'm loving it. It's very... uplifting. Life affirming.'

'Really?' But what was wrong with the classics, with literature...?

'I've nearly finished it. I can drop it in when I take the boys back to school next week. You'll still have a few days to read it before the meeting.' Bex smiled at her. 'Do come along – it's a great way of getting to meet people. Trust me, I know. I was new to Little Woodford last Easter and through the book club and the WI and working at the pub I've made lots of friends.'

But this was a wealthy educated woman with children and yet she was a barmaid? Miranda couldn't help herself and blurted out, 'The pub?'

'Yes, I work there weekday lunchtimes. It gets me out of the house, gives a bit of purpose to the day and Belinda – the landlady – is very good about letting me have the school holidays off because there's always a student or two who'd like a holiday job.'

Involuntarily, Miranda glanced at Bex's tummy. 'But you're...'

'Pregnant? Yes. So?' She sounded a bit prickly; maybe she'd had this criticism before.

'Yes, yes, I know.' But she wasn't going to confide just how much she knew. Besides, she'd been reassured that working during her own pregnancy had had no effect on the tragedy which had subsequently happened – but it had done nothing to assuage the guilt.

'So,' said Bex, obviously wanting to move away from the subject of pregnancy and working motherhood, 'shall I drop the book round next week?'

'Yes, yes, that'd be lovely.'

'And we meet in the function room at the pub the Monday after.'

'I'm looking forward to it.' Miranda wasn't sure she was, if she was brutally honest. But maybe she'd stick out the club for a couple of meetings just to get to know a few people. Maybe next time they'd read something more challenging. If she could exert any influence she'd make sure of it. Some Dostoyevsky maybe, or perhaps Julian Barnes. Anything but chick lit.

44

A few days later, Ashley was questioning his commitment to acting as he stood outside the stage door of the Players Theatre wishing his knees weren't shaking quite so much. Shit, if he was this nervous about an audition for the local am-dram group what would he be like when he went for real parts in real theatres? The stage door was down the side return of an old cinema and the lighting wasn't great. Ashley had deliberately tucked himself in to the deepest shadow he could find while he observed the members of the company arrive, tap the code into the keypad and let themselves in. He'd counted about a dozen people enter and decided that he had to make a move sooner rather than later. Would they laugh at him for turning up on spec? He just needed the courage to find out. Courage which, he'd found out, seemed to be in rather limited supply. He steeled himself, stepped out of the shadow and rapped sharply on the door.

What, he asked himself as he waited to be admitted, was the worst that could happen? And no one had died of rejection. Or, at least, he didn't think they had.

'Pullen?'

Oh, shit a brick. Mr Johnson.

'What are you doing here, Pullen?'

Ashley resisted the urge to give his maths teacher a facetious response. Instead he said, 'Hoping for an audition, sir.'

Mr Johnson stared at him and tapped the keypad, then held the door open for Ashley. 'Much as I'm not a fan of your attitude in school, I have to admit you might be an asset here.'

Ashley was stunned. It was only *faint* praise but Mr Johnson *never* handed out bouquets – only brickbats.

Mr Johnson stopped in the doorway and turned, blocking Ashley's path. 'But if there is *any* repeat of the appalling insolent behaviour you demonstrated at the end of last term I will have you excluded from this company and every other theatre group in the county. Do I make myself clear?'

Ashley swallowed and nodded. This was more like the teacher he knew and hated. What a git. Fuming internally, Ashley followed Mr Johnson into the theatre and found himself walking down a long badly lit corridor. Along one side of the passage were stacked scenery flats – left over, he presumed, from previous productions. And suddenly he was surrounded by dark drapery – the wings – and then, to his right, the brightly lit expanse of the stage. A gaggle of people were standing around chatting in amongst the furniture that presumably set the scene for their next production.

'I've got a new recruit,' said Mr Johnson, suddenly exuding bonhomie and good cheer. He clapped Ashley on the shoulder. 'This is Ashley Pullen, the star of the school's panto in December. He wants to audition.' He gave Ashley a slight shove that propelled him into the middle of the group. It was almost, thought Ashley, as though Mr Johnson, having introduced him, wanted to distance himself from him. Well, if that was the case, it was mutual.

There was a general murmuring of *jolly good* and *that's great* before a stout woman, with a mass of scarves and huge clunky beads draped around her neck, stepped forward.

'I'm Cassandra – the theatre director.' She held out a small, soft, pudgy hand, also decked out in lots of clunky jewellery, to Ashley. He shook it but then, from the expression on her face, got the impression that she'd expected him to kiss it. 'Anyway,' she said, whisking it back out of his grasp, 'I am sure we can fit you in before we start tonight's rehearsal.' She clapped her hands. 'If everyone would like to take a seat in the stalls...'

The cast and crew shuffled off the stage and down the flight of steps at the sides into the gloom of the stalls. They were joined by Cassandra who sat in the middle of the auditorium.

'When you're ready,' she called.

Ashley's heart raced and his palms sweated but he took a deep breath. 'I'm doing a speech from the play of *Kes*, by Barry Hines. It's a speech from a lad called Anderson.' He stared through the brightness of the lights into the darkness, trying to discern if there were any approving nods. But he couldn't see a thing.

'Off you go,' called Cassandra.

And Ashley began to recite his prepared piece. '"Well it was once when I was a kid. I was at Junior School, I think, or somewhere like that, and went down to Fowlers Pond, me and this other kid. Reggie Clay they called him..."' He warmed to his monologue, describing the two kids catching tadpoles and, not having a jam jar to hand, they put them in his wellies. And describing how they filled the boots to the brim with the creatures until there was no water... nothing but tadpoles. And then came the description of putting his foot in the wellington, in amongst the tadpoles. He mimed this bit, screwing up his face as he described the way they squashed between his toes.

A loud clap and 'Thank you,' stopped him.

And then it wasn't just the one pistol-shot of a clap, there was applause; proper applause from the others in the audience.

Ashley felt his face flare with pleasure and relief and with embarrassment. He hadn't been expecting this – not from grown-ups, not at an audition.

Then Cassandra was on stage with him. 'So, Ashley Pullen, when can you start?'

Ashley could remember how thrilled he'd been when the panto had been a success, how chuffed with the applause and praise that he'd received for each performance but it paled into insignificance compared to the unalloyed delight he was experiencing at being accepted by other actors – proper actors, people who knew what they were doing. These weren't other kids, mucking around, pretending to act, and his audience wasn't parents who *had* to say nice things. This was the real deal and he'd been accepted. If he knew how to do a whole series of backflips he'd have flick-flacked across the stage in joy.

'As soon as you want me,' he said. 'Now?' he added hopefully.

'I got it, I got it,' Ashley gabbled as he fell in through the front door, his excitement leaving him uncoordinated and almost incoherent.

Amy looked up from the sofa. 'Got what? A dose of the flu?'

'No, Mum, I got into the theatre group. They liked me. They liked my audition.'

'Oh, is that all.'

Ashley felt suddenly deflated.

'Look,' added his mum seeing her son's expression, 'I get that you like acting and I get that I was wrong about your reasons why.' Which she had been left in no doubt about by her son during a very heated conversation. 'But I still worry about what this is going to do to your school work.'

'It'll be OK, I promise.'

Amy looked supremely unconvinced. 'Oh, yeah.'

'I managed with the panto, didn't I?'

'You weren't doing no mock GCSEs when you did that. It's all different now – and next term with the real thing…'

'You just don't get it, do you?' yelled Ashley as he slammed out of the room and thundered up the stairs. He raced into his room, banged the door shut behind him and threw himself on his bed. Why couldn't she see that this was his future? That acting was the only thing he wanted to do?

At least the bunch at the theatre 'got it'. He thought about his new friends. Well, they weren't friends yet but he was sure they'd become so – he certainly liked them and he was sure they liked him. They liked his acting ability so that was a start. There was Cassandra with all her scarves and beads and bling, and then there was the woman with the Cupid's bow mouth who looked like some sort of forties film idol and dressed like one, too, with retro clothes and waved hair. And the men who were so confident, so self-assured, with their expansive gestures and casual elegance. No one thought acting was dressing up or showing off or 'gay' like his mum and Mags did. No, it was just what they did, how they rolled and, what was more, at the theatre almost everyone seemed to be a bit odd, a bit eccentric, but they were all so proud of their differences. Not like at school were everyone was desperate to fit in, to be the same. Where 'difference' was to be avoided at all costs.

No, he thought, that wasn't strictly true; school was full of kids who were different but they gravitated towards similarly different kids... the Goths, the petrol-heads, the jocks all hung around in their various groups, some of which were cooler than the others. Jocks were definitely cool, the geeks less so. And Ashley had been aware for some time that, although he was reasonably popular, he didn't have a group he fitted right into. He could feign an interest in cars or sports but it was all faked. But now... now he had a gang that was perfect and he hadn't felt happier.

The Sunday after Ashley had auditioned successfully for the Woodford Players, Miranda picked up the book club book. Roderick had gone off for a golf match with some of his colleagues from chambers and she was on her own. She stared at the book as if it was some totally noxious medicine that she'd been told she had to swallow. With a deep sigh she opened the cover and flicked over the pages till she reached the first chapter.

She told herself to switch off the critical part of her brain, the part which she knew would abhor the book. This was, she was certain, going to be the equivalent of eating pappy white bread when she might have been getting stuck into a wonderful artisanal seeded rye loaf. Heigh-ho... she made a start.

At the bottom of the second page the heroine made a pithy comeback to a customer in her shop and Miranda felt her mouth twitch. Yes... well... just as one swallow didn't make a summer, one snappy one-liner was unlikely to make this a great read. She carried on. Three pages later she giggled. OK, she conceded, maybe it wasn't great literature but at least it was entertaining. Miranda glanced at her watch. She'd give it another hour before she went to do something more worthwhile.

The click of the key in the front door startled her so much she almost dropped the book. Dear God, was that Roderick home already? She looked at her watch. Four o'clock! Where had the time gone? Guiltily, she stuffed the book behind the sofa cushions. Roderick would laugh himself silly if he saw what she was reading. And if he did find out she'd lie about how much she'd enjoyed it. Now, if he knew that he'd split his sides.

45

The following evening Miranda pushed open the door of the pub and made her way in. She wasn't a fan of pubs but, to judge by first impressions, this one wasn't all bad. There was a fire burning in the big inglenook and there were no flashing fruit machines or hideous muzak. She supposed that if you liked country pubs, this one was OK. She walked over to the bar.

'Evening,' she said to the woman she remembered greeting on New Year's Day – presumably the landlady.

'Hello. And what can I get you?'

Miranda thought. Did she want a drink? 'Erm... I'm here for the book club.'

'That doesn't mean you're not allowed to drink. In fact there's some members who reckon it's compulsory.'

Bex had said something to that effect – that they had wine and nibbles and chat. It didn't sound as though the conversation was likely to be very cerebral – but then the book hadn't been either. 'Oh. Maybe a small glass of a vegan white wine then.'

The landlady gave her a long stare. 'Listen, m'dear...'

What was it with the people in this town that they couldn't address anyone properly? 'Yes.'

'This is a country pub. We don't do vegan wines. You can have a Cabernet Sauvignon, a white Rioja or a Chardonnay. And they come in three sizes; large, small or a bottle.'

'A bottle!'

'If you're going to have more than one glass, it'll work out cheaper. Or you could share it – help to break the ice, seeing as how you're new here.'

Miranda hadn't thought of that. She needn't drink more than a sip or two. The sky wouldn't fall in if she didn't stick to her principles absolutely.

'A white Rioja, then. A bottle.'

'How many glasses?'

'Four.'

As the landlady found a tray, loaded it up and rang up the purchase on the till she said, 'I'm Belinda. And you are...? Seventeen pounds please.'

'Oh, Miranda Osborne.' She extracted a twenty and handed it over.

'You up at The Grange?'

She nodded.

'You dealt with your... problem yet?' Was the landlady smirking?

'Yes, thank you.'

'Any clue as to who did it?'

'No. I'm sure we'll find out eventually.'

'Doubt it,' said a male voice from across the room.

Miranda spun round and eyeballed the eavesdropper. 'Why, do you know something?' She gave him a gimlet stare – one of the ones she used to use in court.

The old boy appeared unfazed and chuckled by way of response.

'You take no notice of old Harry; he's a troublemaker. Aren't you, you old git?'

The old boy drained his drink and wandered over to the bar where he put his tankard down and then returned Miranda's stare at closer quarters.

'Just remember, what goes around comes around,' he said to her before he shuffled off towards the door.

She had no idea what he meant but she felt slightly rattled all the same. She grabbed the tray and her change. 'The function room?'

Belinda indicated a flight of stairs. 'Up there. It's all laid out ready.'

Which meant she was the first. For some reason, maybe it was the encounter with Harry, she felt nervous. Was this a good idea? Was she walking into a lion's den of people who had already formed a hostile opinion of her?

Miranda went up to the room, dumped the tray, wandered over to the window and looked out. She saw the woman next door open and shut the gate and head for the pub. A few minutes later she heard footsteps on the stairs.

'Hi, Miranda,' she said as she reached the function room. 'Belinda told me you were here ahead of me. She also told me you bought white so I went for red.' Bex waved a bottle before dumping it on the tray and then putting down several glasses she had threaded between the fingers of her other hand.

Miranda was aghast. Wine! While pregnant!

'Not that I'm drinking it.' Bex glanced down at her tummy.

Miranda relaxed and allowed herself to smile in approval.

'I've got a lime and lemonade on the bar. I'll just fetch it.'

Bex shot off back down the stairs and returned a few seconds later with a tall glass containing her drink. 'Cheers,' she said as she took a swig.

Miranda cracked open the screw top on her bottle and poured herself a small glass. 'Cheers,' she replied.

'We've got to hope that not everyone buys a whole bottle. We'll all be under the table if they do.'

How incredibly irresponsible if the group behaved like that. 'Indeed,' was all Miranda could bring herself to say. She fished in her bag for the book. 'Here, I'd better give it back to you.'

More footsteps were heard on the stairs. It was Olivia. The pair stared at each other.

'I think you two have met,' said Bex cheerfully, apparently oblivious to the change in atmosphere. 'But you haven't been formally introduced. Olivia meet Miranda, Miranda this is Olivia. Miranda lives in your old house.'

'Yes, I know,' said Olivia.

'And you work at the hotel,' countered Miranda. The atmosphere was Baltic.

Bex shot worried looks from one to the other. 'Wine?'

Fifteen minutes later everyone had arrived and the noise level in the function room was epic.

Bex picked up a biro and pinged the side of an empty wine glass. The imperious ding-ding-ding cut through the conversations which all gradually petered out.

'Good evening,' said Bex, 'and an especial welcome to our latest member, Miranda Osborne, who has moved into The Grange quite recently.'

A ripple of greetings ran round the room. Olivia scowled.

'So, I think we ought to get started but before we do maybe Miranda would like to tell us a little bit about herself. So if you'd like to top up your glasses and take your seats...'

The women in the book club refilled their glasses and settled down while Miranda worked out which bits of her life she was prepared to share.

'My husband, Roderick, and I moved here from London. We're both lawyers but I don't practise any more. I'm passionate about veganism and animal welfare—'

'Don't we know it,' someone muttered not quite sotto voce.

Miranda raised her voice a fraction, '—and in sustainability in all things. After London, I value the deep peace of the country,' she flashed a look at Heather who stared back, 'as, I am sure everyone does.' Heather looked sceptical. 'As you probably know, I am also against pollution of any sort... noise, air, casual littering. I will do my best to prevent it using any means possible.'

She glared again at Heather who looked coolly back. 'There, I think that covers the important things.'

'Thank you, Miranda.' Bex beamed at the club members and held up her copy of the book. 'Who'd like to open the batting?'

'I would,' said Heather, 'but just before I do I thought I'd share some lovely news with you all – well, Olivia knows this already but I don't think the rest of you do. As you know, we finished the fundraising just before Christmas and the foundry is coming to repair the bell frame in the near future. It's going to be quite a job but we're hopeful we'll be able to ring out the bells again at the Easter service. Won't that be lovely?' As the book group agreed whole-heartedly that it would, indeed, be lovely, Heather gave Miranda her broadest smile and was rewarded with a stony stare back. Did Miranda mouth, 'we'll see about that'?

Downstairs, Amy wandered into the bar.

'Hiya, Belinda. Anyone been asking for me?'

'Another date?'

Amy nodded. 'Thought I might give it one last throw of the dice before I resign myself to being a lonely old maid. And a G and T please.'

'That sounds a bit defeatist.' Belinda put a glass under the optic and gave Amy a double shot. 'And no, no one's been in yet.'

Amy shrugged. 'Why shouldn't I be defeatist? I mean, look at the last two.'

'Third time lucky?' Belinda dropped ice and a slice into the drink and then poured in the tonic.

'Maybe.' Amy didn't sound convinced. 'How much?'

'On the house.'

'Oh, Belinda, you don't have to.'

'No, I don't but you sound as if you need cheering up.'

'Cheers, hon.' Amy took a swig and leaned an elbow on the bar.

'So, what's this one like?'

'Well… he *says* he likes watching soaps, and Sunday lunches at the pub, and he plays rugby for Catteford Extra B. I don't know nothing about rugby but is that good?'

'The Extra Bs?' Belinda giggled. 'No, it's desperate, but it means he plays for the fun of it and there's more beer drinking involved than playing.'

'So, he's not bigging himself up?'

'Not if he's admitting to playing for the Extra B side.'

'Maybe there's hope for this one.'

'Good luck. And, er…' Belinda scratched her nose. 'The usual signal?'

'Might as well.' Amy took her drink and went over to a table near the window and played with her phone as she waited for her date.

She was engrossed in a game of solitaire when a voice said, 'May I join you?'

Startled she glanced up and saw a bloke about her age with a crooked nose, very smiley blue eyes and a devastating smile. He looked like a hero from an action film. No, she couldn't be this lucky.

'Sorry, but I'm waiting for a date.'

'Amy?'

Amy's heart banged against her ribs. Blimey, maybe her luck had changed. 'Ryan?'

'That's me? Drink?' He put his Guinness down on the table.

Amy glanced at her glass and saw it was half empty. She necked the last of it and handed it over. 'G and T, ta.'

'Back in a tick.'

As he turned to go to the bar she caught Belinda's eye and gave her a big thumbs up. Belinda grinned back.

'So,' said Bex, as the discussion about the book came to a close, 'I think we're all in agreement that that book wasn't great literature, but it was a thumping good read.' She grinned at the group who were all feeling happily relaxed after a glass – or several – of wine. 'And I think it would be nice if we invited our newest member to choose our next read. Miranda – have you got a suggestion for us?'

Miranda had been planning to point the group towards something uplifting, something literary, something... worthy. She had a mental list: *One Hundred Years of Solitude*; *Ulysses*; *To the Lighthouse*... So she was a tiny bit surprised when she heard herself say, 'Have you read *Love in a Cold Climate*?'

'Nancy Mitford?' checked Bex.

Miranda nodded and everyone else shook their heads.

'Sell it to us,' said Bex.

Miranda told them about the mad aristocratic family with a myriad of daughters and the efforts made to marry them off. Her audience looked bemused or gobsmacked.

'And the best thing is, it's pretty much an autobiography,' finished Miranda.

'I'm sold,' said Bex.

'And me,' chorused most of the others.

Olivia was conspicuously silent.

'Olivia?' asked Bex.

'If we must. I feel it's a book that's been done to death. TV adaptations, dramatisations... And then there's the endless biographies of the Mitfords.'

Bex and Miranda exchanged a glance before Bex said, 'It's a valid point, Olivia, but I think the majority are in favour.'

'As you wish.' She sniffed. 'Still,' she muttered, 'at least I won't have to waste time reading the wretched book.'

The function room emptied slowly but Olivia deliberately hung back to leave with Bex.

'Fancy a coffee at mine?' offered Bex.

'I'd love one. Now I work I really don't see enough of my old friends.'

The pair walked down the stairs. In the bar they saw Amy chatting animatedly to a good-looking man.

'Do you think that's a date?' said Bex. 'If it is, let's hope he's a better bet than that awful Billy.'

'He can't be worse,' said Olivia.

They thanked Belinda for the use of the function room and made their way next door to Bex's house.

'Did your parents get home OK after Christmas?' asked Olivia as Bex opened the front door.

Bex nodded and said, 'Yes, thanks. It was a lovely Christmas, well... mostly.' She went to the foot of the stairs. 'I'm back,' she called up them.

A just audible, 'OK,' came back from the attic.

'Mostly?' queried Olivia.

Bex led the way into the kitchen. 'I broke the news about the baby to Richard's parents.'

'Oh.'

'Indeed. We've barely spoken since.' She sighed. 'How about yours?'

'So-so. It was cosy but thank God, Jade could go back to the vicarage to sleep. I don't how we'd have coped otherwise. As it was, with Tamsin in the spare room, Mike had to sleep on an airbed in the sitting room, so it wasn't ideal. And then there was the fact that I had to leave them to fend for themselves quite a lot – I had shifts all over the holiday.' Olivia pulled out a chair from under the kitchen table and sat down.

'That can't have been much fun.' Bex filled the kettle and got out the mugs.

Olivia shrugged. 'Well, what can you do? If you work in hospitality it comes with the territory. The money was handy though. And I expect my Christmas was better than Miranda's. At least I didn't have to spend most of my spare time shovelling shit.'

The pair looked at each other and giggled.

'Do you know who did it?' asked Bex.

Olivia shook her head. 'Why, do you?'

Bex wrinkled her nose. 'There's a chap at the pub... called

Harry. I'd bet good money he might have something to do with it. Or knows who did.'

'I must meet him,' said Olivia. 'I'd like to buy that man a drink.'

'Join the queue. There's no two ways about it, she's a tricky customer. That said, I was stunned by her choice of book.'

'Oh, come on…' said Olivia. '*Love in a Cold Climate*?'

'At least it's accessible… and funny. Just think what she *might* have chosen.'

'Point taken. But it's still a cliché.'

'It could still be worse. A *lot* worse.'

'To be honest, I was a little taken aback when she said she wanted to join the book club. Everything she's done so far seems to have been designed to either set herself apart or upset the locals. Do you think she's decided she needs to start accepting the town and the inhabitants for what they are instead of trying to change everything?'

The kettle clicked off. 'Maybe. On the other hand I heard some of the things she said before the meeting started; her hatred of animal husbandry, her veganism, and then there's the bells.'

'Good luck with that.' Olivia snorted.

'That's pretty much what we all told her. But she seems quite determined. It's as if she doesn't want to be popular.'

'So why join the book club?'

'Maybe it's lonely up there on the moral high ground. Or perhaps she hopes to subversively convert us to her way of thinking.'

'Then she's soon going to realise that we don't want to change.'

'Indeed. We like this place the way it is.' Bex poured the boiling water onto the coffee granules and passed a mug and the milk to Olivia.

'Ah, but I think she reckons we'd like it *more* if we took her advice.'

'You mean go meat-free and weave our own lentils?'

'How's her petition against the bells doing?' asked Olivia after she'd had a sip of her coffee.

Bex picked up her iPad off the counter and flipped back the cover before she pressed the 'on' button and tapped in her code. She sat next to Olivia and tapped one of the icons. Then she typed in 'St Catherine's Church bells petition' into a text box.

She looked at the window that popped up and snorted. 'Oh, dear,' she chortled. 'I don't think that's going to cut much ice. Seventy-eight signatures. And I bet half of them aren't local. I think that makes it Little Woodford one–Miranda Osborne nil.'

46

Heather, Brian, Bert and a gaggle of others, including the bell-ringers, stood by the font and gazed towards the roof of the crossing of the nave and the transept at a point which was directly under the tower. They were corralled behind a safety barrier and all sported hard hats as they watched one of the massive bells sway slowly in the trapdoor that was high above a line of pallets waiting to receive them. There was a deal of shouting of instructions from the man from the foundry at the team of volunteers, some of whom were up in the belfry, others were stationed in the ringing chamber and yet more were in the body of the church, and between the three teams they were making sure the bell got a safe passage to ground level. Over and above the shouted instructions – *left a bit... lower away... stop* – came the clank and rattle of the chains that attached the bell and the headstock to the block and tackle so it could be lowered, inch by grinding inch. Finally a couple of helpers were able to reach up and guide it onto the centre of the pallet. It settled on the wooden planks with a gentle thud.

'One down, five to go,' said Brian cheerfully.

'They're big when they're close up, aren't they?' said Heather.

'And this is the treble,' said Pete, the steeple keeper.

'Is that the smallest?' asked Heather. She knew the answer but she also knew how passionate Pete was about the bells and he only needed the smallest of nudges to talk about them.

'Yup,' said Pete. 'That's it. This is number one and they all get bigger and bigger all the way to number six – the tenor.' And as he rambled on about change-ringing, its history and the combinations and permutations that went into ringing peals and rounds, the workers hauled up the chains and made ready to lower another bell and Heather began working out what she needed to add to her shopping list.

'Yes, I see,' said Heather eventually. 'You really know your stuff, don't you?' She glanced at her watch. 'My, is that the time? I've got to go and get lunch on. I've a meeting this afternoon and I can't be late.' She departed out of the church and into the sharp breeze that nipped at her ankles as she made her way back to the vicarage. The meeting she'd alluded to was a bit of a lie but she wanted to go and see Bex after she finished at the pub and before she went to collect the children from school. She hadn't seen her for a while and she'd heard from Olivia, at church on the previous Sunday, that Bex's in-laws weren't exactly happy at the thought of a new step-grandchild. She didn't feel there was much she could do to help but maybe Bex might like the opportunity to sound off a little.

Brian came back for lunch about thirty minutes later and was in a fine mood. The fact that work had actually started on fixing the bell frame had improved his morale immensely.

'And,' he said as he tucked into Heather's home-made vegetable soup, 'it's even better that they'll be ready to ring at Easter. Actually, I think they'll be ready before but we can save the moment for Easter Sunday. It'll be the icing on the cake.'

'Miranda Osborne won't think so. I can see her protesting with a placard in the churchyard. *Ban the Bells!*'

'She can try.'

'She came to the book club last week.'

'It's a free country.'

'Olivia thinks that load of manure was a bit of a wake-up call

– that she might be able to get away with bonkers protests in a place like London where they're used to those sorts of things but here... All she's done is make herself very unpopular. And now she's trying to row back – hence joining the book club.'

Brian looked over his glasses at his wife. 'So she's walked into the lion's den, eh? She's not lacking in courage, is she?'

'We're not fierce,' protested Heather. 'It's a lovely welcoming group.'

'Yes, dear,' said Brian and carried on eating his soup.

An hour later, lunch finished, the washing-up done and a thirty minute postprandial snooze completed, Heather walked up to Bex's house.

'Is this a good time?' she asked Bex, when her friend opened the door.

'Perfect. I've just got back from the pub. Miles is here too.' She shut the door and led the way into the kitchen. 'Excuse the mess – I seem to be running out of energy these days. Miles, bless him, has popped round to cook up a bunch of stuff to go in my freezer.'

Miles was standing by the table dicing carrots and onions. 'Hi, Heather.'

'Hello, Miles. What a kind thing to do.'

'My pleasure. Anyway, I can do this sort of thing in half the time it takes Bex.'

'Bragger,' said Bex smiling. She filled the kettle. 'Tea?'

'Please,' said Heather. 'Are you overdoing things?'

'I don't think so.'

'How long till the baby's due?'

'Five months – give or take. I'll be stopping work at Easter.'

'Good,' said Heather firmly.

'I agree,' said Miles.

'Not that the school holidays mean a rest for me. With the kids around twenty-four seven it's harder work than it is when I'm at the pub. I'd half planned to take them to Cyprus to see Granny Helen and Grandpa Phil...'

'Are those Richard's parents?'

Bex nodded and then patted her belly. 'They're not over the moon about this little one here.'

Miles snorted and chopped even more rapidly.

'Tricky.'

'That's one word for it. It doesn't help matters that I was the hired help before I married Richard. I obviously wasn't good enough for their son.'

'Don't be ridiculous,' said Heather.

Bex sighed. 'OK, maybe I'm exaggerating but Granny Helen's always been a bit tricky where I'm concerned. And I can't cut her out of our lives – she's the kids' granny. But, right now, I can't face a fortnight in Cyprus with her having digs at me all the time and it's too far to go for just a few days. And it's not a situation that's going to go away.'

'I wish I knew what to suggest.'

'It doesn't matter.' Bex sounded resigned and fed up. 'This is why we have friends... because we can't choose our families. In the meantime we'll all just have to make the best of it. I imagine she'll get over it... eventually.'

Miles put down his knife. 'I think you're being an absolute saint. I'd have told Helen to take a hike long since.'

Bex made the tea and passed the mugs around. She paused by Miles and put her hand on his shoulder. 'I love you for your support on this... but I can't. I can't alienate her, and the kids can't know that relations between us are at an all-time low. I think Megan might have picked up a bit of a vibe but the boys are still in blissful ignorance – and I want it to stay that way. Even if, when we FaceTime at Christmas, she can barely bring herself to talk to me. But we can get through this. And I'm so glad I've got you to help me.'

Miles reached up and held her hand and gave her a grin. 'I think you're forgetting that I got you into this mess.'

'And I wouldn't have it any other way.'

Heather smiled at the couple. Yes, she thought, together they were strong enough to weather most things – including a difficult mother-in-law.

Work progressed on the bell frame and the steel girders that were going to underpin it finally got delivered ready to be fitted into the bell tower. Parishioners came and gawped at the bells now they were all on the floor of the church, the local TV station filmed the work as it progressed and Brian longed for it all to be over so his church could be returned to normal. The book club met and discussed *Love in a Cold Climate* and chose another book to read for the March meeting; the snowdrops in the churchyard faded and were replaced by daffs and then suddenly it was almost Easter, the supermarket started to stock Easter eggs and Bex began to think about what she could do to entertain the children for two whole weeks of holiday when good weather wasn't guaranteed. But at least when Easter had come and gone she could look forward to giving up work and being able to put her feet up during the day. Although, while she was looking forward to putting her feet up – her ankles were starting to get quite swollen at the end of each shift – she really wasn't looking forward to stopping working. She loved her job and the locals that frequented the pub. And she really liked working for Belinda.

She told Belinda as much one sunny spring morning as she arrived at work. The door to the kitchen was propped open and Bex could hear the sound of Miles and Jamie working at prepping lunches.

'Not as much as I'm going to miss you,' said Belinda with feeling.

'How's the recruiting going?'

Not brilliant, if I'm honest. There's been a card up in the post office for two weeks now and I've not had one enquiry. You'd think someone would want a part-time job in a nice environment and which slots in with school hours.'

'And with a thoroughly lovely boss.'

'Are you talking about me?' came Miles's voice from the kitchen.

'Certainly not. I haven't forgotten how you used to shout at me when I first started working here.'

Miles came out of the kitchen and leaned against the door jamb. 'I didn't shout; I was offering you advice.'

'Huh!'

'And *huh* from me too,' said Belinda. 'I've lived with you, remember.' She called to Jamie, over Miles's shoulder. 'What do you say, Jamie?'

'Nothing – he's holding a knife,' was the response.

Everyone laughed.

'Three against one,' said Miles. 'That's not fair.' He retreated back into the kitchen and pulled the door shut behind him.

Bex cracked on with her duties before opening time and Belinda went to her office upstairs to chivvy an order for mixers which should have arrived and hadn't.

At midday Bex unlocked the front door and waited for the punters to arrive. And while she waited she thought about something which had been on her mind for some time. She came to a decision and pushed open the door to the kitchen. Miles was working on his own and she could see Jamie in the pub car park dragging on a sneaky fag.

'Come to apologise?' said Miles. But he was smiling.

'What for?'

'Saying I shouted at you.'

'Don't be silly, of course I haven't.' Bex walked around the stainless steel counter and kissed him on the cheek. 'But I have come with a proposal.'

'Propose away.' Miles's eyes widened. 'It's… you're not…'

'No – not *that* sort of proposal.' Bex grinned. 'I've got to wait for a leap year to do that. No, I wondered… well, it seems silly to pay two lots of council tax and two lots of utility bills. So… well, the kids are used to you being around a lot and me living in a big house with loads of space and you living in a shoebox of a flat...'

'Are you inviting me to move in?'

'Yes. I won't be offended if you'd rather not. I do understand that having three kids... four soon... will be a bit of a shock to an old bachelor like you.'

'Hey, less of the old.'

'But what do you think?'

Miles nodded. 'It sounds like a plan. But what about Megan?'

'I think she'd like it. And the boys love having you around.'

'You *think* she'd like it. *I* think you need to ask Megan – just to be sure.'

'And if she says yes, you'd like to move in?'

Miles nodded again. 'Well, I totally understand you want a live-in chef and a reserve babysitter but, as a swap for a few more cuddles and someone to watch telly with, it doesn't seem too lousy a deal.'

Bex kissed him again. 'I don't know why I love you, but I do.'

'Good. I love you too.'

A loud shout of 'Oi!' from the bar broke up their romantic moment. Guiltily Bex shot back out of the kitchen.

'Hi, Harry.'

'What does a man have to do to get a drink around here?'

'Sorry about that. The usual?'

47

Brian and Heather might have been able to relax over the bells and the fundraising but not all was sweetness and light at the vicarage. Despite the fact that, on several occasions, Brian had gently reminded Jade about the house rules, she still seemed to forget that her hosts weren't personal servants whose job it was to clear up after her.

Heather had been out at a meeting of the Little Woodford Historical Society which had involved a visit to an archaeological dig on a farm up near Woodford Priors. All the members of the society had been encouraged to have a go which had been fun – but back-breaking. Heather, despite her elation at finding a flint arrowhead, had come home aching and tired and longing for a hot bath to ease her shoulders and back before she set about cooking supper for them all.

She let herself in through the back door and saw that Jade had already returned from work – the signs were obvious as the kitchen looked like a total tip despite the fact that Heather had left it looking immaculate when she'd gone out after lunch. She sighed but decided she'd have the run-in with Jade after her bath when she felt refreshed. Wearily she climbed the stairs and headed for the bathroom to turn on the taps so it would fill while she got undressed and into her dressing gown. Across the corridor she could hear Radio One blaring out. Never mind, loud music wouldn't spoil her enjoyment of her soak.

Heather's eyebrows shot up when she opened the door. Two wet towels were on the floor, there was a ring an inch wide around the bath and a dusting of talcum powder over everything. Heather blew angrily down her nose and stomped across the landing to Jade's room. She banged on the door.

'Yeah?'

Heather opened the door. 'A word.'

'What?'

'A word,' she shouted.

Jade reached for her laptop and pressed some buttons. The music faded.

'Thank you.'

'What's the matter?'

Heather took a breath before she started. 'Quite a lot actually. The kitchen is a disaster zone yet again. Do you *never* think about looking behind you when you leave a room and wonder if it looks the same as when you entered it?'

Jade looked confused.

'I don't mean the bricks and mortar or the soft furnishings but the mess – the crumbs, the dollops of jam, the dirty plates and cups…'

'Well—'

'No, you don't. And I have just got back and the one thing I was looking forward to was a hot bath and I find the bathroom is even worse than the kitchen.'

'How do you know it's me? Brian used the bathroom this morning and all.'

Heather closed her eyes and counted to three. 'Jade, I have been married to Brian for almost thirty years and never once in that time has he used two towels at once or talcum powder.'

Jade looked sullen.

'I have been patient. And so has Brian, but I am giving you notice, young lady, that one more episode like this and I'll ask you to leave. You can go back to your folks or you can find somewhere else to live – frankly I don't care. But I am not – *not* – putting up with your mess any longer. Do I make myself clear?'

Jade looked as if she might cry. 'But you can't throw me out.'

'Oh, yes I can. I'll give you a fortnight's notice and then you're out on your ear. Shape up or ship out. And you can start shaping up by cleaning the bathroom.'

'But I've just got back from work.'

'No, you haven't because you've had time to make toast, take a bath and trash my home in the process. Sort it.'

Feeling purged by her outburst Heather stamped down the stairs and flung herself on the sofa. 'Wretched child,' she muttered.

Brian came out of his study. 'Well, she paid no attention to me. Maybe she'll listen to you.'

'You heard my outburst.'

'Difficult to miss. It needed saying.'

'I mean it. I'll tell Olivia she'll have to take her daughter back.'

'Poor Olivia.'

Heather snorted. 'Her daughter, her problem.'

'Heather,' admonished Brian.

'Sorry. It's just... it's just...' She sighed. 'Maybe I was a bit harsh.'

'Would a sherry make it better?'

Heather nodded. 'I think it rather might.'

Fifteen minutes later as she and Brian had just refilled their glasses a contrite and bashful Jade appeared.

'I've done the bathroom. Do you want to check if it's OK?'

'I'll go,' said Brian. Two minutes later he returned and gave Heather a thumbs up from the door.

'And I'll get on with the kitchen, shall I?' said Jade.

For a second Heather almost caught herself saying, 'Don't worry dear, it wasn't that bad. It'll only take two ticks to sort,' when she realised that if she did she'd be making matters worse.

'Yes, please,' she said instead. Adding, 'And make sure you deal with the crumbs on the floor too.'

'Yes, Heather.'

Brian came into the sitting room and pushed the door shut with his foot. 'By George, I think she's got it.'

'Humph,' said Heather. 'Time will tell.'

The following week Megan and Sophie trailed out of school, their backpacks slung over one shoulder, and feeling happy that school was over for two whole weeks.

'What are you doing over Easter?' asked Megan.

Sophie shrugged. 'Not a lot. You?'

'I'd hoped we might be going to Cyprus – to see Granny and Grandpa – but Bex hasn't mentioned anything. Besides, it'd be a bit awkward taking Miles along.'

'That'd be weird.' They walked a few paces in silence before Sophie asked, 'What's it like, now he's actually moved in?'

'It was strange at first but he cooks some well-lush food and it's nice for Bex because he takes the boys to school in the morning so she can have a bit of a lie-in. She's been getting really tired.'

'Maybe we can make some plans for things we can do together – go shopping in Cattebury maybe. Or do you think our mums would let us get the train to London? I mean, we're sixteen and you know your way about. You understand how the Tube works.'

Megan stared at her friend, excited by the audaciousness of the idea. 'I suppose... I mean if we promised to only go to Westfield and be home by six...' The two girls stared at each other, their eyes bright with excitement at the idea.

'But what about your mum?' asked Megan.

'She's OK during the day. We have a carer who pops in at lunchtime every day. Just as long as I'm back to cook supper and get her to bed.'

They heard the sound of feet pounding behind them.

'Megs, Soph, stop,' panted Ashley. 'Can I walk home with you?'

Megan and Sophie exchanged a glance. 'I suppose,' said Sophie. The girls shelved further discussion about their planned trip – they tacitly understood that they wanted this to be an outing just for them and they didn't want hangers-on tagging along too.

The threesome ambled along the pavement. 'How's the theatre group?' asked Megan.

Ashley's face lit up. 'Oh, it's so brilliant. Even Mr Johnson isn't the git he is in school – he can be quite nice when he's not teaching. I love it and I'm learning so much – all the backstage stuff and tips about techniques with make-up and wigs and... oh, everything.'

'Mum was saying that she might be able to do something for the theatre,' said Sophie.

'Really?' Ashley's bafflement was plain. 'I don't see—'

'Not acting, but she could prompt, or do make-up. Something where she doesn't have to be too mobile. She'd love to get involved with a company again.'

'I suppose.'

'The thing is,' continued Sophie, 'in the past it hasn't really been an option – she wasn't keen on me going out alone late in the evening to help her get back from the theatre. But as you're there already, you could give her a hand to get home.'

'Maybe.'

'Well, don't be too enthusiastic,' snapped Sophie. 'I mean, after all the help she gave you at the panto...'

'I didn't mean it like that. It's just... well, what sort of help would she need?'

'It's just getting up and down kerbs and steps and that sort of thing. It's nothing difficult. Why don't you come back to mine and talk to her about it?'

'Now?'

Sophie began to lose patience. 'No, in a month. Yes, now, of course now, why not?'

'OK,' said Ashley.

'I'll leave you to it,' said Megan hitching her backpack higher onto her shoulder.

'I'll come round to yours later,' said Sophie. 'You know... to ask Bex about...'

'That'd be nice,' said Megan. 'She might say *no way*.' Ashley looked at her curiously. 'None of your business, Ash – this is girl stuff.'

He and Sophie strolled through the town to the side road that led to Sophie's house. She let them in.

'Mum, I'm back,' she called. 'Ashley's come to have a word.'

'Hiya,' came Lizzie's cheerful acknowledgement from the sitting room.

'You go through,' instructed Sophie. 'I'll make us all a cuppa.'

Ashley sidled into the sitting room. 'Hello, Lizzie.'

'How's things?'

'All right, I guess. I think Mum might have a new boyfriend.'

'Oh?'

'I've not met him yet.'

'And?'

'Her last bloke was a total loser.'

'It doesn't mean this guy will be too.'

Ashley shrugged. 'My dad didn't hang around and Billy – her ex – was a lowlife.' He gave Lizzie an ironic smile. 'Her track record ain't good. Anyway, let's not talk about that; Soph was saying you were thinking about joining the theatre company.'

'It depends if they want me. What do you think?'

Ashley wasn't sure what to say. It wasn't his call and besides, being a newbie, he really didn't know how the old-timers would react.

'It's all right, you don't have to answer that,' said Lizzie, sensing his unease.

'And Soph said you might need a hand getting home again, after rehearsals.'

'Getting around in this thing,' she patted the arm of her chair, 'can be a right pain in the backside. In an old town like this there aren't as many dropped kerbs as there ought to be. And then there's getting in and out of the theatre itself; two steps at the front door and several at the back, so I've been told.'

'I think they've got a ramp.'

'They might have but I haven't got the upper-body strength to get up it. I haven't got the upper-body strength to do lots of things. That's why I'll need a hand. So maybe if you can take me along to one of the rehearsals…'

Ashley nodded. 'Why not? You say when.'

'Maybe the next one?'

Ashley nodded.

'Anyway, enough about me, how are you getting on there?'

'I love it.'

'You've found your tribe.'

'I have. I so fit in. I just know this is how I want to spend my life. Even if I don't earn a living I want to be a part of acting somehow.'

'I completely get that. It's how I felt. And if I can do anything to help you get there, I will.'

'Would you?'

'No problem. You can repay me by giving me a hand to the theatre next Tuesday.'

'Deal.'

Bex and Megan eyeballed each other in the kitchen and Soph stood by the door, looking embarrassed. The pair looked like a couple of cats, squaring up for a fight. If they'd had tails, they'd have been all fluffed up like bottlebrushes.

'No,' said Bex. 'Which syllable of that word don't you understand?'

'But, Bex, that's so unfair.'

'I don't think so. London is a long way off, and I'm not prepared to let the pair of you go there on your own. Cattebury yes, London no. Understand?'

'We'll only be going to the Westfield Centre.'

'I know, but you're barely sixteen. What if something happened? What if you got mugged… or worse.'

'Oh, come off it, Bex. That could happen in Cattebury.'

'I agree. But at least I'd be close enough to be able to help. No, I'm sorry, no means no and I'm not budging.'

'Miles would let us go.'

'I very much doubt that. And if you ever try and play him off against me you'll find yourself in very hot water.'

Megan glowered and Sophie went even redder.

'Come on, Megs,' she said quietly. 'Going to Cattebury will be fine. There's lots to do there.'

'Huh,' was all Megan gave as an answer.

'Now, if you've quite finished shouting at me,' said Bex, 'I've got a splitting headache.' She sat down at the table and rubbed her forehead with her hand.

'Can we get you a painkiller?' asked Sophie.

'That's very sweet of you, my dear, but I think I'll go for a lie-down for a few minutes. Tell the boys that if they need me I'm on my bed, having a rest.'

Megan and Sophie watched Bex make her way out of the kitchen and up the stairs.

'You shouldn't have shouted at her,' said Sophie.

Guilt made Megan defensive. 'I didn't.' Sophie gave her a look. 'Well, not very loudly. Not enough to get a headache.'

'Does she often get headaches?'

Megan shook her head.

'We ought to tell the boys, like your stepmum said. Where are they?'

'In the garden. Miles built them a den out of old pallets – they have almost moved in there, full time.'

'Sounds fun.'

'I suppose – if you're their age.'

The girls passed the message to the two lads and then returned to Megan's bedroom to remake their plans for a shopping trip now that London had been ruled out.

'Shit,' said Sophie, catching sight of Megan's alarm clock after a while. 'I need to run – got supper to make.'

Off she dashed with plans only half-made and leaving Megan with a faint sense of resentment that Sophie had to put her mother's needs first. She knew it wasn't Sophie's fault but she wished it were otherwise.

As Miles pulled into the pub car park he saw Sophie close the gate to The Beeches then sprint down the road towards her house. He glanced at the clock on the dash and saw it was later than he thought. Damn – he'd meant to be back in time to give Bex a hand with the kids' supper before he started at the pub. And he still had to unload the shopping from the cash and carry. He jumped out of the car and unlocked the back door to the kitchen and then began to ferry in the giant jars of mayonnaise, pickled onions and the like, the catering packs of paper napkins, bacon and sausages and sacks of frozen chips. He dumped the frozen goods in the huge freezer, put the meat in the fridge but everything else he left stacked tidily in a corner of the kitchen. Ten minutes later he was scooting over the gravel and in through Bex's front door.

The house was quiet. Not a sound.

'Hello?' No reply.

Surely Megan had to be in; her friend, Sophie, had left only minutes earlier. Miles raced up the stairs, taking them two at a time. He got to the bottom of the attic flight. 'Megan,' he shouted.

A second later she was at the top. 'Yeah, what?'

'Where is everyone?'

'Oh, Bex had a headache and is having a lie-down and the boys are in the den in the garden.'

Miles felt a whoosh of relief. 'Oh, fine.' And then he felt a bit shamefaced for having a panic. But for some reason, even though he'd only been a member of the household for a ridiculously short time, he felt strangely responsible for them all. Now he lived with them he was becoming more and more besotted with the little family. God help him, he thought, when the baby arrived. If he felt like this about kids he had no actual physical connection to, what would he be like when he had his very own son or daughter to take care of? 'Sorry to have bothered you,' he said and made his way to the bedroom he now shared with Bex.

He pushed open the door and in the gloom – the curtains had been drawn – saw her, spark out, on the bed. He tiptoed across the room and felt her forehead. Well, she wasn't feverish. He wondered what had made her feel poorly.

Bex opened her eyes. She yawned and then sat bolt upright. 'Hell's bells – what's the time?'

'It's OK, it's not six yet.'

She began to scramble out of bed and then stopped. 'Shit.' She held her head.

'Still got a headache? Megan said you weren't feeling well.'

'Hmm.' She took stock. 'Yes and no. Yes, I've still got a head but it's a lot better.'

'Then you stay here. I'll get Jamie in to do the prep for tonight and I'll cook the kids' supper and make something light for you.'

'No, no, I'm not hungry.'

'You've got to keep your strength up.'

'Missing one meal won't matter.'

'How about scrambled eggs on toast?'

'How about I take a paracetamol and man up?'

'Paracetamol? Is that OK? It won't do any harm…'

'I've done this before, Miles. How many times do I have to tell you I am pregnant, not ill.'

'Apart from the headache.'

'Yes, apart from that.'

'So, what brought it on?'

'I had a bit of a niggle this afternoon when I got back from the pub and then Megan and I had words on the subject of her and Sophie going up to London on their own to go shopping in the Easter holidays.'

'Ah.'

'It wasn't really a row. Just a difference of opinion.'

'Even so.'

'Even so, I don't think the argument was responsible. I'm just getting to that stage in a pregnancy when I don't sleep that well because the baby is doing gym, or I've got heartburn or I just can't get comfortable. It'll all be better in June when it's here.'

Miles kissed her on the nose and stroked her hair. 'You're the expert. And, June! Not long now.'

'Eleven weeks – give or take.'

'I can't wait.'

'I'll remind you of that when we're both sleep-deprived and wading in nappies.'

48

Bert and Brian stood in the nave and looked at the space that had appeared now the bells had been hoisted back into the bell tower. All that was left as a reminder of their recent presence were the six pallets they'd rested on.

'Pete will be pleased they're back in their rightful place in time for Easter,' observed Bert.

'I think we all are. It'll be wonderful to have them ring out on Easter morning for the first time.'

'Well, I hate to disappoint you, Reverend, but they're going to have to do some bell-ringing practice first. Easter Sunday ain't going to be the first time the bell-ringers get to swing 'em.'

'Yes, but you know what I mean.'

'It's been a long time since they last rang out.'

'Seven months. Services haven't been the same without them. Heather and I thought we'd have an informal party at the community centre on Easter Monday – to thank all the people who supported the bell fund. Nothing elaborate and there's no budget so it'll be bring and share. But we've asked the bell-ringers if they would ring the bells again for us and maybe take some of the party-goers up the bell tower for a guided tour – Pete and the others were very keen to do that. I think they see it as an opportunity to have a bit of a recruiting drive. Heather's made all the invitations. There's one for you and Joan, naturally.'

'That sounds like a right good idea, Reverend. My Joan'll be delighted. I expect she'll make one of her pork pies if we ask her nicely.'

'That would be splendid. And if I can ask you to take a couple of other invitations to drop off at your end of town…?'

'My pleasure.'

A few days after the start of the school holidays, Bex was sitting with her feet up while rain lashed at the windows and the boys watched *Cars* yet again when she heard the letter box clatter. The post had already been, it wasn't the day for the local rag so it was probably some flyer for the local pizza parlour or someone advertising gardening services. But even so, Bex's curiosity got the better of her so she swung her feet off the sofa and padded out into the hall to see what had been delivered. A cream envelope with handwriting on it lay in the middle of the Victorian tiles. Bex bent down with an audible 'oof' to pick it up. Now she was into her third trimester, bending down was getting progressively harder but at least her head hadn't thumped, as it did sometimes when she moved suddenly. And her ankles, she noticed, while she was down there, were getting puffy. Maybe, now she had more time to take it easy, now she was no longer working at the pub, they'd revert to the slim lines they'd once had rather than trying to emulate small beach balls. She scanned the envelope. *The Millar Family (and Miles!)*. Bex grinned and opened it.

Please come to a Bring-and-Share party at the Community Centre on Easter Monday at 2.00pm to celebrate the reinstallation of St Catherine's Church bells. All welcome. RSVP The Vicarage

Then in Heather's handwriting it said – *Do come and if you'd like to make a cake or two… *hopeful face**

Bex pottered into the kitchen, picked up the phone and dialled.

'Hello, the vicarage.' The voice wasn't Heather's.

'Can I speak to Heather please?'

'Sure. who's calling?'

'Bex.'

'Oh, hi, Bex – it's Jade.'

'Hello, and how are you getting on...' And so the conversation continued for some minutes as Bex asked after the family – all well – and if they had plans for Easter – not really, Mum's working – until Jade said that Heather wanted a word too.

'Sorry,' said Bex, 'gabbling on like that. You must have far better things to do than talk to me.'

But whether Jade did was lost in the handover of the phone.

'Hi, Bex,' said Heather cheerily. 'I trust you've rung to say you're coming?'

'Wouldn't miss it for the world and yes, I can do some cakes – shall I do several? Something like a Victoria sponge, a chocolate cake and a fruit loaf? And how about a quiche or a pavlova?'

'That's too much to ask.'

'No, it's not. You know how much I love baking. And, anyway, Miles might lend a hand too.'

'Well, I'm not going to turn you down.'

'I didn't think you would.'

'But don't you overdo things. I know what it's like at that stage of pregnancy – the lack of sleep, the aches and pains—'

'The indigestion.'

'Don't remind me. But you're keeping well.'

'Mostly. I don't feel a hundred per cent, if I'm totally honest – like I'm about to go down with something. But I don't.'

'Have you been to see the doctor?'

'I'll only be wasting his time. I've got no temperature, no other symptoms – well apart from indigestion, swollen ankles and insomnia.'

'Even so.'

'I'll just be cluttering up his waiting room. No, as I said to Miles, it'll all be fine once the baby is born and I'm not sharing my body with something out of the film *Alien*. Anyway, I can't wait for the party and to have a catch-up with everyone. Will Olivia be there? I haven't seen her for an age.'

'I get to see her at church now and again but her shift pattern means she misses out on so many other things. But yes, she says she's got Easter Monday off – all of it.'

'Good. I miss her.'

'So do I,' said Heather. 'And when she was on all those committees and – ahem – quite bossy, I never thought I'd say that.'

Bex laughed. 'I know what you mean. I imagine Miranda didn't get an invite.'

'Heavens, no. But I wouldn't put it past her to turn up and try and spoil it. She might have joined the book club but she doesn't exactly "join in" does she?'

'She chose a book.'

'That's not the same as joining in. She's present and she contributes, but that is all. It's almost as if she doesn't know how to.'

Bex knew what Heather meant; Miranda had hardly divulged anything that could be described as personal information. She'd told them nothing they didn't already know beyond the name of her husband and the fact she'd been a lawyer. She never commented on a book beyond what was factual and maybe, *maybe*, a very objective reason as to why she did, or didn't enjoy it – usually based on the quality of the prose or the accuracy of descriptions. 'She doesn't exactly encourage any of us to cosy up and pop round for a girls' night in.'

Heather snorted. 'And what a barrel of laughs that evening would be.'

'Anyway, stuff Miranda. Let's look forward to Easter Monday.'

★

Amy let herself into Miranda's house and called out a loud 'Coo-ee,' before she slipped off her coat and hung it over the back of a chair. There was no hook near the front door – apparently Miranda didn't believe in coat hooks or hat stands. They came under the heading of clutter. There was a cupboard for guests' coats but as she wasn't a guest she hadn't been told where to find it. Of course, she *had* found it. There wasn't much she hadn't found. She'd had a good rummage through most of Miranda's minimalist, hidden cupboards but Miranda's minimalism wasn't just outward – it also seemed to extend to other possessions and food. She hadn't found anything very nice in that department; certainly nothing she fancied helping herself to. Well... perks of the job, wasn't it? Dear God, wondered Amy, what on earth did that woman survive on? Lentils and fresh air? No wonder she was in a permanent bad mood. So, if it pissed off Miranda that she dumped her coat wherever it suited her, then so be it.

Amy had dusted, polished and swept and was about to start mopping the bleached birch planking – about the only thing that had survived Miranda's extreme makeover of Olivia's old house – when the door opened and in came her boss.

'Hello, Mrs Osborne.' Amy had long since learnt that Mrs O was even more blooming formal than Mrs L had been. Well, posh houses were bound to be inhabited by snobs. Amy didn't stop to think that Bex wasn't snobby not in the least.

'Amy, I've heard a rumour that the bells are going to be rung again at the weekend.'

'Easter Sunday? Yes, that's right. Heather – the vicar's wife – says they're all finished and back up in the tower. She says the foundry did a right good job.'

'Did she now.'

Amy could see Miranda's mind working; she could almost hear the cogs turning. She decided to bung a drop of something combustible onto the flames. 'Yeah, the locals are all dead keen to hear them ring again. It ain't been the same without them. Of course, there'll have to be a practice first, then they're ringing on

Easter Sunday and, on the Monday, Heather's having a party to thank all the fundraisers.' Miranda pursed her lips so tight Amy was reminded of a cat's arse. 'Heather's using the community centre by the cricket pitch for that do.'

'Really,' said Miranda.

Amy couldn't resist a naughty suggestion. 'It's bring-and-share so I don't suppose it'd matter if you wanted to go along too as long as you take a contribution. It'll be a cracking way of meeting people. Bex'll be there and Mrs L. I expect some of the other book club ladies will be and all. And the bells are going to ring a quarter peal and Bert say that goes on for about forty minutes, just to make sure everyone knows everything is back in tip-top condition.' Amy beamed disingenuously at Miranda and wondered if her boss was going to self-combust. She was almost throbbing with pent-up anger and annoyance.

She saw Miranda take a deep breath and exhale slowly. 'Then it might be fun to attend.'

Amy thought it almost certainly would be – for the onlookers. Nothing like a mad woman throwing a hissy fit to give everyone something to talk about for days – possibly even weeks.

'Oh, go on,' urged Amy. 'You'll have a blast.'

49

The schools might have broken up for Easter but the Woodford Players had a production coming up and the rehearsal schedule couldn't afford to stop so, the following Tuesday evening, Ashley made his way to Sophie and Lizzie's house and rang the bell. Lizzie, ready and waiting, opened it.

'I am stupidly excited about this,' she admitted to Ashley, as he helped manoeuvre her out of the house.

'It's only the theatre,' said Ash. He pushed the chair down the path, through the open gate and onto the pavement.

'It's not just that... it's being out and about, meeting new people. I mean, I'm not a recluse and I do go out but it's not easy for Sophie and I hate it that I cramp her style so much. She's OK pushing me on the flat but she'd never get me up the Cattebury road and as for anything with steps...'

'I know it wouldn't solve the problem of the steps but what about an electric wheelchair?'

'I wish. Do you know how much they cost?'

'A lot, I suppose.'

'And some. It's no picnic, living on benefits.'

'I kinda know that,' said Ashley. 'Sometimes, when one of Mum's ladies moves or goes away and she's not wanted for a week or two, we really have to tighten our belts. Come the summer, once I've done my GCSEs, I'm going to look for a job. Something like Sophie's got – shop work maybe.'

'That'll make a big difference to your mum.'

'I'll give her half and save half. I'll need money if I'm going to do drama school.'

'You'll always need money if you're going to go into acting.'

Ashley stopped the chair at the main road and waited for a gap in the traffic before he pushed Lizzie across. 'So you never made it big?'

'Ha!' said Lizzie. 'That's the irony. I worked my way out of a provincial theatre to a bit part in a West End production, only a few lines but the rest of the cast were all household names. Obviously their mates came to see the show and one of them asked me to go and do a screen test for a film he was going to be in.'

'Wow,' said Ashley, genuinely impressed.

'Yeah, that was about two weeks before I got the diagnosis for multiple sclerosis. After that my life became a bit of a car crash.'

'I'm sorry.'

'Yeah. So was I.' Lizzie gave a hollow laugh. 'I couldn't cope with it and I hit the bottle, tried drugs, did all sorts of stupid things – oh, don't worry, I don't do any of that now. But I decided that if my life was ruined I might as well try the live-fast-die-young approach. Trust me, it's not a good idea. All I did was rinse my savings and wind up in a lot of situations I shouldn't have done. The only good thing to come out of it was, as a result of a very hazy weekend, I found I was pregnant. I went home, told my parents, straightened myself out and promised myself that I'd do the best I could, for as long as I could, to take care of my kid. So, using my office skills, I got a job which I held down till things got too bad and then it was benefits.'

'Right, well, here we are,' said Ashley. He pushed the chair down the side passage that led to the stage door. He was quite glad they'd reached their destination – he wasn't overly comfortable with having a grown-up confide in him. It had been one thing him telling Lizzie about his worries and problems – but somehow it didn't seem right that she was reciprocating.

He pulled open the door and turned the wheelchair around so he could heave it up the steps. Using all his strength he managed to haul it into the building and then he pushed Lizzie behind the stage and into the big room that served as the dressing room. Cassandra was already there being pinned into her costume by Debs, the wardrobe mistress, and the woman with the Cupid's bow mouth – Evie – was leaning in towards a mirror and applying lots of kohl.

'Evening,' said Ashley. 'This is Lizzie. She used to act—'

'Used to,' interrupted Lizzie, 'being the operative words. But I know a certain amount about theatre production and if I can do anything – front of house, backstage, anything – I'd really like to get involved again.'

Evie put down her kohl pencil and swivelled around in her chair. 'Darling, we can always use another pair of hands.'

'Good, because the legs aren't much cop,' said Lizzie.

'I'm Evie, Evie Fairbairne.' Languidly she extended a hand for Lizzie to shake.

'And I'm Cassandra. Director, actor, Jack-of-all-trades.' Cassandra waved at Lizzie because, with the wardrobe mistress pinning up a hem she couldn't move. 'So, any specific skills?'

'Typing and accountancy qualifications but I'm good at make-up, I can operate a sewing machine so I could help out with costumes and I'd be happy to prompt or sell tickets or … anything.' She grinned up at the other two women. 'I'm trying not to sound too needy but I'd love to be a part of this company.'

'You joining us isn't a problem. As we're all volunteers we're not constrained by the wages bill.'

'Wages! I wish,' said Evie. 'No, we do this because we're artistes.' She waved her hand theatrically. She then returned to her mirror and carried on painting her eyes.

'I am sure,' continued Cassandra, 'we'll be able to find plenty of jobs for you round and about. I mean, if you'd like, you could prompt at tonight's rehearsal. I usually do it but, as you can see,' she plucked at her costume, 'I'm in this production so it's a tad tricky when I'm on stage myself.'

'Oh, I'd love to!'

'Ash, be a love and find Lizzie a copy of the script. I think there's one by the props' table.'

Ashley scurried off to find it.

'Now, that's a lad who might go far in acting,' said Cassandra to Lizzie. 'Really talented.'

'He says he wants to go to drama school.'

'He should.'

'Finance will be a problem.'

'It will be the same if he goes to uni. The only advantage of uni is that he's more likely to get a steady job after. Acting is so precarious.'

'Tell me about it,' said Lizzie.

When Ashley returned with the script Cassandra and Lizzie were chatting as if they'd been mates for ten years, not ten minutes.

Later that evening, as Ash wheeled Lizzie home again, she said, 'Thanks for that, Ash. I really appreciated it. It was such fun being with actors again – I'd forgotten how much I missed it. And Cassie thinks a lot of you.'

'Does she? Really!'

Ashley saw Lizzie nod her head. 'She thinks you have real talent. You ought to stick with the theatre group till you leave school and decide what you really want to do.'

'Yeah, I kinda worked that out for myself. And I thought I might try and get an apprenticeship in a trade. Like you said, then I'll always have something to fall back on. I'm not stupid, I know there's a lot of actors who never make it.'

'It's a tough profession. You need buckets of luck as well as talent. And you must never lose sight of the fact that luck comes in two flavours – good luck—'

'And bad.'

'Indeed.'

Ashley turned into the road that led to Lizzie's house. 'All I have to do now is persuade Mum that uni isn't the be-all and end-all.'

'Get the teachers to have a word with her. I'm sure that nice Miss Watkins will back you. Mums only want what's best for their kids, you know. Trust me.'

'Maybe.'

They reached Lizzie's front door.

'Right,' said Ashley after he'd pushed her up the ramp and over the threshold, 'I'll be off. Glad you enjoyed it.'

'I loved it. Night, Ash.'

While Ashley was out Amy contemplated whether she had the brass neck to gatecrash Heather's party. She knew Miranda wouldn't give a tuppenny toot about upsetting people – besides, she was, as Amy knew only too well, under the misguided impression that it was open-house. But Amy had dusted the invitations on enough mantelpieces to know that it was definitely invitation only and she also knew she'd done nothing to merit one. And if she did gatecrash would Heather be sufficiently hacked off to throw her out? Was it worth the risk to get a ringside seat to see what Miranda did?

Amy thought about taking along a cake or a bottle of wine on the pretext that, while she understood she wasn't invited, she thought it would be a nice gesture to help out with the food. And then keep everything crossed that Heather would suggest she should stay. That might work.

The next morning, on her way back from work, Amy popped into the bakery and bought a cake. When she got it home she transferred it from the silver-covered cake board onto one of her own plates and then picked a few bits off the edge to give it a home-made appearance. She admired her handiwork before she slipped it into an airtight tin and popped it in the fridge.

Over at The Beeches, Bex was working hard in her kitchen baking the cakes she'd promised Heather, while Megan revised for her GCSEs in her room and the boys played in the garden. The weather was kind and she had the back door open so she could keep a vague eye on them while she cooked. She promised them that, if they played nicely and let her get on, she'd take them up to the swings later. There was a part of her that really regretted her promise because, if she were honest with herself, she didn't feel completely well. She had a niggling headache and felt slightly sick. A bug, she told herself as she bent down to open the oven door to get out the two sponges she'd just baked. The gust of super-hot air didn't help matters and, as soon as she'd released the cakes from their tins and turned them out onto a couple of wire cooling racks, she poured herself a glass of water and drank it. Her head swam and she sat down with a bump. She folded her arms on the table and rested her head on them. Two minutes, she told herself, just two minutes.

'Mummy, Mummy, when can we go to the swings?' Alfie tugged at her sleeve.

Wearily she raised her head and glanced at the kitchen clock. The two minutes had turned into twenty. And she needed to get going with lunch for everyone except the very thought of lunch made her feel sicker.

'After lunch. And I'm just about to make it for everyone.' She forced a smile. 'I thought we could have pizzas.' Well the kids could, Bex thought she'd pass.

50

'You going to be in for supper?' Amy asked Ashley later that day.

'Yeah. Why?'

'Cos there's someone I'd like you to meet.'

'Oh yeah.' Ashley sounded wary. 'This your new bloke?'

'Might be. Anyway, he's not "my bloke", he's a friend.'

Ashley shrugged. 'If you say so. So what's this one do?'

'He's a fireman.' Amy said it with pride and she stared at Ashley, wanting him to be impressed.

Ashley considered this. 'I suppose that's better than being a thief.'

'Too right it is.'

Ashley still looked unimpressed.

'OK, so I made a mistake with Billy. This guy's different.'

'Really.'

'You'll see, when you meet him. So, you'll be here for supper. You ain't got a rehearsal or nothing.'

Ashley shook his head. 'I'll be here.'

'And you'll be nice.'

Ashley sighed. 'I suppose.'

*

Sharp at six the doorbell rang and Amy yelled to Ashley, 'Get that, would you, I'm busy in the kitchen.'

Ashley, revising in his bedroom, threw down his pen and crashed down the stairs, two at a time. He knew who it was going to be and, although he'd promised his mum he'd be 'nice', all he was prepared to be was polite. He certainly wasn't going to be any more accommodating than that. His mother had had some crap boyfriends in the past and he wasn't expecting this new guy to be any better than that git Billy. So he was quite surprised, when he opened the door, to see a bloke carrying a massive bunch of flowers and a bottle of wine standing on the doorstep looking rather nervous.

'Hello,' said Ashley. 'You must be Ryan.'

'And you must be Ashley.'

'You'd better come in.' Ashley opened the door as Amy came out of the kitchen, wiping her hands on a tea towel.

'Hello, Ames,' said Ryan. He proffered his gifts.

'Oooh, lovely. You shouldn't have,' she said, taking them. 'I don't know if I've got a vase big enough. No one's never given me flowers before.'

'Really?' Ryan was genuinely surprised. 'Never?'

Amy shook her head. She led the way back into the kitchen and handed Ashley the bottle. 'You pour us all a drink while I sort out the flowers.'

'Actually,' said Ryan, 'I don't suppose you've got a beer?'

Amy nodded as she began to open cupboards, searching for something suitable for her bouquet. 'Ash, there's some cans on the floor in the cupboard under the stairs. You can have one too if you like. And when you've done that, pour me a glass of vino, there's a love.'

Five minutes later they were in the sitting room with the flowers in a plastic jug – the only suitable thing that Amy could find – and sipping their drinks.

Amy looked at her guest with a big grin on her face. 'Well, ain't this nice.'

'It's grand,' said Ryan.

'And I hope you like shepherd's pie.'

'Love it, my favourite.'

'Really? It's yours too, isn't it, Ash?'

'It's OK.'

'I'll dish up when we've had our drinks.' Silence fell. 'Tell Ash about being a fireman, Ryan.'

'There's nothing much to tell – we get a shout, we go to the emergency, deal with it, we come back to the station.'

Ashley sipped his beer but caught his mother glaring at him. Her expression plainly said, *show an interest*.

'Have you been to any big fires, then?' said Ashley.

'A few. I was at that warehouse fire on the other side of Cattebury a few weeks ago. You know, the one that made the local news.'

Ashley nodded. It had been massive. 'Cool.'

'And then we had to deal with that pile-up on the motorway last winter. That was nasty – several dead who we had to cut out of their cars but we got half a dozen badly injured out first.'

'Yuck,' said Amy.

Ryan nodded. 'It's horrible but someone has to do it.'

'I bet you've seen some well-gross things,' said Ashley.

Ryan nodded again. 'But maybe it's not something to talk about before dinner, eh?'

Ashley took a gulp of his beer. 'I think I'd be sick.'

'You get used to it. So, you don't fancy being a firefighter?'

Ashley shook his head.

'Nah,' said Amy. 'He still wants to act.'

Suddenly Ashley felt a bit self-conscious about doing a job that was basically trivial and unimportant when he was talking to someone who actually saved lives. 'But I know I've got to get a proper job as well. Everyone says actors get crap pay – well, unless you're Patrick Stewart or Christian Bale.'

'Yeah, I don't imagine they're short of a bob or two. But being an actor sounds like a great job even if the pay is shit... for most people. And let's face it, I didn't become a firefighter for the money. You've got to do something you like – you spend a lot of your life working.'

'Exactly!'

Amy drained her glass. 'It's all very well for you to say that but some of us don't get much choice. Being a cleaner ain't much cop but the rent's got to be paid and food put on the table. Talking of which…' She got up and went into the kitchen where the two men could hear her banging around, getting the pie out of the oven and draining the vegetables.

'What have you got in mind?' asked Ryan.

Ashley warmed to him. His mum was right, he did seem nice. And he was taking an interest. Billy had never done that and his dad certainly hadn't; in fact, he'd never met his dad which just showed how little interest he had in his son. 'I don't know. I thought I might do an apprenticeship.'

'In what?'

'Mum says everyone always needs plumbers. Not sure I could deal with other people's toilets though.' Ashley wrinkled his face.

'Gross,' agreed Ryan. 'But what about being an electrician? And it's a skill that theatres and film sets need too. I mean, I'm sure you'll make a fine actor but if you didn't you might still be able to work in the industry – just not in the limelight.'

Ashley stared at Ryan. 'That's a wicked idea. Genius. Thank you.'

Ryan gave Ashley a big smile then drained the last of his drink. 'Glad to have been of service.'

As Ashley and Ryan were bonding over shepherd's pie and beer, Miranda was in her state-of-the-art kitchen, listening to Radio Three while she made a sweet potato and bean chilli. Suddenly, over the music, she heard the church bells clanging away. For crying out loud! She left the pot simmering on the hob as she strode to the huge bi-fold doors and flung them open. No, the noise wasn't deafening but it shattered the tranquillity of the evening. How on earth could she be expected to entertain friends, out here on the patio, with that going on? She stormed back into the house and picked up her phone. She scrolled down her contacts list – the vicarage – and hit the call button. It was answered on the second ring.

'Hello, the vicarage.'

'Good evening. This is Miranda here.'

'Miranda, how lovely to hear from you.'

'I haven't rung you to exchange pleasantries.'

'Oh?'

'No – the bells.'

'Yes, isn't it a joy to hear them ringing again?'

'A joy?' Miranda's voice was almost a squeak. 'No, it isn't. It's an abomination.'

'Oh, dear,' said Heather. 'Then I'm afraid we have to agree to disagree.'

'We'll do no such thing. I am going to monitor the noise level and as soon as this ridiculous bank holiday is over I am going to report it to the district council. So, if you don't want a noise abatement order I suggest you tell the ringers to cease and desist forthwith.'

'Cease and desist? No, I don't think I'm going to do that. And it isn't, as you put it, a "ridiculous bank holiday" but Easter – the main festival of my faith. So, if that's everything...?' Miranda wasn't used to people not being intimidated by her and was stunned into momentary silence. 'Good. Goodbye,' finished Heather.

The connection was severed and Miranda was left fuming. Her temper wasn't improved when she returned to her saucepan of chilli to find it had stuck to the bottom and had burnt. Ruined! If she hadn't been so angry she would have cried.

If the bell practice had enraged Miranda on the Friday evening, it was nothing to the incandescent wrath she felt on the Sunday morning when the bells rang out joyously to celebrate Easter.

The weather seemed to be celebrating along with the church as the sun shone, the temperature rose and the sky was a flawless blue.

'This is intolerable,' she grumbled at Roderick, over breakfast. 'I want to go into the garden and work out in the fresh air but goodness knows what that racket will do to my hearing.'

Roderick looked at her over the top of the *Observer*. 'Is it that bad?'

'Is it that bad?' Miranda stared at her husband incredulously. She pushed her chair back and pulled open the patio doors. 'Listen!' She turned to him. 'It might not be quite so intolerable if they were any good.'

'They sound fairly competent to me.'

Miranda snorted and narrowed her eyes. 'You are going to back me, aren't you – when I make a formal complaint?'

'Of course, dear.'

'Good. And you'll come with me tomorrow to talk to the vicar at their wretched party they're throwing to thank people who were misguided enough to support the wretched bells? I want him left in no doubt that bells are an anachronism and are a serious cause of noise pollution.'

'Of course, dear.'

Miranda stared at her husband. She couldn't fault him as a breadwinner but sometimes, *sometimes*, she did wonder if he was quite on-message.

'Listen,' said Miles as he served up scrambled eggs for everyone's breakfast at The Beeches.

'To what?' said Lewis as he buttered some toast.

'The bells.'

Lewis cocked an ear. 'And?'

'I just think they're rather lovely,' said Miles.

'I do too,' said Megan taking the plate Miles offered her. 'What about you, Bex?' Bex seemed miles away. 'Bex?'

'Oh... yes, I suppose.'

'Do you want eggs?' asked Miles.

Bex shook her head. 'Not for me. I don't feel very hungry.'

'Then what about some toast?'

'Maybe.' She took a slice and broke off a corner to nibble.

'Dry toast?' Miles gave her a questioning look.

'Don't fuss,' she warned. 'I'm fine.'

'Why don't you go back to bed if you're not feeling great? I can look after the kids till I have to go to the pub, Megan can help me prep the lamb for tonight's supper and I can rustle up something cold to leave everyone for lunch.'

'Miles! I said *I'm fine.*'

Miles piled the last of the eggs on his own plate and sat at the table. The family ate in slightly uneasy silence, broken only by the sound of the bells, and the scraping of cutlery on china.

When everyone had finished and Miles had loaded the dishwasher, the boys ran out into the garden to play and Megan muttered something about revision and went off to her room.

'Anything else?' offered Miles. 'Tea, maybe?'

'No, I'm good.'

Miles opened his mouth to say Bex didn't look it but changed his mind. Instead he said, 'So, what are your plans for this morning?'

'I'm going to make a couple of quiches – one for lunch and one for Heather's party tomorrow.'

'Would you like me to do it?'

'Oh, for God's sake, Miles, just stop fussing.'

'Fine. In which case I've got some things to sort out at the pub before the lunch service. I'll be back about two thirty.'

'I'll see you then.' Bex still sounded hacked off.

Miles dropped a kiss on her forehead and left. As soon as he'd gone Bex slumped forward and rested her head on her arms. Shit, she felt crap.

Somehow she managed to find the energy to make the flans and later give the children their lunch. After they'd eaten the weather began to cloud over so, while Megan went out to see Sophie, Bex put a DVD on for the boys, toed off her slippers and put her feet up on the sofa.

'Good,' said Miles, startling her into instant wakefulness, 'you're taking it easy.'

'Hi, sweetheart,' said Bex. She glanced at the clock and saw it was coming up for two thirty. 'You're early.'

'I left Jamie to clear down.' He leaned over the back of the sofa and gave her a kiss. 'How are you feeling?'

'Very relaxed,' she lied. Her back ached. She must have slept uncomfortably – which was hardly surprising given she was on the sofa and not in bed. 'Be a love, put the kettle on.'

Bex didn't actually fancy tea much but she wanted Miles out of the way while she got herself upright. He'd only fret if he saw how stiff and achy she was. Miles tramped off to the kitchen while Bex managed to swing her feet to the floor. Very slowly and trying not to groan she levered herself into a sitting position. When Miles came back with her drink she had moved to an armchair and had propped a couple of cushions behind her to make herself as comfortable as possible. She'd be better in the morning, she told herself. All she needed was a half-decent night's sleep.

51

Easter Monday was another bobby-dazzler of a day for which Heather offered up a short prayer of thanks. Hosting a party was going to be so much easier if the sun shone. Sure, they had the community centre and all the guests had promised to bring food so she didn't have that much to do but it would be so much nicer for everyone to be able to spill out onto the outfield of the cricket pitch rather than being confined in the ancient prefab. The kids would be able to run about, people could stretch out on the grass... there was no doubt about it, in Heather's mind, the fine weather was going to be the icing on the cake of a very jolly day.

She hummed as she finished making sausage rolls and a fruit salad, put them in suitable containers and then shoved cling film over them.

'Brian,' she called. A faint response came back from the study. She walked down the hall and put her head round the door. 'I'm just nipping over to the community centre for a few minutes.'

'OK, dear. I'll see you when you get back.'

Heather picked up the food and the key to the hall and made her way down the path and across the road to the cricket pitch. She picked her way over the grass and listened to the cawing of the rooks as they fussed and flapped over their nests in the big trees around the cricket ground and the church. Smaller birds twittered in the understorey and above her a few fluffy clouds that resembled picture-book sheep drifted aimlessly across a delphinium blue sky. Such a perfect day. As she let herself into the community centre she found she was humming the old Lou Reed classic. And why not? she thought. Why not?

Heather dumped her plates down on a shelf and began to pull trestle tables out of the stack at the side of the room and click the legs into position before she deftly turned them the right way up and arranged them round the edge of the room. Once she'd put up a dozen or so tables she found the banqueting roll from the store cupboard in the little kitchen at the back of the building and began to cover them with clean white paper. After about half an hour she had most of the room sorted and as she finished other townsfolk began arriving with their contributions – cakes, vol-au-vents, salads of various descriptions, sandwiches, savoury snacks... it was going to be quite a spread.

As Heather moved the dishes into a vaguely logical arrangement – sweet things on one table, savoury on another and cakes on the third, Bex came in with a couple of the things she was contributing.

'Goodness me,' said Heather. 'How you've suddenly bloomed.'

'You mean the bump is huge.'

Heather grinned. 'I wouldn't have put it quite like that.'

'No, you're far too diplomatic but I bet it's what you're thinking. And I've still got almost a couple of months to go – well, seven weeks and a few days, to be precise. I tell you, Heather, I can't wait to have my body back. I know everyone says babies are easier to look after on the inside than the outside but I swear, even with feeds, I'm going to get more sleep than I am at the moment.'

'You do look tired,' said Heather.

'Don't you start. Miles – bless him – is being a total old mother hen; always clucking and fussing around me. I know he cares but I have done this before.'

'He's just so thrilled he's going to be a dad.'

Bex nodded. 'I get that and it's lovely that he is so completely excited…'

'But it's a bit wearing?'

'Exactly. Anyway…' Bex dumped her plates on a table. 'I'll go and get the other stuff.'

'Do you want a hand?'

'I brought the car down.' She was back in a couple of minutes with two more cakes, and then did a third trip to fetch the quiche and a fruit flan.

'Bex! That's far too generous of you.'

'It's nothing. You know me, any excuse to bake.' She looked about her. 'What else needs doing?'

'Nothing, or nothing you need to worry about. I'm going to faff about putting out plates and glasses and then we'll be ready for the kick-off at one.'

'I hope it stays nice.'

Heather was befuddled. 'But it's a glorious day.'

'The weatherman said there might be thunderstorms later. You know what they say about the British summer – three fine days and a thunderstorm.'

'Oh well. We'll just have to keep our fingers crossed it misses us.'

An hour later Bex returned on foot with her brood. As she crossed the cricket club she wished she was wearing something smarter than her old Crocs but her ankles didn't allow her to slip into some of her more stylish and prettier sandals. She was going to be *so* glad when this baby was born and she got her figure back again. As she trudged over the grass she could see someone hovering in the trees at the edge of the outfield. She stopped and stared. Amy? But this wasn't her sort of thing. Besides, Bex knew for a fact that Amy hadn't been invited because Heather had told her so. Heather had said that her milk-of-human-kindness had curdled somewhat when Amy hadn't offered to deliver leaflets around the council estate. Heather said that she knew Amy was a busy person, 'but we're all busy people and it wouldn't hurt Amy to spare half an hour to drop off a few flyers through a few letter boxes.'

So, wondered, Bex, was Amy planning on gatecrashing? Frankly, knowing Amy as she did, she wouldn't put it past her. *Shameless* was a word that sometimes sprang to mind where her cleaner was concerned. Bex paused halfway across the outfield and slipped her shoes off. She wished her feet didn't ache quite so much. Carrying an extra stone was bad enough but this heat was putting the tin lid on things.

Bex put her shoes back on again and plodded on, waving at others from the town that she knew or recognised; Bert and Joan, Olivia, Dr Connolly and Jacqui, Harry from the pub, Jo from the PTA... The kids had already scattered to hang out with friends but Bex wasn't concerned. They'd been told they could go where they liked as long as they didn't stray beyond the cricket pitch. She made her way into the community centre to find a cold drink. The rundown old prefab was stiflingly hot, even with all the windows open, and most of the guests who had already arrived had collected a drink and a plate of food and were lounging on the grass outside the building, some on portable picnic chairs, some on rugs, some just sprawled out on the outfield. The kids were more active with the boys running around after a football while the girls either seemed to be making daisy chains or were practising their handstands up against the side of the building. It was, thought Bex, a lovely scene, the epitome of English village life.

The building was almost empty. There were a couple of small groups of people standing around chatting or collecting plates of food from the impressive spread while Heather, the host, was busy topping up the tea urn with more water. Bex couldn't imagine why *anyone* would want tea on a day like this but then it *was* England so presumably there were those who did.

'Hi, Heather,' she said as she made her way to one of the tables to collect a glass of squash. Heather, she noticed, was looking quite pink. No surprise given that she was partially enveloped in steam from the boiler. 'Hot, isn't it,' said Bex.

'Isn't it just. I really don't want to sound as if I am complaining but there's a tiny bit of me that would be quite grateful if we got one of those threatened thunderstorms – just to clear the air, you understand.'

'I know what you mean and I agree. I'd forgotten just how hot having a baby makes you.'

'Oh, yes. You poor thing, you must be boiling.'

Olivia came over and joined them. 'Goodness, Bex…'

'I know, I'm vast.' She tried to sound as if she didn't care but the joke was wearing a bit thin. 'Anyway, how's life with you?'

'Good, thanks. We're settling down to the new routine.'

'And Jade?'

Olivia shot a look at Heather. 'Fine as far as I know. We don't see much of her these days now she's at the vicarage.'

'She's a model tenant,' said Heather. 'She even cooks supper if I'm going to be late back.'

Olivia's jaw dropped. 'Really?'

'Really,' said Heather firmly.

Bex took a gulp of her drink. 'That's wonderful. I long for the day when Megan looks after me – although I am *very* lucky that Miles is pretty handy in the kitchen.' Movement near the door caught her eye. Miranda Osborne was hovering on the threshold. Bex looked at Heather and raised a questioning eyebrow. Surely Heather hadn't invited her. Heather responded with an infinitesimal shake of her head before she swept forward.

'Miranda – what a surprise. Have you come to join us?'

'Not really. I have a bone to pick with you.'

'Oh, that sounds ominous.'

'Excuse me,' said a voice from behind Miranda which Bex recognised as Amy's. Amy pushed her way past and came into the hall carrying a cake on a plate.

'I know I've not had no invite,' she said, ignoring the fact that she was interrupting. 'But as I didn't do nothing much for the bells, I thought the least I could do was to help out now with the party.' She thrust the cake at Heather.

'Oh... Amy, that's very generous of you. Thank you.'

Amy looked at Heather expectantly. 'Yeah, well...'

Heather got the hint. 'Would you like to join us?'

'Oh – don't mind if I do.' She toddled off across the room and began piling a plate with sandwiches and cocktail sausages. Bex stared at the spread laid out on the table and found that she didn't really fancy any of it. In fact, the very thought of eating made her feel a touch bilious.

'As I was saying...' said Miranda.

'Oh, yes, you said you have a bone to pick. Let me guess, it's about the bells.'

'Indeed. Yesterday and last week, when they were practising, the noise was intolerable.' Miranda glared at Heather. 'I was completely unable to enjoy my garden because of them.'

'I live much closer to the church than you do,' said Bex, 'and I love them.'

Miranda gave Bex a withering look. 'I am not prepared to be deafened on a regular basis by that racket.' As she finished the sentence, right on cue, the bells began to ring the promised quarter peal to celebrate the success of the fundraising.

'I think you'll find you are in a minority and as the bells have been in existence for centuries, I think, as an incomer, you have very little right to criticise our tradition.'

Bex's feet began to ache again so she made her way to the edge of the room to find a seat. She could have taken herself off to the slightly cooler temperature outside but she wasn't going to miss this showdown between Miranda and Heather for the world. She noticed Amy was blatantly eavesdropping too.

'Just because something is a tradition,' said Miranda, 'doesn't make it right or acceptable in the modern age.'

'I disagree,' said Heather firmly.

'It used to be traditional to burn Catholics at the stake but we live in more enlightened times.'

'That's hardly comparable.'

'I think that these wretched bells are inflicting a cruel and unnatural torture on anyone in earshot – just like an ordeal by fire.'

'That's a total overreaction,' snapped back Heather.

Bex was aware of her head starting to throb. Was it the heat... the noise...? She took another gulp of her drink.

Row or no row Bex needed some fresh air. Much as she was loath to miss the action she had to get outside. She made her way to the door, leaving Heather and Miranda hissing at each other like a pair of cats. If anything it was almost as bad outside as it was in – the temperature was truly oppressive and the air was sticky with humidity to boot. Bex plonked down on the steps to the community centre and toed off her shoes. What she wanted, she thought, was to be drenched in cold water but the only place she would achieve that was to go home and have a shower. Only she didn't have the energy. She leaned against the door jamb and shut her eyes. Even blotting out the glare of the sun didn't ease her head and she began to feel dizzy. Across the other side of the pitch the bells continued to ring out their joyous message that they were back in action and although Bex was a fan of the bells, on this occasion she wished they'd stop. She wanted everything to stop – the heat, the noise, the sunshine... everything.

She sat on the step, her eyes shut, and waited for the world to stop rocking and rolling. She'd be better in a minute, she told herself. It was nothing and it was going to pass.

'Are you all right?' asked Amy.

'I'm fine,' lied Bex opening her eyes and trying to look more chipper than she felt. 'Just needed to get the weight off. You know how it is at this stage of being pregnant.'

Amy nodded as a low rumble of thunder reached them. As it did the sun was blotted out by a cloud. 'Yeah, I do. I was always needing a sit-down when I was pregnant with my Ashley and I was a lot younger than you. That and always wanting the lav. It's no picnic, is it?' There was another rumble – louder and more sustained. 'Looks like we're in for a storm,' she observed.

For Bex, it couldn't break soon enough. Maybe her wish to be drenched in cooling water was about to be granted. She felt a bit sorry for Heather as it would put a damper on the party but Bex was feeling too ropy to care about being selfish. People began to drift off the cricket pitch towards the sheltering safety of the community centre. Bex moved over a little on her step so as not to be in the way.

'Well, I'll leave you to it. I could murder a glass of wine. Can I get you anything?'

'No thanks,' said Bex.

The first fat drops of rain began to splash down onto the grass and a gust of cooler air made the leaves shiver. Bring it on, thought Bex. She leaned against the building as the trickle of people echoed the rainfall which was rapidly becoming a torrent. In a couple of minutes the area was empty and everyone had crowded into the building. The sound of the party, of people having fun, eating and drinking swelled but Bex sat alone on the step in the rain. She jumped when there was a bolt of lightning and an almost simultaneous crash of thunder which managed to utterly drown out the bells. Bex thought her head was going to split but at least she was cooler. Feeling ghastly, she waited for the rain to have an effect and wondered if maybe she ought to ask for help but by now she was feeling so dreadful she didn't even have the strength to do that. She lay down on the step and curled up, willing the pain and the nausea to go away.

'Oi, Bex! You all right?' asked Amy.

Bex wasn't going to risk opening her eyes as she replied. 'No,' she admitted.

Behind Bex, in the body of the community centre, came the sound of the townsfolk chattering and laughing, in front of her was the hiss of the rain and the clanging of the bells, interrupted by the rumbles and crashes of the storm but she was oblivious to almost all of it as the throbbing in her head grew.

Miranda's cut-glass voice sliced through the noise. 'Amy says you're not well. I'm calling you an ambulance.'

'Don't be silly,' croaked Bex, 'I'll be fine in a minute.'

But Miranda had obviously ignored her as she then heard, 'Yes please, an ambulance. It's an emergency – I think it might be pre-eclampsia... Yes, the cricket pitch at Little Woodford. Yes... as quick as you can.'

52

Miles got to the hospital just as Bex was being taken into theatre for an emergency caesarean.

He'd driven like a loon through the storm to the hospital in Cattebury and had abandoned his car in the car park and raced in with no thought to buying a ticket. He pounded through the puddles, coatless, and arrived at reception sodden and dripping. His anxiety was at an epic level where it had been since Heather had phoned the pub and told him of the situation.

'And don't worry about the children. Jade and I have them safe at the vicarage. The boys haven't a clue as to what is going on and Megan is being very brave.'

Miles had gabbled his thanks, told Jamie and Belinda they'd have to cope without him, to which Belinda told him to take as long as he needed and, if necessary, she'd get a temp chef in to help Jamie.

'Now go!' she'd ordered.

Miles didn't need telling twice.

'Bex Millar,' he said to the receptionist at the entrance to the maternity department. 'Where is she?'

'Take a seat, Mr Millar – she's being taken to theatre.'

'She's what?'

'She's very poorly and we need to deliver the baby.'

'But... but...'

'She's in safe hands, Mr Millar.'

Miles didn't think to point out that he wasn't called Millar but Patterson and anyway, what did it matter? All he could think about was Bex and the baby and the danger they were both in. He paced up and down the corridor a couple of times before he slumped in a chair. He'd never been the least bit religious but he was praying right now and making promises to a God he'd never really acknowledged before. If Bex and the baby pull through I promise I'll never swear again. If Bex and the baby pull through I promise I'll never get angry again. If Bex and the baby pull through... And so it went on as he checked the clock every few seconds and his worry and the fear of what might happen went off the scale. Minute by interminable minute ticked past. The nurses on duty offered him a cup of tea but he declined. Somewhere down a corridor he heard the cries and groans of a mother giving birth and he tried to shut out the sound. Bex wasn't doing that – she was unconscious, under the knife.

'Mr Millar?'

Miles jumped. 'Yes?'

'The baby has been delivered and she's fine. A little on the small side but she's breathing on her own. We're taking her down to the neonatal unit and your wife is in the recovery room. She's just coming round and you can see her in just a few minutes.'

Miles felt almost weak with relief. 'Thank God,' he whispered.

'You're lucky your wife's friend recognised the symptoms and called for an ambulance when she did.'

'Yes, yes, that was wonderful.'

Miles went back to his chair, light-headed, blinking back tears of happiness at the reprieve he'd been given and thought about the news. He was a father. He had a baby girl. Oh, my God, he thought. He had given up hope of this ever happening. And now... now he had a daughter. His very own little girl. And he was going to be the best father ever. He fast-forwarded to the future; he'd teach her to cook, he'd walk her down the aisle... He was dizzy with happiness.

'Mr Millar? You can see your wife now.'

The nurse led him along the corridor and opened a door.

'Not too long,' she warned. 'Your wife is very tired. She was very poorly.'

In the centre of the opposite wall Bex was sitting up in bed, propped up on pillows, a drip in her arm. She looked exhausted and groggy.

Miles rushed across the room and took her hand. She looked so weak and vulnerable.

He clasped her hand and leaned forward and kissed her gently. 'Oh, my darling girl. How are you?'

'I'm feeling much better than I did. We've got a little girl.'

'They said. Oh, Bex…' Miles felt his eyes welling up again as he thought about what might have happened.

'Hey,' said Bex. 'Everything's fine.'

'But it might not have been.'

'And the baby is doing really well. She's four and a half pounds they say – which is good for someone so prem.'

'But she's not with you.'

'She needs to be kept warm and they need to give her a little help with her feeding but they tell me she's going to be fine – she just needs a little bit of extra care for a few days, maybe a couple of weeks.'

'And you?'

'Still drugged to the eyeballs.' She gave him a wan smile.

The nurse came back in. 'Mr Millar, I need to check on Bex, here. If you'd like to go down to the neonatal unit and meet your daughter while I do that and then I think it'll be time for Bex to get some rest. Come back this evening.'

Miles kissed Bex again. 'The nurses here have married us off. Maybe we ought to make it official when you're up and about.'

'Is that a proposal?'

'I rather think it might be.'

'Then I rather think I'd like to say yes.'

The nurse cleared her throat. Miles took the hint and edged towards the door.

'But I'm going to get hold of Richard's folks,' he said. 'They need to know what happened.'

'OK,' said Bex. 'You're right. Good luck with that.'

'Love you.'

'Love you too.'

It was two days before Bex was allowed home but she'd not been bored in hospital as there had been a near-constant stream of visitors to see her and when she wasn't seeing her friends and family she was in the intensive care unit gazing at her daughter and wondering how anything so tiny could be so perfect. Miles gave her updates on how they were coping at home without her, including a blow-by-blow account of his FaceTime call to Granny Helen.

'She was concerned about you, obviously,' said Miles.

Bex found that hard to believe – except that her stay in hospital meant she was falling down in her duties as the live-in carer for Helen's grandchildren. And, if something happened to her, who would there be to look after them. She didn't think Helen would let Miles take over.

'And the baby,' asked Bex.

Miles rolled his eyes.

And why would Helen care? The baby wasn't a blood relative, she mistrusted her daughter-in-law and had made her views on Miles pretty clear. Oh, the joys of happy families. Bex dreaded having to take the children to the Med to see their grandparents but in fairness to the children it would have to happen. Maybe she could put them on a plane on their own – find an excuse as to why she couldn't go… She'd think about it.

She arrived back at The Beeches to a houseful of flowers, cards and presents that had been delivered by, so it seemed, half the residents of the town. She was completely overwhelmed by everyone's generosity and felt suddenly rather teary as she contemplated the gifts.

'It hormones,' she told Miles as she blew her nose. 'They're all out of kilter.'

'Why's Mummy crying?' asked Alfie.

'Mummy's not crying,' said Bex. 'Not really.' She gave Alfie a gentle hug. 'I'm just a bit sad that your sister has to stay in hospital a little longer. We'll go and see her later today, shall we?'

'When is she coming home?' Alfie wanted to know.

'In a little while. Promise.'

'You go and sit on the sofa,' said Miles, 'and I'll bring you a nice cuppa.'

As Bex made her way to the sitting room the doorbell rang.

'And don't you answer that. I'll get it, you put your feet up,' instructed Miles.

Bex did as she was told and sat down gingerly. The scar was healing nicely but her tummy was still very sore. Quite apart from a zipper of stitches she had hideous trapped wind – which really didn't help matters. Anyone who thought a caesarean section was easier than pushing had to be off their trolley. She could hear voices out in the hall and wondered who it was who had come round. She imagined it would be someone like Heather or Olivia or one of her other friends from the town. She rearranged the cushions to make herself comfortable and waited for her visitor to come into the sitting room.

'I am very glad to hear you're home,' said a cut-glass accent.

Bex twisted to look over the back of the sofa and instantly regretted it. 'Ouch.' Then she recovered her manners. 'Miranda. How lovely to see you. I was going to come and see you in the next couple of days. I think I owe you a vast amount – you saved two lives on Monday.'

Miranda walked around the sofa and perched on the armchair. 'I'm actually rather surprised you didn't recognise your symptoms, yourself,' she said. Her tone of disapproval was unmistakable.

Bex was a tiny bit taken aback at being ticked off like that. 'I... well...' She stopped and started again. 'I'd had two children with no complications or difficulties and I assumed that this baby would be the same.'

'Which it patently wasn't.'

'Yes, I know that now.'

'But you must have had symptoms; felt unwell.'

Bex shrugged and winced. 'I did, but I put it down to the heatwave, to being a bit under the weather, to being that much older and running around after three other children. You know, I was busy and not really paying attention.'

'You were pregnant and not *paying attention*?' Miranda was incredulous.

'Yes, and I'm sorry.' Although Bex wondered why on earth she was apologising to Miranda. She decided to shift the focus away from herself. 'But what fascinates me was how on earth did you know what was wrong with me? I thought you said you're a lawyer, not a doctor.'

'I am... was. I dealt with medical negligence cases mostly.' There was a pause. 'Including my own.'

'Oh.' Bex didn't know what else to say.

'I lost my own daughter.'

'Oh, Miranda.' Bex's eyes filled. Ignoring the discomfort she leaned forward and clasped Miranda's hand. 'Oh, Miranda, I am so desperately sorry.'

'I had pre-eclampsia. I didn't know it but I went to my midwife to say that I didn't feel right. She said all the things I had were normal – back pain, swollen ankles, nausea...' Miranda stopped while she composed herself. 'Only they weren't.' The two women gazed at each other, their faces wet with tears. 'But it was a long time ago now.'

'But that's not something you'd get over, is it?'

Miranda shook her head. 'No. So that was how I knew.'

'And you saved me and my baby.'

'All I did was ring for an ambulance. I think anyone would have done the same, I just happened to be the person who did.'

'Even so… I am totally indebted.'

'It's kind of you to say so. Anyway, I gather you had a baby girl, which is wonderful. Miles is like a dog with two tails.'

'He is, isn't he?'

'And have you decided on a name yet?'

'We're inclined towards Emily. Such a pretty name, don't you think?'

'Yes, I love that name.'

'And Miles and I would like to ask you to be a godmother to her.'

Miranda began to cry again. 'I would utterly love to be her godmother. But only if I'm allowed to spoil her.'

'Of course.'

'Then, thank you.'

It was early evening when the family returned to the house after visiting little Emily at the hospital. The visit had taken some time as Bex and Miles had to take turns to amuse the other children as Emily's siblings were only allowed on the unit one by one. They were still completely fascinated by her daintiness and her tiny fingernails but almost more fascinated by the bleeps and other rhythmical noises that were the constant background to life on this ward.

When they got home Bex, who still tired easily, returned to her place on the sofa, Miles went into the kitchen to knock up some supper for them all and Megan supervised Alfie's bath. Lewis sat on the sofa by Bex and read to her from his school library book. It was, thought Bex, an almost perfect scene of domestic harmony – and it would be total domestic harmony when Emily came home.

The peace was shattered by the doorbell. Bex sighed. Who the hell was it at this hour?

'Run and see who it is, Lewis,' she said.

Obediently he jumped up and ran to get it.

'Granny! It's Granny!' he shrieked.

'Mum?' called Bex. She was bewildered. Obviously there had been loads of phone calls between them as Granny May had wanted daily updates on Bex's baby but she'd never mentioned coming down. And if Granny May was here, who was looking after Grandpa?

Bex heaved herself off the sofa and tottered into the hall.

'Helen.' She just managed to stop herself from exclaiming, *What the fuck?* Instead she managed to say, 'How lovely.' She noticed the huge suitcase at Helen's feet.

Lewis was jumping up and down hanging onto her arm and then there was a commotion on the stairs as Alfie, dripping wet and stark naked, came bounding down them, followed by Megan clutching his towel.

'I tried to call from the airport but I couldn't get a reply,' said Granny Helen.

Megan managed to catch Alfie, pick him up and swaddle him in the towel before she proffered him to Granny Helen for a kiss.

'We've just got back from the hospital,' explained Bex. Then she added, 'How long are you staying for?' She didn't mean the question to come out quite as it did. Even to her own ears it sounded rather graceless.

Helen sniffed. 'I can always find a hotel.'

Megan put Alfie down and he held his towel around him with one hand while he grabbed Helen's other arm.

'No. No, I didn't mean it like that. No, you absolutely must stay here. We've masses of space.' She glanced again at the gigantic case. Oh, dear Lord, it looked as if she was planning on staying for weeks.

'Good. I came over to make sure that my grandchildren are being properly looked after.' There was a pause before Helen added, 'You must be so distracted and run off your feet with the baby in hospital and everything.'

There was a definite inference, thought Bex, that she and Miles couldn't be trusted. That she was an unfit mother. She decided to ignore it. Pick your battles, she told herself.

Miles came out of the kitchen. 'Ah, I thought I heard the bell ring. Helen, how lovely.'

For a second Bex was baffled. How the hell did Miles know who she was? Then she remembered they'd had a video call.

'Why don't you go and sit in the sitting room with Bex while I make up the spare bed and take your case upstairs? It's spag bol for supper – I trust that's OK? If not you must say and I'll prepare something else. Would you like a drink?'

'No, that's fine. Megan, could you put some clothes on Alfie before he catches his death. And no, I don't need a drink. I can wait for dinner.'

Bex led the way into the sitting room and sat down gingerly. She decided she needed to build bridges. 'It's so thoughtful of you to come over to help us. As you said, we're quite busy. It'll be easier tomorrow as the schools go back.'

'So… how is the baby?'

'Emily is doing really well. The doctors are very pleased with her progress.'

'Good, I'm glad.' She didn't sound it. 'And you?'

'Oh… still sore. Miles is being wonderful.'

'Is he?'

'I don't know how I'd manage without him.'

'Well, if it hadn't been for him you wouldn't be in this situation, would you?'

Bex forced a smile. 'No, but I am so pleased to have another daughter. I think my family is now totally perfect and complete.' Apart from you, you old bag. 'And the boys and Megan adore Emily. Things couldn't be more lovely.' Suck on that.

53

Megan met Sophie on the corner of Sophie's road, like they always did, and the pair headed towards the comp for the first day of the summer term.

'How's Bex and the baby?' asked Soph.

'They're good. Emily is still in hospital and I think she'll be there for a bit but the nurses say she's doing really well for her size.'

'That's great. Everyone says that it was really scary at the time.'

Megan nodded. She didn't want to relive the moment when the ambulance raced onto the cricket pitch and Heather had found her and told her to be brave and everyone else was staring at her and the boys … and then she realised it was her stepmother who was on the stretcher. And then she remembered how it had been when her dad had been killed. 'The paramedics are with her. She's getting the best treatment,' Heather had said. But that didn't mean it would turn out well – Megan was only too well aware of that.

'Yeah, well it's fine now.' And Megan told Sophie about baby Emily and how dinky she was and Sophie got all clucky and gooey.

'I can't wait to see her.'

'And my gran from Cyprus has come over to help.'

'That must be nice.'

'Kind of. I don't think she likes Miles.'

Sophie was aghast. 'Not like Miles?'

'It's complicated.'

They were joined by Ashley who'd been waiting for them at the end of his road.

'So what happened?' he asked Megan outright. 'Mum said your mum was taken really poorly and rushed into hospital.'

Megan really didn't want to go into the whole incident again. 'The baby came early but all is well now.'

'Oh…' Ashley sounded as if he didn't believe her. 'Oh, Mum made it sound more serious than that.'

No surprise there – everyone knew Amy exaggerated everything.

Helen was sitting at the kitchen table at The Beeches watching Miles and the two boys romp around in the garden. Alfie and Lewis were letting off steam after a day at school and, even though Helen heartily disapproved of Miles and his unfortunate liaison with her daughter-in-law, she was hard put to fault the way he looked after the children. Lewis and Alfie obviously adored him to the extent that they preferred him to read them a bedtime story over herself. And that rankled, if she was honest. As did the fact that he was a far superior cook to her and that Megan – whom Helen had thought would side with her over Miles usurping Richard's position – seemed very fond of him too.

Bex came into the kitchen. 'I'm going to pop over to the hospital again for a few minutes. I thought you might like to come and meet Emily.'

Helen contemplated the invitation and rather wished it hadn't been extended as it would be churlish to say no. 'I'd love to,' she lied.

'Good. Miles is going to supervise the boys' homework while

he cooks supper. He's going to go over to sit with her later while I do baths and bed.'

Twenty minutes later Bex keyed in the code to get them onto the NICU, they slathered their hands in the antiseptic liquid and then she led Helen to the cot. Bewildered, Helen looked at the technology, took in the noise and the incessant bleeping and the general air of bustle.

'You get used to it,' said Bex, reading Helen's mind. 'And the babies don't care. And this,' she said, lifting a tiny scrap out of its cot, 'is Emily.' She held her daughter out to Helen. 'Would you like to hold her?'

The minute baby was swaddled in a blanket and had a tube up her nose held in place by a sliver of sticky tape. Hesitantly Helen took her and looked down at her grandchildren's half-sister. She wanted to dislike the child – it wasn't Richard's but *that man's* – but her size and vulnerability shoved all of that away.

'Oh,' she said. 'She's sweet.'

Bex raised an eyebrow. 'Don't sound so surprised,' she said wryly.

Helen looked at her daughter-in-law. 'I am sorry, I didn't mean to. It's just… it's just…'

'She's not Richard's? No, I know that and a part of me wishes she was. But I can't turn the clock back and neither can you. Nothing can bring Richard back and I still miss him. Even with Miles in my life I miss him. And Lewis and Alfie need a father figure. Megan does too, but less so because she's older – although in some way I think that also makes things harder for her. She has more memories; is more aware of what she's lost. I tried to be both parents and, while I didn't fail, Miles can give them so much more. *I* need so much more. And I like to think that Richard, being the lovely man he was,' which made Helen preen, 'would approve too.'

Helen nodded. 'Maybe.' She gazed again at her step-granddaughter. 'She reminds me of Lewis when he was tiny.'

'Same mother,' Bex reminded her.

'Yes, I suppose so.'

The next day, Miranda parked her car in the town centre and made her way to the little boutique that was situated down a side road behind the town hall. One thing she really did like about Little Woodford was the fact that, with the exception of the Co-op, the place contained very few chain stores. No, the shopping wasn't great when she compared it with London, and the Co-op was a joke compared to the supermarkets she'd been used to but, equally, she didn't have to battle with traffic fumes and overcrowded pavements. And these little indy stores did sell some lovely, quirky, eclectic and original things.

She headed along the road towards her destination hoping that the baby-clothes shop would have something suitable – otherwise she'd have to find a gift for baby Emily online. While Miranda had no aversion at all to internet shopping, she wanted to pick something out herself; to feel the quality, to check the suitability and to be certain that it was perfect.

'Miranda.'

She stopped in her tracks and turned. The vicar's wife. She suppressed a sigh and waited for some sort of smug dig about the bells.

'Miranda, I've been wanting to see you. I meant to walk up to your home and call but… well… Easter is our busy time and everything just got away from me.'

Which showed a deplorable lack of planning, in Miranda's opinion. 'And what can I do for you?' she asked warily.

'I wanted to thank you for your amazing quick-witted response to Bex's illness. I am very fond of her, as are many local people and if the unthinkable had happened…'

'But it didn't.'

'Because of you.' Heather clasped Miranda's hand and shook it warmly. 'I know we've had our differences but maybe we can start again.' She looked at Miranda hopefully.

'I'm... I'm not sure.'

'You may find you get used to the bells. You may find you come to like them. People do, you know.'

Miranda rather doubted that and was wondering how to respond when Belinda joined them. 'Miranda – just the person. The next time you're in the pub, the drinks are on me. I owe you.'

'What on earth for?'

'For what you did for Bex.'

'But...?'

'No *buts* about it, dearie. You're on free booze for quite a while.'

'Thank you.'

'I've got to get on,' said Belinda. 'I've got the banking to do but you make sure you come along sometime soon. It isn't just me that wants to thank you, quite a lot of our regulars do too. Promise?'

Oh, why not. 'Promise.'

'They all want to shake your hand.'

It was nice to suddenly be Mrs Popular. Miranda didn't think she'd ever been in this position before. 'OK, I'd like that.'

'Good.'

As Miranda continued her way to the boutique, she recalled her visit to the town several months previously, on New Year's Eve, when she'd felt such envy at the friendships of the other residents. Maybe being called 'dearie' by the pub landlady was meant as a compliment, a hand of friendship, a sign of being accepted. It was how she referred to people she liked – people like Bex, who was undeniably popular. Maybe informality wasn't such a bad thing after all.

*

It was a fortnight later that Miles and Bex were allowed to take Emily out of hospital and bring her home. The two weeks had definitely been made easier all round by the presence of Granny Helen who had helped with the childcare when Miles or Bex had wanted to be at the hospital. She was still undeniably tricky and could be prickly but relations between her and Bex had thawed. Maybe Helen, Bex had mused to Miles one night in bed, had realised that she wasn't the mother from hell and had her children's best interests at heart and that Miles was a nice guy and a brilliant dad.

'It's also been getting on for two years since Richard died,' Miles had pointed out. 'I imagine she's coming to terms with what happened.'

'I swear, when it first happened, she thought I had something to do with it. It was like she suspected me of putting out a contract on Richard — like I'd got him run over just to get my hands on the life insurance.'

Miles had propped himself up on one elbow to look at Bex better. 'You're kidding me?'

'That's what it felt like.'

'No wonder you two weren't exactly bosom buddies.'

'And we'd probably still be circling each other like cats about to fight if it hadn't been for little Emily.'

'I still can't believe I'm really a dad,' said Miles.

'Well, you are. And you just wait till this apple-of-your-eye becomes a teenager and is all hormonal and slams doors and flounces.'

'Emily will never do that.'

Bex raised an eyebrow. 'Good luck with that,' was all she said.

The next morning, after Emily had had her morning feed and was back in her Moses basket by the Aga fast asleep, Miles had got the children to school and Helen had got the washing out of the machine and was hanging it up in the garden in the late April sunshine, the doorbell rang.

Bex stopped making a shopping list and went to answer it. Belinda was on the doorstep.

'Hello,' said Bex. 'Come in and I'll put the kettle on.'

'I won't stop – I should think you've got more than enough to do with four kids and a visitor.'

Bex led the way into the kitchen. She pointed out the window. 'Actually,' she said, 'my visitor is being more than helpful.'

Belinda raised an eyebrow in disbelief and went over to the basket on the counter to coo over Emily.

'I can't believe how she's growing.'

'It's what babies do best. Well, that and create utterly disproportionate piles of washing.'

'Bless her,' said Belinda. 'Anyway, Emily is mostly the reason I'm here. I was hoping you might agree to me throwing a small party at the pub to welcome her to the world.'

'What a lovely idea.'

'There's a bunch of the regulars who are longing to meet her. You wouldn't have to stay long and Jamie and I will do everything...'

'Belinda, I honestly don't need persuading. We've decided that we're going to ask Brian to christen her and we'll obviously have a party then but I want my folks there and Miles has got a whole bunch of relations he wants to show his daughter off to—'

'As he jolly well ought to.'

'So we need to find a date that suits everyone. It might take a while – in fact, at the rate we're going we might be able to combine it with Emily's eighteenth.'

Belinda laughed. 'So how about we say this Saturday coming.'

'That'd be perfect. Helen is going back to Cyprus on Sunday so we can make it a farewell to her as well.'

Right on cue Helen reappeared in the kitchen with the empty laundry basket. 'What's this about my farewell?'

Bex explained about Belinda's offer.

'Oh.' Helen sounded totally underwhelmed. 'I suppose. Don't you think that taking the children to a pub at their age is inappropriate?'

'It's not the pub – it's the upstairs function room,' said Bex. 'In a place this size there are precious few public spaces and while this house is big enough for us to host a party for all my friends, Belinda is offering to do it to spare me the trouble.'

Helen remained silent.

'Which is very kind of her, isn't it?' prompted Bex.

'Yes, yes it is.' But she still sounded dubious.

Obviously, thought Bex, Helen was still doubting the wisdom of some of her daughter-in-law's decisions. But then it was still very early days in their recent rapprochement. There were bound to be glitches.

54

The day of the party arrived and Belinda and Jamie had produced a magnificent spread between them, aided by Miles who had insisted on cooking a selection of vegan snacks for Miranda who had promised to attend along with Roderick. Bex had to admit to being agog with curiosity at the thought of meeting him. Who, she wondered, would take on a lifetime commitment to being married to scary Miranda? She had begun to warm to Miranda after getting to know her a bit better, but she still felt a little intimidated by her. Olivia had done her best to describe her husband after her encounters at the hotel but her word-picture had only made matters worse. Now Bex could only imagine some downtrodden lackey.

At midday Bex and her family made their way to the pub, Miles proudly carrying Emily in her Moses basket while Bex and Megan each carried a plate of food Miles had made and Granny Helen shepherded the boys. The party was only just getting going when they arrived although they hadn't been there long when the room began to fill up. Olivia arrived with Nigel and Zac, Dr Connolly and Jacqui followed a couple of minutes later and then Amy, Mags and Ashley joined them. Soon almost all their friends and acquaintances were squashed into the room and the noise level rocketed. Although Emily, asleep in her cot, was oblivious.

Down one side of the room were two tables, one for all the food and another with bottles of wine, soft drinks and a barrel of beer on it. Belinda stood by the second table dispensing drinks and bonhomie and encouraging people to help themselves to the buffet.

'I really don't want leftovers,' she told her guests. 'So no one goes till it's all eaten.' Given the wonderful spread that was on offer there were a number of townsfolk who reckoned that to carry out Belinda's wishes they might have to end up with a lock-in.

Bex, still feeling a bit sore when she stood around for too long, sat on a chair at the side and chatted to Bert and Joan while the boys made a den under the buffet table. Every now and again one of other of them would creep out, bob up, grab a couple of cocktail sausages or vol-au-vents and then disappear back underneath again. Granny Helen had commented that they appeared to be stuffing themselves with unsuitable food but then surprised Bex by saying, 'But I suppose it doesn't matter once in a while. I've noticed their diet is pretty good the rest of the time.'

Blimey, thought Bex, praise indeed.

Miranda appeared with her husband just as Bex was beginning to wonder where they were. Roderick, was wearing mustard trousers with an open-neck shirt. He certainly chimed with Olivia's description of someone wanting to look like the local squire but not quite hitting the mark. On the other hand he didn't look downtrodden or like a lackey but rather patrician. Leaving Roderick to introduce himself to Miles, Miranda approached Bex rather awkwardly and handed over the most beautifully wrapped package that was finished off with a broad silk ribbon in pink and silver.

'I hope I haven't overstepped the mark but I did warn you that when I agreed to be Emily's godmother I would spoil her shamelessly.'

'Oh, Miranda, you shouldn't have,' murmured Bex as she pulled the two loose ends of the bow. The ribbon fell away and she began to unfold the tissue on the neatly wrapped package to reveal the softest, most gorgeous white cashmere matinée jacket, bootees, scarf and hat. Bex had seen the set in the window of the little boutique in town and had also seen the ridiculous price tag. At the time she wondered just who might be daft enough or rich enough to buy such an expensive outfit – now she knew.

'That is just lovely,' she said, shaking out the folds of the jacket and holding it up to admire. And it was. It was exquisite and now she could examine the detail and feel the quality the price tag made sense. 'Just the most perfect present ever.' Gathering up the dainty little items she stood up and gave Miranda a kiss on the cheek. 'I can't thank you enough.'

'My pleasure,' said Miranda. She looked genuinely touched by Bex's obvious gratitude.

'I must show Miles what you've given Emily and you and Roderick must help yourselves to some food. Miles made some stuff specially for you. I do hope you enjoy it.'

Having shown Miles the present Bex felt she ought to circulate a little. Besides, Emily had woken up and this was the perfect opportunity to show her off to the guests. Bex picked her out of her crib and, holding her in the crook of her arm she went around the room to introduce her new daughter to her friends.

'So this is the little minx who caused all the trouble,' said Jacqui as she stroked her tiny cheek.

'It is indeed. Worth it though,' said Bex happily as she moved on.

Bert, Joan and Harry all had their hearts melted by Emily.

'She'll be a little beauty when she grows up,' said Harry.

'A right little heartbreaker,' agreed Bert.

Amy and Mags both said she was the prettiest baby in Little Woodford and Olivia, who had already seen her numerous times, told Bex that she became sweeter and sweeter every time she clapped eyes on her.

And Bex hoovered up the praise on behalf of her daughter as she gazed down at her until she began to tire again and took Emily back to her doting father.

'Here you go,' she said, handing her over.

Miles was only too happy to take her and looked as if he would burst with pride as he cradled the tiny infant.

Zac sought out Megan. 'Glad your mum's OK.'

'Stepmum,' she responded automatically. 'But yes, it's great. I mean, what would have happened to me and the boys if...'

'Don't go there,' said Zac.

Megan eyeballed him. 'By the way, have you apologised to Ash? It's been weeks and weeks since you were such a total twat and upset him.'

Zac coloured.

'Then you must,' she insisted. 'Now. He's over there.'

Zac bit his lip.

Megan grabbed his arm. 'Do it. Do it now.' She tugged on his sleeve.

Miserably, Zac followed her across the room. 'What am I going to say?' he asked her.

'That you were a twat, that you're sorry, that you're still friends...' They reached their quarry. 'Here, Zac wants to say something.' She gave him a shove.

Zac didn't look Ashley in the eye as he said, 'I'm sorry.'

'Yeah, well I was being a bit of a git too.'

'No, you weren't. I was the one being an arse.'

Ashley nodded.

'You're not supposed to agree.'

'Well, you were being a git, weren't you?'

'So were you.'

The pair grinned at each other. Megan left them to their renewed bromance.

*

Bex looked around the room and decided it was a lovely party. Everyone was chatting and getting on, the mix of people from across the town was perfect, everyone seemed to be enjoying themselves... even Helen, which was a triumph in its own way. She looked around for her mother-in-law to make sure she still was.

Oh, Lordy, she was chatting to Miranda. Helen and Miranda. Two strong-minded and rather prickly women – not really a match made in heaven. Quite apart from the fact that, even though there was a hint of rapprochement, Helen still seemed to harbour a mostly low opinion of her daughter-in-law, and Bex wasn't entirely sure what she might divulge to Miranda. She didn't want Miranda thinking that she'd promised to be the godmother to the daughter of a crap parent. She sidled over to eavesdrop and had to strain to hear what was being said. She pretended to be deciding what she wanted to eat as she earwigged.

'... and I can't think why Bex wanted to move here,' said Helen. 'They had everything in London and quite apart from all the culture on offer. So much more stimulating for the children, don't you think? After all, one reason why my late son lived there was because of the opportunities that were right on the doorstep. I mean, I know Richard was brought up in a small town like this but we always made sure there were plenty of educational outings. I'm not entirely sure, what with the new baby and everything, that my grandchildren will get the same opportunities. To be honest, I don't think Bex can be bothered.'

Actually, thought Bex, the reason Richard had lived in London was because he worked there. He always said that if he found the right job away from the capital he'd take it in a heartbeat. And he'd also always said that, as a kid, he'd dreaded weekends and the obligatory trip to some dull gallery or museum. He'd said it had put him off history and art for life.

'I worry,' continued Helen, 'about my grandchildren being deprived of the right sort of cultural exposure.'

Bex waited for Miranda to agree with Helen, to side with her about the horrors of living in a backwater, about rubbing shoulders with oiks and bumpkins, about the lack of facilities, or anything else that had apparently annoyed Miranda since she'd moved in. And it wasn't that Bex didn't know about Miranda's opinions – she made them pretty plain on more than one occasion at the book club.

'Oh, Helen, you can't mean that,' said Miranda. 'Just think about the positives; the clean air, the low crime rate, the sense of community...'

Bex's jaw dropped. And then she butted in, she couldn't help herself.

'Miranda!'

'What?' said Miranda turning.

'I can't believe you've just said what you did. '

'You mean about the town?'

Bex nodded. 'But all those things you hate... the bells, the smells, the market.'

'I know, I know, you're right.' She sounded quite apologetic.

'So?'

'So, I've come to appreciate some of the other aspects.' Miranda sighed. 'It's different here. People know each other. People have friends. When we lived in London, the only people we associated with were our work colleagues. It seemed to be the same for most people. Mothers didn't gather at the school gate because almost none of the children in a street went to the same school as other children in the street and anyway they didn't walk they went by car. It was all about one-upmanship, about getting ahead, about having more, bigger, better. It was all we knew.' She sighed. 'And in London I was anonymous.'

'Well, you certainly aren't in a place like this,' said Bex.

'So I have discovered.'

'And it's not such a bad thing if people know who you are.'

Miranda gave her a wry smile. 'It is if it means getting a midden delivered to your door.'

'No. I can see that. I expect it was a one-off.'

'It better had be.'

'But,' said Helen, butting in, 'I still think London is a better, more vibrant, place.'

'I don't,' said Bex. 'The kids love it here, they love the nature reserve, the play park, the school, they have some wonderful friends, and they're safe. When Alfie went walkabout last year he was brought home by a friend's son. Like that would have happened in London.'

'Bex is right,' said Miranda. 'I was wrong about this place when I moved here. I thought the locals just needed educating to make their lives better. It's taken me a while to realise that their lives are pretty good.'

'Even if they eat meat?' Bex was incredulous.

'I have to accept that some people do. I may not like it but there it is.'

It was Amy's turn to but in. 'I never thought you were a proper veggie, anyway.'

'I beg your pardon?' Miranda might have been prepared to be a bit more conciliatory where carnivores were concerned but she wasn't going to take criticism from her cleaner!

'I said, you're not a proper veggie.'

'No, I'm a vegan.'

Amy shrugged. One and the same as far as she was concerned. 'Course you're not. You've got all them Milano Blahnik shoes. Everyone knows if you're a veggie you can't wear leather shoes.'

'Have you been going through my cupboards?' Miranda was incensed.

Bex was getting worried. The last thing she wanted at the celebratory party was a bust-up between Amy and one of her guests.

'I'm sure Amy just had to tidy something away. She's always having to put things away for me.'

'Yeah, that's it.' Amy latched onto the excuse like a drowning man onto a life raft.

'I don't leave things lying around,' said Miranda.

'What, *never*?' Bex couldn't believe that. No one on the planet was *that* tidy.

'Hardly ever.'

'Well, there you go then,' crowed Amy.

Miranda sniffed. 'And for your information they are *not* by Manolo Blahnik but Nemanti Milano. They are made entirely from non-animal and cruelty-free products.'

'Really.' Amy sounded disbelieving.

'Yes, really.'

Roderick wandered over. He could see that his wife seemed to be in a rather hostile situation. He had no doubt she would be able to cope but a little moral support never did anyone any harm.

'You'll be telling us next,' said Amy, 'that you've changed your mind about the bells.'

'I certainly have not. I will be doing everything in my power to get them silenced.'

'No, you won't,' said Roderick.

It was Miranda's turn to let her jaw drop. 'Roderick?'

'Miranda, you know I support you in everything you do and I am the most ardent admirer of your strength of mind, your passionately held beliefs and your courage. But you are wrong about the bells. They've been here for centuries and we are – to coin a phrase – blow-ins—'

'But…'

'Don't argue.' Roderick's voice cut across the party and silence fell as Miranda seemed to shrink. 'The bells are part and parcel of this community, change-ringing is an ancient and wonderful tradition and I, for one, *like* the bells.'

'Oh.'

'And I am not prepared to support your campaign and, if you insist on continuing, I will take counter-measures.'

Miranda was ashen. 'Roderick?'

He nodded. 'I will act *pro bono* for the town and against you. And I think you'll find I'll win.'

'Oh.'

'Bloody hell,' whispered Heather.

'I see,' said Miranda. She stared sightlessly at her glass before she looked up and shook her head. 'Never let it be said I don't know when I'm beaten.' She smiled ruefully. 'And I have been – well and truly.'

'Good,' said Harry. 'Cos you wouldn't want another delivery.'

Miranda's eyes widened. 'You?'

'Nope,' lied Harry cheerfully. 'I'm just saying that you didn't like the last one much, did you?'

'Hmmm.'

'On the bright side,' said Harry, 'it gave us all something to talk about.' He chuckled at the memory.

'It was quite funny,' agreed Roderick.

Miranda stared at him.

'Come off it,' said her husband. 'It was almost worth it just to see the reaction of the Clifton-Prices. Candida's face was a picture. I never have liked her much.'

'But, Roderick – I don't understand.'

'Valentine's not too bad but that wife of his…'

'But I only invited them for Christmas because I thought you adored them both.'

'No! I thought you did.'

Miranda began to laugh. 'How utterly ridiculous.'

Others in the room giggled nervously. It certainly did seem pretty ridiculous.

'Maybe,' said Harry, 'you two ought to try talking to each other. And while you're at it, you might try listening to us locals – stop trying to make us change our ways. It won't do no good and it won't make you no friends.'

Miranda nodded. 'Yes, I get that. And I'd like to be friends.'

'Then you come into the pub tomorrow evening and I'll buy

'ee a drink. Tell you all you need to know about this place, and mebbe I'll introduce you to some other locals.'

Miranda looked at her husband. 'Roddy?'

'I think that sounds like a grand idea,' he said. 'But I think the drinks'll be on us.'

Harry wasn't going to argue.

The sound at the party began to rev up again and this time it woke Emily and she began to grizzle.

Time to go, thought Bex. She told Miles that Emily needed a feed and a change, then she picked up the baby and slipped out of the room leaving her family enjoying themselves along with all their friends. As she got to her gate she looked back up at the open window of the function room and heard the laughter and the chatter and realised that she'd never felt more at home, more accepted, anywhere in her life. And now Little Woodford seemed to have worked its magic on the Osbornes of all people.

Good for Little Woodford, she thought. Long may it continue to thrive.

Acknowledgements

When I began to write this book I knew nothing about church bells, change-ringing, bell-related problems and the concomitant fundraising required to solve them but thanks to some incredibly kind, patient and knowledgeable people I hope anything that I have written regarding bell-ringing isn't too wide of the mark. If I have got anything wrong, it's because I didn't listen hard enough.

So thank you to, Rosalie Gibson, Anita Clayton, Hilary Ely, Hilarie Rogers and Bernadette O'Dwyer. And thank you to Kirsty for advice on things theological and other, general, church-related matters. I am also indebted to the support and encouragement of everyone at Head of Zeus but especially Rosie, and also to my agent, Laura, for wise words of advice.

About the Author

CATHERINE JONES lives in Thame, where she is an independent councillor. She is the author of nineteen novels, including the Soldiers' Wives series, written under the pseudonym Fiona Field.